Size 14 is not Fat Either

A Heather Wells Mystery

Also by Meg Cabot

The Guy Next Door
Boy Meets Girl
Every Boy's Got One
Size 12 Is Not Fat

and published by Macmillan Children's Books

All American Girl
Nicola and the Viscount
Victoria and the Rogue
All American Girl: Ready or Not
Avalon High
Teen Idol

The Mediator: Love You to Death
The Mediator: High Stakes
The Mediator: Mean Spirits
The Mediator: Young Blood
The Mediator: Grave Doubts
The Mediator: Heaven Sent

The Princess Diaries Guide to Life
The Princess Diaries
The Princess Diaries: Take Two
The Princess Diaries: Third Time Lucky
The Princess Diaries: Mia Goes Fourth
The Princess Diaries: Give Me Five
The Princess Diaries: Sixsational
The Princess Diaries: Seventh Heaven

Meg Cabot

Size 14 is not Fat Either

A Heather Wells Mystery

PAN BOOKS

First published 2006 by Avon Books,
an imprint of HarperCollins Publishers, USA

First published in Great Britain 2007 by Pan Books
an imprint of Pan Macmillan Ltd
Pan Macmillan, 20 New Wharf Road, London N1 9RR
Basingstoke and Oxford
Associated companies throughout the world
www.panmacmillan.com

ISBN 978-0-330-44394-4

3 5 7 9 8 6 4

A CIP catalogue record for this book is available from
the British Library.

Printed and bound in Great Britain by
Mackays of Chatham plc, Chatham, Kent

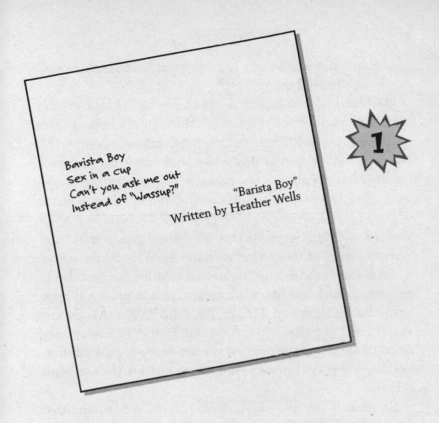

Barista Boy
Sex in a cup
Can't you ask me out
Instead of "Wassup?"

"Barista Boy"
Written by Heather Wells

The guy behind the counter is checking me out. No, really.

He's hot, too. Well, in a twenty-year-old barista kind of way. I bet he plays the guitar. I bet he stays up way too late at night, strumming, the way I do. I can tell by the slight shadows under his long-lashed green eyes, and the way his curly blond hair is sticking up in spikes all over his head. Bed head. No time to shower before work, because he was up so late practicing. Just like me.

"What'll it be?" he asks me. But with a look. A look that definitely says, *I'm checking you out*.

I know I'm the one he's checking out because there's no one in line behind me.

Well, and why *shouldn't* he check me out? I look good. I mean, the parts of me you can see through my bulky winter outerwear, anyway. I fully put on mascara *and* cover-up this morning (unlike Barista Boy, I like to disguise my undereye circles). And what with my parka, you can't see the four—well, okay, ten—pounds I put on over the holidays. Because who counts calories when it's Christmas? Or New Year's? Or after New Year's, when all that Christmas candy is on sale? There's plenty of time to get in shape again for bikini season.

And, okay, I've been telling myself that for the past five or six years, and I still haven't actually tried it yet—getting in shape for bikini season, I mean. But who knows? Maybe this year. I have two days of vacation due to me, all I've accrued since passing my employment probationary period in October. I could go to Cancún. And, okay, just for the weekend. But still.

So what if I'm five—well, maybe eight—years older than Barista Boy? I've still got it. Obviously.

"Grande café mocha, please," I say. I'm totally not into foamy drinks with whipped cream on top of them, but it's the first official day of spring semester (spring! Right!), and it's really cold out and supposed to blizzard later, and Cooper left this morning (for destinations unknown, as usual) without turning on the coffeemaker, and my dog Lucy wouldn't go out because it was so cold, so I'll probably find a nice surprise from her when I get home, and I REALLY need a little pick-me-up to help me quit feeling so sorry for myself.

Plus, you know, as long as I'm blowing five bucks on a cup of coffee, I might as well go for the gold.

"One grande café mocha, coming up," Barista Boy says,

doing one of those flippy things with my cup. You know, twirling it, like it's a gun and he's an outlaw in a western.

Oh, yeah. He *definitely* plays guitar. I wonder if he sits around writing songs he can never work up the guts actually to perform, like me? I wonder if he's constantly second-guessing his songwriting talent, like I am?

No. He's got the guts to get up in front of a crowd with a guitar and his own lyrics. I mean, just look at him.

"Soy or nonfat?" he asks.

Oh, God. I can't face my first day back to work after break on nonfat milk. And soy? *Soy?*

"Whole milk, please," I say. I'll be good later. At lunch I'll just have a chicken parm and a salad, and maybe just a BITE of lo-cal frozen yogurt. . . .

Mmmm, unless Magda got in more Dove Bars. . . .

"You know," Barista Boy says, as he rings me up, "you look really familiar."

"Oh," I say. I'm blushing with pleasure. He remembers me! He must see hundreds, maybe THOUSANDS of caffeine-starved New Yorkers a day, but he remembers ME! Fortunately it's so cold outside, and so warm in here, my red cheeks could easily be taken for the fact that I'm overheating in my coat, and not that I'm kvelling over his remembering me.

"Well, I live and work in the neighborhood," I say. "I'm in here all the time." Which isn't strictly true, since I'm keeping to a pretty tight budget (due to my pitiful salary), which foamy coffee drinks are definitely not part of, since I can get free coffee anytime I want from the cafeteria.

They just don't have mocha syrup in them. Or whipped cream. We tried to keep whipped cream canisters in the caf, but people kept swiping them in order to do whip-its.

"No," Barista Boy says, shaking his lusciously shaggy head. "That's not it. Actually, has anybody ever told you that you look a lot like Heather Wells?"

I take my drink from him. This, of course, is always the tricky part. What do I say? *Yes, actually . . . because I* am *Heather Wells*, and then run the risk of him asking me out simply because he thinks I still have connections in the music industry (so not. See above, re: fear of being booed off the stage)?

Or do I just laugh and say, *Why, no?* Because then what happens later, after we start dating, and he finds out I *am* Heather Wells? I mean, I could probably keep it a secret for a little while, but eventually he's going to find out my real name. Like when we're in Customs coming back from Cancún. Or when we're signing the marriage certificate. . . .

So I settle for saying, "Really?"

"Sure. Well, if you were thinner," Barista Boy says, with a smile. "Here's your change. Have a good one!"

What I can't believe is how the entire city can be gearing up for a predicted snowstorm—I mean, trucks filled with salt and sand can be lumbering down Tenth Street, breaking off tree limbs as they go by; the grocery stores can have already sold out of bread and milk; the television can show nothing but Storm Watch updates—and still, the drug dealers are out in full force in and around Washington Square Park.

I guess it just goes to show that we Americans still have a lot to learn from our hardworking immigrant population.

But there they are, standing on the sidewalk in their Perry Ellis parkas, enjoying some fresh mochaccinos of their own. Since it's the morning a significant—for New York City, anyway—amount of snow is being predicted to come down at any moment, very few people are walking by, but those who do are greeted with cheerful offers of sensimilla.

And okay, those offers are unanimously declined. But when the drug dealers notice me shuffling dejectedly toward them, they kindly shout a list of their wares in my direction.

I would laugh if I didn't still feel so grumpy about Barista Boy. Plus the fact that, every single time I step out of my house, I am accosted by these guys. It doesn't seem to matter to them that I have never once made a purchase. They only shrug as if I'm lying or something when I tell them that the strongest artificial stimulant I've consumed lately is caffeine. Sadly.

I'm not lying, though. A beer now and then is about as adventurous as I get.

Light beer, of course. Hey, a girl's gotta watch her figure.

"How you feelin' about all this white stuff that's supposed to fall from the sky soon, Heather?" one of the drug dealers, an affable guy named Reggie, steps away from his compatriots to ask me, with courtly solicitude.

"Better'n the white stuff you and your scum posse are peddling, Reggie," I am shocked to hear myself growl. God, what is *wrong* with me? Ordinarily, I'm super-polite to Reggie and his colleagues. It doesn't pay to antagonize your local dealer.

But ordinarily, I have not just been called fat by my favorite Barista Boy.

"Hey, baby," Reggie says, looking hurt. "There is no call to be offensive."

He's so right. It's wrong to call Reggie and his friends scum, while referring to those middle-aged men who toil away for the tobacco industry as senators.

"I'm sorry, Reggie," I say, meaning it. "You're right. It's just that for nine months now, you've been trying to hustle me right outside my front door, and for nine months now, I've been telling you no. What do you think is going to happen? I'm gonna turn into a raging cokehead overnight? Gimme a break."

"Heather." Reggie sighs, looking toward the thick gray clouds overhead. "I am a businessman. What kind of businessman would I be if I let a young woman like yourself, who is going through a very trying period in her life and could probably use a little pick-me-up, walk by without makin' an attempt to engage her business?"

And, to illustrate his meaning, Reggie takes a copy of the *New York Post* he's kept tucked under his arm, and opens it to the front page. There, in two-inch letters, screams the headline, *It's On Again*, over a black-and-white photo of my ex-fiancé hand in hand with his on-again, off-again bride-to-be, pop princess Tania Trace.

"Reggie," I say, after taking a restorative sip of my café mocha. But only because I'm so cold. I don't actually want it anymore, because it's covered with the taint of Barista Boy. Well, maybe I still want the whipped cream. Which is sort of good for you. I mean, it's dairy. And dairy's an important part of a well-balanced breakfast. "Do you really think I sit around all day fantasizing about getting back together with my ex? Because nothing could be further from the truth."

The fact is, I sit around all day fantasizing about getting together with my ex's brother, who continues to remain stubbornly immune to my charms.

But there's no reason my local drug dealer needs to know this.

"My apologies, Heather," Reggie says, refolding the paper. "I just thought you'd want to know. This morning on New

York One, they said the wedding is still scheduled to go on in St. Patrick's Cathedral, with the reception at the Plaza this Saturday."

I goggle at him. "Reggie," I say, stunned. "You watch New York One?"

Reggie looks mildly affronted. "I check the weather, like any New Yorker, before I leave for work."

Wow. That is so cute. He watches the weather before leaving for work to deal drugs on my street corner!

"Reggie," I say, impressed, "my apologies. I admire your dedication. Not only do you refuse to let the elements keep you from your work, but you're up on your local gossip. Please go right ahead and keep on trying to sell me drugs."

Reggie smiles, showing all of his teeth, many of which are capped—festively—in gold. "Thank you, baby," he says, as if I have just bestowed on him some very great honor.

I smile back at him, then continue my slog to my office. I shouldn't really call it a slog, though. I actually have a very short commute, which is good, since I have a problem getting up on time in the morning. If I lived in Park Slope or the Upper West Side or something, and had to take the subway to work every day, forget it (although, if I lived in Park Slope or the UWS, I'd be required by law to have a child, so it's just as well). I guess I'm really lucky, in a way. I mean, sure, I can barely afford a café mocha, and thanks to all of the holiday parties I attended, I can't fit into my size 12 stretch cords unless I'm wearing a pair of Spanx.

And okay, my ex is about to marry one of *People* magazine's 50 Most Beautiful People, and I don't even own my own car, let alone my own home.

But at least I get to live rent-free in a kick-ass apartment on the top floor of a brownstone two blocks from where I work in the coolest city in the entire world.

And okay, I only took my job, as the assistant director of a New York College dormitory, in order to get tuition remission benefits and actually attain the BA I lied about already having on my résumé.

And yeah, all right, so I'm having a little trouble getting into the School of Arts and Sciences due to my SAT score, which was so low that the dean won't admit me until I take—and pass—a remedial math course, despite my explaining to her that, in lieu of paying rent, I do all the billing for a very cute private detective, and have never once made an accounting error, that I know of.

But it is useless to expect a coldhearted bureaucracy—even the one you work for—to treat you as an individual.

So here I am, at nearly twenty-nine, about to learn the FOIL method for the first time (and let me tell you, I'm having a pretty hard time imagining a situation in which I might actually have to employ it).

And yeah, I write songs until late into the night, even though I can't, for the life of me, find the guts to actually sing them in front of anyone.

But still. My commute only takes two minutes, and I get to see my boss/landlord, on whom I have a major crush, wearing nothing but a towel from time to time as he darts from the bathroom to the laundry room to look for a clean pair of jeans.

So life's not *too* bad. In spite of Barista Boy.

Still, living super-close to my place of work has its drawbacks, too. For instance, people seem to have no compunction about calling me at home about inconsequential matters, like backed-up toilets or noise complaints. Like just because I live two blocks away, I should be able to come over at any hour to rectify matters my boss, the live-in building director, is supposed to handle.

But all in all, I like my job. I even like my new boss, Tom Snelling.

Which is why when I walk into Fischer Hall that arctic morning and find that Tom isn't there yet, I'm kinda bummed—and not just because that means there's no one to appreciate the fact that I'd made it in to the office before nine-thirty. No one except Pete, the security guard, who's on the phone, trying to get through to one of his many children's principals to find out about a detention one of them has been assigned for.

And I guess there's the work-study student manning the reception desk. But she doesn't even look up as I go by, she's so engrossed in a copy of *Us Weekly* she's stolen from the mail-forwarding bin (Jessica Simpson's on the cover. Again. She and Tania Trace are neck and neck for Tabloid Skank of the Year).

It's not until I turn the corner and pass the elevators that I see the line of undergrads outside the hall director's office. And I remember, belatedly, that the first day of spring semester is also the first day a lot of kids come back from Winter Break—the ones who didn't stay in the dorm (I mean, residence hall) to party until classes started again today, the day after Martin Luther King Day.

And when Cheryl Haebig—a New York College sophomore desperate for a room change because she's a bubbly cheerleader and her current roommate is a Goth who despises school spirit in all its guises, plus has a pet boa constrictor—leaps up from the institutional blue couch outside my office door and cries, "Heather!" I know I'm in for a morning of headaches.

Good thing I have my grande café mocha to keep me going.

The other students—each and every one of whom I recognize, since they've been in the office before due to roommate conflicts—scramble up from the cold marble floor on which they've been waiting, the couch being only a two-seater. I know what they've been waiting for. I know what they want.

And it's not going to be pretty.

"Look, you guys," I say, wrestling my office keys out of my coat pocket. "I told you. No room changes until all the transfer students are moved in. Then we'll see what's left."

"That's not fair," exclaims a skinny guy with large plastic disks in his earlobes. "Why should some stupid transfer student get dibs on all the open spaces? We got here first."

"I'm sorry," I say. I really am, because if I could just move them all, I wouldn't have to listen to their whining anymore. "But you're going to have to wait until they've all checked in. Then, if there are any spaces left, we can move you guys into them. If you can just hang on until next Monday, when we know who's checked in and who hasn't shown up—"

I am interrupted by general moaning. "By next Monday I'll be dead," one resident assures another.

"Or my roommate will," his friend says. "Because I'll have killed him by then."

"No killing your roommate," I say, having gotten the office door open and flicked on the lights. "Or yourself. Come on, guys. It's just another week."

Most of them go away, grumbling. Only Cheryl continues to hang around, looking excited as she follows me into my office. I see that she has a mousy-looking girl in tow.

"Heather," she says again. "Hi. Listen, remember when you

said if I found someone who would swap spaces with me, I could move? Well, I found someone. This is my friend Lindsay's roommate, Ann, and she said she'd swap with me."

I've peeled off my coat and hung it on a nearby hook. Now I sink into my desk chair and look at Ann, who appears to have a cold, from the way she's sniffling into a wadded-up Kleenex. I hand her the box I keep handy in case of Diet Coke spills.

"You want to trade spaces with Cheryl, Ann?" I ask her, just to make sure. I can't imagine why anyone would want to live with a person who painted the walls of her side of the room black.

Then again, it was probably annoying to Cheryl's roommate that Cheryl's side of the room was decorated with so many pansies, the New York College mascot.

"I guess," Ann says, looking wan.

"She does," Cheryl assures me brightly. "Don't you, Ann?"

Ann shrugs. "I guess," she says again.

I begin to sense Ann might have been coerced into agreeing to this room change.

"Ann," I say. "Have you *met* Cheryl's roommate, Karly? You know she, er . . . likes the color black?"

"Oh," Ann says. "Yeah. The Goth thing. I know. It's okay."

"And . . ." I hesitate to bring it up, because, ew. "The snake?"

"Whatever. I mean"—she looks at Cheryl—"no offense, or anything. But I'd rather live with a snake than a cheerleader."

Cheryl, far from being offended, beams at me.

"See?" she says. "So can we do the paperwork for our swap now? Because my dad is here to help me move, and he wants to get back to New Jersey before this big blizzard hits."

I pull out the forms, finding myself shrugging, just like Ann—it's sort of catching.

Meg Cabot

"Okay," I say, and hand them the papers they have to fill out to make the switch. When the girls—Cheryl giddy with excitement, Ann decidedly more calm—finish filling out their forms and leave, I look over last night's briefing forms. Fischer Hall is staffed round-the-clock by a security guard, student front desk receptionists, and resident assistants, students who, in exchange for free room and board, act as sort of house mothers on each of the hall's twenty floors. They all have to fill out reports at the end of their shifts, and my job is to read and follow up on these briefings. This always makes for an interesting morning.

The reports range from the ludicrous to the banal. Last night, for instance, six forty-ounce bottles of beer were hurled from an upper-story window onto the roof of a cab passing on the street below. Ten cops from the Sixth Precinct arrived and ran up and down the stairs a few times, unsuccessfully trying to figure out who the pitcher had been.

On the other end of the spectrum, the front desk apparently lost someone's Columbia House CD of the Month, causing much consternation. One of the RAs somberly reports that a resident slammed her door several times, crying, "I hate it here." The RA wishes to refer the student to Counseling Services.

Another report states that a small riot occurred when a cafeteria worker chastised a student for attempting to make an English muffin pizza in the toaster oven.

When my phone jangles, I pounce on it, grateful for something to do. I do love my job—really. But I have to admit it doesn't tax my intellect overly much.

"Fischer Hall, this is Heather, how may I help you?" My last boss, Rachel, had been very strict about how I answered the phone. Even though Rachel's not around anymore, old habits die hard.

"Heather?" I can hear an ambulance in the background. "Heather, it's Tom."

"Oh, hi, Tom." I glance at the clock. Nine-twenty. Yes! I was in when he'd called! If not on time, then at least before ten! "Where are you?"

"St. Vincent's." Tom sounds exhausted. Being the residence hall director of a New York College dormitory is a very demanding job. You have to look out for about seven hundred undergraduates, most of whom, with the exception of summer camp or maybe a stint in boarding school, have never been away from home for an extended period of time before in their lives—let alone have ever shared a bathroom with another human being. Residents come to Tom with all of their problems—roommate conflicts, academic issues, financial concerns, sexual identity crises—you name it, Tom has heard it.

And if a resident gets hurt or sick, it's the residence hall director's job to make sure he or she is okay. Needless to say, Tom spends a lot of time in emergency rooms, particularly on weekends, which is when most of the underage drinking goes on. And he does all this—is on duty twenty-four hours a day, three hundred and forty-three days a year (all New York College administrators get twenty-two vacation days)—for not much more than I make, plus free room and board.

Hey, is it any wonder my last boss only lasted a few months?

Tom seems pretty stable, though. I mean, as stable as a six-foot-three, two-hundred-pound former Texas A&M linebacker whose favorite movie is *Little Women* and who moved

to New York City so he could finally come out of the closet
can be.

"Look, Heather," Tom says tiredly. "I'm gonna be stuck
here for a few more hours at least. We had a twenty-first
birthday last night."

"Uh-oh." Twenty-first birthday celebrations are the *worst*.
Inevitably, the hapless birthday boy or girl is urged to slam
back twenty-one shots by his or her party guests. Since the
human body cannot process that much alcohol in such a
short period of time, most of the time the resident ends up
celebrating his or her big day in one of our local emergency
rooms. Nice, huh?

"Yeah," Tom says. "I hate to ask, but would you mind going
through my appointment books and rescheduling all my ju-
dicial hearings this morning? I don't know if they're gonna
admit this kid or not, and he won't let us call his parents—"

"No problem," I say. "How long you been there?"

Tom exhales gustily. "He only got up to seven before he
passed out. So since midnight, or thereabouts. I've lost all
track of time."

"I'll come spell you if you want." When a student is in the
emergency room but hasn't been admitted, it's policy that a
New York College representative stay with him or her at all
times. You can't even go home to take a lousy shower unless
there's someone there to take your place. New York College
does not leave its students alone in the ER. Even though the
students themselves will frequently check out without even
bothering to tell you, so you're sitting there watching Spanish soaps for an hour before you find out the kid isn't even
there anymore. "Then at least you can get some breakfast."

"You know, Heather," Tom says, "I think I'll take you up on
that offer, if you really don't mind."

I say I don't and am taking money out of petty cash for cab fare before I've even hung up. I love petty cash. It's like having your own bank, right in the office. Unfortunately, Justine, the girl who'd had my position before me, had felt the same way, and had spent all of Fischer Hall's petty cash on ceramic heaters for her friends and family. The Budget Office still scrutinizes our petty cash vouchers with an eagle eye every time I take them over for reimbursement, even though each and every one of them is completely legit.

And I still haven't figured out what a ceramic heater is.

I finish rescheduling all of Tom's appointments, then polish off my café mocha in a gulp. *If you were thinner.* You know what, Barista Boy? With those long nails you won't trim because you're too poor to afford a new guitar pick, you look like a girl. Yeah, that's right. A girl. How do you like *that*, Barista Boy?

Quick stop at the cafeteria to grab a bagel to eat on the way to the hospital, and I'll be ready to go. I mean, café mochas are all well and good, but they don't supply lasting energy . . . not like a bagel does. Particularly a bagel smothered in cream cheese (dairy) over which several layers of bacon (protein) have been added.

I've grabbed my coat and am getting up to get my bagel when I notice Magda, my best work bud and the cafeteria's head cashier, standing in my office doorway, looking very unlike her usual self.

"Morning, Magda," I say to her. "You will never believe what Barista Boy said to me."

But Magda, normally a very inquisitive person, and a big fan of Barista Boy, doesn't look interested.

"Heather," she says. "I have something I have to show you."

"If it's the front page of the *Post*," I say, "Reggie already beat you to it. And really, Mags, it's okay. *I'm* okay. I can't believe she took him back after that whole thing at the Pussycat Dolls with Paris. But, hey, his dad owns her record label. What else is she going to do?"

Magda shakes her head.

"No," she says. "Not the *Post*. Just come, Heather. Come."

Curious—more because she still hasn't cracked a smile than because I actually think she has something so earth-shattering to show me—I follow Magda down the hall, past the student government office—closed this early in the morning—and Magda's boss's office, which, oddly, is empty. Normally, the dining office is filled with kvetching cafeteria workers and cigarette smoke, Gerald Eckhardt, the dining hall director, being an unapologetic smoker. He's only supposed to light up outside, but invariably I catch him puffing away at his desk, then blowing the smoke out the open window, like he doesn't think anyone is going to catch on.

But not today. Today the office is empty—and smoke-free.

"Magda," I say, as her pink smock disappears through the swinging doors to the cafeteria's loud, steaming kitchen, "what is going on?"

But Magda doesn't say anything until she's standing beside the massive industrial stove, on which a single pot has been set to boil. Gerald is standing there as well, looking out of place in his business suit among his pink-smocked employees, dwarfing everyone else with his massive frame—a result of sampling his own recipe for chicken parm a little too often.

Gerald looks—well, there's only one word for it: frightened. So does Saundra, the salad bar attendant, and Jimmy, the hotline server. Magda is pale beneath her bright makeup. And Pete—what's *Pete* doing here?—looks like he wants to hurl.

"Okay, you guys," I say. I am convinced whatever is going on has to be a joke. Because Gerald, being in food services, is a prankster from way back, a master of the rubber rat in the desk drawer, and plastic spider in the soup. "What gives? April Fool's isn't for another three months. Pete, what are you doing back here?"

Which is when Pete—who's wearing, for some reason, an oven mitt—reaches out and lifts the lid from the merrily boiling pot, and I get a good look at what's inside.

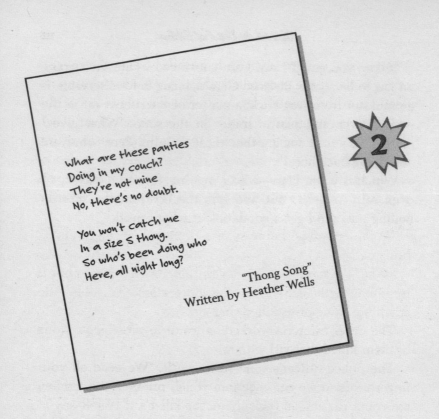

What are these panties
Doing in my couch?
They're not mine
No, there's no doubt.

You won't catch me
In a size S thong.
So who's been doing who
Here, all night long?

"Thong Song"
Written by Heather Wells

2

The Fischer Hall cafeteria is crowded, but not with students. We told the residents there was a gas leak—not one big enough to evacuate the whole building, but one that necessitated closing down the caf.

The sad thing is, they were all so bleary-eyed from partying the night before, the residents actually seemed to believe us. At least, no one protested—once I started handing out the free-meal voucher cards, so they could go eat in the student union.

Now the dining hall is still packed—but with college presidents, administrators, cafeteria workers, police officers, and homicide detectives, instead of hungry eighteen-year-olds.

Even so, the room is strangely hushed, so that the energy-saving bulbs in the chandeliers above our heads—casting reflections in the stained-glass windows near the edges of the high ceiling—seem to be humming more noisily than usual. Above the humming, I can hear Magda sniffling. She's sitting on one side of the cafeteria with the rest of her fellow workers, in their hairnets and pink uniforms and French manicures. A city police officer is speaking to them in a gentle tone.

"We'll let you go home soon as we get your fingerprints," he says.

"What do you need our fingerprints for?" Magda's chin is trembling with fear—or maybe indignation. "We didn't do anything. None of us killed that girl!"

The other cafeteria workers murmur in agreement. None of them killed that girl, either.

The police officer's tone stays gentle. "We need all your fingerprints so we can ascertain which prints in the kitchen are yours, ma'am, and which are the killer's. If he left any."

"Ascertain away," Gerald says, coming to the defense of his employees. "But I'm tellin' you right now, none of my folks is a murderer. Am I right, people?"

Everyone in a pink smock nods solemnly. Their eyes, however, are shining with something a little more than just tears. I suspect it might be excitement: Not only had they found a murder victim in their kitchen, right there amid the corn dogs and peanut-butter-and-jelly bars, but now they are valuable witnesses to a crime, and as such are being treated not as cafeteria workers—untouchables, as far as the students they serve are concerned—but as actual thinking human beings.

For a few of them, this might actually be a first.

I spot the head of the Housing Department, Dr. Jessup, at a table with several other administrators, all looking dazed. The discovery of a corpse's head on campus has worked as an expedient in getting the administrative staff to work before ten, despite the impending blizzard. Even the college president, Phillip Allington, is there, seated next to Steven Andrews, the new head basketball coach, who looks worried. He has good reason to: The entire New York College varsity basketball team—not to mention the varsity cheerleading squad—is housed in Fischer Hall, thanks to the building's close proximity to Winer Complex, the college sports center.

After the two student deaths in this building during the first semester—winning Fischer Hall the nickname Death Dorm—all the university employees (including sport coaches) seem to be feeling a little jumpy. And who can blame them? Especially President Allington. His tenure hasn't been an easy one. No one knows that better than me, assistant director of Death Dorm.

And now it looks as if things have just gotten immeasurably worse, not just for the president, but for my boss's boss, the head of Housing . . . and he knows it. The show-hanky tucked into his breast pocket is crumpled, as if someone—exercising my superlative investigative skills, I surmise that someone was Dr. Jessup himself—has actually been using it. Sitting slumped in a chair at a sticky cafeteria table for the past half hour hasn't done much for the creases in Dr. Jessup's suit, either.

"Heather," Dr. Jessup says to me, a little too heartily, as I come toward his table, having been summoned away from my desk—where I went directly after Pete's revelation to begin calling everyone I could think of, including Dr. Jessup and my boss, Tom—by one of the police officers. "Detective Canavan wants to talk to you. You remember Detective Canavan from the Sixth Precinct, don't you?"

Like I could forget.

"Detective," I say, extending my right hand toward the slightly rumpled-looking middle-aged man with the graying mustache, who stands with one foot resting on the seat of an empty cafeteria chair.

Detective Canavan looks up from the cup of coffee he's holding. His eyes are the color of slate, and the skin around them is wrinkled from overexposure to the elements. It's no joke, being a New York City homicide detective. Sadly, not all of them look like Chris Noth. In fact, none of them do, that I've noticed.

"Nice to see you again, Heather," the detective says. His grasp is as formidable as ever. "I understand you've seen it. So. Any ideas?"

I look from the detective to the head honcho of my department and back again.

"Um," I say, not sure what's going on. Wait—do Dr. Jessup and Detective Canavan actually want my help in solving this heinous crime? Because this is so the opposite of how they were about my helping them out last time. . . . "Where's the rest of her?"

"That isn't what Detective Canavan meant, Heather," Dr. Jessup says, with a forced smile. "He meant, do you recognize . . . it?"

Carol Ann Evans, dean of students—yeah, the same one who won't admit me into her college until I show her I can multiply fractions—happens to be seated nearby, and makes a kind of gagging noise and covers her mouth with a wadded-up tissue when she hears the word *it*.

And, to my certain knowledge, she hasn't even taken a peek at what's inside that pot.

Oh. They don't really want my help. Not THAT way.

I say, "Well, it's kinda hard to tell." No way am I going to announce, in front of all these people, that Lindsay Combs, homecoming queen and (now no longer) future roommate of her best friend Cheryl Haebig, had apparently been decapitated by person or persons unknown, and her head left in a pot on the stove in the Fischer Hall cafeteria.

I know. Ew.

"Come, now, Heather," Dr. Jessup says, with a smile that doesn't quite reach his eyes. To Detective Canavan he says, loudly enough for everyone in the caf to hear, apparently in an effort to impress President Allington, who wouldn't know me from Adam—though his wife and I were once nearly murdered by the same person—"Heather here knows every single one of Fischer Hall's seven hundred residents by name. Don't you, Heather?"

"Well, generally speaking," I say uncomfortably. "When they haven't been set on simmer for a few hours."

Did that sound flip? I guess it did. Dean Evans is gagging again. I didn't mean to be flip. It's just that . . . come *on*.

I hope the dean isn't going to hold this against me. You know, admission-to-the-College-of-Arts-and-Sciences-wise.

"So who is she? The girl." The detective seems unconscious of the fact that nearly everyone in the cafeteria is eavesdropping on our conversation. "A name would be nice."

I feel my stomach roll a little, like it had back in the kitchen when Pete had lifted the lid and I'd found myself staring into those unseeing eyes.

I take a deep breath. The air in the cafeteria is pungent

with ordinary breakfast smells . . . eggs and sausage and maple syrup. You can't smell *her.*

At least, I don't think so.

Still, I'm thankful that I haven't had time this morning for my customary cream-cheese-and-bacon bagel breakfast. The café mocha has—so far—been more than enough. The parquet of the dining hall floor is swimming a little before my eyes.

I clear my throat. There. That feels a little better.

"Lindsay Combs," I say. "She dates—dated—the Pansies' point guard." The Pansies is the (sad) name of the New York College Division III basketball team. They lost their real name, the Cougars, in a cheating scandal in the fifties, and have been stuck with being Pansies ever since—to the amusement of the teams they play, and their own everlasting chagrin.

Everyone in the room sucks in their breath. President Allington—dressed, as usual, in his interpretation of what one of his college's students might wear (if it were 1955), a New York College letter jacket and gray cords—actually cries, "No!" Beside the president, Coach Andrews—as I'd known he would—goes pale.

"Oh, God," he says. He's a big guy—around my own age—with spiky dark hair and disarmingly blue eyes . . . what they call Black Irish. He'd be cute if he wasn't so muscle-bound. Oh, and if he ever actually noticed I was alive.

Not that, if he did, anything would ever come of it, since my heart belongs to another.

"Not Lindsay," he says, with a groan.

I feel for him. I really do. Cheryl Haebig isn't the only one who liked Lindsay . . . we all did. Well, everyone except our office graduate student assistant, Sarah. Lindsay was an immensely popular girl, the captain of the New York College cheerleading squad, with waist-length honey-colored hair and grapefruit-sized breasts that Sarah maintained were the result of plastic surgery. While Lindsay's excessive school spirit could be annoyingly perky (to me, anyway) at times, it was at least a pleasant change from the usual type of New York College students we saw in our office—spoiled, dissatisfied, and threatening to call their lawyer father if we didn't get them a single or an extra-long bed.

"Jesus Christ." Dr. Jessup hadn't believed it when I'd called to say that he needed to get to Fischer Hall as soon as possible, due to the fact that one of our residents had lost her head . . . literally. Now he looks as though it's finally sinking in. "Are you *sure*, Heather?"

"Yeah," I say. "I'm sure. It's Lindsay Combs. Head cheerleader." I swallow again. "Sorry. No pun intended."

Detective Canavan has removed a notepad from his belt, but he doesn't write anything in it. Instead, he flips slowly through the pages, not looking up. "How could you tell?"

I'm trying hard not to remember those unseeing eyes looking up at me—only not. "Lindsay wore contact lenses. Tinted. Green." Such an unnatural shade of green that Sarah, back in the office, always asked, whenever Lindsay left, "Who the hell does she think she's fooling? That color does *not* occur in nature."

"That's all?" Detective Canavan asks. "Tinted contact lenses?"

"And the earrings. She's got three on one side, two on the other. She came down to my office a lot," I say, by way of explaining how I was so familiar with her piercings.

"Troublemaker?" Detective Canavan asks.

"No," I say. Most students who end up in the office of the

residence hall director are either there because they're in trouble, or they've got a problem with their roommate. Or, as in Lindsay's case, because they want the free birth control I keep in a jar on my desk instead of Hershey's kisses (lower in calories). "Condoms."

Detective Canavan raises his gray eyebrows. "I beg your pardon?"

"Lindsay stopped by a lot for free condoms," I say. "She and her boyfriend were pretty hot and heavy."

"Name?"

I realize, belatedly, that I've just managed to incriminate one of my residents. Coach Andrews realizes it, too.

"Aw, come on, Detective," he says. "Mark isn't capable of—"

"Mark what?" Detective Canavan demands.

Coach Andrews, I see, is looking panicky. Dr. Allington rushes in to his favorite employee's rescue. Well, sort of.

"The Pansies do have a very important ball game tomorrow night," the president begins worriedly, "against the Jersey College East Devils. We're eight-and-oh, you know."

To which Coach Andrews adds defensively, "And none of my boys had anything to do with what happened to Lindsay. I don't want them dragged into it."

Detective Canavan—not even sounding like he's lying, which I know he is—says, "I sympathize with your dilemma, Coach. You, too, Dr. Allington. But the fact is, I have a job to do. Now—"

"I don't think *you* understand, Detective," Dr. Allington interrupts. "Tomorrow night's game is being televised on New York One. Millions of dollars of commercial advertising is at stake here."

I stare at the president, openmouthed in astonishment. I

notice Dean Evans is doing the same thing. She meets my gaze, and it's clear we're both thinking: *Whoa. He did* not *just say that.*

You would think, considering we're both on the same cognitive wavelength, she'd be a little more sympathetic about the remedial math thing. But I guess not.

"*You're* the one who doesn't understand, Doctor." Detective Canavan's voice is hard, and loud enough to make Magda and her fellow cafeteria workers stop crying and lift up their heads. "Either your people give me the name of the girl's boyfriend now, or you'll be sending more girls home later this semester in body bags. Because I can guarantee, whatever sick bastard did this to Miss Combs, he will do it again, to someone else."

Dr. Allington stares hard at the detective, who stares even harder back.

"Mark Shepelsky," I say quickly. "Her boyfriend's name is Mark Shepelsky. He's in Room Two-twelve."

Coach Andrews slumps across the tabletop, burying his head in his arms. Dr. Allington groans, pinching the bridge of his nose between his thumb and index finger as if stricken by a sudden sinus headache. Dr. Jessup just looks at the ceiling, while Dr. Flynn, the Housing Department's on-staff psychologist, smiles sadly at me from the table where he sits with the other school administrators.

Detective Canavan looks a bit calmer as he flips his notepad back open and jots down the name.

"There," he says. "That didn't hurt, now, did it?"

"But," I say. Detective Canavan sighs audibly at my *But*. I ignore him. "Lindsay's boyfriend couldn't have had anything to do with this."

Detective Canavan turns his rock-hard stare on me. "And just how would you know that?"

"Well," I say, "whoever killed her had to have access to a key to the cafeteria. Because he'd need one to sneak in before the caf was open in order to hack up his girlfriend, clean the place up, and get out by the time the staff arrived. But how would Mark get hold of a key? I mean, if you think about it, Fischer Hall employees ought to really be your primary suspects—"

"Heather." Detective Canavan's already squinty eyes narrow even further. "Do not—I repeat, do not—be getting any ideas that you're going to be launching your own personal investigation into this girl's murder. This is the work of a sick and unbalanced mind, and it'd be in the best interest of everyone, yourself most particularly, if this time you left the investigating to the professionals. Believe me, we have things under control."

I blink at him. Detective Canavan can be scary when he wants to be. I can tell that even the deans are scared. Coach Andrews looks terrified. And he's about a foot taller than the detective, and about fifty pounds heavier . . . all of it muscle.

I long to point out to the detective that I would not have had to launch my own personal investigation into last semester's murders if he had actually listened to me from the beginning that they *were*, in fact, murders.

But it's pretty obvious he seems to get it this time around.

I should probably tell him that I have absolutely no desire at all to get involved with *this* particular criminal case. I mean, throwing girls down an elevator shaft is one thing. Chopping their heads off? So not something I want to involve myself in. My knees are still shaking from what I saw inside that pot. Detective Canavan so doesn't need to worry about me doing any investigating this time. The professionals are *welcome* to this one.

"Are you listening to me, Wells?" the detective demands. "I said I do not want a repeat performance—"

"I got it," I interrupt quickly. I'd elaborate—like how about no way do I want anything to do with headless cheerleaders—but decide it would be wiser simply to retreat.

"Can I go now?" I ask—I direct the question more at Dr. Jessup, since he is, in fact, my boss—well, Tom's my direct boss, but since Tom's busy trying to figure out if there are any cafeteria keys missing (a task he seems to relish, since it keeps him well away from what they found on the stove—and the fact that he's been asked to look is also proof that Detective Canavan is right . . . the NYPD *does* have things under control), Stan's the closest thing I've got nearby.

But Stan is staring at *his* boss, President Allington, who is trying to get Detective Canavan's attention. Which is sort of a relief, since I've had all of Detective Canavan's attention I can take for the moment. That dude can be *scary*.

"So what I hear you telling me, Detective . . ." Dr. Allington is saying, his careful phrasing illustrative of the training that had earned him his PhD. "What I hear you saying is that this unfortunate matter will most likely not be cleared up by lunch today? Because my office was planning on hosting a special function this afternoon to honor our hardworking student athletes, and it would be a shame to have to postpone it. . . ."

The look the detective levels at the college president might have frozen lava. "Dr. Allington, we're not talking about some kid barfing up his breakfast in the locker room after gym class."

"I realize that, Detective," Dr. Allington says. "However, I had hoped—"

"For Christ's sake, Phil," Dr. Jessup interrupts. He's had enough. Finally. "Someone tried to fricassee a kid, and you wanna open up the salad bar?"

"All I'm saying," Dr. Allington says, looking indignant, "is that, in my professional opinion, it would be best not to allow this incident to interfere with the residents' normal routine. You'll recall that a few years ago, when the school had that rash of suicides, it was the publicity about them that generated so many of the copycat attempts—"

Detective Canavan apparently can't help raising an incredulous gray eyebrow at that one. "You think half a dozen coeds are gonna rush home and whack off their own heads?"

"What I'm trying to say," Dr. Allington continues haughtily, "is that if the luncheon is canceled—not to mention tomorrow night's game—the truth about what's happened here is going to be impossible to keep from leaking. We're not going to be able to keep something like this quiet for long. I'm not talking about the *Post*, either, or even 1010 WINS. I'm talking about the *New York Times*, maybe even CNN. If your people don't find that girl's body soon, Detective, we may even attract the networks. And that could be very damaging to the school's reputation—"

"Corpseless head found in dorm cafeteria," Carol Ann Evans, to everyone's surprise, says. When we all turn our heads to blink at her, she adds, in a choked voice, "Tonight on *Inside Edition*."

Detective Canavan shifts his weight and removes his foot from the chair seat.

"President Allington," he says. "In about five minutes, my people are going to seal this entire wing off from the public.

And by public, I am including your employees. We are launching a full-scale investigation into this crime. We ask that you cooperate.

"You can do so, firstly, by removing yourself and your employees from the immediate vicinity as soon as my men are through with them. Secondly, I'll have to ask that this cafeteria remain closed until such time as I deem it safe to re-open. Unless I'm mistaken"—the detective's tone implies that this is hardly likely—"you've had a student murdered on school grounds this morning, and her killer is still at large, possibly right here on campus. Possibly even here in this very room. If there's anything that could be more damaging to your school's reputation than that, I can't think of it. I really don't think postponing a luncheon—or a basketball game—is comparable, do you?"

I guess I can't really blame Dean Evans for bursting into a fit of nervous giggles just then. The suggestion that there might be a killer on the New York College student life administrative staff is enough to send even the most staid individual into hysterical laughter. A more boring group of people could hardly be found anywhere on the planet. Gerald Eckhardt, with his surreptitious smoking and cross-shaped tie tack, wielding a meat cleaver? Coach Andrews, in his jogging pants and letter jacket, hacking a young girl to death? Dr. Flynn, all hundred and forty pounds of him, using a circular saw to dismember a cheerleader?

It just isn't within the realm of the possible.

And yet.

And yet even Carol Ann Evans must have figured out by now that whoever killed Lindsay had complete access to the cafeteria. Only someone who works at Fischer Hall—

or in the Student Life Department—would have access to the key.

Which means someone on the Housing staff could be a killer.

The sad part is, this doesn't even surprise me.

Wow. I guess I really *am* a jaded New Yorker.

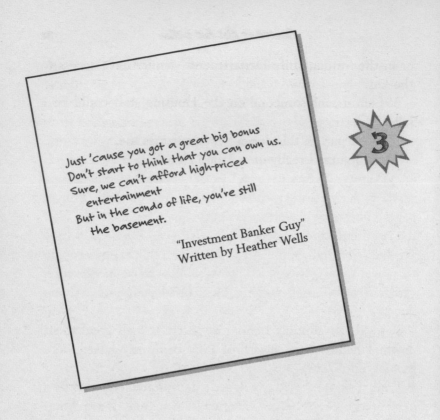

Just 'cause you got a great big bonus
Don't start to think that you can own us.
Sure, we can't afford high-priced
   entertainment
But in the condo of life, you're still
   the basement.

"Investment Banker Guy"
Written by Heather Wells

3

"You have a bunch of messages," Sarah, our office's graduate student assistant—every residence hall is assigned a GA, who, in exchange for free room and board, helps run the administrative aspects of the hall office—informs me tersely as I come in. "The phones are ringing off the hook. Everyone wants to know why the caf is closed. I've been using the gas leak excuse, but I don't know how long people are going to believe us, with all these cops traipsing in and out. Have they found the rest of her yet?"

"Shhh," I say, looking around the office, in case there's a resident lurking.

But the office (still festooned with garlands of fake ever-green, a menorah, and Kwanzaa gourds, thanks to my slightly manic and clearly overzealous holiday decorating) is empty, except for Tom, who is back in his office—separated from the outer office, in which I sit, by a metal grate—murmuring into the phone.

"Whatever," Sarah says, rolling her eyes. Sarah is getting a master's in psychology, so she knows a lot about the human psyche and how it works. Or thinks she does, anyway. "Half the people in the building aren't even awake yet. Or, if they are, they've hurried off to class. So do you think they're going to cancel tomorrow night's game? Not because of this bliz-zard we're supposed to be getting, but because of . . . you know. Her?"

"Um," I say, slipping behind my desk. It feels good to sit down. I hadn't been aware of how badly my knees were shaking until now.

Well, it's not every day you see a decapitated cheerleader's head in a pot. Especially a cheerleader you knew. It's no won-der I'm a little shaky. Plus, except for the café mocha, I still haven't had breakfast.

Not that I feel like eating. Well, very much.

"I don't know," I say. "They want to question Mark."

Sarah looks annoyed. "He didn't do it," she says scornfully. "He's not smart enough. Unless he had help."

It's true. The admission standards for New York College are some of the highest in the country . . . except when it comes to athletes. Basically any semi-decent ballplayer who wants to come to New York College is accepted, since, as a Division III school, all the best athletes tend to go to colleges in Division I or II. Still, President Allington is determined to have his legacy at New York College be that he turned it into an actual contender in the world of college ball—his ultimate goal, it's rumored, is to have the school's Division I rating reinstated.

Though the likelihood of this happening—especially in light of today's events—seems slim.

"I still can't get over it," Sarah is saying. "Where could her body be?"

"Where all bodies in New York City turn up," I say, looking at my phone messages. "In the river somewhere. No one'll find it till spring, when the temperature rises enough to cause the body to bob."

I'm no forensic expert, of course, and I haven't even been able to enroll in any criminal justice courses yet, thanks to the remedial math I need to get through first.

But I've watched a lot of *Law and Order* and *CSI*.

Plus, you know, I live with a private detective. Or "share a domicile with," I should say, since "live with" sounds like we share more than that, which we don't. Sadly.

Sarah shudders elaborately, even though it's warm in the office and she's wearing one of the thick striped sweaters woven for her by a fellow member of the kibbutz upon which she spent the summer of her freshman year. It looks quite fetching over her overalls.

"It just doesn't make any sense," she says. "How can there be another murder in this building? We really ARE turning into Death Dorm."

I'm looking at my messages. My best friend Patty—she's no doubt seen the cover of today's *Post*, and is as worried as Reggie was about how it's affected me. Someone who wouldn't give his name and said he'd call back later—creditor, no doubt. I'd maxed out the cards a little in my preholiday gift-buying frenzy. If I can hold them off until March, I'll pay it all back when I get my tax refund. And—

I wave the slip at Sarah. "Is this for real? Did he really call? Or are you yanking my chain?"

Sarah looks surprised. "Honestly, Heather," she says. "Do you think I'd joke around on a day like today? Jordan Cartwright really did call. Or, at least, someone who *claimed* to be Jordan Cartwright called. He wants you to call him back right away. He said it was vitally important. Emphasis on the vitally."

Well, that sounds like Jordan, all right. Everything is vitally important to Jordan. Especially if it involves humiliating me in some way.

"What if," Sarah says, "Lindsay's body isn't in the river? Supposing it's still in the building. Supposing . . . my God, supposing it's still in Lindsay's room!"

"Then we'd have heard from Cheryl already," I say. "Since she and Lindsay's roommate swapped spaces first thing this morning."

"Oh." Sarah looks disappointed. Then she brightens. "Maybe it's somewhere else in the building! Like in someone else's room. Could you imagine coming home from class and finding a headless body in your swivel chair, like in front of your computer?"

My stomach twists. The café mocha is not resting well.

"Sarah," I say. "Seriously. Shut up."

"Oh, my God, or what if like we find it in the game room, propped up against the foosball table?"

"Sarah." I glare at her.

"Oh, lighten up, Heather, " she says, with a laugh. "Can't you tell I'm resorting to gallows humor in an effort to break the connection between such a horrifying stimulus and an unwanted emotional response, such as revulsion or fear, which in this case wouldn't be helpful or professional?"

"I'd prefer revulsion," I say. "I don't think anyone has to be professional when there's a headless cheerleader involved."

It's at this moment that Tom chooses to appear in the doorway to his office.

"Can we not say that word?" he asks queasily, grasping the doorframe for support.

"What?" Sarah flicks some of her curly hair off her shoulder. "*Cheerleader?*"

"No," Tom says. "*Headless.* We *have* her head. Just not the rest of her. Oh, God. I can't believe I just said that." He looks at me miserably. There are purple shadows under his bloodshot eyes from his night spent at the hospital, and his blond hair is plastered unattractively to his forehead from lack of product. Under ordinary circumstances, Tom wouldn't be caught dead looking so unkempt. He's actually fussier about his hair than I am.

"You should go to bed," I say to him. "We've got things covered in here, Sarah and I."

"I can't go to bed." Now Tom looks shocked. "A girl's been found dead in my building. Can you imagine how that would look to Jessup and everybody? If I just . . . went to bed? I'm still on employment probation, you know. They'd just decide I can't hack it and—" He swallows. "Oh, my God, did I just say the word *hack?*"

"Go back in your office, shut the door, and close your eyes for a while," I say to him. "I'll cover for you."

"I can't," Tom says. "Every time I close my eyes, I see . . . her."

I don't have to ask what he means. I know, only too well. Since the same thing keeps happening to me.

"Hey." A kid in a hoodie, with a tiny silver pair of barbells pierced through the bottom of his nose, leans his head into the office. "Why's the caf closed?"

"Gas leak," Sarah, Tom, and I all say at the same time.

"Jesus," the kid says, making a face. "So I gotta walk across campus to get breakfast?"

"Go to the student union," Sarah says quickly, holding out a meal pass. "On us."

The kid looks down at the voucher. "*Sweet*," he says, because with the voucher, the meal won't be subtracted from his daily quota. Now he can have TWO dinners, if he wants to. He shuffles happily away.

"I don't see why we can't just tell them the truth," Sarah declares, as soon as he's gone. "They're gonna find out anyway."

"Right," Tom says. "But we don't want to cause a panic. You know, that there's a psychopathic killer loose in the building."

"And," I add carefully, "we don't want people finding out who it was before they've gotten hold of Lindsay's parents."

"Yeah," Tom says. "What she said." It's weird having a boss who doesn't actually know what he's doing. I mean, Tom's great, don't get me wrong.

But he's no Rachel Walcott.

Which, on balance, is something to be grateful for. . . .

"Hey, you guys," Sarah says. "What am I? Ha, ha, ha, thump."

Tom and I look at one another blankly.

"I don't know," I say.

"Someone laughing his head off. Get it? Ha, ha, ha,

thump." Sarah looks at us reprovingly when we don't laugh. "Gallows humor, people. To help us COPE."

I glance at Tom. "Who's with the birthday kid?" I ask him. "The one at the hospital? If you and I are here, I mean?"

"Oh, crap," Tom says, looking ashen-faced. "I forgot about him. I got the call, and—"

"You just *left* him?" Sarah rolls her eyes. Her contempt for our new boss isn't something she tries to hide. She thinks Dr. Jessup should have hired *her* to take over, even though she's a full-time student. A full-time student whose part-time hobby is analyzing the problems of everyone she meets. I, for instance, allegedly have abandonment issues, due to my mother running off to Argentina with my manager . . . and all of my money.

And because I have not pursued the issue as aggressively as Sarah thinks I should via the courts, I allegedly suffer from low self-esteem and passivity, as well. At least according to Sarah.

But I feel like I have a choice (well, not really, because it's not like I've got the money to pursue it in the courts, anyway): I can sit around and be bitter and resentful over what Mom did. Or I can put it behind me and just get on with my life.

Is it wrong I choose the latter?

Sarah seems to think so. Although this is only the stuff she tells me when she's not busy accusing me of having some kind of Superman complex, for wanting to save all the residents in Fischer Hall from ever coming to harm.

It really isn't any mystery to me why Sarah didn't get the job and Tom did. All Tom ever says to me is stuff like he likes my shoes, and did I see *American Idol* last night. It's much easier to get along with Tom than it is with Sarah.

"Well, I think murder trumps alcohol poisoning," I say, coming to Tom's defense. "But we still need to have someone there with the resident, especially if he doesn't end up getting admitted. . . ." If Stan finds out we have a resident in the ER with no one there to supervise his care, he will flip out. I don't want to lose my new boss just when I'm starting to like him. "Sarah—"

"I have a lab," she says, not even looking up from the sign-in sheets she's gathering to photocopy, ostensibly so the police can check to see if Lindsay had any guests the night before who might have decided to repay her hospitality by cutting her head off.

Except, of course, Lindsay hadn't. We'd been over the logs twice. Nothing.

"But—"

"I can't miss it," Sarah says. "It's the first one of the new semester!"

"I'll go, then," I say.

"Heather, no." Tom looks panicky. I can't tell if it's because he genuinely doesn't want to put me through a New York City ER waiting room after what I've already been through this morning, or if it's just that he doesn't want to be left alone in the office, considering the fact that he's so new to his job. "I'll get one of the RAs. . . ."

"They'll all have classes, too, just like Sarah," I say. I'm already on my feet and reaching for my coat. The truth is, I'm not trying to be a martyr. I'm actually seriously welcoming the chance to get out of there. Though I try not to act like it. "Really, it's fine. They'll have to admit him soon, right? Or let him go. So I'll be back soon. It *is* a he, right?"

"What girl would be stupid enough to try to drink twenty-one shots in one night?" Sarah asks, rolling her eyes.

"It's a guy," Tom says, and hands me a slip of paper with a name and student ID number on it, which I shove into my pocket. "Not the most scintillating conversationalist, but then, he was still unconscious when I was there. Maybe he's awake by now. Need petty cash for cab fare?"

I assure him I still have what I'd grabbed from the metal box earlier, when I'd been on my way to spell him . . . before we'd found out about Lindsay.

"So," Tom says to me in a quiet voice, as I'm about to head out the door. "You've dealt with this before." We both know what he means by *this*. "What, um, should I *do*?"

He looks really worried. That and the bed head make him seem younger than he really is . . . which, at twenty-six, is still younger than me. Almost as young as Barista Boy.

"Be strong," I say, laying a hand on his massive, Izod-sweater-clad shoulder. "And whatever you do . . . don't try to solve the crime yourself. *Believe* me."

He swallows. "Whatever. Like I want to end up with *my* head in a pot? No, thanks."

I give him a reassuring pat. "I'll be on my cell if you need to reach me," I say.

Then I beat a hasty retreat into the hallway, where I run into Julio, the head housekeeper, and his newly hired nephew—nepotism is as alive and well at New York College as it is anywhere else—Manuel, laying rubber-backed mats along the floor in order to protect the marble from salt the residents will track in when it finally starts snowing.

"Heather," Julio says to me worriedly as I breeze past, "is it really true, what they say? About . . ." His dark eyes glance toward the lobby, in which police officers and college administrators are still swarming like fashionistas at a sample sale.

"It's true, Julio," I stop to tell him, in a low voice. "They found a . . ." I'm about to say *dead body*, but that isn't strictly true. "Dead girl in the cafeteria," I settle for finishing.

"Who?" Manuel Juarez, an outrageously handsome guy I'd heard some of the female—and even some of the male—student workers sighing over (I don't bother, because of course I don't believe in romance in the workplace. Also because he's never looked twice at me, and isn't likely to, with so many nubile nineteen-year-olds in belly-baring tees around. I haven't bared my belly since, um, it started jutting over the waistband of my jeans), appears concerned. "Who was it?"

"I can't really say yet," I tell them, because we're supposed to wait until the deceased's family has been informed before giving out their name to others.

The truth, of course, is that if it had been anyone but Lindsay, I'd have told them in a heartbeat. But everyone—even the staff, whose tolerance for the people whose parents provide our paychecks is minimal, at best—liked Lindsay.

And I'm not going to be the one to tell them what happened to her.

Which is one of the reasons I'm so grateful to have this chance to be getting out of here.

Julio shoots his nephew an annoyed look—I guess because he knows as well as I do that I'm not allowed to give out the name—and mutters something in Spanish. Manuel flushes darkly, but doesn't reply. I know Manuel, like Tom, is still so new that he's on employment probation. Also that Julio is the strictest of supervisors. I wouldn't want to have him as *my* boss. I've seen the way he gets when he catches the residents Rollerblading across his newly waxed floors.

"I have to go to the hospital about a different kid," I tell

Julio. "Hopefully I'll be back soon. Keep an eye on Tom for me, will you? He's not used to any of this stuff."

Julio nods somberly, and I know my request will be carried out to the letter . . . even if it means Julio has to fake a spilled can of soda outside the hall director's door, so he can spend half an hour cleaning it up.

I manage to make it past all the people in the lobby and out into the cold without being stopped again. But even though—miraculously—there's a cab pulling up in front of Fischer Hall just as I walk out, I don't hail it. Instead, I hurry on foot around the corner, back toward the brownstone I left just a couple of hours before. If I'm going to be sitting in the hospital all day, there are a couple of things I need—like my remedial math textbook so I can be ready for my first class, if it isn't canceled due to snow, and maybe my Game Boy, loaded with Tetris (oh, who am I kidding? Between studying and Tetris, it's a solid bet I'll be spending my morning trying to beat my high score). Still, maybe I can convince Lucy to come outside and get her business done, so I don't have to worry about finding any surprises later.

The clouds above are still dark and heavy with unshed moisture, but that isn't, I know, why Reggie and his friends are nowhere to be seen. They've scattered thanks to the heavy police presence around the corner, at Fischer Hall. They're probably in the Washington Square Diner, taking a coffee break. Murder's as tough on the drug business as it is on everything else.

Lucy is so puzzled to see me home this early that she forgets to protest about being let outside into Cooper's grandfather's cold back garden. By the time I've retrieved my textbook and Game Boy and come back downstairs, she's sitting by the back door, her business steaming a few yards away. I let her back in and hastily clean up her mess, and am about to tear from the house when I notice the message light blinking on the machine in the hall—our house phone, as opposed to Cooper's business line. I press PLAY, and Cooper's brother's voice fills the foyer.

"Um, hi," my ex-fiancé says. "This message is for Heather. Heather, I've been trying to reach you on your cell as well as your work phone. I guess I keep missing you. Could you call me back as soon as you get this message? I have something really important I need to talk to you about."

Wow. It really must be important, if he's calling me on Cooper's house line. Cooper's family haven't spoken to him for years—since they learned the family patriarch, Cartwright Records founder Arthur Cartwright, had left his black sheep grandson his West Village brownstone, a prime piece of New York City real estate (valued at eight million dollars). Relations hadn't exactly been warm before that, though, thanks to Cooper's refusal to enter the family business (specifically, Cooper refused to sing bass in Easy Street, the boy band his father was putting together).

In fact, if it wasn't for me—and my best friend Patty and her husband Frank—Cooper would have spent Christmas and New Year's by himself (not that the prospect of this seemed to have bothered him very much), instead of basking in the warm glow of family . . . well, Patty's family, anyway, my own family being either incarcerated (Dad) or on the lam with my money (Mom. It's actually probably good I'm an only child).

Still, I'd found during the years I'd dated Cooper's brother that what was important to Jordan was rarely important to me. So I don't exactly scoop up the phone and call him right back. Instead, I listen to the rest of the messages—a series of hang-ups: telemarketers, no doubt—and then head back out into the cold toward St. Vincent's.

Now that I want one, of course I can't find a cab, so I have to hoof it the five or six blocks (avenue blocks, not short street blocks) to the hospital. But that's okay. We're supposed to get a half hour of exercise a day, according to the government. Or is it an hour? Well, whatever it is, five blocks in bitter cold seem more than enough. By the time I get to the hospital, my nose and cheeks feel numb.

But it is warm in the waiting room—if chaotic . . . though not as much as it normally is: the weather forecast has apparently frightened most of the hypochondriacs into staying home—and I'm able to find a seat with ease. Some kindly nurse has turned the channel on the waiting room television set from Spanish soaps to New York One, so everyone can keep abreast of the coming storm. All I need to get comfy is a little hot cocoa—and I come by that easily enough, by slipping some coins into the coffee vending machine—and some breakfast.

Food, however, is less easy to come by in the St. Vincent's ER waiting room, unless I'm willing to settle for Funyuns and Milk Duds from the candy machine. Which, under ordinary circumstances, I would be.

But in light of this morning's events, my stomach is feeling a little queasy, and I'm not sure it can handle a sudden influx of salt and caramel with its usual ease.

Plus, it's five of the hour . . . the time when the security guards open the ER doors and allow each patient inside to have visitors. In the case of my student, that visitor would be me.

Of course, when I need it, I can't find the slip of paper Tom had handed to me, the one with the student's name and ID number on it. So I know I'll have to wing it when I get into the ER. Hopefully there won't be that many twenty-one-year-olds in there, sleeping off way too many birthday shots from the night before. I figure the nurses might be able to help me out. . . .

But in the end, I don't need any help. I recognize my student the minute I lay eyes on him, stretched out on a gurney beneath a white sheet.

"Gavin!"

He groans and buries his face in his pillow.

"Gavin." I stand beside the gurney, glaring down at him. I should have known. Gavin McGoren, junior, filmmaking student, and the biggest pain-in-the-butt resident in Fischer Hall. Who else would keep my boss up all night?

"I know you're not asleep, Gavin," I say severely. "Open your eyes."

Gavin's lids fly open. "Jesus Christ, woman!" he cries. "Can't you see I'm sick?" He points at the IV sticking out of his arm.

"Oh, please," I say disgustedly. "You're not sick. You're just stupid. Twenty-one shots, Gavin?"

"Whatever," he mutters, folding his IV-free arm over his eyes, to block out the light from the fluorescents overhead. "I had my boys with me. I knew I'd be all right."

"Your boys," I say disparagingly. "Oh, yeah, your boys took great care of you."

"Hey." Gavin winces as if the sound of his own voice hurts. It probably does. "They brought me here, didn't they?"

"*Dumped* you here," I correct him. "And left. I don't see any of them around anymore, do you?"

"They had to go to class," Gavin says blearily. "Anyway, how would you know? You weren't here. It was that other tool from the hall office—where'd he go?"

"If you mean Tom, the hall director," I say, "he had to go deal with another emergency. You're not our only resident, you know, Gavin."

"What are you riding on me for?" Gavin wants to know. "It's my birthday."

"What a way to celebrate," I say.

"Whatevs. Not for nothing, but I was filming it for a class project."

"You're always filming yourself doing something stupid for a class project," I say. "Remember the reenactment you did of the scene from *Hannibal*? The one with the cow brain?"

He lifts his arm to glare at me. "How was I supposed to know I'm allergic to fava beans?"

"It might surprise you to know, Gavin," I say, as my cell phone vibrates in my coat pocket, "that Tom and I actually have better things to do than hold your hand every time you pull some stunt that ends up with you in the emergency room."

"Like what?" Gavin asks, with a snort. "Let those ass-kissing RAs suck up to you some more?"

It is very hard for me not to tell Gavin about Lindsay. How can he lie there, feeling so sorry for himself—especially after having done something so incredibly stupid to get himself into this position in the first place—when back in the building a girl is dead, and we can't even find her body?

"Look, can you just find out when I can get out of here?" Gavin asks, with a moan. "And spare me the lectures, for once?"

"I can," I say, only too happy to leave him to himself. Among other things, he doesn't smell too good. "Do you want me to call your parents?"

"God, no," he groans. "Why would I want you to do *that*?"

"Maybe to let them know how you celebrated your birthday? I'm sure they'll be very proud. . . ."

Gavin pulls the pillow over his head. I smile and go over to one of the nurses to discuss the possibility of his being released. She tells me she'll see what the doctor says. I thank her and go back out into the waiting room, pulling out my cell phone to see who called me . . .

. . . and am thrilled to see the words *Cartwright, Cooper* on my cell phone's screen.

I'm even more thrilled when, a second later, a voice says, "Heather."

And I look up and find myself staring into the eyes of the man himself.

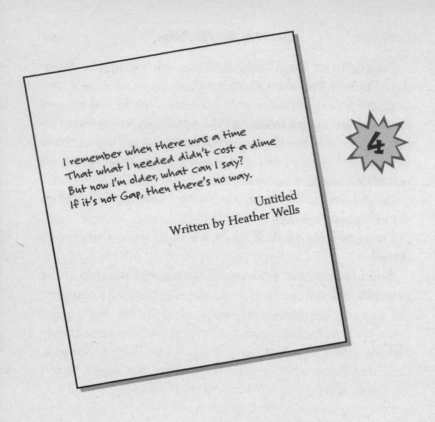

I remember when there was a time
That what I needed didn't cost a dime
But now I'm older, what can I say?
If it's not Gap, then there's no way.

Untitled
Written by Heather Wells

4

Oh, whatever. So I'm in love with him, and he has shown absolutely zero interest in reciprocating my feelings. So what? A girl can dream, right?

And at least I'm dreaming about someone age-appropriate, since Cooper's over thirty—a decade older than Barista Boy.

And it's not like Cooper's earning minimum wage in some coffee shop. He owns his own business.

And, okay, he won't actually TELL me what it is he does all day, because he seems to think it's not fitting for someone of my tender sensibilities to know. . . .

But that just means he cares, right?

Except that I know he cares. Why else would he have asked me to move in with him (well, into the top-floor apartment of his brownstone, anyway) after Jordan kicked me out (even though Jordan maintains he did no such thing, that I'm the one who left. But, I'm sorry, he was the one who let Tania Trace fall face first into his crotch—in our own apartment, no less. Who wouldn't interpret something like that as an invitation to leave)?

But Cooper's made it VASTLY clear that he only cares about me as a friend. Well, insofar as he has never hit on me, anyway.

And, okay, Cooper *did* sort of mention once—when I was in a state of severe shock from having been nearly murdered, and was only semiconscious—that he thinks I'm a nice girl.

But am I really supposed to think of that as a good thing? I mean, *nice*? Guys never go for nice girls. They go for girls like Tania Trace, who, in the video for her last single, "Bitch Slap," was rolling around in an oil slick wearing nothing but leather panties and a wife-beater.

They don't MAKE leather panties in my size. I'm pretty sure.

Still, there's always a chance Cooper isn't the leather panties type. I mean, he's already proved he's nothing like the rest of the family by being so nice to me. Maybe there's hope. Maybe that's why he's here at the hospital right now, to tell me that he can't stand to be without me a second more, and that his car is waiting outside to whisk us to the airport for a Vegas wedding and a Hawaiian honeymoon—

"Hey," Cooper says, holding up a paper bag. "I figured you hadn't eaten. I brought you a sandwich from Joe's."

Oh. Well, okay. It's not a Vegas wedding and a Hawaiian honeymoon.

But it's a sandwich from Joe's Dairy, my favorite cheese

shop! And if you've ever tried Joe's smoked mozzarella, you know it's just as good as a Hawaiian honeymoon. Possibly better.

"How'd you know I was here?" I ask dazedly, taking the bag.

"Sarah told me," Cooper says. "I called your office when I heard what happened. It was on the police scanner."

"Oh." Of course. Cooper listens to a police scanner while he's on stakeouts. That or jazz. He's a nut for Ella Fitzgerald. If Ella wasn't dead, I'd be jealous.

"Aren't your clients going to wonder where you are?" I ask. I can't believe he's blowing off a case for me.

"It's okay," Cooper says with a shrug. "My client's husband is occupied for the moment." I don't even bother asking what he means, since I know he won't tell me. "I was going for lunch, anyway, and I figured you hadn't eaten," he says.

My stomach rumbles hungrily at the word *lunch*. "I'm famished," I confess. "You're a lifesaver."

"So." Cooper leads me to an empty set of orange plastic seats in the waiting room. "What's the kid in for?"

I glance at the emergency room doors. "Who, Gavin? Chronic stupidity."

"Gavin again, huh?" Cooper produces two Yoo-Hoos from his parka pockets and hands me one. My heart lurches. YOO-HOOS! God, I love this man. Who wouldn't? "If that kid lives to graduation, I'll be surprised. So. How you hanging in there? I mean, with the dead girl."

I've sunk my teeth into the crunchy baguette—filled with freshly made smoked mozzarella, garlicky roasted peppers, and sun-dried tomatoes. It is impossible to speak after that, of course, because the inside of my mouth is having an orgasm.

"I actually put in a call," Cooper goes on, seeing that my

mouth is full (though ignorant, hopefully, of all the fireworks going on inside of it), "to a friend at the coroner's office. They got over there pretty quickly, you know, on account of business being slow, thanks to this storm we're supposed to get. Anyway, they're pretty sure she was dead well before she was . . . well, you know."

Decapitated. I nod, still chewing.

"I just thought you'd want to know," Cooper goes on. He's unwrapping a sandwich of his own. Prosciutto, I think. "I mean, that she didn't . . . suffer. They're pretty sure she was strangled."

I swallow. "How can they tell?" I ask. "Considering . . . well, there's no neck?"

Cooper has just taken a bite of his own sandwich as I ask this. He chokes a little, but manages to get it down.

"Discoloration," he says, between coughs. "Around the eyes. It means she quit breathing before death occurred, due to strangulation. They call it vagal inhibition."

"Oh," I say. "Sorry." I mean about making him choke.

He swills some Yoo-Hoo. As he does, I have a chance to observe him without his noticing. He hasn't shaved this morning . . . not that it matters. He's still one of the hottest-looking guys I've ever seen. His five o'clock—more like noon—shadow just makes the angular planes of his face more defined, bringing into even more definition his lean jaw and high cheekbones. Some people—like his father, Grant Cartwright—might think Cooper needs a haircut.

But I like a guy with hair you can run your fingers through.

You know, if he'd let you.

Still, though to me that slightly overlong dark hair gives him the appearance of a friendly sheepdog, Cooper must strike an imposing figure to others. This becomes obvious when a homeless guy carrying a bottle in a paper bag, coming into the hospital to get out of the cold for a little while, spies an empty chair next to me and wanders toward it . . .

. . . only to change his mind when he gets a look at Cooper's wide shoulders—made even more intimidating-looking by the puffiness of his anorak—and massive Timberlands.

Cooper doesn't even notice.

"They think she'd been there awhile," he says, having successfully forced down whatever it was he'd been choking on. "On the, er, stove. Since before dawn, at least."

"God," I say.

But though back in the dorm—I mean, residence hall—I couldn't think about what had happened to Lindsay without feeling a wave of nausea, I have no trouble finishing my sandwich. Maybe it's because I really *was* starving.

Or maybe it's because of Cooper's soothing presence. Love does funny things to you, I guess.

Speaking of love . . .

My cell phone chirps, and when I take it out of my pocket, I see that Jordan is calling me. Again. I hastily shove the phone back into the recesses of my coat.

Not quickly enough, though.

"He must really need to talk to you about something," Cooper says mildly. "He left a message at home, too."

"I know," I say sheepishly. "I heard it."

"I see." Cooper looks amused about something . . . at least by the way the corners of his mouth curl up beneath the quarter inch of dark fuzz growing around them. "And you aren't calling him back because . . . ?"

"Whatever," I say, annoyed. But not with Cooper. I'm annoyed with his brother, who refuses to realize that a breakup is just that: a breakup. You don't keep on calling your ex, especially when you're engaged to someone else, after you've broken up. I mean, it's common courtesy.

I guess it doesn't help that I keep sleeping with him. Jordan, I mean.

But seriously, it was just that one time on Cooper's hallway runner, and in a moment of total weakness. It's not like it's ever going to happen again.

I don't think.

I guess you could also say I'm a little annoyed with myself.

"So did you know her?" Cooper asks, artfully changing the subject, most likely because he can tell it's not one I'm relishing.

"Who? The dead girl?" I take a slug of Yoo-Hoo. "Yeah. Everyone did. She was popular. A cheerleader."

Cooper looks shocked. "They have cheerleaders in college?"

"Sure," I say. "New York College's team made it to the finals last year."

"The finals of what?"

"I don't know," I admit. "But they're proud of it. Lindsay—that's the dead girl—was especially proud of it. She was studying to be an accountant. But she had tons of school spirit. She—" I break off. Even Yoo-Hoo doesn't help this time. "Cooper. Who would *do* something like that to someone? And *why*?"

"Well, what do you know about this girl?" he asks. "I mean, besides that she was a cheerleader studying to be an accountant?"

I think about it. "She was dating one of the basketball players," I say, after a while. "In fact, I think he might be a suspect. Detective Canavan seems to think so, anyway. But he didn't do it. I *know* he didn't. Mark's a nice kid. He'd never kill any-one. And certainly not his girlfriend. And not that *way*."

"It's the *way* that strikes me as . . ." Cooper shrugs beneath his anorak. "Well, the word *overkill* comes to mind. It's al-most as if the killer left her that way as a warning."

"A warning to who?" I ask. "Jimmy the line cook?"

"Well, if we knew that," Cooper says, "we'd have a good idea who did it, wouldn't we? And why. Canavan's right to start with the boyfriend. He any good? As a ballplayer, I mean?"

I look at him blankly. "Coop. We're Division Three. How good can he be?"

"But the Pansies have been playing a lot better since they got that new coach, this Andrews guy," Cooper says, with a slight smile . . . I guess at my sports ignorance. "They've even started broadcasting the games. Locally only, I know. But still. I take it tomorrow night's game will be canceled, in light of all this?"

I snort. "Are you kidding? We're playing the New Jersey East Devils at home. Don't you know we're eight-and-oh?"

Cooper's smile broadens, but his voice is tinged with frost. "The head of one of the cheerleaders was found in her dorm cafeteria, but they aren't canceling tomorrow night's ball game?"

"Residence hall," I correct him.

"Heather Wells?" A doctor has come out of the ER, hold-ing a clipboard.

"Excuse me," I say to Cooper, and hurry over to the ER doc, who informs me that Gavin is recovering nicely and that she's releasing him. He'll be out as soon as he's signed the ap-propriate forms. I thank the doctor and return to Cooper's side, only to find he's already on his feet, scooping up the de-bris from our picnic and stuffing it into a nearby trash can.

"Gavin's ready to go," I say to him.

"So I gathered." Cooper pulls his gloves back on, readying himself for the plunge back into the arctic weather. "You guys need a lift back?"

"I doubt Gavin's up to walking," I say. "But we'll grab a cab. I'm not running the risk of him barfing in your car."

"For which I thank you," Cooper says gravely. "Well, see you at home, then. And, Heather . . . about Lindsay—"

"Don't worry," I interrupt. "In no way am I going to interfere with the investigation into her death. I totally learned my lesson last time. The NYPD is on their own with this one."

Cooper looks serious. "That wasn't what I was going to say," he informs me. "It never occurred to me that you would even consider getting involved in what happened at Fischer Hall today. Especially not after what happened last time."

It's ridiculous. And yet, I feel stung.

"You mean last time, when I figured out who the killer was before anybody else did?" I demand. "Before anyone else even realized those girls were *being* killed, and not dying of their own recklessness?"

"Whoa," Cooper says. "Slow down, slugger. I just meant—"

"Because you do realize that whoever did this to Lindsay had to have access to the keys to the caf, right?" I don't care that the homeless guy with the bottle-in-the-bag is now giving ME the wary eye he'd given Cooper just minutes before. What I lack in shoulder breadth, I make up for with hip girth. Oh, and pure shrillness.

"Because there was no sign of forced entry," I go on. "Whoever put Lindsay's head in there had to have had access to a master key. We're talking about three or four individual locks. No one could've picked three or four different locks, not in one night, not without somebody noticing. So it *had* to be somebody who works for the school. Somebody with access to the keys. Somebody I KNOW."

"Okay," Cooper says, in a soothing voice . . . probably the same voice he uses on his clients, hysterical wives who are convinced their husbands are cheating on them, and need to hire him to prove it in order to get custody of the Hamptons beach house. "Calm down. Detective Canavan is on it, right?"

"Right," I say. I don't add that my faith in Detective Canavan's investigative skills is not high. I mean, I *did* almost die once because of them.

"So don't worry about it," Cooper says. He's laid a hand on my shoulder. Too bad I'm wearing so much—coat, sweater, turtleneck, undershirt, bra—I can barely even feel it. "Whoever it was, Canavan'll catch him. This isn't like last time, Heather. Last time, no one but you was even sure there'd been a crime. This time . . . well, it's pretty obvious. The police will take care of it, Heather." His fingers tighten on my shoulder. His gaze is intent on mine. I feel like I could dive into those blue eyes of his and just start swimming, and go on and on and never reach the horizon.

"Yo, Wells."

Trust Gavin McGoren to pick *that* moment to come limping out of the ER.

"This guy bothering you, Wells?" Gavin wants to know, thrusting his wispily goateed chin in Cooper's direction.

I restrain myself—barely—from hitting him. College staff is forbidden from striking students, no matter how sorely tempted we might be. Interestingly, we aren't allowed to kiss them, either. Not that I've ever wanted to, at least where Gavin is concerned.

"No, he isn't *bothering* me," I say. "This is my friend Cooper. Cooper, this is Gavin."

"Hey," Cooper says, holding out his right hand.

But Gavin just ignores the hand.

"This guy your *boyfriend*?" he demands of me, rudely.

"Gavin," I say, mortified. I can't look anywhere in the vicinity of Cooper's face. "No. You know perfectly well he's not my boyfriend."

Gavin seems to relax a little. "Oh, that's right," he said. "You like those pretty-boy types. Jordan Cartwright. Mr. Easy Street."

Cooper has dropped his hand. He is staring at Gavin with an expression of mingled amusement and derision. "Well, Heather," he says. "Delightful as it's been meeting one of your infant charges, I think I'll be going now."

"Hey!" Gavin looks insulted. "Who you calling an infant?"

Cooper barely acknowledges Gavin's presence, saying only, "I'll see you at home," to me, with a wink, then turning to leave.

" 'See you at home'?" Gavin is staring daggers at Cooper's departing back. "You guys live together? I thought you said he wasn't your boyfriend!"

"He's my landlord," I say. "And he's right. You *are* an infant. Ready to go? Or do you want to stop by the liquor store on the way back to the hall so you can buy a bottle of Jägermeister and finish off the job?"

"Woman," Gavin says, shaking his head, "why you gots to be that way? Always up in my business?"

"Gavin." I'm rolling my eyes. "Seriously. I'll call your parents. . . ."

He drops the gangbanger act at once.

"Don't," he says, the goatee drooping. "My mom'll kill me."

I sigh and take his arm. "Come on, then. Let's get you home, before it starts snowing. Did you get a note from the doctor, to excuse you from class?"

He scowls. "They won't give notes for alcohol poisoning."

"Poor baby," I say cheerfully. "Maybe this will teach you a lesson."

"Woman," Gavin explodes again, "I don't need you to tell me how to act!"

And we walk out into the cold together, bickering like a brother and sister. At least, *I* think that's how we sound.

Little do I know Gavin thinks something entirely different.

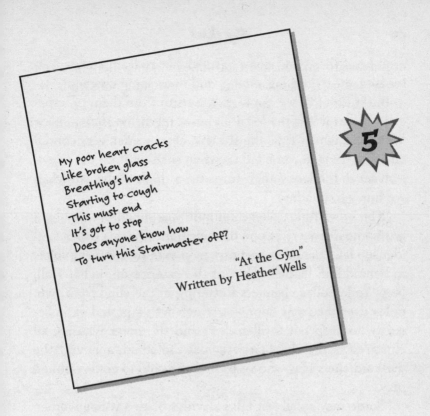

5

My poor heart cracks
Like broken glass
Breathing's hard
Starting to cough
This must end
It's got to stop
Does anyone know how
To turn this Stairmaster off?

"At the Gym"
Written by Heather Wells

The rest of the day does not exactly fly by. It's amazing, in fact, how slowly time can pass when all you want to do is go home.

At least, when I get back to Fischer Hall from the hospital, the deed has been done—Lindsay's family has been notified of her death . . . which means it's okay for us to start telling the building staff and residents about what happened to her.

But this, as I'd suspected, does not exactly make things any better. Reactions upon being told the truth—that the cafeteria is closed because of the discovery of a cheerleader's severed head there, and not a gas leak—vary from stunned astonishment to giggling, crying, and even some gagging.

But it isn't like we can keep the truth from them . . . especially when it hits the local all-news television station, New York One, which Tina, the student desk worker, very conscientiously runs to come tell us when she sees it on the television set in the lobby, then turns up as high as she can when we hurry to join her:

"The New York College campus was shocked today by a gruesome discovery at one of their dormitories, Fischer Residence Hall," the news anchorperson says, in an urgent voice, as behind him flashes a shot of the exterior of Fischer Hall, New York College banners fluttering in the wind from twin poles over the front door—at which we've posted extra security, to keep out thrill-seekers and the press, who are all clustered in the chess circle across the street, annoying the die-hard chess fans who've braved the cold to come out and play.

"Some may recall last fall's slayings of two young women in this very same dormitory," the reporter intones, "a tragedy that has led some on campus to refer to the building as Death Dorm."

I glance at Tom when the announcer says this. He presses his lips together, but otherwise says nothing. Poor guy. His first professional gig out of grad school, and it has to be at Death Dorm. I mean, residence hall.

"This morning, Fischer Hall cafeteria workers arrived at work to make another grisly discovery: a human head in a pot on the school stove."

This is met by a collective "EW!" by Tina and most of the rest of the students—not to mention a few administrators—gathered in the lobby to watch the broadcast. Tom actually groans and drops his face in his hands in anguish. Pete, the security officer, doesn't look too happy, either.

"The head has been positively identified by grieving family members as belonging to New York College sophomore and varsity cheerleader Lindsay Combs," the reporter goes on, as a photo of Lindsay fills the screen. It's the photo that was taken the night she was crowned Homecoming Queen. Her smile is as dazzling as the tiara in her honey-colored hair. She's dressed in white satin and holding a dozen red roses in her arms. Someone outside the frame of the photo had flung an arm around her shoulders and the tiara had tipped rakishly over one of Lindsay's unnaturally green eyes. I seriously don't understand why she thought this was a good look.

"According to witnesses, Lindsay was last seen yesterday evening. She left her room at approximately seven o'clock in the evening, telling her roommate she was going to a party. She never returned."

This much we already knew. Cheryl had come by the office in tears earlier, heartbroken over what had befallen her friend—and roommate . . . a roommate she'd never even gotten a chance to swap midnight giggles or shots of Southern Comfort with, since Lindsay had been dead before Cheryl ever even moved in.

Lindsay's original roommate, Ann, had taken the news a little less hysterically, and had been able to give the police their only lead . . . the one about the party. Of course, relations between Ann and Lindsay apparently not having been the best, the girl hadn't been able to tell Detective Canavan WHICH party Lindsay had been going to . . . and Cheryl, incoherent with sobs, hadn't been much help in that department, either. In fact, Tom had had one of the RAs escort Cheryl to Counseling Services, where she's hopefully getting the help she needs to cope with her grief . . . and the fact that she's pretty much guaranteed a single room for the rest of the year.

Of course, Cheryl is the one person on campus who didn't want one.

"How Lindsay ended up in the Fischer Hall cafeteria kitchen is a mystery that has authorities here baffled," the reporter goes on. The shot shifts to one of New York College President Phillip Allington standing at a podium in the library lobby, Detective Canavan looking rumpled and cranky at his side. Coach Andrews, for some reason, is standing on the president's other side, managing to look calm, but at the same time somewhat confused. But then, that's how a lot of athletic coaches look, I've noticed, as I've flipped past ESPN.

The anchorman's voice goes on, "A spokesperson from the New York City Police Department insists that even though no arrests have been made, the police have several suspects and are following more than a dozen leads. There is, college President Phillip Allington assured the academic community at a press conference earlier this afternoon, no need for alarm."

Footage from the press conference begins to run.

"We would like to take this opportunity," President Allington says woodenly, obviously reading from something that he'd had someone else write for him earlier in the day, "to reassure our students, and the public in general, that the law enforcement officials in this city are using every measure available to us to track down this vicious criminal. At the same time, we'd like to urge our students to take extra safety precautions until Lindsay's killer is apprehended. Although it is the goal of our residence halls to foster a feeling of community—which is why we call them residence halls and not dormitories—it's important for students to keep their doors locked. Do not allow strangers into your room or into any campus building. While the police believe this senseless crime to be, at this time, an isolated act of random violence, we cannot stress enough the necessity of exercising caution until the individual responsible is brought to justice. . . ."

No sooner were the words "keep their doors locked" out of President Allington's mouth than half the students in the lobby abruptly disappeared, heading toward the elevators with anxious looks on their faces. It's the habit of a lot of kids in buildings like Fischer Hall to leave the door to their room propped open to welcome drop-by visitors.

This is apparently about to change.

Of course, the fact that Lindsay hadn't been killed in her room didn't appear to occur to any of them. Any more than the fact that there hadn't been anything "random" about the act of violence that had ended Lindsay's life. Her killer had obviously known her—and also the Fischer Hall cafeteria—at least passably well.

But if this fact hadn't sunk in to the student population, it had been driven home to the cafeteria staff, who were only just now being allowed to go home after a day's worth of grueling questioning. I'm shocked to see them come streaming out of the cafeteria shortly after the end of President Allington's press conference, at quarter to five o'clock . . . well after those who were assigned to the breakfast shift usually got off work. Detective Canavan and his colleagues had really grilled them . . . no pun intended.

Still, tired as she must have been, Magda manages a smile as she comes toward me. She's slathered her fingers with Purel, and is wiping them with a Kleenex. As she gets closer, I see why: her fingertips are black with ink.

Magda's been printed.

"Oh, Magda," I say, when she's close enough. I put an arm around her shoulder, leading her out of the lobby and back toward my office, where it's quieter. "I'm so sorry."

"It's all right," Magda says, with a sniffle. The whites of her eyes are pink, her eyeliner and mascara smudged. "I mean, they are only doing their jobs. It isn't their fault one of my little movie stars—"

Magda breaks off with a sob. I hustle her into the hall office, where at least she'll be hidden from the inquiring gazes of the residents gathered in front of the elevator bank, home after their first day of classes—only to discover that they'll have to seek their evening meal elsewhere.

Magda sinks into the institutional orange couch in front of my desk and buries her head in her hands, sobbing. I hasten to shut the outer office door, which locks automatically when closed. Tom, having heard the disturbance, comes out of his own office and stands, looking at Magda uncomfortably as the words "Little movie star," and "Byootiful little baby" drift up incoherently from her knees, which is where she's sunk her face.

Tom looks at me. "What's the deal again with the movie star thing?" he whispers.

"I told you," I whisper back. For a gay guy, Tom can be surprisingly clueless sometimes. "They filmed a scene from *Teenage Mutant Ninja Turtles* here at Fischer Hall. Magda was working here at the time."

"Well." Tom stares at her some more as she cries. "It certainly seems to have made an impression. Considering it's a movie no one ever saw."

"People saw it," I say to him crossly. "Don't you have something you should be doing?"

He sighs. "I'm waiting for someone from Counseling Services. We're going to be holding grief counseling here in the office from five to seven, to help residents cope with what happened to Lindsay."

I don't say anything. I don't have to. He already knows.

"I told them no one was going to show up," he says beleagueredly. "Except maybe Cheryl Haebig and the RAs. But it came down from the president's office. The administration wants to look like we care."

"Well." I nod at a sobbing Magda. "Here's someone who needs some grief counseling."

Tom pales at my suggestion. "She's your friend," he says accusingly.

I glare at him. "You're the one with the master's degree."

"In college student personnel! I have to tell you, Heather." He looks frightened. "I don't know about this. I mean, any of this. Things were a lot simpler back in Texas."

I glare at him even harder. "Oh, no," I say. "You are *not* quitting on me, Tom. Not because of one little murder."

"Little!" Tom's face is still ashen. "Heather, nobody back home ever got their head whacked off and left in a pot on a stove. Sure, couple kids got crushed to death every year under the bonfire structure. But murdered? Honestly, Heather. Home's looking pretty good right now."

"Oh, right," I say sarcastically. "If it was so much better back there, how come you waited until you got here to come out of the closet?"

Tom swallows. "Well . . ."

"Let's talk about your quitting later, okay?" I flop down on the couch beside Magda. "I've got other things to worry about right now."

Tom throws Magda one last panicky look, then mutters,

"Okay, I'll just, um, finish up this paperwork," and disappears back into his office.

I sit beside Magda, resting a hand on her back as she cries. I know this is the right thing to do as a friend . . . but as someone who works in a helping field, I'm not sure this is what I'm supposed to do. *How could Dr. Jessup have hired someone like me?* I wonder. I mean, I know I'm the only who applied, and all. But I am thoroughly unfit for this job. I don't have the slightest idea what to do in the face of sorrow like Magda's. Where *is* that grief counselor, anyway?

"Magda," I say, patting her back through her pink cafeteria smock. "Um. Look, I'm sure they don't really suspect you. I mean, anyone who knows you knows you couldn't have had anything to do with . . . what happened. Really, don't worry about it. No one thinks you did it. The police are just doing their job."

Magda raises her tear-stained face to peer at me astonishedly.

"That's . . . that's not why I'm upset," she says, shaking her head until her—tiger-striped blond, this week—curls swing. "I *know* they're just doing their job. That's all right. None of us did it—none of us *could* do that."

"I know," I say hastily, still rubbing her back. "It's horrible of them to suspect you. But, you see—"

"It's just," Magda goes on, as if I hadn't spoken, "I heard . . . I heard it was *Lindsay*. But that couldn't be. Not little Lindsay, with the eyes, and the hair? The cheerleader?"

I stare at her. I can't believe she didn't recognize Lindsay back when she'd been looking into the pot. It's true I probably saw Lindsay more often than Magda did, on account of her affection for my condom jar. So it isn't any wonder I had no problem recognizing her. Is it?

Or is *this* the job I'm suited for? Recognizing the faces of dead people who've been boiled for a while? What kind of position would this even qualify me for? I mean, there can't be any demand for someone with a skill like this, except maybe in the few societies that are left that still practice cannibalism. *Are* there even any of these?

"Yes," I say, in answer to Magda's question. "Yes, I'm sorry. But it was Lindsay."

Magda's face crumples again. "Oh, no!" she says, with a wail. "Heather, no!"

"Magda," I say, alarmed by her reaction. Which, really, if you think about it, is way more natural than mine—which had been to flee the area for the warmth of the St. Vincent's ER. Or Sarah's, which had been to make bad jokes. "I'm so sorry. But if it's any consolation, Cooper told me the coroner thinks she was strangled first. I mean, she didn't die from . . . from having her head chopped off. That didn't happen until later."

Not surprisingly, Magda seems to find little comfort in this piece of information. I really do suck at grief counseling. Maybe I should go into accounting.

"It's just . . ." Magda sobs, "it's just that Lindsay—she was so sweet! She loved it here so much! She always wore her uniform on game days. She never did anything to anybody. She didn't deserve to die like that, Heather. Not Lindsay."

"Oh, Magda." I pat her arm. What else can I do? I notice that each of Magda's nails has been painted in the New York College school colors of gold and white. A major college basketball fan, Magda never misses a game, if she can help it. "You're right. Lindsay never did anything to deserve what happened to her." That we know of.

Oh, see? There it is again! Where does that kind of jaded cynicism even come from? It can't be because I'm a washed-up former pop star trying to put my life together, only to be told I have to take remedial math.

Can it?

"People are gonna try to make things up." Magda's gaze on mine is intense. "You know how people are, Heather. They're gonna try to say, *Well, she shouldn't have been seeing so many boys*, or something like that. But it wasn't Lindsay's fault she was so pretty and popular. It wasn't her fault boys buzzed around her like bees to honey."

Or flies around horse manure.

God, what is *wrong* with me? Why am I blaming the victim? I'm sure Sarah, if she were here, could tell me. Is it out of some desire to distance myself from what happened to Lindsay, so I can be, like, *Well, that could never happen to me, because the boys aren't exactly buzzing around me like bees to honey. So no one will ever strangle me and then chop my head off?*

Or is there some other reason I can't help thinking there might be something more to Lindsay's death than a "random act of violence"? Was she really all sunshine and school spirit? Or was she actually hiding something behind those iridescently green contact lenses?

Magda reaches out and grasps my hand in a grip so tight that it hurts a little. Her eyes—still swimming with tears—are bright as the rhinestones she sometimes has implanted in her nail tips.

"Listen to me, Heather." Magda's carefully lined lips tremble. "You've got to find the person who did this to her. You've got to find him, and bring him to justice."

I'm on my feet at once. But I can't go far due to Magda's death grip on my hand.

"Mags," I say. "Look, I appreciate your faith in my investigative abilities, but you've got to remember, I'm just the assistant hall director. . . ."

"But you're the only one who believed those other two girls, last semester, were murdered! And you were right! Smart as he is, that Detective Canavan, he couldn't've caught their killer—because he didn't even think they'd been killed. But you, Heather . . . you knew. You've just got this way with people. . . ."

"Oh," I say, rolling my eyes. "Yeah. Right."

"You may not think so, but you do. That's why you're so good at it. Because you don't *know* you can do it. I'm tellin' you, Heather, you're the only one who can catch the person who did this to Lindsay—who can prove she really was a nice girl. I'm begging you to at least *try*. . . ."

"Magda," I say. My hand is starting to sweat from her grip on it. "I'm not a cop. I can't involve myself in their investigation. I promised I wouldn't. . . ."

What is Magda even thinking? Doesn't she know that this guy, whoever it is, isn't shoving people down elevator shafts? He's strangling them, and chopping their heads off, then hiding their bodies. Hello, that is a lot different. It's a lot more deadly, somehow.

"That little pom-pom girl has the right to a good and proper rest," Magda insists. "And she can't have it until her murderer is found and brought to justice."

"Magda," I say uncomfortably. How would a grief counselor respond, I wonder, if one of his patients demanded that he solve the brutal slaying of the individual the patient was grieving over? "I think you've been watching a few too many episodes of *Unsolved Mysteries*."

Apparently this was not the proper way to respond, since Magda just clutches my hand harder and says, "Will you just think on it, Heather? Just think on it for a while?"

Magda had once told me that, in her youth, she had been a beauty queen, runner-up for Miss Dominican Republic two years in a row. It isn't actually that hard to believe now, as she gazes up at me with all the intensity of a pair of headlights set on high. Beneath all that makeup, the drawn-on eyebrows, and the six-inch-high hair, there's a dainty loveliness that the entire contents of the Duane Reade cosmetics aisle couldn't hide.

I sigh. I've always been a sucker for a pretty face. I mean, that's how I ended up saddled with Lucy, for God's sake.

"I'll think about it," I say, and am relieved when Magda loosens her grip on my hand. "But I'm not promising anything. I mean, Magda . . . I don't want to get *my* head chopped off, either."

"Thank you, Heather," Magda says, her smile beatific despite the fact that her lipstick is smeared. "Thank you. I'm sure Lindsay's spirit will rest easier knowing that Heather Wells is looking out for her."

I give Magda a final pat on the shoulder and with a little smile she gets up to go, wandering down the hallway to the dining office, where the staff hangs their coats. I look after her, feeling . . . well, a little strange.

Maybe that's because all I've had to eat today is a smoked mozzarella sandwich—with roasted peppers and sun-dried tomatoes, which are sort of vegetables, I guess—and a grande café mocha.

Then again, maybe it's because I've made her feel so much better, and I don't even know how. Or, actually, because I *do* know how. I just can't believe it. Does she honestly think I'm going to launch my own private investigation into Lindsay's death? If so, she's been inhaling way too much nail-gel dust.

I mean, what am I supposed to do, go around looking for

a guy with a cleaver and a girl's body in a fresh grave in his backyard? Yeah, right. And get my head chopped off, too. The whole thing is ridiculous. Detective Canavan isn't stupid. He'll find the killer soon enough. How can anyone hide a headless corpse? It's going to have to turn up sometime.

And when it does, I just hope I'm somewhere far, far away.

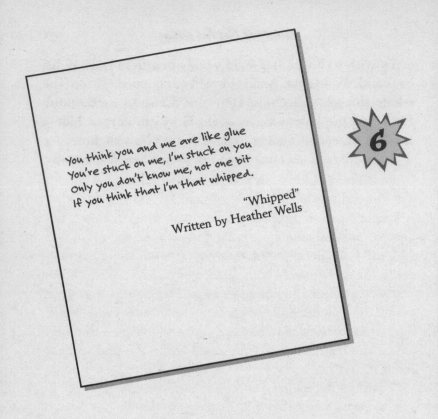

You think you and me are like glue
You're stuck on me, I'm stuck on you
Only you don't know me, not one bit
If you think that I'm that whipped.

"Whipped"
Written by Heather Wells

6

It still isn't snowing by the time I leave work, but it *is* pitch-black outside, even though it's just a little past five o'clock. The news crews are still parked along Washington Square Park, across the street from Fischer Hall—in fact, there are more of them than ever, including vans from all the major networks, and even CNN . . . just as President Allington had predicted.

The presence of the news vans isn't doing much to deter the drug trafficking in the park, though. In fact, I run into Reggie as I turn the corner to Cooper's brownstone. Although at first he hisses, "Sens, sens," to me, when he recognizes me, his expression turns grave.

"Heather," he says. "I am very sorry to hear about the tragedy in your building."

"Thank you, Reggie." I blink at him. In the pink glow from the street lamp, he looks surprisingly harmless, though I've heard from Cooper that Reggie carries in an ankle holster a .22 that he has, upon occasion, been called upon to use. "Um . . . you wouldn't happen to have heard anything about why the girl was killed? Or by whom? Would you?"

Reggie's grin is broad. "Heather," he says, sounding delighted, "are you asking me what the word on the street is?"

"Um," I say. Because put that way, it sounds so terrifically dorky. "Yeah. I guess I am."

"I haven't heard anything about it," Reggie says, and I can tell by the way his smile has faded—but, more to the point, the way he maintains steady eye contact with me—that he's telling the truth. "But if I do, you will be the first to hear about it."

"Thanks, Reggie," I say, and start back down the street . . . only to pause when I hear Reggie call my name.

"I hope you are not thinking about getting involved in whatever this young lady was messing with, Heather," he says to me. He's not smiling at all now. "Because you can bet she was messing with something . . . and that is what got her killed. I would not like to see that happen to a nice lady like yourself."

"Thanks, Reggie," I say. Which is not what I want to say. What I want to say is, *I wish people would have a little faith in me. I'm not that stupid.* But I know everyone is only trying to be nice. So instead I say, "Don't worry, I'm leaving the investigating to the professionals this time. Anything you tell me that you hear, I'm taking straight to them."

"That's good," Reggie says. And then, seeing a group of

typical West Village dot commers, he hastens away from me, murmuring, "Smoke, smoke. Sens, sens," at them.

I smile after him. It's always nice to see someone so dedicated to his calling.

When I finally finish undoing all the locks to the front door of Cooper's brownstone, I can barely get it open because of all the mail that's piled up beneath the slot. Turning on the lights—Cooper must still be away on his little stakeout—I scoop up the enormous pile, grumbling at all the coupon packs and AOL trial disks. I'm asking myself why we don't ever get any *real* mail—just bills and savings offers—when Lucy comes careening down the stairs, having heard me come in. In her jaws is a Victoria's Secret catalog that she's apparently spent the afternoon savaging into a droolly mess.

Lucy is truly a remarkable animal, given this special ability she has of singling out the sole catalog most likely to make me feel inadequate, and destroying it before I ever even get a chance to open it.

It's as I'm trying to wrestle it away from Lucy—to keep her from leaving chunks of Heidi Klum's torso all over the place—that the hallway phone rings, and I pick it up without even checking the caller ID.

"Hello?" I say distractedly. There is dog spit all over my fingers.

"Heather?" The voice of my ex-fiancé—sounding worried—fills my ear. "Heather, it's me. God, where have you been? I've been trying to reach you all day. There's something . . . there's something I really need to talk to you about—"

"What is it, Jordan?" I ask impatiently. "I'm kind of busy." I don't say what I'm busy doing. He doesn't need to know I'm busy trying to get my dog to stop eating a lingerie catalog. Let him think I'm busy being made love to by his brother.

Ha. I wish.

"It's just," Jordan says, "Tania told me the other day that you RSVP'd no to the wedding."

"That's right," I say. I'm starting to piece together what all this might be about. "I have plans on Saturday."

"Heather." Jordan sounds wounded.

"Seriously, I do," I insist. "I have to work. It's check-in day for the transfer students."

This isn't a complete lie. Check-in day for the transfer students is on a Saturday. It's just that it was last Saturday, not this coming Saturday. Still, Jordan will never know that.

"Heather," he says, "my wedding is at five o'clock. Are you telling me you will still be working at five o'clock?"

Damn!

"Heather, I don't understand why you don't want to come to my wedding," he goes on. "I mean, I know things were rocky between us for a while—"

"Jordan, I walked in on you getting head from the bride-to-be," I remind him. "Which, at the time, I mistakenly thought *I* was. So I think my indignation was pretty understandable."

"I realize that," Jordan says. "And that's why I thought you might feel . . . awkward about coming. To the wedding, I mean. That's why I'm calling, Heather. I want to make sure you know how important you are to me, and how important your coming to the wedding is to me, and to Tania, too. She still feels terrible about what happened, and we'd really like to show you how truly—"

"Jordan." By this time, I've made it into the kitchen with the cordless phone clutched in one hand, Lucy trailing behind me with her tongue lolling excitedly. After throwing away the damp Victoria's Secret catalog, I flip on the light and reach for the handle to the fridge. "I'm not going to your wedding."

"See," Jordan says, sounding frustrated, "I knew that's what you were going to say. That's why I called. Heather, don't be this way. I really thought we'd managed to put all that behind us. My wedding is a very important event in my life, Heather, and it's important to me that the people I care about are there with me when it happens. *All* the people I care about."

"Jordan." There, behind the milk (I went grocery shopping yesterday, when I heard about the impending blizzard, so the milk carton is full and actually well before the expiration date, for once), it sits: a white cardboard box of leftover bodega fried chicken. In other words, a box of heaven. "I'm not going to your wedding."

"Is it because I'm not inviting Cooper?" Jordan wants to know. "Because if it is—if it means that much to you—I'll invite him, too. Heck, you can bring him as your escort. I don't understand what it is you see in him, but I mean, the two of you *are* living together. If you really want to bring him—"

"I'm not bringing your brother to your wedding, Jordan," I say. I've removed the white cardboard box from the fridge, along with a hunk of goat's milk gouda from Murray's Cheese Shop, a hard red apple, and the milk. I'm holding the phone to my face with my shoulder, and have to kick the fridge door to get it to close. Lucy is not helping by sticking to my side like glue. She loves bodega fried chicken (peeled from the bone) as much as the next person. "Because I'm not going to your wedding. And quit acting like you want me there because you care, Jordan. I know perfectly well your publicist suggested I come, to make it look like I've forgiven you for cheating on me, and that we're pals again."

"That's not—" Jordan sounds affronted. "Heather, how can you imply such a thing? That is totally ridiculous."

"Is it?" I plonk everything I've gathered from the fridge onto the butcher-block kitchen table, then grab a plate and a glass and sit down. "Didn't your solo album tank? And wasn't it partially because your boy-next-door image got slightly tarnished by all the headlines when it got out that you'd been cheating on me, the Mall Princess, with your dad's latest discovery?"

"Heather," Jordan cuts me off tersely. "No offense, but the American public's memory is not quite that sharp. By the time you and I split, you hadn't had an album out in years. It's true you were once beloved by a certain segment of the population, but that segment has long since moved on—"

"Yeah," I say, stung in spite of myself. "They've moved on to wanting nothing to do with either of us. Good thing you're attaching yourself to Tania's shiny star. Just don't ask me to watch you do it."

"Heather." Now Jordan sounds long-suffering. "Why do you have to be this way? I thought you'd forgiven me for what happened with Tania. It certainly seemed as if you'd forgiven me that night in Cooper's hallway—"

I feel myself blanch. I can't believe he has the nerve to bring that up.

"Jordan." My lips feel numb. "I thought we agreed we were never going to speak about that night again." Never speak of it, and never, ever allow it to happen again.

"Of course," Jordan says soothingly. "But you can't ask me to act like it didn't happen. I know you still have feelings for me, Heather, just like I still have feelings for you. That's why I really want you there—"

"I'm hanging up now, Jordan."

"No, Heather, wait. That thing I saw on the news just now, about some girl's head. Was that your dorm? What the hell kind of place do you work in, anyway? Some kind of death dorm?"

" 'Bye, Jordan," I say, and press OFF.

I put down the phone and reach for the chicken. Lucy takes up position at my side, alert for any food that might not make it from my plate to my lips, and instead fall haphazardly onto my lap or the floor. We work as a team that way.

I know there are some people out there who prefer their fried chicken hot. But they've probably never had the fried chicken from the bodega around the corner from Cooper's brownstone—or, as Cooper and I call it, bodega fried chicken. Bodega fried chicken isn't just for everyday consumption. It's definitely comfort food on a different scale than your ordinary fried chicken, your KFC or Chicken Mc-Nuggets. I'd bought a nine-piece the day before, knowing today would be hellish, on account of it being the first day of the new semester.

I just hadn't anticipated it would be *this* hellish. I might have to eat all nine pieces myself. Cooper was just going to have to suffer. A little salt, and . . .

Oh. Oh, yes. No mouth orgasm, but close enough.

I'm plowing through my second bodega fried chicken leg—Lucy starting to whimper because I haven't dropped anything yet—when the phone rings again. This time—after I've wiped my hands on a paper towel—I check the caller ID before answering. I'm relieved to see that it's my best friend, Patty. I answer on the second ring.

"I'm eating bodega fried chicken," I tell her.

"Well, I certainly would if I were you, too"—Patty's voice, as always, is as warm and comforting as cashmere—"considering the day you've had."

"You saw the news?" I ask.

"Girl, I've seen the news *and* the newspapers from this morning. And you will not believe who called me a little while ago."

"Oh, my God, he called you, too?" I'm stunned.

"What do you mean, me, too? He called *you*?"

"To make sure I was coming. Even though I RSVP'd no."

"No!"

"Yes! Then he even said I could bring Cooper as my date."

"Holy Christ." That's what I love about Patty. She knows all the appropriate responses. "His publicist must have put him up to it."

"Or Tania's," I say, finishing off the chicken leg and reaching into the box for a thigh. I know I should probably eat the apple instead. But I'm sorry, an apple just isn't going to cut it. Not after the day I've had. "It would make her look like less of a skank if I showed up. Like I don't blame her for breaking Jordan and me up."

"Which you don't."

"Well, we were destined for Splitsville, USA, anyway. Tania just hastened our arrival. Still, I'm not going. How gross would that be? It's all well and good to invite the ex, to show there's no hard feelings and all. But the ex isn't supposed to actually *go*."

"I don't know," Patty says. "It's the in thing to go now. According to the Styles section in the *Times*."

"Whatever," I say. "I haven't been stylish since the nineties. Why should I start now? You're not going, are you?"

"Are you insane? Of course not. But, Heather, can we

please talk about what happened in your dorm today? I mean, residence hall. Did you know that poor girl?"

"Yeah," I say, picking a stringy chicken piece from between my teeth. Fortunately we're not on video phone. "Sort of. She was nice."

"God! Who would do such a thing? And why?"

"I don't know," I say. I break off a chunk of thigh meat for Lucy, after making sure it contains no cartilage or bone, and give it to her. She inhales it, then looks at me sadly, like, *Where'd it go?* "That's for the police to figure out."

"Wait." Patty sounds incredulous. "What did you just say?"

"You heard me. I'm not getting involved in this one."

"Good for you!" Patty takes the phone from her mouth and says to someone in the background, "It's all right. She isn't getting involved in this one."

"Say hi to Frank for me," I say.

"She says hi," Patty says to her husband.

"How's the new nanny working out?" I ask, since the two of them have just hired a real British nanny—a middle-aged one, because Patty swore what happened to Sienna Miller was never going to happen to her.

"Oh," Patty says. "Nanny is fine. We're both terrified of her, but Indy seems to adore her. Oh, Frank says to tell you that he's very proud of you. Leaving the murder investigation to the police . . . this shows real growth on your part."

"Thanks," I say. "Magda doesn't agree, though."

"What do you mean?"

"She thinks the cops are going to blame the victim. Which is probably true. I mean, even Reggie said something about what happened to Lindsay looking as if it might be retribution for something she did."

"Reggie . . . the drug dealer on *your street corner?*" Patty asks, in an incredulous voice.

"Yeah. He's going to ask around. You know, find out the word on the street for me."

"Heather," Patty says, "I'm sorry, I'm confused. But when you say things like that, it makes it sound like you really do plan on getting involved in the investigation."

"Well," I say, "I'm not."

There is a masculine mumble in the background. Then Patty says to Frank, "Fine, I'll ask her. But you know what she's going to say."

"Ask me what?" I want to know.

"Frank has a gig at Joe's Pub next week," Patty says, in a tense voice. "He wants to know if you'd like to join him."

"Of course I'll come," I say, surprised she feels like she has to ask. "I love that place."

"Um, not come to the performance," Patty says, still sounding tense. "He wants to know if you'll join him onstage."

I practically choke on the piece of chicken I'm swallowing. "You mean . . . *sing?*"

"No, perform a strip tease," Patty says. "Of course sing." Suddenly Frank's voice fills the phone.

"Before you say no, Heather," he says, "think about it. I know you've been working on your own stuff—"

"How do you know that?" I demand hotly, although I know perfectly well. Patty's mouth is even bigger than mine. She just doesn't tend to stuff hers with as many Dove Bars as I do mine, which is why she's a size 6 and I'm a 12. And growing.

"Never mind how I know," Frank says, ever the loyal husband. "You haven't been up on a stage in years, Heather. You've got to get back up there."

"Frank," I say, "I love you. You know I do. That's why I'm saying no. I don't want to ruin your gig."

"Heather, don't be like that. You got burned by that asshole Cartwright. Senior, not junior. But don't listen to him. I'm sure your stuff is great. And I'm dying to hear it. And the guy's'd get a kick out of playing it. Come on. It'll be a fun crowd."

"No, thank you," I say. I am trying to keep my tone light, so he won't hear the panic in my voice. "I think my songs are a little too angry-rocker-chick for a Frank Robillard crowd."

"What?" Frank sounds incredulous. "No way. They'll love you. Come on, Heather. When else are you going to get a chance to play the pub? It's a perfect venue for angry-rocker-chick stuff. Just you, a stool, and a microphone—"

Fortunately, at that moment, the call waiting goes off.

"Oops," I say. "That's the other line. I have to grab it. It could be Cooper."

"Heather. Listen to me. Don't—"

"I'll call you back." I click over to the other line, my relief over my narrow escape palpable. "Hello?"

"Heather?" a semi-familiar male voice asks hesitantly.

"This is she," I say, with equal hesitance. Because not that many guys I don't know call me. On account of I don't give out my home number. To anyone. Because no one ever asks for it. "Who is this?"

"It's me," the voice says, sounding surprised. "Your dad."

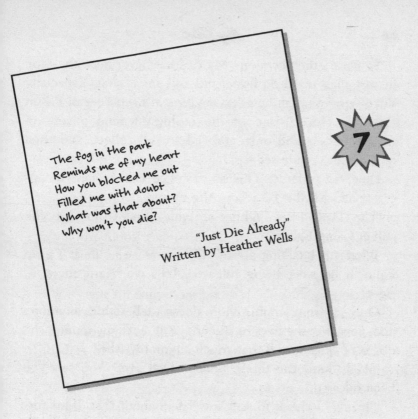

7

The fog in the park
Reminds me of my heart
How you blocked me out
Filled me with doubt
What was that about?
Why won't you die?

"Just Die Already"
Written by Heather Wells

I sit there in stunned silence for maybe three seconds.

Then I go, "Oh! Dad! Hi! Sorry, I didn't recognize your voice right away. It's—it's been a really long day."

"So I heard," Dad says. He sounds tired. Well, you would, too, if you were serving ten to twenty in a federal prison for tax evasion. "That's the dorm where you work, right? The one where they found the girl's head?"

"Residence hall," I correct him automatically. "And yeah. It was pretty upsetting." I'm frantically trying to figure out why he's calling. It's not my birthday. It's not a holiday. It's not *his* birthday, is it? No, that's in December.

So what's the occasion? My dad has never been the type to just pick up the phone and call for a chat. Especially since—even though he's serving time at Eglin Federal Prison Camp in Florida, one of the cushiest federal prisons in America—he's still only allowed to call collect, and then only during certain set—

Hey, wait a minute. This isn't a collect call. At least, no operator had asked if I'd accept the charges.

"Um, Dad," I say. "Where are you calling from? Are you still at Camp Eglin?"

What am I talking about? Of *course* he's still at Camp Eglin. If he were being released, I'd have heard about it, right?

Only . . . from whom? Mom doesn't talk to him anymore, and, now that she lives in Buenos Aires with my money, she doesn't talk to me all that much anymore, either. . . .

"Well, that's the thing, honey," Dad says. "You see, I've been released."

"Really?" I check to see how I feel about that. I am surprised to find that I feel . . . nothing. I mean, I love my dad, and all. But the truth is, I haven't seen him in so long—Mom would never take me to visit him, of course, since she hated his guts for losing all his money and forcing her to have to work (as my agent and promoter).

And once I got old enough to go by myself, I was too broke ever to make it to Florida. Dad and I were never that close, anyway . . . more like polite acquaintances, really, than parent and child. Thanks to Mom.

"Wow," I say, looking in the cardboard box to see how much dark meat is left. I am determined to save the breasts for Cooper, since they're his favorite. "That's great, Dad. So, where are you now?"

"Funny you should ask. I'm actually calling you from down the street—the Washington Square Diner. I was wondering if you wanted to get together for coffee."

Seriously. I just don't get it. I go for months—literally—where nothing at all unusual happens to me. My days are a blur of dog-walking, work, and *Golden Girl* reruns. And then WHAM! In one day, I find a head in a pot on a stove; get asked to play my songs at Joe's Pub with none other than super-mega-rock-star Frank Robillard; and my dad gets out of jail, shows up in my local coffee shop, and asks to see me.

Why can't things happen a little at a time? Like one day I find the head; another day Frank asks me to jam with him onstage; and another day my dad calls to let me know he's out of jail and in my hometown.

But I guess we don't get to choose how things transpire.

Because if we did, I definitely wouldn't have eaten all that chicken before going to see my dad. Because the sight of him sitting there in that booth—before he notices me, so I have a chance to study him before he knows he's being observed—causes my gut to twist. Not in the same way it twisted when I saw Lindsay's head in that pot—that was horror. The sight of my dad just saddens me.

Maybe because *he* looks sad. Sad and thin. He's not the robust golf player I knew from two decades ago—the last time I saw him outside of Camp Eglin's visitors' center—but a sort of shell of that man, reed-thin, with graying hair and the even whiter beginnings of a beard and mustache.

Still, that face transforms when he glances my way and finally notices me in the doorway. Not that he is overcome with joy or anything. He just plasters a grin on his face—a grin that doesn't reach his sad, tired eyes—every bit as blue as my own.

And every bit as cautiously guarded.

What do you say to the father you haven't seen for so long, with whom your relationship has always been . . . well, nonexistent, even when you lived together?

I say, "Hey, Dad," and slide into the booth across the table from him. Because what else am I *supposed* to say?

"Heather," he says, and reaches across the table to squeeze my hand, once I've stripped off my gloves. His fingers feel warm against mine. I squeeze back, with a smile.

"So this is a surprise," I say. "When did you get out?"

"Last week," he says. "I thought about calling you then, but . . . well, I wasn't sure you'd be too happy to see me."

"Of course I'm happy to see you, Dad." Dad's not the one I have a beef with. Well, not really. I mean, it wasn't exactly cool of him not to pay taxes all those years. But it wasn't MY money he wasn't paying taxes on. Or, in the case of Mom, stole. "When did you get here? To the city, I mean?"

"This morning. I took the bus. Lovely way to see the country." The waitress comes up as he's saying this, and he looks at me questioningly. "Have you had dinner?"

"Oh, yes," I say. "I'm good. Just hot chocolate would be nice"—I say this last to the waitress—"with whipped cream."

Dad orders chicken noodle soup to go with his coffee. The waitress nods and goes away. She looks distracted. She's probably worrying about the impending snowstorm, which a weatherman on New York One, playing on the TV hanging over the counter, assures us is due at any moment.

"So," I say. "The bus." For some reason I can't stop thinking about Morgan Freeman's ride to freedom on that bus in the movie *The Shawshank Redemption*. Well, I guess it isn't too surprising. Morgan Freeman had been a prisoner, too. "Isn't that like a parole violation? I mean, for you to leave the state of Florida?"

"Don't worry about me, kiddo," Dad had said, patting my hand. "I've got things under control. For a change."

"Great," I say. "That's great, Dad."

"So what do you hear from your mother?" he wants to know. I notice that he doesn't make eye contact when he asks this. He busies himself adding more half and half to his coffee.

"Well," I say, "you mean since she took off for Buenos Aires with the contents of my bank account? Not a whole heck of a lot."

Dad purses his lips and shakes his head. Now he makes eye contact. "I'm sorry about that, Heather," he says. "You can't know how much. Your mother isn't like that. I don't know what could have come over her."

"Really? Because I have a pretty good idea," I say, as the waitress comes back with his soup and my hot chocolate.

"Oh?" Dad digs into his soup like it's his first food of the day. For such a skinny guy, he has a pretty good appetite. "What's that?"

"Her meal ticket lost her recording contract," I say.

"Oh, now, Heather," Dad says, looking up from his soup. "Don't say that. Your mother loves you very much. She's just never been a strong woman. I'm sure it wasn't her idea—taking your money, I mean. I'm positive that Ricardo character put her up to it."

And I'm positive it was the other way around, actually, but I don't say so, because I don't feel like getting into an argument about it.

"How about you?" I ask instead. "Have you heard from her?"

"Not in quite some time," Dad says. He opens one of the

packs of crackers that came with his soup. "Of course, given the way I let her down, I don't suppose I deserve to."

"I wouldn't beat yourself up over that one, Dad," I say, feeling that twinge in my stomach again. Only this time, I realize the twinge is actually north of my stomach. It's more in the vicinity of my heart. And it appears to be pity. "She hasn't exactly been Miss Parent of the Year herself."

Dad shakes his head over his soup. "Poor Heather," he says, with a sigh. "When they were handing out parents up in heaven, you certainly got the short end of the stick."

"I don't know," I say, surprised to find myself prickling a little. "I think I've done all right for myself. I mean, I've got a job, and a nice place to live, and . . . well, I'm getting my BA."

Dad looks surprised . . . but pleasantly so. "Good for you!" he says. "At New York College?"

I nod. "I get tuition remission through my job," I explain. "I have to take this remedial math course before I can start taking real courses, but—"

"And what are you going to study?" Dad wants to know. His enthusiasm about the subject takes me aback, a little. "Music? I hope you're studying music. You've always been so very talented."

"Uh," I say. "Actually, I was thinking more of criminal justice."

Dad looks startled. "Good heavens," he says. "Why? Do you want to be a policewoman?"

"I don't know," I say. I'm too embarrassed to tell him the truth . . . that I'd hoped, with a BA in criminal justice, Cooper might take me on as a partner in his business, and the two of us could detect crimes together. Like *Remington Steele*. Or *Hart to Hart*.

It's a little sad that all my fantasies are rooted in eighties television shows.

"You should study music theory," Dad says firmly. "To help with your songwriting."

I flush. I forgot that I sent Dad a tape of myself singing some of my own stuff for Christmas one year. What had I been thinking?

"I'm too old for a singing-songwriting career," I tell him. "I mean, have you seen those girls on MTV? I can't wear short skirts anymore. Too much cellulite."

"Don't be silly," Dad says dismissively. "You look fine. Besides, if you're self-conscious, you can just wear slacks."

Slacks. Dad kills me sometimes. He really does.

"It would be a shame," Dad says. "No, not just a shame—a sin—to let God-given talent like yours go to waste."

"Well," I say, "I don't think I have. I did the singing thing already. I think maybe now it's time to try a different talent."

"Criminal justice?" Dad looks confused. "That's a talent?"

"Well, at least one where no one's going to boo me off a stage," I point out.

"No one would dare!" Dad cries, laying down his spoon. "You sing like an angel! And those songs of yours—they're much better than some of that garbage I hear on the radio. That girl, going on about her lumps, or her humps, or whatever she's talking about. And that other one—that Tracy Trace, the one that old boyfriend of yours is marrying this weekend. Why, she's half naked in that video!"

I have to repress a smile. "Tania Trace," I correct him. "And that's the number one video on *TRL* right now."

"Well," Dad says firmly, "regardless. It's trash."

"What about you, Dad?" I ask, thinking I'd better change the subject before he gets too overexcited. "I mean, you were at Camp Eglin for . . . gosh. Almost twenty years. What are you going to do now that you're out?"

"I have a few irons in the fire," Dad says. "Some of which look quite promising."

"Yeah?" I say. "Well, that sounds good. Here in New York?"

"Yes," Dad says. But I notice he's gotten more hesitant in his replies. And he's not making eye contact with me anymore.

Uh-oh.

"Dad," I say. Because suddenly I have a new feeling in my stomach. And it isn't horror or pity. It's dread. "Did you really call me because you wanted to see me and catch up on old times? Or was there something else?"

"Of course I wanted to see you," Dad says, with some asperity. "You're my old daughter, for goodness' sake."

"Right," I say. "*But . . .*"

"What makes you think there's a *but?*" Dad wants to know.

"Because," I say, "I'm not nine anymore. I know there's always a *but.*"

He lays down his spoon. Then he takes a deep breath.

"All right," he says. "There's a but."

Then he tells me what it is.

8

Tick-tock
Alarm clock
Doesn't ring
Funny thing
I wake
No break
Somebody please
Shoot me.

"Morning Song"
Written by Heather Wells

I'm fifteen minutes late to work the next day. Personally, I don't think fifteen minutes is all that long. Fifteen minutes shouldn't even count as tardy . . . especially when you take into account what happened to me the night before—you know, the whole return of the prodigal dad thing.

But fifteen minutes can be quite a long time in the life cycle of a residence hall. Fifteen minutes is long enough, in fact, for a representative from Counseling Services to find my desk and station herself at it.

And when I run breathlessly into the office and see her there, and go, "May I help you?" those fifteen minutes she's been at my desk are apparently long enough to make her feel enough at home at it to go, "Oh, no, thank you. Unless you're going for coffee, in which case I could use one, light, no sugar."

I blink at her. She's wearing a tasteful gray cashmere sweater set—with pearls, no less—and is making me feel quite underdressed in my professional wear of jeans and chunky cable-knit sweater. She doesn't even have hat hair. Her chestnut curls are swept into a perfect chignon. How the hell did she make it across the park—or, as I've been calling it lately, the Frozen Tundra—from Counseling Services without freezing her head off?

Then I spy them, sticking out of the black wool trench she's hung on the coat rack—on *my* peg. Earmuffs. Of course.

Tricky fashionista.

"Oh, Heather, there you are," Tom says, coming out of his office. He looks much better today than he did yesterday, now that he's gotten some sleep and actually washed and styled his blond hair. He is even wearing a tie.

And okay, he's wearing it with a bright pink oxford and jeans. But it's an improvement.

"This is Dr. Gillian Kilgore from Counseling Services," he goes on. "She's here to offer grief counseling to any residents who feel they might need it, in light of yesterday's events."

I smile briefly at Dr. Kilgore. Well, what else am I supposed to do? Spit at her?

"Hi," I say. "You're in my seat."

"Oh." Tom seems to notice for the first time where Gillian Kilgore has stationed herself. "That's right. That's Heather's desk, Dr. Kilgore. I meant for you to take the GA's desk—"

"I like this desk better," Dr. Kilgore stuns us both (I can tell Tom is stunned because his face goes as pink as his shirt) by saying evenly. "And of course, when students do come by for their appointments, Mr. Snelling, I'll be meeting with them in your office. For more privacy."

This is clearly news to Tom. He is standing there kind of bleating, like a lost sheep—*Baaah . . . baaah . . . but*—when Gillian Kilgore's first victim, I mean appointment, comes loping into the office. Mark Shepelsky is the Pansies' six-foot-seven power forward, and current resident of Room 212, one of the most sought-after doubles in the entire building due to its view of the park and the fact that, being on the second floor, its occupants can take the stairs instead of depending on the elevators, which are crowded at best, broken most of the rest of the time.

"Someone needed to see me?" Mark says. More like grunts, really. A skinny, pasty-skinned kid, he's good-looking in a crew-cutted ballplayer way.

But he can't hold a candle to Barista Boy, if you ask me.

Not that I like Barista Boy. Anymore.

"You must be . . ." Dr. Kilgore glances down at the appointment book open on her desk. Excuse me, I mean, *my* desk. "Mark?"

Mark shuffles his size-fourteen feet. "Yeah. What's this about?"

"Well, Mark," Dr. Kilgore says, slipping a pair of reading glasses over her nose, I guess in an attempt to look empathetic (it doesn't work), "I'm Dr. Kilgore. I'm here from Student Counseling Services. I understand that you were close with Lindsay. Lindsay Combs?"

Mark does not exactly break down in tears at the mention of his beloved's name. In fact, he looks indignant.

"Do we gotta do this?" he demands. "I already talked to the cops all day yesterday. I got a game tonight. I gotta practice."

Gillian Kilgore says soothingly, "I understand, Mark. But we're concerned about you. We want to make sure you're all right. Lindsay was, after all, important to you."

"Well, I mean, she was hot and everything," Mark says, looking confused. "But we weren't even dating. We were just playing. You know what I mean?"

"You two weren't exclusive?" I hear myself asking.

Both Tom and Gillian Kilgore turn to look at me, Dr. Kilgore with seeming annoyance, Tom with a wide-eyed, *Are you trying to get yourself in trouble?* look, which I ignore.

Mark says, "Exclusive? No way. I mean, we fooled around a little. I already told that detective dude, lately the only time I've seen her is at games, and over break I hardly saw her at all. . . ."

"Well, let's talk about that," Dr. Kilgore says, taking hold of Mark's arm and attempting to steer him toward Tom's office for some privacy (which, good luck, with that grate between his office and the outer one where I sit).

"Was Lindsay seeing anybody else?" I ask, before Mark can be pulled away.

He shrugs. "Yeah, I guess. I don't know. I heard she was doing—I mean, seeing—some frat guy."

"Really." I plunk down onto my desktop. "What frat?"

Mark looks blank. "I don't know."

"Well." It's hot in my office. I begin peeling off my coat. "Did you tell Detective Canavan about this?"

"He didn't ask."

"Mark." Gillian Kilgore's voice has gotten almost as cold as it is outside. "Why don't you step in here and we'll—"

"Detective Canavan didn't ask if you and your girlfriend were exclusive?" I demand incredulously. "And you didn't mention that you weren't?"

"No." Mark shrugs again. He's big with the shrugging, I see. "I didn't think it was important."

"Mark." Dr. Kilgore's voice is sharp now. "*Come with me, please.*"

Mark, looking startled, follows Dr. Kilgore into Tom's office. She practically slams the door behind them—but not before giving me a withering stare. Then, through the grate, we hear her say, "Now, Mark. Tell me. How are you feeling about all this?"

Has she not noticed the grate? Does she really think we can't hear her?

Tom looks at me, his expression noticeably miserable. "Heather," he says. We don't have to worry about Dr. Kilgore overhearing us, because she's chattering away so loud behind the grate. "What are you doing?"

"Nothing," I say. I get up from my desk and hang up my coat on the peg next to the one where Dr. Kilgore has hung hers. "Is it hot in here? Or is it just me?"

"It's hot," Tom says. "I turned the radiator off, but it's still . . . radiating. Seriously, though. What was all that about?"

"Nothing," I say, with a shrug. It's catching, I guess. "I was just curious. Have they reopened the caf?"

"Yes. For breakfast. Heather, are you   "

"Great. Have you had coffee yet?"

Tom sends a scowl in the direction of his office door. "No. I came in and *she* was already here. . . ."

"How'd she get in?" I ask in surprise.

"Pete let her in, with the master." Tom sighs. "Would you really bring me back a cup of coffee? With milk and sugar?"

"You got it," I say, with a smile.

"Have I told you today that you're my favorite assistant dorm director? Seriously?"

"Tom, Tom, Tom," I say. "Don't you mean I'm your favorite assistant RESIDENCE HALL director?"

Not surprisingly, when I get to the caf, it's practically empty. I guess the discovery of a severed head in the kitchen has a way of putting off your pickier eaters. Except for a few lone diners, I'm the only person in there. I stop by the register to say hi to Magda on my way in. She does not look good. Her eyeliner has already faded, and her lip liner is on crooked.

"Hey," I say to her, in my warmest voice. "How are you, Mags?"

She doesn't even crack a smile. "None of my little movie stars will come in," she says mournfully. "They're all eating at *Wasser Hall.*" She says the words like they contain poison.

Wasser Hall, a residence hall across the park that was recently renovated to include its own pool in the basement, is our bitterest rival. After the press—and students—started calling Fischer Hall Death Dorm, I got a lot of calls from parents demanding their kids be moved to Wasser Hall. Can I just say that the assistant hall director there thinks she's all that because of it?

I got her back, though, during a trust exercise we were all required to do at in-staff training over Winter Break, when we each had to fall back into each other's arms and I accidentally-on-purpose dropped her.

"Well," I say soothingly, "it's only natural. They're scared. They'll come back after the police figure out who the killer is."

"*If* the police figure out who the killer is," Magda says gloomily.

"They will," I assure her. Then, to cheer her up, I add, "Guess who I had dinner with last night."

Magda brightens. "Cooper? He finally asked you for a date?"

It's my turn to look gloomy. "Um, no. My dad. He got out of jail. He's here, in the city."

"Your dad's out of the pen?" Pete is walking by, an empty coffee mug in his hand. He's on his way in for a refill. "No kidding?"

"No kidding," I say.

"So." Pete has forgotten about his coffee. He looks intrigued. "What'd you two talk about?"

I shrug. Damn that Mark and his contagious shrugging. "I don't know," I say. "Him. Me. Mom. A little of everything."

Magda is equally fascinated. She leans forward and says, "I read a book once where the man, he goes to prison, and when he gets out, he's . . . you know. Like your boss, Tom. On account of not having been with a woman in so long."

I raise my eyebrows. "I'm pretty sure my dad's not gay now, Magda," I say. "If that's what you mean."

Magda looks disappointed and leans back into her seat. "Oh."

"What's he want?" Pete asks.

"Want?" I stare at him. "He doesn't want anything."

"The man comes to see you first thing out of jail," Pete says, looking incredulous. "Says that he doesn't want anything from you . . . and you *believe* him? What's wrong with you?"

"Well," I say hesitantly. "He did say he just needed a place to stay for a few days while he gets on his feet."

Pete lets out a bark of *I told you so* laughter.

"What?" I cry. "He's my *father*. He raised me for my first ten years or so."

"Right," Pete says cynically. "And now he wants to mooch off your fame and fortune."

"What fortune?" I demand. "He knows perfectly well his ex-wife stole all my money."

Pete, chuckling, heads for the coffee machine.

"Why can't he just want to rebuild his relationship with the daughter he barely knows?" I shout after him. Which just makes him laugh harder.

"That's all right, honey," Magda says, patting my hand. "Ignore him. I think it's nice your daddy came back."

"Thank you," I say indignantly. "Because it is."

"Of course it is. And what did Cooper say when you asked him if your daddy could move in?"

"Well," I say, unable to meet Magda's gaze all of a sudden. "Cooper hasn't said anything about it yet. Because I haven't asked him."

"Oh," Magda says.

"Not," I say quickly, "because I don't believe my dad is totally on the up and up. I just haven't actually *seen* Cooper yet. He's busy with a case. But when I do see him, I'll ask. And I'm sure he'll say it's all right. Because my dad really wants to turn his life around."

"Of course," Magda says.

"No, Magda. I really mean it."

"I know you do, honey," Magda says. But her smile doesn't reach her eyes. Kind of like Dad's, as a matter of fact.

But that, I tell myself, has nothing to do with anything I've just said to her. It has to do with what happened yesterday, with Lindsay.

And as for Pete . . . well, let him laugh. What does *he* know?

Although considering he's a widower with five kids to support on his own, he might actually know quite a lot.

Dang.

Scowling, I head for the bagel bar and pop a plain in the toaster. Then I hit the coffee dispenser. I make one for Tom—

with cream and sugar—and one for me, half coffee, half hot cocoa, lots of whipped cream—then return to the bagel bar as mine pops up from the toaster, slather each side in cream cheese, slap on some bacon, then meld. Voilà, the perfect breakfast treat.

I put it on a plate, the plate on a tray with the coffees, and am heading out of the caf when I happen to spy, out of the corner of my eye, a flash of gold and white. I turn my head, and see Kimberly Watkins, one of the Pansies' varsity cheerleaders—in uniform because it's a game day—sitting by herself at a table, a large textbook open in front of her, alongside a plate appearing to contain an egg-white omelet and half a grapefruit.

And before I think about what I'm doing, I find myself plonking my tray across the table from hers and going, "Hey, Kimberly."

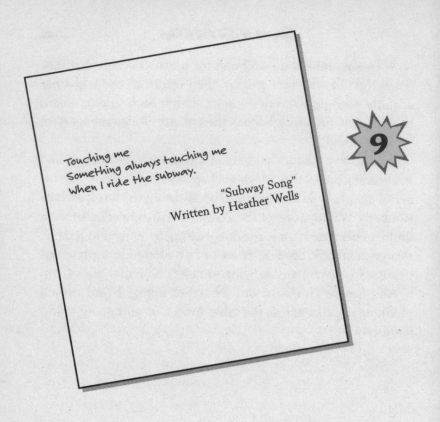

Touching me
Something always touching me
When I ride the subway.

"Subway Song"
Written by Heather Wells

9

"Um," Kimberly says, looking up at me suspiciously, clearly uncertain who I was, and why I was suddenly sitting across from her. "Hi?"

"I'm Heather," I say. "Assistant hall director?"

"Oh!" Kimberly's suspicious expression changes to one of recognition, even casual welcome. Now that she knows I'm not there to try to—well, whatever it was she thought I was there to do . . . hit on her? proselytize?—she seems to relax. "Hi!"

"Listen," I say. "I just wanted to see how you were doing. I mean, about this whole thing with Lindsay. I know you two were friends. . . ."

Actually, I don't know this. But I just assume two girls who were on the same cheerleading team would be friends. Right?

"Oh," Kimberly says, in a different tone, and the bright, Crest-Whitestrip smile she'd flashed me vanishes. "I know. It's so awful. Poor Lindsay. I . . . I can't even think about it. I cried myself to sleep last night."

For a girl who'd cried herself to sleep the night before, Kimberly looks pretty good. She apparently spent her break somewhere warm, because even though it's winter, Kimberly's bare legs are tanned. Apparently she isn't too concerned about the cold outside, or the blizzard New York One still insists we're supposed to be getting at any moment, but which has currently stalled over Washington, DC.

She doesn't seem too concerned about eating breakfast in the place where, twenty-four hours ago, her good friend's severed head was found, either.

"Wow," I say. "You must be devastated."

She crosses her long, coltish legs beneath the table and begins to twist a strand of her long black hair—straightened, naturally—around and around one finger.

"Totally," she says, her doe eyes wide. "Lindsay was, like, my best friend. Well, after Cheryl Haebig. But Cheryl doesn't really like to hang out anymore, 'cause, you know, she spends most of her free time with Jeff. Jeff Turner." Kimberly blinks at me. "You know Jeff, right? He's one of Mark's roommates, in Two-twelve."

"Sure, I know Jeff," I say. I know all the basketball players, they've been down to the office so many times for disciplinary hearings, primarily of the keg-smuggling variety. Fischer Hall is supposed to be dry.

"Well, the two of them, they're, like, practically married. They hardly ever want to party anymore."

And now that Cheryl's moved into Lindsay's room and will most likely not receive a new roommate, she and Jeff will be able to canoodle uninterrupted. . . .

But wait. That's no reason so kill someone.

"So, after Cheryl, Lindsay was your best friend," I say. "Gosh, that must be awful, to lose someone that close. I'm surprised you can—no offense—even eat in here."

Reminded of her food, Kimberly takes a big bite of her egg-white omelet. Inspired by this, I take a bite of my bacon-and-cream-cheese bagel. Mmm. *Heaven.*

"Yeah, well," Kimberly says, "I don't go in for ghosts, and all of that. When you're dead, you're dead."

"That's very practical of you," I say, after taking a sip of my cocoa-coffee.

"Well," Kimberly says, with a shrug, "I'm in fashion merchandising." And indicates the intimidating-looking textbook in front of her. *Introduction to Managerial Accounting.*

"Oh," I say. "So since you knew Lindsay so well, would you know of anyone who maybe had a grudge against her? Maybe wanted her out of the way? Enough to kill her, I mean?"

Kimberly twists the long strand of dark hair around her other finger for a while. "Well," she says slowly. "A lot of people hated Lindsay. I mean, they were jealous of her, and stuff. I did tell that policeman, the one who came by last night, about her roommate, Ann."

"Ann hated Lindsay?"

"Well, maybe not hate. But they didn't get along. That's why Lindsay was so psyched when Ann finally agreed to swap rooms with Cheryl. Even though Cheryl doesn't hang out with us much anymore, at least Lindsay didn't have to worry about all the stupid shit Ann was doing to annoy her."

"Stupid shit like what?" I ask, taking another bite of my bagel.

"Oh, just dumb stuff. Erasing messages people left for Lindsay on her dry-erase board on the door. Drawing devil horns on all of Lindsay's photos in the school paper before handing it to her. Using all of Lindsay's tampons and not replacing the box. Stuff like that."

"Well, Kimberly," I say, "it sounds like Ann and Lindsay didn't exactly get along. But you don't really think Ann actually killed her, do you? I mean, why would she? She knew she was moving out, right?"

Kimberly looks thoughtful. "Well, yeah, I guess. But anyway, I told that detective guy to make sure she's got a, whadduya call it? Oh, yeah, an alibi. 'Cause you never know. It could be one of the *Single White Female*–type thingies."

I'm sure Detective Canavan jumped on the "*Single White Female*–type thingie" lead. Not.

"What about boyfriends?" I ask.

This cognitive leap is too much for Kimberly's tender young brain to process. She knits her slender eyebrows in confusion. "What?"

"Was Lindsay seeing anybody? I mean, I know she was dating Mark Shepelsky. . . ."

"Oh." Kimberly rolls her eyes. "Mark. But Lindsay and Mark, I mean, they were pretty much over, you know. Mark's so . . . immature. Him and Jeff—you know, Cheryl's boyfriend—all they're into is drinking beer and watching sports. They never took Lindsay and Cheryl out clubbing, or whatever. Which I guess is fine for Cheryl, but Lindsay . . . she wanted more excitement. More sophistication, I guess you could say."

"So is that why she started seeing someone else?" I ask.

When Kimberly's eyes widen, I explain, "Mark stopped by the office this morning and mentioned something about a frat guy?"

Kimberly looks contemptuous. "Is that what Mark called him? A frat guy? He didn't mention he's a *Winer*?"

"A what?" For a minute, I think she's saying Lindsay's new boyfriend complains a lot.

"A Winer. W-I-N-E-R. You know." When I continue to regard her blankly, she shakes all her long hair in disbelief. "Gawd, don't you know? *Doug Winer*. The *Winer* family. Winer *Construction*. The Winer Sports Complex, here at New York College?"

Oh. Now I know what she's talking about. You can't pass by a building under construction in this city—and, despite the fact that Manhattan is an island and you'd think every piece of usable land on it has been developed already, there are quite a few buildings under construction—without noticing the word WINER written on the side of every bulldozer, spool of wire, and piece of scaffolding connected with the job site. No building in New York City goes up unless Winer Construction puts it up.

And apparently the Winers have earned a bit of money because of that fact. They may not be Kennedys or Rockefellers, but apparently, to a New York College cheerleader, they come close. Well, they did donate a big chunk of cash to the college. Enough to build the sports complex, and everything.

"Doug Winer," I repeat. "So . . . Doug's well off?"

"Um, if you call being filthy rich well off," Kimberly says, with a snort.

"I see. And were Doug and Lindsay . . . close?"

"Not engaged or anything," Kimberly says. "Yet. But Lindsay thought Doug was getting her a tennis bracelet for her birthday. A diamond one. She saw it in his dresser." Momentarily, the pathos of Lindsay's death strikes, and Kimberly looks a little less bubbly. "I guess he'll have to take it back now," she adds mournfully. "Her birthday was next week. God, that's so sad."

I agree that the fact Lindsay did not live to receive a diamond tennis bracelet for her birthday is a shame, then ask her if Lindsay and Doug had had any disagreements that she knew of (no), where Doug lives (the Tau Phi Epsilon House), and when Doug and Lindsay had last seen each other (sometime over the weekend).

It soon becomes clear that though Kimberly claims to have been Lindsay's best friend, either the two of them hadn't been all that close, or Lindsay had led a remarkably dull life, because Kimberly is unable to reveal anything more about Lindsay's last week on earth. Anything more that could help me to figure out who killed her, anyway.

Except, of course, that's not what I'm doing. I'm not getting involved in the investigation into Lindsay's death. Far from it. I'm just asking a few questions about it, is all. I mean, a person can ask questions about a crime without actually launching a private investigation into said crime. Right?

I'm telling myself this as I walk back into the hall director's office, holding Tom's coffee (I got him a new one, after the original went cold while I was talking to Kimberly) in one hand, and a new coffee-cocoa-whipped-cream concoction for myself in the other. I'm not too surprised to see that Sarah, our grad assistant, has shown up to work wearing an unhappy expression. Sarah's unhappy most days.

Today, her bad mood appears to be catching. Both she and Tom are slumped at their desks. Well, technically, Tom is slumping at *my* desk. But he looks plenty unhappy, until he sees me.

"You," Tom says, as I plop his coffee in front of him, "are a lifesaver. What took you so long?"

"Oh, you know," I say, sinking onto the couch next to my desk. "I had to comfort Magda." I nod at Tom's office door, which is still closed. Behind it, and through the grate, I hear the low murmur of voices. "She still in there with Mark?"

"No," Sarah says disgustedly. "Now she's in there with Cheryl Haebig."

"What's with you?" I ask Sarah, because of the scowl.

"Apparently," Tom replies in a long-suffering voice, since Sarah just sinks more deeply into her chair, refusing to speak, "Dr. Kilgore is one of Sarah's professors. And not one she likes very much."

"She's a Freudian!" Sarah bursts out, not even attempting to lower her voice. "She actually believes that sexist crap about how all women are in love with their fathers and secretly want a penis!"

"Dr. Kilgore gave Sarah a D on one of her papers last semester," Tom informs me, with only the tiniest of smirks.

"She's anti-feminist!" Sarah asserts. "I went to the dean to complain. But it was no use, because she's one of *them*, too." *Them*, apparently, referred to Freudians. "It's a conspiracy. I'm seriously considering writing a letter to the *Chronicle of Higher Education* about it."

"I've suggested," Tom says, still with that very slight smirk, "that if Dr. Kilgore's presence is such an aggrievance to Sarah, she take the petty cash vouchers over to Budget for disbursement. . . ."

"It's like five degrees outside!" Sarah yells.

"I'll go," I volunteer sweetly.

Both Sarah and Tom stare at me incredulously.

"Seriously," I say, setting down my coffee-cocoa and getting up to grab my coat. "I mean, it's not like I'll be able to get any work done, with you at my desk, Tom. And I could use some fresh air."

"It's like five degrees out!" Sarah shouts again.

"It's no big deal," I say. I wind my scarf around my neck. "I'll be back in a jiff."

I scoop up the petty cash vouchers sitting on Sarah's desk, and sail from the office. Out in the lobby, Pete starts laughing when he sees me. Not because I look comical in all my outside layers, but because he's remembering what I'd said about my dad.

Well? Why *can't* he just want to rebuild his relationship with the daughter he barely knows?

Seriously, with friends like Pete, who needs enemies?

Ignoring Pete, I go outside—and almost turn back, it's so cold. The temperature seems to have plummeted since my walk to work an hour ago. The cold sucks the breath from my chest.

But I've made up my mind. There's no turning back now.

Lowering my head against the wind, I start across the park, ignoring the offers of "smoke, smoke," from Reggie's compatriots as I make my way toward the other side of campus—the opposite direction from the Budget Office. Which also happens to be the direction from which the wind is blowing in subarctic blasts.

Which is why, when I hear my name being called out from behind me, I don't turn around right away. My ears are so numb beneath my knit cap, I think I must be hearing things. Then I feel a hand on my arm and whip around, expecting to see Reggie with his gold-toothed grin.

I don't think it's necessarily the wind that sucks away my breath when I see that it's Cooper Cartwright.

"Oh," I say, goggling at him. He's as bundled up as I am. Except for the squirrels (and the drug dealers) we're the only two living beings stupid—or desperate—enough to be in the park on this frosty morning.

"Cooper," I say, through wind-chapped lips. "What are you doing here?"

"I stopped by to see you," Cooper says. He's breathing slightly heavily. Apparently he's been running to catch up with me. Running. In this weather. In all those clothes. If it were me, I'd have collapsed into a gelatinous heap. But since it's Cooper, he's just breathing slightly harder than usual. "And Sarah and Tom said you were on your way to the Budget Office." He jerks a gloved thumb over his shoulder. "But isn't the Budget Office that way?"

"Oh," I say, thinking fast. "Yeah. It is. But, uh, I thought I'd kill two birds with one stone and just stop by to see this one guy about this thing. Was there something important you needed to see me about?" *Please*, I'm praying. *Please don't let him have spoken to my dad before I've gotten a chance to speak to him about my dad.* . . .

"Yeah," Cooper says. He hasn't shaved again this morning. His dark razor stubble looks delectably prickly. "My brother. And why he might have left a message asking to speak to me about you. Any idea what that might be about?"

"Oh," I say, feeling slightly sick with relief. Although possibly that's from all the whipped cream. "Yeah. He wants me to come to his wedding. You know, to show there's no hard feelings—"

"In front of the photographers from *People*," Cooper finishes for me. "I got it. I should have known it wasn't anything important. So." His icy blue gaze focuses on me like a laser. "You're stopping by to see this one guy about *what* thing?"

Damn! How does he always know? *Always*?

"Well," I say slowly. "See, it turns out Lindsay was seeing a new guy before she died. A Winer."

"A what?"

"You know." I spell it. "As in Winer Construction."

His dark-lashed eyelids narrow. "Heather. Why does this sound to me like you're investigating that dead girl's murder?"

"Because I am," I say, then hold up both gloved hands in protest when he inhales to begin his tirade. "Cooper, think about it! Winer Construction? The Winer Sports Complex? They're bound to have skeleton keys to locks all over the city. Doug could totally have had access to the caf—"

"Did anyone sign him in that night?" Cooper demands.

Damn. He knows the workings of Fischer Hall almost as well as I do.

"Well, no," I say. "But there's a thousand ways he could have snuck in. Chinese food deliverymen do it all the time, to slip menus under the kids' doors—"

"No." That's all Cooper says. He accompanies the word with a single head shake.

"Cooper, listen to me," I say, even though I know it's pointless. "Detective Canavan isn't asking any of the right questions. He doesn't know how to get information out of these kids. I do. I swear that's all I'm doing. Gathering information. Which I will fully turn over to him."

"Do you honestly believe I'm that gullible, Heather?" Cooper demands.

He is glaring down at me. The wind is biting into my face and making my eyes sting, but it doesn't appear to be bothering him at all. Possibly because he's got all that razor stubble to protect him.

"You know, it's very stressful to work in a place people are calling Death Dorm," I say. "Tom only just started working there, and he already wants to quit. Sarah's being impossible. I'm just trying to make Fischer Hall a fun place to work again. I'm just trying to do my job."

"Counseling some kid because she put Nair in her roommate's shampoo bottle," Cooper says, mentioning an all-too-frequent form of roommate torture around New York College, "and finding the person responsible for boiling a cheerleader's head on a cooking range are two entirely different things. One of them is your job. One is not."

"I just want to talk to the Winer kid," I say. "What harm can TALKING do?"

Cooper continues to stare down at me, as the wind goes on whistling. "Please don't do this," he says, so quietly I'm not entirely sure he's said it at all. Except that I saw his lips move. Those oddly lush (for a guy) lips that sometimes remind me of pillows, against which I'd like to press my—

"You can come with me," I offer brightly. "Come with me and you'll see. All I'm doing is talking. Not investigating. Not at all."

"You've lost it," Cooper says. Not without some disgust. "I mean it, Heather. Sarah is right. You *do* have some kind of Superman complex."

"Up, up, and away," I say. And take his arm. "So. Coming?"

"Do I have a choice?" Cooper wants to know.

I think about it.

"No," I say.

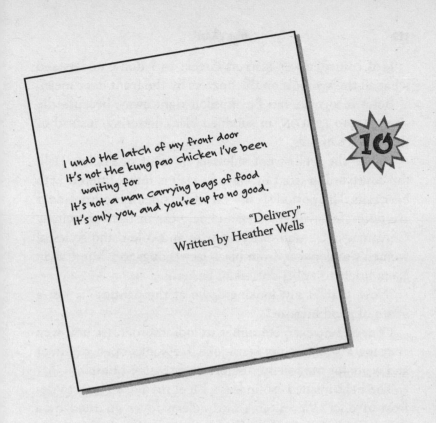

I undo the latch of my front door
It's not the kung pao chicken I've been
waiting for
It's not a man carrying bags of food
It's only you, and you're up to no good.

"Delivery"
Written by Heather Wells

Fraternity Row, otherwise known as Waverly Hall, is a huge
building on the opposite side of Washington Square Park
from Fischer Hall. Set back from the street by a stone wall
around a courtyard, and entered beneath an archway, it's
more Parisian in style than other buildings around the square,
and for that reason, more distinctive. Maybe that's why it
was determined by the trustees that this building would
house the college's Greek fraternities (the sororities, of
which there are fewer, are housed in a more modern building on Third Avenue), one frat per floor.

I, of course, never learned Greek, so I don't understand what all the symbols on the buzzers by the front door mean.

But I recognize Tau Phi Epsilon right away, because the sign TAU PHI EPSILON, in subdued black lettering, instead of the Greek symbols.

Unlike the well-swept sidewalk in front of Fischer Hall, the courtyard in front of Waverly Hall is filthy, littered with beer cans. The potted shrubs on either side of the front door are decorated with women's underwear instead of twinkly Christmas lights—all different sizes and colors and styles of women's underwear, from black lacy thongs to white Calvin Klein briefs to polka-dot bikini bottoms.

"Now, that," I say, looking down at the panties, "is just a waste of good lingerie."

Cooper, however, continues to look murderous, not even cracking a smile at my semi-joke. He yanks open the door and waits for me to enter before going inside himself.

The heat inside is so intense, I feel my nose begin to defrost at once. We enter a fairly clean foyer guarded by a gray-haired New York College security officer, whose face is crisscrossed by so many broken capillaries that his off-duty (one can only hope) predilection for whiskey is plainly obvious. When I show him my staff ID and tell him we're there to see Doug Winer of Tau Phi Epsilon, he doesn't even bother buzzing up to see if Doug's there. He just waves us toward the elevator. As we pass, I realize why: he's busy watching soap operas on one of his desk monitors.

Joining Cooper in the tiny, three-person elevator, I'm silent during the bouncy ride . . . until the cab lurches to a stop on the fifth floor, and the door opens to reveal a long, somewhat dingy hallway, along which someone has spray-painted in three-foot-high flourescent pink letters: FAT CHICKS GO HOME.

I blink at the letters, which reach nearly to my hip, and are scrawled across doors and walls indiscriminately. The Tau Phi Epsilons are going to have some pretty hefty floor damage charges come the end of the school year.

"*Well*," I say, staring at the wall.

"This," Cooper bursts out, "is *exactly* why I don't think you ought to be getting involved in this investigation."

"Because I'm a fat chick, and I ought to go home?" I ask, struck to the quick.

Cooper's expression darkens even further . . . a feat I hadn't thought possible.

"No," he says. "Because . . . because . . . guys like this . . . they're *animals*."

"The kind of animals who would chop off a cheerleader's head and cook it on a stove in a dorm cafeteria?" I ask him pointedly.

But he's apparently speechless with indignation. So I knock on the door closest to the elevator, the one with TAU PHI EPSILON written over the frame.

The door swings open, and a dark-haired woman in an honest-to-God maid's uniform—not one of those sexy ones they sell on Bleecker Street, but a real one, with long sleeves and a skirt below the knees—blinks at us. She's fairly young, probably early forties, and has a dust rag in one hand. She's not wearing a lace cap, though. Thank God.

"Yes?" she says. She has a heavy Spanish accent. Heavier than Salma Hayek's, even.

I show her my staff ID. "Hi," I say. "I'm Heather Wells, and this is my friend Cooper Cartwright. I'm with the Housing Department. I just wanted to—"

"Come in," the woman says disinterestedly. She steps out of the way so that we can enter, then closes the door behind us. We find ourselves in a spacious, well-lit loft—the old-fashioned kind, with high ceilings, crown molding, and parquet floors—in a foyer surrounded by doors on all four sides.

"They're in there." She nods her head toward a set of closed French doors off to the right.

"Um, well, we're actually looking for someone in particular," I say. "Doug Winer. Do you know which room is—"

"Look," the woman says, not unpleasantly. "I just clean here. I don't actually know any of them by name."

"Thank you for your time," Cooper says politely, and, taking me by the arm, steers me toward the closed French doors. He's muttering something beneath his breath that I don't quite catch . . . possibly because the minute his hand closed over my arm, my heart began to drum so loudly in my ears, it drowned out all other sound. Even through seven layers of material, Cooper's touch excites me no end.

I know. I really *am* pathetic.

Rapping sharply on the glass panes of the double doors, Cooper calls out, "Hello, in there."

A voice from within hollers something indistinguishable. Cooper looks down at me, and I shrug. He throws open the French doors. Through the thick gray fog of marijuana smoke, I'm able to make out the green felt of a billiard table, and, in the background, a wide-screen TV transmitting the flickering images of a football game. The room is lit by a bank of windows that let in the uneasy gray of outdoors, and by the warm glow of a brass and stained-glass lamp that hangs over the pool table. In a far corner, a spirited game of air hockey is taking place, and to my immediate left, someone opens a mini-fridge and pulls out a beer.

That's when I realize Cooper and I must have just died—possibly on that rickety old elevator—and I'd somehow ended up in Guy Heaven by mistake.

"Hey," says a blond kid leaning over the pool table to make a difficult shot. He has a joint pressed between his lips, the tip of which glows red. Incredibly, he's dressed in a red satin smoking jacket and a pair of Levi's. "Hang on."

He draws back the cue and shoots, and the click of balls is drowned out by the sudden thunder of the football fans as they cheer on a favorite player. Straightening, the kid removes the joint from his mouth and studies Cooper and me from behind a hank of blond hair. "What can I do you for?" he inquires.

I look longingly at the beer the kid reaches for and sucks back while he waits for our response. A glance at Cooper tells me that he, too, is fondly recalling a time in his life when it was okay—even encouraged—to drink beer before lunchtime. Although I never actually lived through a time like that, never having gone to college.

"Um," I say, "we're looking for Doug Winer. Is he here?"

The kid laughs. "Hey, Brett," he calls over his red satin shoulder. "This babe wants to know if Doug's here."

Brett, at the air hockey table, snorts. "Would we be enjoying this excellent ganja if the Dougster wasn't here?" he inquires, raising his beer bottle in the air like that guy in that play who held up the skull and said he knew him well. "Of course the Dougster is here. The Dougster is, in fact, everywhere."

Cooper is staring longingly at the wide-screen TV, apparently unaware that I've just been called a babe—which, while still sexist, is a nicer welcome than I'd have expected, based on the signage outside.

Still, with my partner apparently in a trance, I feel it's up to me to steer the conversation in a more profitable direction.

"Well," I say. "Could you tell me where, specifically, I might find Mr. Winer?"

One of the guys in front of the TV suddenly swivels around and barks, "Christ, Scott, it's a cop!"

Every joint in the room, and a surprising amount of beer, disappears in a split second, crushed under Docksiders or stashed behind sofa cushions.

"Cops!" Scott, the kid at the pool table, throws down his joint disgustedly. "Aren't you guys supposed to announce yourselves? You can't peg me for nothing, man, 'cause you didn't announce yourself."

"We're not cops," I say, holding up both gloved hands. "Relax. We're just looking for Doug."

Scott sneers. "Yeah? Well, you gotta be buyin', 'cause in threads like those, you sure ain't sellin'." A number of snickers sound in agreement.

I look down at my jeans, then glance surreptitiously at Cooper's anorak, which he has unzipped to reveal a Shetland sweater featuring a green reindeer leaping over a geometric design in which the color pink figures prominently, a sweater I happen to know he received for Christmas from a doting great-aunt. Cooper is quite popular with the more elderly of his relatives.

"Um," I say, thinking fast, "yeah. What you said."

Scott rolls his eyes and pulls his beer out from the ball socket in which he'd stashed it. "Outside and down the hall, first door on your left. And be sure to knock, okay? The Winer usually has company."

I nod, and Cooper and I retrace our steps back to the FAT CHICKS GO HOME hallway. The maid is nowhere to be seen. Cooper looks as if someone has hit him.

"Did you," he breathes, "smell that?"

"Yeah," I say. "Why am I thinking they've got a slightly better source for their weed than Reggie?"

"Isn't this part of the Housing Department?" Cooper wants to know. "Don't they have an RA?"

"A GA," I say. "Like Sarah. But in charge of the whole building, not one for each floor. He can't be everywhere at once."

"Especially," Cooper says, under his breath, "when Tau Phis are obviously paying him not to be."

I don't know what makes him think that . . . but I'm willing to bet he's right. Hey, grad assistants are students, too, and more often than not, financially insolvent ones.

The first door on the left is covered with a life-sized poster of Brooke Burke in a bikini. I knock politely on Brooke's left breast, and hear a muffled "What?" in response. So I turn the knob and go in.

Doug Winer's room is dark, but enough gray light spills from around the shade to reveal a very large water bed, on which two figures recline, amid a plethora of beer cans. The predominant decorating theme, in fact, seems to be beer, as there are piles of beer cans, bottles, and cases strewn about the room. On the walls are posters of beer, and on the shelves creative stacks of it. I, who like beer just as much as the next person, if not slightly more, feel a little embarrassed for Doug.

After all, drinking beer is one thing. Decorating with it is quite another.

"Uh, Doug?" I say. "Sorry to wake you up, but we need to talk to you a minute."

One of the figures on the bed stirs, and a sleepy male voice asks, "What time is it?"

I consult Cooper's watch—since I don't own one—after he presses the button on it that lights up the face. "Eleven," I say.

"Shit." Doug stretches, then seems to become aware of the other presence in his bed. "Shit," he says, in a different tone, and pokes the figure—rather sharply, in my opinion.

"Hey," Doug says. "You. Get up."

Mewling fitfully, the girl tries to roll away from him, but Doug keeps poking, and finally she sits up, blinking heavily mascaraed eyes and clutching the maroon sheets to her chest. "Where am I?" she wants to know.

"Xanadu," Doug says. "Now get the hell out."

The girl blinks at him. "Who are you?" she wants to know.

"Count Chocula," Doug says. "Get your clothes and get out. Bathroom's over there. Don't flush any feminine hygiene products down the john or you'll clog it."

The girl blinks at Cooper and me in the doorway. "Who're they?" she asks.

"How the hell should I know?" Doug says crankily. "Now get out. I got stuff to do."

"All right, Mr. Cranky Pants." The girl swings herself out of bed, awarding Cooper and me with a generous view of her heart-shaped backside as she struggles into a pair of panties that didn't make it to the shrubs outside. Clutching a spangly-looking dress to her chest, she simpers as she wriggles past

Cooper on her way to the bathroom, but gives me a narrow-eyed glare as she passes.

Well, same to you, sister.

"Who the hell are you?" Doug demands, leaning over and lifting the blind just enough to allow me to see that he's built like a lightweight wrestler, small, but muscular and compact. In the odd New York College campus fashion of the day, his head is shaved on all sides, but rises in a spiky blond flattop at the crown. He appears to be wearing a St. Christopher medallion and little else.

"Hello, Doug," I say, and I'm surprised when my voice comes out dripping with animosity. I hadn't liked the way Doug had treated the girl, but I'd hoped I'd be able to hide it better. Oh, well. "I'm Heather Wells and this is Cooper Cartwright. We're here to ask you a few questions."

Doug is fumbling along his bedside table for a pack of cigarettes. His square, stubby fingers close around a pack of Marlboros.

That's when Cooper takes two long strides forward, seizes the kid's wrist, and squeezes very hard. The kid yelps and turns a pair of angry pale blue eyes up at the larger man.

"What the fuck do you think you're doing?" he brays.

"Smoking stunts your growth," Cooper says, reaching down and pocketing the cigarette pack. He doesn't let go of Doug's wrist, but subtly begins applying pressure to it, in response to the kid's trying to pull it away. "And have you ever seen a photograph of a smoker's lungs?"

"Who the fuck do you guys think you are?" demands Doug Winer.

I think about saying something smart like, *Your worst nightmare*, but I glance over at Cooper and realize that what we are, really, is an assistant hall director whose BMI is in the overweight range, and a Shetland-sweater-wearing private detective, neither of whom has ever belonged to a fraternity.

Still, Cooper could intimidate by his sheer size alone, and apparently chooses to do so, looming over the kid's bed like a six-foot-three headboard.

"Who we think we are doesn't much matter," Cooper says, in his scariest voice. And that's when I realize Cooper hadn't liked the way Doug had treated the girl, either. "I happen to be a detective, and I have few questions I'd like to ask you concerning the nature of your relationship with Lindsay Combs."

Doug Winer's eyes widen perceptibly, and he says, in a high voice, "I don't have to tell the cops shit. My dad's lawyer said so!"

"Well," Cooper says, lowering himself onto the pitching water mattress, "that's not strictly true, Douglas. If you don't tell the cops shit, they'll have you arrested for obstruction of justice. And I don't think either your dad or his lawyer is going to like that."

I have to hand it to Cooper. He's scared the living daylights out of the boy, and without even lying to him. He *is* a detective . . . and the cops *could* arrest Doug for obstruction of justice. It's just that Cooper isn't a *police* detective, and wouldn't be able to do any arresting himself.

Seeing the kid's truculent expression go suddenly soft with fear, Cooper lets go of his wrist and stands back, folding his arms across his chest and looming quite menacingly. He manages to look as if he feels like breaking Doug Winer's arm—and might still do it, if provoked.

Doug massages his wrist where Cooper grasped it, and

looks up at him resentfully. "You didn't have to do that, man," he says. "It's my room, I can smoke if I want to."

"Actually," Cooper says, with the same amiableness that, I'm sure, always misleads his less savory clients into thinking he was secretly on their side, "this room belongs to the Tau Phi Epsilon Association, Douglas, not you. And I think the Tau Phi Epsilon Association might be interested to learn that one of their pledges is conducting a lucrative business in dealing controlled substances from their property."

"What?" Doug's jaw drops. In the gray light, I can see now that the kid's chin is peppered with acne. "What are you talking about, man?"

Cooper chuckles. "Well, let's leave that aside for a while, shall we? How old are you, Douglas? Tell the truth, now, son."

To my surprise, the kid doesn't say, *I'm not your son*, the way I would have, if I'd been him. Instead, he sticks out his pimpled chin and says, "Twenty."

"Twenty," Cooper echoes, looking pointedly about the room. "And are all these beer cans yours, Douglas?"

Doug isn't quite as stupid as he looks. His face grows dark with suspicion as he lies sullenly, "No."

"No?" Cooper looks mildly surprised. "Oh, I beg your pardon. I suppose your fraternity brothers, the ones who are over twenty-one, I mean, which is the legal drinking age in this state, drank all these beers and left them in your room as a little joke. Forgive me if I'm wrong, but isn't the New York College campus a dry one, Heather?" Cooper asks me, though he knows the answer very well.

"Why, yes, I believe it is, Cooper," I reply, seeing his game and playing along. "And yet, in this young man's room, there are many, many empty beer containers. You know what, Cooper?"

Cooper looks interested. "No, what, Heather?"

"I think that Tau Phi Epsilon is perhaps in violation of that dry campus ordinance. I think the Greek Association will be very interested to hear about your room, Mr. Winer."

Doug props himself up on his elbows, his bare, hairless chest heaving suddenly. "Look, I didn't kill her, all right? That's all I'll tell you. And you guys had better stop harassing me!"

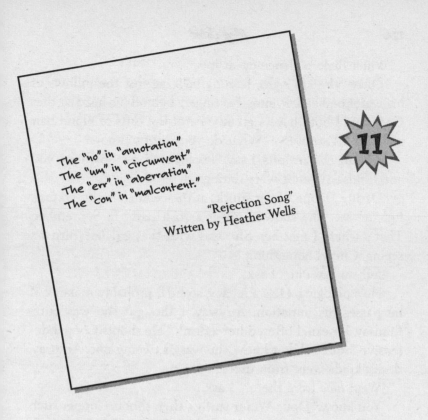

The "no" in "annotation"
The "um" in "circumvent"
The "err" in "aberration"
The "con" in "malcontent."

"Rejection Song"
Written by Heather Wells

Cooper and I exchange astonished glances. The astonishment, anyway, isn't feigned.

"Did anyone here accuse you of killing anyone, Douglas?" Cooper spreads out his hands innocently.

"Yeah, really." I shake my head. "We were only accusing your fraternity of supplying alcohol to their underaged brother."

Doug scowls. "You leave my fraternity out of this, okay?"

"We might be able to do that," Cooper says, stroking his whiskered jaw thoughtfully. "If you could be a little more forthcoming with the information my friend here requested."

Winer flicks a glance up at me.

"Okay," the kid sighs, leaning back against the pillows of his water bed and twining his fingers behind his head so that Coop and I both have a great view of the tufts of blond hair beneath his arms. Ew. "What do you want to know?"

Ignoring the armpits, I say, "I want to know how long you and Lindsay Combs were dating."

"Dating." Doug Winer smirks at the ceiling. "Right. Dating. Let me see. She showed up at a rush party in September. That's where I met her. She was with that girl Jeff Turner's seeing. Cheryl Something."

"Jeff's a Tau Phi?" I ask.

"He's pledging. He's a legacy, so he'll probably make it, if he passes his initiation. Anyway, I thought she was cute. Lindsay, I mean. I offered her a drink." He shoots Coop a defensive look. "I didn't know she wasn't twenty-one. Anyway, things kinda went from there."

"Went *how* from there?" I ask.

"You know." Doug Winer shrugs, then shoots Cooper such a smugly superior smile that I feel hard-pressed not to launch myself at the guy, tear a hole in the water mattress, and hold the kid's head in it until he drowns.

Not, of course, that I would ever do something like that. Because then I'd probably get fired.

"No, I don't know," I say, through gritted teeth. "Please explain it to me."

"She gave me head, okay?" Winer snickers. "Fucking homecoming queen, my ass. And she was a pro, let me tell you. I never had it like that from any girl—"

"Okay," Cooper interrupts. "We get the picture."

I feel my cheeks burning and curse myself. Why do I have to respond like such a Goody Two-shoes to words like *head*?

Especially around Cooper, who is already convinced I'm "a nice girl." By going around blushing all the time, I'm just reinforcing the image.

I try to make out as if I'm not blushing, just flushed. It *is* warm in Doug's room—especially since, judging from the sound of water coming from his bathroom, his girlfriend (or whatever she is) appears to be showering. I start unwinding my scarf.

"Never mind," I say to Cooper, to show him I'm all right with the gritty language. To Doug I say, "Go on."

Douglas, still looking smug, shrugs. "So I thought it'd be a good idea to keep her around, you know? For emergencies."

I'm so surprised by the coldness of this that I can't think of anything to say. Cooper's the one who inquires, calmly examining his own cuticles, "What do you mean, keep her around?"

"You know. Put her number in the little black book. For a rainy day. Whenever I was feelin' down, I'd give ol' Lindsay a call, and she would come over and make me feel better."

I really can't remember the last time I'd felt so much like killing someone—then recall that only an hour or so ago I'd wanted to pummel Gillian Kilgore with almost the same intensity as I now longed to throttle Doug Winer.

Maybe Sarah is right. Maybe I *do* have a Superman complex.

Cooper glances at me, and seems to sense that I'm having a difficult time restraining myself. He looks back down at his fingernails and asks Doug casually, "And Lindsay didn't have any complaints about this kind of relationship?"

"Shit, no," Doug says with a laugh. "And if she had complained, she'd've regretted it."

Cooper's head turns so fast in Winer's direction that it's nothing but a blur. "Regretted it how?"

The kid seems to realize his mistake and takes his hands away from his head, sitting up a little straighter. I notice that his abdomen is perfectly flat, except where it's ridged with muscles. I had abs that tight once. When I was eleven.

"Hey, not like that, man." Winer's blue eyes are wide. "Not like that. I mean, I'd've stopped calling her. That's all."

"Are you trying to tell us"—I've found my voice at last—"that Lindsay Combs was perfectly willing to come up here any old time you called and give you—ahem—oral sex?"

Doug Winer blinks at me, hearing the hostility in my voice, but apparently not understanding where it's coming from. "Well. Yeah."

"And she did this because?"

The kid stares at me. "What do you mean?"

"I mean that girls do not generally perform oral sex for no reason." At least, no girl with whom I was acquainted. "What did she get out of it?"

"What do you mean, what did she get out of it? She got *me* out of it."

It was finally *my* turn to smirk. "*You?*"

"Yeah." The kid sets his jaw defensively. "Don't you know who I am?"

Cooper and I, as if on cue, exchange blank stares. The kid says insistently, "I'm a Winer."

When we both continue to look uncomprehending, Doug prompts, as if he thinks we're slow, "Winer *Construction.* Winer Sports Complex? You guys haven't heard of it? We fucking own this city, man. We practically built this fucking college. At least the new buildings. I'm a Winer, man. A *Winer.*"

He certainly sounds like one.

And if this was the reason Lindsay Combs had been bestowing blow jobs so liberally upon this kid, I for one didn't believe it. Lindsay hadn't been that type of girl.

I don't think.

"Plus, I gave her shit," Doug admits grudgingly.

Now we were getting somewhere.

Cooper raised his eyebrows. "You what?"

"I gave her shit." Then, seeing Cooper's expression, Doug glances nervously in my direction, and says, "I mean, stuff. I gave her stuff. You know, the kind of stuff girls like. Jewelry and flowers and stuff."

Now, Lindsay was *that* kind of girl. At least, from what I knew of her.

"I was even gonna give her this bracelet for her birthday—" Suddenly the kid slings himself out of bed, affording us a view I'd have preferred not to have of his snug black Calvin Klein briefs. He goes to a dresser and draws a small black velvet box from a drawer. Turning, he casually tosses the box to me. I fumble, but manage to catch it. "I don't know what I'm gonna do with it now."

I open the black velvet lid and—I will admit it—my eyes widen at the slender strand of diamonds lying inside the box on a bed of royal blue silk. If this is the kind of payback Lindsay was routinely receiving for her services, I guess I could understand it a little better.

Stifling a desire to whistle at the costliness of such a gift, I tilt the box at Cooper, who raises his dark eyebrows. "That's quite a trinket," he comments mildly. "You must have some allowance."

"Yeah." Doug shrugs. "Well, it's just money."

"Is it Dad's money?" Cooper wants to know. "Or your own?"

The kid had been rooting around, looking for something

on top of the dresser. When his fingers close around a bottle of aspirin, Doug Winer sighs.

"What difference does it make?" he wants to know. "My money, my dad's money, my grandfather's money. It's all the same."

"Is it, Doug? Your father and grandfather's money comes from construction. I understand that you traffic an entirely different substance."

The kid stares. "What are you talkin' about, man?"

Cooper smiles affably. "The boys down the hall intimated that you know your way around certain hydroponics."

"I don't give a shit what they intimidated," Doug declares. "I do not deal drugs, and if you accuse me of selling so much as one of these to someone"—He shakes the bottle of aspirin at us—"my dad'll have your ass in a sling. He's friends with the president, you know. Of this college."

"That's it," I say, feigning terror. "I'm scared now."

"You know what? You better be. . . ." Doug starts toward me. But he gets no farther than a step before Cooper blocks his path, a hulking mass of muscle, anorak, and razor stubble.

"Just where do you think you're going?" Cooper asks lightly.

As Cooper had evidently hoped he would—guys are so predictable—the kid takes a swing at him. Cooper ducks, his grin growing wider. Now he has license to beat the crap out of Winer, as he'd no doubt been longing to do.

"Coop," I say. Because suddenly I realize things are not going at all the way I'd hoped. "Don't."

It's useless. Cooper takes a step toward the kid just as Doug is taking a second swing, catches the kid's fist in his hand, and, by applying steady pressure with his fingers alone, sends Winer to his knees.

"Where were you," Cooper growls, his face inches from the kid's, "the night before last?"

"What?" Doug Winer gasps. "Man, you're hurtin' me!"

"Where were you the night before last?" Cooper demands, evidently increasing the pressure on the kid's hand.

"Here, man! I was here all night, you can ask the guys! We had a bong party. Jesus, you're gonna break my hand!"

"Cooper," I say, my heart beginning to drum. Hard. I mean, if I let Cooper hurt a student, I'll be in serious trouble. Fired, even. Also . . . well, much as I dislike him, I find I can't stand by and see Doug Winer get tortured. Even if he deserves it. "Let the kid go."

"All night?" Cooper demands, ignoring me. "You were at a bong party all night? What time did it start?"

"Nine o'clock, man! Lemme go!"

"Cooper!" I can't believe what I'm seeing. This is a side of Cooper I've never witnessed before.

And am pretty sure I never want to see again. Maybe this is why he won't tell me what he does all day. Because what he does all day is stuff like this.

Cooper finally releases the kid, and Winer slumps to the floor, clutching his hand and curling into a fetal position.

"You're gonna regret this, man," the kid wimpers, fighting back tears. "You're gonna be real sorry!"

Cooper blinks like someone coming out of a daze. He looks at me and, seeing my expression, says sheepishly, "I only used one hand."

I am so stunned by this explanation—if that's even what it is—that I can only stare at him.

A tousled blond head peeks in from the bathroom doorway. The girl from the water bed has managed to pour herself back into a bright orange party dress, but she's barefoot, her wide eyes focused on Doug's prone form.

But she doesn't ask what happened. Instead, she asks, "Are my shoes in there?"

I lean down and lift up two orange high-heeled pumps. "These them?"

"Oh, yes," the girl says gratefully. She takes a few hesitant steps around her host and seizes the shoes. "Thank you very much." Slipping the pumps onto her feet, she says to Doug, "It was very nice meeting you, Joe."

Doug just moans, still clutching his injured hand. The girl scoops some of her blond hair from her eyes and leans down, displaying an admirable amount of cleavage.

"You can reach me at the Kappa Alpha Theta House anytime. It's Dana. Okay?"

When Doug nods wordlessly, Dana straightens, grabs her coat and purse from a pile on the floor, then wiggles her fingers at us.

" 'Bye, now!" she says, and jiggles away, her backside swaying enticingly.

"You get out, too," Doug says to Cooper and me. "Get out or I'll . . . I'll call the cops."

Cooper looks interested in this threat.

"Really?" he says. "Actually, I think there are a few things the cops need to know about you. So why don't you go right ahead and do that?"

Doug just whimpers some more, clutching his hand. I say to Cooper, "Let's just go."

He nods, and we step from the room, closing Doug's door behind us. Standing once again in the Tau Phi House's hallway, inhaling the rich odor of marijuana and listening to the sounds of the football game drifting out from the game room, I study the spray paint on the wall, which the maid who'd answered the door is trying to wipe off with paint remover and a rag. She's barely started on the F in FAT CHICKS. She has a long way to go.

She has a Walkman on, and smiles when she sees us. I smile automatically back.

"I don't believe a word that kid said," Cooper says, as he zips up his anorak. "How 'bout you?"

"Nope," I say. "We should check his alibi."

The maid, who apparently hadn't had the volume on her Walkman turned up very high, looks at us and says, "You know those guys are gonna back him up whatever he says. They're his fraternity brothers. They have to."

Cooper and I exchange glances.

"She has a point," I say. "I mean, if he didn't talk when you had him in that hand lock, or whatever it was . . ."

Cooper nods. "The Greek Association really is a marvelous institution," he remarks.

"Yes, it is," the maid says, just as gravely. Then she bursts out laughing and goes back to scrubbing the F.

"About what happened back there," Cooper says to me, in a different tone of voice, as we stand waiting for the elevator. "That kid . . . he just . . . the way he treated that girl   I just . . ."

"Now who's got the Superman complex?" I want to know.

Cooper smiles down at me.

And I realize I love him more than ever. I should probably just tell him that, and get it out in the open so we can stop playing these games (well, okay, maybe he's not playing games, but Lord knows I am). At least that way I'll know, once and for all, if I have a chance.

I'm opening my mouth to do just that—tell him how I

really feel about him—when I notice he's opening his mouth, too. My heart begins to thump—what if he's about to tell me that *he* loves *me*? Stranger things have happened.

And he *did* ask me to move in with him, pretty much out of the blue. And okay, maybe it was because he felt bad about the fact that I'd just walked in on my fiancé, who happens to be his brother, getting a blow job from another woman.

But still. He *could* have done it because he's secretly always been in love with me. . . .

His smile has vanished. This is it! He's going to tell me!

"You'd better call your office and tell them you're going to be late getting back," he says.

"Why?" I ask breathlessly, hoping against hope that he's going to say, *Because I plan on taking you back to my place and ravishing you for the rest of the day.*

"Because I'm taking you over to the Sixth Precinct, where you're going to tell Detective Canavan everything you know about this case." The elevator doors slide open, and Cooper unceremoniously propels me into the car. "And then you're going to keep out of it, like I told you."

"Oh," I say.

Well, okay. It isn't a declaration of love, exactly. But at least it proves he cares.

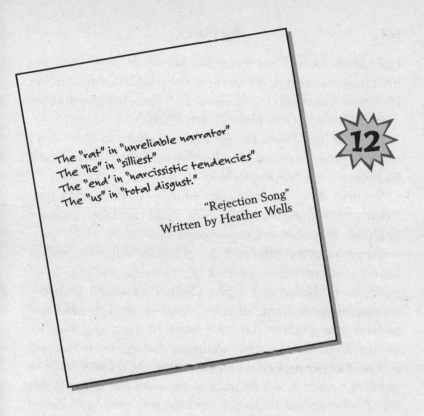

The "rat" in "unreliable narrator"
The "lie" in "silliest"
The "end' in "narcissistic tendencies"
The "us" in "total disgust."

"Rejection Song"
Written by Heather Wells

"What do you mean, we *have* to go to tonight's game?"

"Departmental memo," Tom says, flicking it onto my desk. Or should I say his desk, since he's apparently taking it over for the duration of Gillian Kilgore's stay? "Mandatory attendance. To show our Pansy Spirit."

"I don't have any Pansy Spirit," I say.

"Well, you better get some," Tom says. "Especially since we're having dinner beforehand with President Allington and Coach Andrews here in the caf."

My jaw drops. "WHAT?"

"He thinks it's just the ticket," Tom says, in a pleasant voice

I happen to know is solely for the benefit of Dr. Kilgore, behind the grate next door, "to show the public that the Fischer Hall cafeteria is safe to eat—and live—in. He's upset about everybody calling this place Death Dorm."

I stare at him. "Tom, I'm upset about that, too. But I don't see how eating warmed-over beef stroganoff and watching a basketball game is going to help."

"Neither do I," Tom says, dropping his voice to a whisper. "That's why I'm taking a little peppermint schnapps with me in a flask. We can share, if you want."

Generous as this offer is, it doesn't quite make the evening sound more palatable. I'd had big plans for tonight: I was going to go home and make Cooper's favorite dinner—marinated steak from Jefferson Market, with a salad and roasted new potatoes—in the hope of buttering him up enough to ask how he'd feel about my dad moving in for a bit.

And Cooper needed major buttering up, if I was going to get him to quit being so mad at me over the Doug Winer thing. After his initial chagrin over the way he'd manhandled the kid (or over me *witnessing* the way he'd manhandled the kid) had worn off—about midway through our meeting with Detective Canavan—Cooper had been quite vocal in his disapproval over my involving myself in the investigation into Lindsay's death at all. I believe the words "damned stupid" were mentioned.

Which did not bode well for my plan of bearing Cooper's children, much less asking him if my dad could move in.

Sadly, Detective Canavan was not in the least bit interested in any of the information I was able to impart pertaining to Lindsay's complicated love life. Or at least, if he was, he didn't act like it. He sat at his desk with a bored expression on his face through my entire recitation, then, when I was done, all he said was, "Ms. Wells, leave the Winer boy alone. Do you have any idea what his father could do to you?"

"Chop me up into little pieces and bury them in cement beneath the concrete foundation of one of the buildings he's constructing?" I asked.

Detective Canavan rolled his eyes. "No. Sue you for harassment. That guy's got more lawyers than Trump."

"Oh," I said, deflated.

"Was the Winer boy signed in the night Lindsay was killed?" the detective asked, though he clearly already knew the answer. He just wanted me to say it. "Not just by Lindsay, but by anyone else? Anyone at all?"

"No," I was forced to admit. "But like I was telling Cooper, there are tons of ways people can sneak into the building if they really want—"

"You think whoever killed that girl acted alone?" the detective wanted to know. "You think the murderer and his accomplices all snuck in past a guard who is paid to keep people from sneaking in?"

"Some of his accomplices could live in the building," I pointed out. "That could be how they got the key. . . ."

Detective Canavan gave me a sour look. Then he went on to inform me that he and his fellow investigators were already aware of Doug Winer's relationship with the victim, and that I should—in fancy detective-speak—butt out, a sentiment that was echoed by a still-steaming Cooper on our way home.

I tried to explain to him about Magda and her request—that Lindsay's character need not be assassinated during the investigation into her death—but this only resulted in Cooper's pointing out that beautiful girls who love too

much, as Lindsay appeared to have done, often meet unpleasant ends.

Which really only served to illustrate Magda's point.

Cooper, however, was of the opinion that if the shoe fit,
Lindsay was going to have to wear it. To which I replied,
"Sure. If anyone could find her foot."

Our parting, at the front door of Fischer Hall, was not
what anyone would reasonably call amicable. Thus the need
for steak before I introduced the topic of my father.

"I have to go home and walk my dog," I say to my boss,
making one last effort to get out of what I just know is going
to be an evening filled with hilarity. Not.

"Fine," Tom says. "But be back here by six. Hey, don't give
me that look. You were at the 'Budget Office' "—He makes
air quotes with his fingers—"for two hours this morning, and
I didn't say anything about it, did I?"

I make a face at him but don't protest further, because he's
got a point. He could have busted me for my disappearing
act earlier in the day, but he didn't. Possibly he's the coolest
boss in the world. Except for the part where he wants to quit
and go back to Texas, where girls apparently don't get decapitated in their residence hall cafeteria.

Having to attend this mandatory dinner and game is putting a serious crimp in my groveling plans. But when I get
home to let Lucy out, I see that Cooper's not around, anyway. The message light on the machine is blinking, and when
I press PLAY, I realize why Coop might be avoiding home. I
hear Jordan's voice, saying irritably, "Don't think you can just
hang up on me like that, Cooper, and that it's all over. Because it's not. You have a real opportunity here to show the
family that you can be a stand-up fellow. Don't blow it."

Wow. *Stand-up fellow*. No wonder Cooper hung up on him.

Poor Cooper. Having me around has put a real crimp in his resolve never to speak to his family again. I mean, considering that my living with him basically drives Jordan crazy. So instead of ignoring his black sheep brother, as he might have were I not around, Jordan instead focuses inordinate amounts of attention on trying to figure out what's going on between us.

Which, sadly, is nothing.

But I don't have a problem with Jordan thinking otherwise. The only problem, of course, is that it's highly unlikely Cooper is ever going to fall in love with me if he's constantly being harangued about me by his brother. That, and my annoying tendency nearly to get myself killed all the time, has to be extremely off-putting. Not to mention the fact that he's seen me in sweats.

There are no other messages on the machine—not even, weirdly, from my dad, though he'd said he was going to call. A quick scan of New York One shows the meteorologist still talking about this blizzard we're supposed to get—now it's hovering somewhere over Pennsylvania. I lace on my Timberlands, fully expecting that I'll just be taking them off later that night without having encountered a flake of snow. On the plus side, at least my feet will get gross and sweaty from wearing snow boots inside a hot, crowded gymnasium.

Back outside, I'm hurrying around the corner to Fischer Hall when I spy Reggie conducting a transaction with someone in a Subaru. I wait politely for him to finish, then smile as he approaches.

"Business is picking up," I observe.

"Because this storm they predicted is holding off," Reggie agrees. "If we're lucky, it will pass us by completely."

"From your lips to the weather god's ears," I say. Then,

pushing aside my—only slightly—guilty conscience, since I knew I was about to do something both Cooper and Detective Canavan wouldn't like (but really, if either of them would show just a modicum of respect for the deceased, I wouldn't feel obligated. I mean, how come guys who have a lot of sex are considered players, while girls who have a lot of sex are considered sluts?), I continue, "Listen, Reggie. What do you know about a kid named Doug Winer?"

Reggie looks blank. "Never heard of him. Should I have?"

"I don't know," I say. "He appears to be Big Man on Campus. He lives over at one of the fraternities."

"Ah," Reggie says knowingly. "A party kid."

"Is that what they're calling them these days?"

"That's what *I* call them," Reggie says, looking mildly amused. "Anyway, I haven't heard of him. But then, party kids and me? We travel in vastly different social circles."

"Probably not as different as you might think," I say, thinking about the marijuana haze hanging over the Tau Phi Epsilon pool table. "But will you ask around about him, anyway?"

"For you, Heather?" Reggie gives a courtly bow. "Anything. You think this boy has something to do with the young lady who lost her head?"

"Possibly," I say carefully, conscious of Detective Canavan's threat about the litigiousness of Doug's father.

"I'll see what I can do," Reggie says. Then he knits his brow. "Where are you going? Back to work? They're making you keep very long hours this week."

"Please," I say, rolling my eyes. "Don't even get me started."

"Well," Reggie says, "if you need a little pick-me-up . . ."

I glare at him. "*Reggie.*"

"Never mind," Reggie says, and drifts away.

Back at Fischer Hall, the excitement about the staff's Dinner and B-Ball Game With the President is palpable. Not. In fact, entirely the opposite is true. Most of the staff are milling around the lobby looking disgruntled. The cafeteria staff—day shift—are being particularly vocal in their protest that, as this is a mandatory function, they should be receiving overtime pay for it. Gerald, their boss, is maintaining that they're getting a free meal out of it, so they should just shut up. Understandably, his employees seem to feel that eating the food they helped prepare in the cafeteria they help maintain and which was, just the day before, the sight of a grisly murder is not as great a treat as he seems to feel it is.

It's odd to see the maintenance staff out of uniform. I barely recognize Carl, the chief engineer, in his leather jacket and jeans (and multiple gold neck chains). Head housekeeper Julio and his nephew Manuel are almost unrecognizable in sports coats and ties. Apparently they went home to change before coming back.

And Pete, out of his security uniform, looks like any other father of five . . . harried, rumpled, and anxious about what the kids are up to back home. His cell phone is glued to his ear, and he's saying, "No, you have to take them out of the can first. You can't microwave SpaghettiOs still in the can. No, you can't. No, you— See? What did I tell you? Why don't you listen to Daddy?"

"This," I say, coming up to Magda, who is resplendent as usual in tight white jeans and a gold lamé sweater (the school colors), "sucks."

But there are bright spots of color in each of Magda's cheeks . . . and not the painted-on kind, either.

"I'm seeing so many more of my little movie stars, though," she says excitedly, "than come in during the day!"

It's true that the dinner hour is the most highly attended meal of the day at Fischer Hall. And it looks as if the president's decision to set an example, by boldly taking a tray to the hot food line and choosing the turkey with gravy, has had an impact: the residents are trickling in, getting over their skittishness about eating in Death Dorm.

Or maybe they just want to see the president's expression when he takes a bite of the caf's (in)famous potatoes au gratin.

Tom sidles up to me, looking grim-faced. A second later, I notice why. Gillian Kilgore is following him, looking unnaturally perky.

"See, wasn't this a good idea?" she asks, looking at everyone milling around the tray cart, trying to grab forks and knives. "This shows that you all have some real bonding in the workplace. Now the healing can begin."

"Apparently nobody told her attendance is mandatory," Tom whispers to me as he slips into line behind me.

"Are you kidding me?" I whisper back. "This had to have been all her idea. You think the president came up with this one on his own?"

Tom glances over his shoulder back at Dr. Kilgore. She's at the salad bar, checking out her lettuce options (iceberg and . . . iceberg). "*Evil*," Tom says, with a shudder.

We're joined, a second later, by a panting Sarah. "Thanks for telling me," she says sarcastically to Tom, as she slides her empty tray next to his.

"Sarah," Tom says, "this is just for full-time staff, not students."

"Oh, right," Sarah says. "Because we're second-class citizens? We don't get to share in the therapeutic benefits of bonding together over shared pain? Was that Kilgore's idea?

Excluding the student workers? God, that is so typical of a Freudian—"

"Shut up," Tom says, "and eat."

We find a table at what we consider a safe distance from the president's and start to sit down, but President Allington catches us.

"Over here," he says, waving to Tom. "Come sit over here by us, Scott."

"Tom," Tom corrects him nervously. "It's, um, Tom Snelling, sir."

"Right, right," the president says, and beside him, Dr. Jessup—who clearly felt it important to show support for Dr. Allington's plan and was attending both the dinner and game with the Fischer Hall staff—points out, "Tom's the director of Fischer Hall, Phillip."

But it's futile. President Allington isn't listening.

"And you're Mary, right?" he says to me.

"Heather," I say, wishing there was a hole nearby I could crawl into. "Remember me? From that time in the penthouse, when you used to live here in Fischer Hall?"

His eyes glaze over. President Allington doesn't like being reminded of that day, nor does his wife, who rarely, if ever, comes into the city from their summer home in the Hamptons anymore because of it.

"Right, right," President Allington says, as Dr. Kilgore joins us with her tray, apparently not noticing she is being followed by an angry-faced Sarah. "Well, I think we all know each other—"

"Excuse us, President Allington?"

Five cheerleaders are lined up in front of our table, all staring at the president.

"Uh," he says, looking anxiously at Dr. Kilgore, as if for assistance. Then, remembering he's supposed to have a reputation for being accessible to the students, Dr. Allington attempts a smile and says, "Hello, girls. What can I do for you?"

Beside the president, Coach Andrews heaves a sigh and lays down his fork.

"Look, girls," he says to them slowly, clearly continuing a conversation that had started elsewhere, "we already discussed this. And the answer is—"

"We aren't talking to you," Cheryl Haebig says, a slight flush rising on her cheeks. Still, she holds her ground. "We're talking to President Allington."

The president glances from the girls to the coach and back again.

"What's this all about, Steve?" he wants to know.

"They want to retire Lindsay's cheerleading sweater," Coach Andrews says, beneath his breath.

"They want to *what*?" President Allington looks confused.

"Let me handle this," Coach Andrews says. To the girls in front of the table, he says, "Ladies, I feel as bad as all of you do about Lindsay. Really, I do. But the thing is, I think a formal memorial service, with input from Lindsay's family—"

"Her family's all here tonight," Megan McGarretty—Room 1410—informs him tersely. For such a tiny thing, she looks pretty intimidating, with her arms folded across the big letter P on her chest, and one hip jutting out like a warning. "And they don't want a memorial service. They're expecting somebody to say something tonight at the game."

"Oh." President Allington's eyes widen. "I'm not sure that would be appropriate."

"You can't just pretend like it didn't happen," Hailey Nichols—Room 1714—declares.

"Yeah," Cheryl Haebig says, her luminous brown eyes swimming with tears. " 'Cause we won't let Lindsay be forgotten. She was as much a part of your team as any of the boys."

"I believe we all recognize that," Dr. Kilgore says, trying to come to the president's rescue. "But—"

"If any of the boys on the team died," Tiffany Parmenter—Megan's roommate—interrupts, "you'd retire his number. You'd hang his jersey from the rafters, along with the championship banners."

"Er." Dr. Kilgore appears flummoxed by this. "That is certainly true, girls. But basketball players are athletes, and—"

"Are you saying cheerleaders aren't athletes, Dr. Kilgore?" Sarah's voice is icy.

"C-certainly not," Dr. Kilgore stutters. "Only that—"

"So why can't you retire Lindsay's sweater?" Hailey wants to know, her blond ponytail swinging in emphasis of her words. "Why can't you?"

I glance at Kimberly Watkins to see if she's going to chime in, but she remains uncharacteristically silent. All five girls are in their cheerleading uniforms, white sweaters with gold letter P's on the fronts, and very short, pleated gold and white skirts. They have on flesh-colored hose beneath their skirts, and white footies with fuzzy gold balls on the back of them. Their white sneakers are by Reebok and their hair color almost unanimously by Sun-In. Except Kimberly's, which is dark as midnight.

"Look." Coach Andrews looks tired. There are dark circles under his eyes. "It's not the jerseys themselves we retire when a player dies. It's the player's number. And Lindsay didn't have a number. We can't retire an article of clothing."

"Why not?"

All eyes turn toward Manuel, who, from the table he's sharing with his uncle and various other members of the custodial staff, blinks back.

"Why not?" he asks again, as his uncle Julio, beside him, looks mortified with embarrassment.

I glance around the table and happen to see Magda at the far end of it, watching the cheerleaders with a troubled gaze. I know what she's thinking without even having to ask. Because I'm thinking the same thing.

"I agree with Manuel," I hear myself say.

Of course, everyone turns to look at me. Which must be a relief to Manuel. But which causes me a certain amount of discomfort.

But I hold my ground.

"I think it could be a lovely gesture," I say. "If done tastefully."

"Oh, it will be," Cheryl assures us. "We already asked if the band can play the school song real slow. And we all chipped in and bought a wreath made out of gold and white roses. And I've got Lindsay's sweater, all nice and pressed."

I notice that everyone—including Dr. Jessup, the head of Housing—is staring at me.

But what's the big deal? It's just a stupid basketball game. Who cares if they—what is it again? Oh, yeah—retire a girl's sweater during it?

"I think it would be a touching tribute to a girl who had more Pansy spirit than just about anybody else in this school," I say to President Allington, who is still looking confused.

"But"—he looks worried—"the game is going to be televised. Live. The entire tri-state area will see Lindsay Combs's cheerleading sweater being retired."

"We'll be the laughingstock of college basketball," Coach Andrews mutters.

"And you're not already," I say, genuinely curious, "with a name like the Pansies?"

Coach Andrews looks sad. "True," he says. I'm sure when he was applying for coaching positions, he never dreamed he'd end up at a Division III school with a flower for a mascot.

He sighs, looking heavenward, and says, "It's all right with me if it's all right with President Allington."

The president looks startled—mostly because he's just taken a big bite of potatoes au gratin, and, from his expression, it's clear the bite included a big clump of flour.

After chugging half a glass of water, the president says, "Whatever. Do whatever you want." He's been beaten, by five cheerleaders and a lump of flour.

Cheryl Haebig immediately stops crying. "Rilly?" she asks brightly. "Rilly, Mr. President? You mean it?"

"I mean it."

Then, as Cheryl and her friends scream—shrilly enough to cause Dr. Kilgore to put her hands over her ears reflexively—Coach Andrews, raising his voice to be heard above the ruckus, says, "They won't broadcast the halftime show, anyway."

President Allington looks relieved. "Well," he says. And brings a forkful of turkey to his mouth. Then, relief turning quickly to disgust, he says, "Well," in a different tone of voice.

And reaches hastily for his water glass again, signifying to all that this will probably be the last meal the president will choose to enjoy in the Fischer Hall cafeteria.

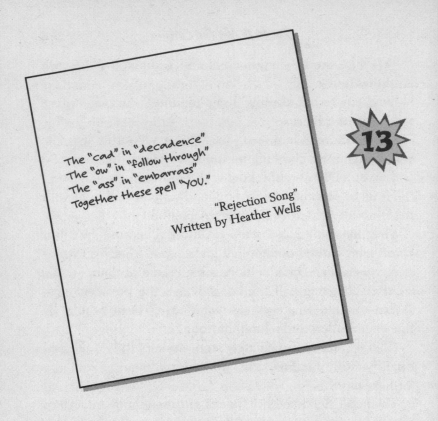

The "cad" in "decadence"
The "ow" in "follow through"
The "ass" in "embarrass"
Together these spell "YOU."

"Rejection Song"
Written by Heather Wells

13

Okay, so I'll admit it. I've never been to a basketball game before. Not a professional one (although Jordan used to beg me to accompany him to Knicks games all the time. Fortunately, I was usually able to come up with a good excuse . . . such as needing to wash my hair), not a high school game (I dropped out of high school after my first album took off), and certainly not a college game (I have generally been able to find other ways to occupy my time).

I can't really say what I'd been expecting, except . . . not what greeted me as I came through the gymnasium doors, which was hundreds of fans—because Division III games evidently do not attract thousands of fans, even if they are being held in the busiest metropolis in the world—with their faces painted the colors of their team—or, in some cases, wearing basketballs split in half, with little slits cut out for eye holes, as masks—stomping their feet against the bleachers, impatient for the game to begin.

Magda, however, a hardened veteran of the sport—all three of her brothers played in high school—takes it all in stride, steering me, followed by Tom ("Don't leave me alone"), Sarah ("Basketball is so sexist"), and Pete ("I told you. Don't put your brother's hamster in there"), toward some bare spots on the bleachers that aren't too high up, because we don't want to have to walk too far to get to the bathroom, according to Magda, and not too low, either, because we don't want to be hit by any balls.

The rest of the representatives from Fischer Hall—including President Allington, who goes to a section reserved just for him, Drs. Kilgore and Jessup, and the trustees, looking relieved to finally be brushing off the residue from Death Dorm—stream into the bleachers, and, since the impulse is contagious, begin stomping their feet as well, until the steel rafters a hundred feet overhead seem to reverberate.

It's only after the band starts the first few notes of "The Star Spangled Banner" that the crowd quiets down, then sings happily along with a pretty blond musical theater major who seems to give the tune her all. Probably she thinks there's a representative from a major record label in the audience, who's going to sign her then and there to a contract. Or maybe a Broadway producer who is going to come up to her when she's done singing and be all, "You were brilliant! Won't you star in the revival of *South Pacific* that I'm planning?"

Yeah. Good luck with that, honey.

Then, when the last echo of "brave . . . brave . . . brave . . ." dies away, the band rips into the school song, and Cheryl and her sister cheerleaders appear, flipping and cartwheeling their way across the court. They really are very impressive. I've never seen such flexibility—outside of a Tania Trace video, I mean.

The cheerleaders are followed by the gangly-legged Pansies team, in their gold and white jerseys. I hardly recognize Jeff and Mark and the other residents of Fischer Hall. On the court, in their uniforms, they look less like hapless sophomores and juniors, and more like . . . well, athletes. I guess because that's what they are, really. They high-five each of the New Jersey East Devils, in their red and gold jerseys, as they stream by. I'm impressed by this good sportsmanship, even though I know they've been told they *have* to do it. The television cameras swirl around Coach Andrews as he and several other men—assistant coaches, no doubt—walk to their seats on the sideline, and shake hands with the opposing team's coach before something happens that Magda explains is called the tip-off.

Despite the subzero temperatures outside, it's overly warm in the gym, what with all the people and their winter coats and the screaming and all. Tempers are short. Sarah, in particular, seems to feel the need to complain. She expresses strong opinions on multiple subjects, including but not limited to the fact that the money spent on athletics at New York College would be better spent helping to fund the psychology labs, and that the popcorn tastes stale. Beside her, Tom placidly sips from his flask, which he informs Sarah he needs for medicinal purposes.

"Yeah," Sarah replies sarcastically. "Right."

"I could use some of that medicine," Pete observes, after finally hanging up his cell phone. The hamster crisis has been averted.

"Be my guest," Tom says, and passes the flask to Pete. Pete takes a sip, makes a face, and passes it back.

"It tastes like toothpaste," he rasps.

"I told you it's medicinal," Tom says happily, and swills some more.

Meanwhile, Sarah has started paying attention to the game.

"Now, why'd that kid get a foul?" she wants to know.

"Because that boy was charging," Magda explains patiently. "When you have the ball, you can't knock people out of the way if they've established defensive position—"

"Oh!" Sarah cries, seizing Magda's wrist with enough force to cause her to slosh some of her soda. "Look! Coach Andrews is yelling at one of the umpires! Why's he doing that?"

"Ref," Magda mutters. She dabs at her white pants with a napkin. "They're referees, not umpires."

"Oh, what's that man saying?" Sarah bounces up and down excitedly on the bleacher bench. "Why's he look so mad?"

"I don't know," Magda says, flashing her a look of annoyance. Her endless patience isn't so endless, it turns out. "How should I know? Would you stop that bouncing? You made me spill my soda."

"Why is that boy getting a free throw? Why does he get to do that?"

"Because Coach Andrews called the ref a blind son of a—" Magda breaks off, her eyes getting wide. "Holy Mary, mother of God."

"What?" Sarah frantically scans the court. "What, what is it? A steal?"

"No. Heather, is that *Cooper?*"

I feel my insides seize up at the sound of the word. "Cooper? It can't be. What would *he* be doing here?"

"I don't know," Magda says. "But I could swear that's him down there, with some older man. . . ."

At the words *some older man*, my heart grows cold. Because there's only one older man Cooper could be with—with the exception of Detective Canavan, of course.

Then I spot them both, down by the Pansies bench. Cooper is scanning the crowd, obviously looking for me, while Dad is . . . well, Dad seems to be enjoying the game.

"Oh, my God," I say, dropping my head to my knees.

"What?" Magda lays a hand on my back. "Honey, who is it?"

"My father," I say to my knees.

"Your *what?*"

"My father." I lift up my head.

It didn't work. He's still there. I'd been hoping, by closing my eyes, I'd make him disappear. No such luck, apparently.

"That's your dad?" Pete is craning his neck to see. "The jailbird?"

"Your dad was in jail?" Tom wasn't out of the closet back when I was a household name, and so knows nothing about my past life. He wasn't even a secret Heather Wells fan back then, which is odd, because most of my most diehard supporters were gay boys. "What for?"

"Would you guys lean back?" Sarah complains irritably. "I can't see the game."

"I'll be right back," I say, because Cooper has finally spotted me in the crowd and is making his way determinedly toward me, my dad following, but slowly, his gaze on the game. The last thing I need is my friends witnessing what I'm sure is going to be a fairly unpleasant scene.

My heart pounding, I hurry to meet Cooper before he can join us in our room. His expression is inscrutable. But I can see that he's taken the time to shave. So maybe the news isn't all bad. . . .

"Heather," he says coolly.

Well, okay. It's pretty much all bad.

"Look who I found ringing our doorbell a little while ago," he goes on. And although my heart thrills at his use of the word *our*, I know he doesn't mean it in the domestic bliss kind of way I'd like to hear it. "When were you going to tell me your dad was in town?"

"Oh," I say, glancing behind me to see if anyone from my gang is eavesdropping. Not surprisingly, they *all* are . . . with the exception of Sarah, who seems to have been hypnotized by the game.

"I was just waiting for the right moment," I say, realizing even as the words are coming out of my mouth how lame they sound. "I mean . . . what I meant to say was. . . ."

"Never mind," Cooper says. He seems to be as hyper-aware as I am that everyone is listening to our conversation—well, what they can hear of it above the screaming and the band. "We'll talk about it at home."

Hideously relieved, I say, "Fine. Just leave him here with me. I'll look after him."

"He's not bad company, actually," Cooper says, gazing down at my dad, who is standing stock-still in the middle of the bleachers—unconscious that all the people behind him are trying to see around him—staring at the game. I guess it's been a while since he's been at a live sporting event. And the game *is* pretty exciting, I guess, if you're into that kind of thing. We're tied at twenty-one. "Hey. Is that popcorn?"

Sarah surprises everyone—well, okay, me, anyway—by

showing she was paying attention to us all along when she shakes her head and says, not taking her gaze from the court, "It's almost gone. Make Heather go get more."

"Get me a soda," Pete says.

"I could use some nachos," Tom adds.

"No!" Magda shrieks, apparently at a call down below. "He really *is* blind!"

Cooper says, "What?" and slides down into the seat I've vacated. "What was the call?"

"Offensive foul," Magda spits. "But he barely touched the kid!"

Shaking my head in disgust, I turn and make my way down the bleachers toward my father. He is still staring, enraptured, at the ball court.

"Dad," I say, when I reach him.

He doesn't take his eyes off the game. Nor does he say anything. The scoreboard over the middle of the court is counting down the time left in the game. There appear to be nine seconds left, and the Pansies have the ball.

"Dad," I say again. I mean, it really isn't any wonder he doesn't realize I'm talking to him. No one has called him dad in years.

Mark Shepelsky has the ball. He's taking it down the court, dribbling hard. He has a look of concentration on his face I've never seen him wear before . . . not even when he's filling out a vending machine lost-change report.

"Dad," I say for a third and final time, this time much louder.

And my dad jumps and looks down at me—

Just as Mark stops, turns, and throws the ball across the court, sinking it into the basket right before the halftime buzzer goes off, and the crowd goes wild.

"What?" Dad asks. But not me. He's asking the fans around him. "What happened?"

"Shepelsky made a three-pointer," some helpful soul shrieks.

"I missed it!" Dad looks genuinely upset. "Damn!"

"Dad," I say. I can't believe this. I really can't. "Why'd you come to the house? You said you were going to call first. Why didn't you call?"

"I did call," he says, watching as the Pansies run from the court, high-fiving one another, their expressions ecstatic. "No one answered. I thought you might be trying to avoid me."

"Did it ever occur to you I might not be avoiding you?" I ask. "That I just might not have gotten home yet?"

Dad realizes, I guess from the stress in my voice, that I'm not happy. Plus, all the action on the court is over for the moment, so he actually spares a second to look down at me.

"What's the matter, honey?" he asks. "Did I screw up?"

"It's just," I say, feeling idiotic for getting so upset, but unable to help myself, "things with Cooper, my landlord . . . I mean, they're *delicate*. And you showing up like that, out of the blue—"

"He seems like a nice guy," Dad says, glancing over at where Cooper is sitting "Smart. Funny." He grins down at me. "You certainly have your old man's approval."

Something inside me bursts. I think maybe it's an aneurism.

"I don't need your approval, Dad," I practically shout. "I've been getting along fine for the past twenty years without it."

Dad looks taken aback. I guess I shouldn't blame him. It's not his fault what he seems to think is going on between Cooper and me isn't.

"What I mean is," I say, softening my tone guiltily, "it's not like that. With Cooper and me, I mean. We're just friends. I do his billing."

"I know," Dad says. He looks confused. "He told me."

Now *I'm* confused. "Then why'd you say you approve? Like you thought we're dating?"

"Well, you're in love with him, aren't you?" Dad asks simply. "I mean, it's written all over your face. You might be able to fool him, but you aren't fooling your old dad. You used to get that same look on your face back when you were nine years old and that Scott Baio fellow would come on TV."

I gape at him, then realize my mouth is hanging open. I close it with a snapping sound probably only I can hear over the din of the gymnasium. Then I say, "Dad. Why don't you go sit down with Cooper? I'll be back in a minute."

"Where are you going?" Dad wants to know.

"To get the nachos," I say.

And stagger away to do so.

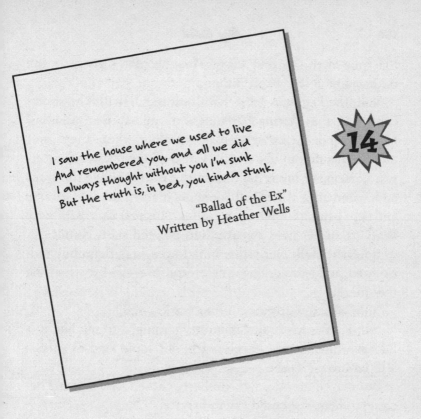

I saw the house where we used to live
And remembered you, and all we did
I always thought without you I'm sunk
But the truth is, in bed, you kinda stunk.

"Ballad of the Ex"
Written by Heather Wells

14

I'm not totally unfamiliar with the layout of the Winer Sports Complex. I'd signed up for a twenty-five-dollar-a-semester aerobics class there last semester, after passing my employment probation, and had even shown up for one session.

Unfortunately, I'd soon learned that only skinny girls take aerobics at New York College, and that larger young ladies like myself—if the waifish young things were to be able to see the instructor around me—had to stand in the back, where we, in turn, couldn't see anything, except tiny arms flailing around.

I quit after the first class. They wouldn't give me my twenty-five dollars back, either.

Still, the lesson at least familiarized me with the sports center, so that during halftime I'm able to find a ladies' room deep in the bowels of the building, where there isn't a mile-long line to use a stall. I'm washing my hands afterward, gazing at my reflection in the mirror above the sinks and wondering if I should just let nature take its course and go brunette, when a toilet flushes and Kimberly Watkins, in her gold sweater and pleated skirt, comes out of a nearby stall. Her red-rimmed eyes—yes, definitely red-rimmed, and from crying, I'm pretty sure—widen when she sees me.

"Oh," she says, freezing in her tracks. "You."

"Hi, Kimberly," I say. I'm pretty surprised to see her, too. I'd have thought the cheerleaders got some kind of special VIP bathroom to use.

But maybe they do, and Kimberly chose to use this one because in here, she could cry in private.

She seems to recover herself pretty quickly, though, and starts washing her hands at the sink next to mine.

"Enjoying the game?" she wants to know. She apparently thinks I can't see that her mascara is smudged where she's wiped away her tears.

"Sure," I say.

"I didn't know you were a fan," she says.

"I'm not, really," I admit. "They're making us attend. To show everyone that Fischer Hall isn't really a Death Dorm."

"Oh," Kimberly says. She turns off the water and reaches for the paper towels at the same time I do.

"Go ahead," she says to me.

I do.

"Listen, Kimberly," I say, as I dry. "I paid a little call on Doug Winer today."

Kimberly's eyes go very wide. She seems to forget her hands are dripping wet. "You *did?*"

"I did."

"*Why?*" Kimberly's voice breaks. "I *told* you, it was her freaky roommate who killed her. Her roommate, not Doug."

"Yeah," I say, tossing the wadded-up paper towels I'd used into the trash. "You said that. But it just doesn't make sense. Ann's no killer. Why would you say she was? Except maybe to throw the police off the scent of the person who *really* did it."

This gets to her. She averts her gaze, and seems to remember her hands. She pulls out a wad of paper towels from the dispenser on the wall. "I don't know what you're talking about," she says.

"Oh," I say. "So you're saying you didn't know Doug deals?"

Kimberly purses her perfectly made-up lips and stares at her reflection. "I guess. I mean, I know he's always got coke, I guess. And E."

"Oh," I say sarcastically. "Is that all? Why didn't you say something about this before, Kimberly? Why were you trying to make me think Ann was the guilty party, when you knew all this about Doug?"

"Geez," Kimberly cries, tearing her gaze away from her reflection and glaring at me. "Just 'cause a guy deals drugs doesn't mean he's a murderer! I mean, heck, a lot of people deal. A *lot* of people."

"Distribution of controlled substances is illegal, you know, Kimberly," I say. "So's possession. He could go to jail. He could get *expelled.*"

Kimberly's laugh is like a hiccup, it's so brief. "But Doug Winer'll never go to jail or get expelled."

"Oh? And why is that?"

"He's a *Winer*," Kimberly says, as if I were supremely stupid.

I ignore that. "Did Lindsay do drugs, Kimberly?"

She rolls her eyes. "Geez. What's *wrong* with you? Why do you care so much? I mean, I realize you're, like, a frustrated ex-rock star or something. But nobody listens to your music anymore. Now you're just a desk jockey at a Division III school. I mean, a monkey could do your job. Why are you *trying* so hard?"

"*Did Lindsay do drugs?*" My voice is so loud and so cold that Kimberly jumps, her eyes wide.

"I don't know," she shouts back at me. "Lindsay did a lot of things . . . and a lot of people."

"What do you mean?" I narrow my eyes at her. "What do you mean, a lot of people?"

Kimberly gives me a very sarcastic look. "What do you think? Everyone's trying to make out like Lindsay was some kind of saint. Cheryl and those guys, with that stupid sweater thing. She wasn't, you know. A saint, I mean. She was just . . . Lindsay."

"What people was she doing, Kimberly?" I demand. "Mark and Doug and . . . who else?"

Kimberly turns back to her reflection with a shrug and dabs at her lip gloss. "Ask Coach Andrews," she says, "if you want to know so badly."

I stare at her reflection. "Coach *Andrews*? How would *he* know?"

Kimberly just smirks.

And my mouth falls open.

I can't believe it. "No, come on," I say. Lindsay and *Coach Andrews*? "Are you serious?"

It's right then that the ladies' room door opens and Megan McGarretty pokes her head in.

"Gawd," she says to Kimberly. "There you are. We've been looking all over. Come on, it's time to do Lindsay's sweater."

Kimberly flashes me a knowing glance, then turns and heads for the door, her pleated skirt swishing behind her.

"Kimberly, wait," I say. I want to ask her what she means about Lindsay and Coach Andrews. She can't possibly mean what I think she means. Can she? I mean, Coach Andrews? He seems like such a . . . well . . . putz.

But Kimberly just sashays out of the room. Not surprisingly, she doesn't even say goodbye.

I stand there, staring at the door the girls have just disappeared through. Lindsay and *Coach Andrews*?

But even if it were true, and he's a potential suspect, I can't think of a reason why Coach Andrews might kill Lindsay. Lindsay's over eighteen. Yeah, okay, the college disapproves of faculty sleeping with their students. But it isn't like Coach Andrews would ever get fired over it. He's Phillip Allington's golden boy, the man who is going to lead New York College back to Division I glory . . . somehow. Or something. Coach Andrews could sleep his way through the entire Women's Studies Department and the trustees wouldn't blink an eye, so long as the Pansies keep winning games.

So why would he kill Lindsay?

And what had that little brat called me? Desk jockey? I'm *way* more than just a desk jockey. Fischer Hall would fall apart if it weren't for me. Why does she think I'm asking so many questions about Lindsay, anyway? Because I *care* about that place, and the people who live in it. If it weren't for me, how many more girls would have died last semester? If it weren't for me, nobody would get their vending machine refunds. How would Kimberly Watkins like living in Fischer Hall *then*?

Fuming, I leave the ladies' room. The hallway outside is dead silent. That's because, I realize, the girls have started their tribute to Lindsay back in the gym, and everyone has hurried back to their seats to watch it. I can hear the faint strains of the school song, played real slow, just like they'd said they'd have the band do it. I sort of want to be in there watching, too.

But I haven't gotten Tom's nachos yet, or Pete's soda. Not to mention Cooper's popcorn. Now is actually a good time to do so, with everyone inside watching Lindsay's sweater ascend to the rafters. Maybe there won't be a line at the concession stand.

I turn the corner, hurrying past empty squash court after empty squash court—if Sarah ever took a serious look around the sports center, she'd come up with a lot more reasons to complain about how the Psychology Department is treated. There must be twenty or thirty million of the Winer family's dollars poured into this building alone. It's almost brand-new, with special ID card scanner gates you have to pass through to get in. Even the soda machines have built-in scanners so you can buy a can of Coke using your dining card. . . .

Except, for such fancy, new-fangled soda machines, they sure seem to be making a funny noise. Not the usual electronic—and, let's admit it, to a soda-lover, comforting—hum, but a sort of thud—thud—thud.

But soda machines don't thud.

Then I see, suddenly, that I'm not the only person in the

hallway. When I come around the side of the bank of soda machines, I see that the thudding noises are coming from the hilt of a long kitchen knife as it repeatedly strikes the ribs of a man in a sports coat and tie. The man lies slumped against the wall to one side of the soda machines, and above him crouch three other men, each wearing half a basketball over his face, with small slits cut out in the rubber so that they can see.

When all three men hear my scream—because if you come across a scene like this when you are just walking along minding your own business, thinking about nachos, you're going to scream—they turn their heads toward me—three half basketballs, with eye slits cut in them, swiveling my way.

Of course, I scream again. Because, excuse me, but, creepy.

Then one of the men pulls the knife out of the man on the floor. It makes a sickening sucking sound. The blade that has just come out of the man is dark and slick with blood. My stomach lurches at the sight of it.

It's only when the man with the knife says, "Run," to his companions that I realize what I've just done—stumbled across the scene of a crime.

But they don't seem interested in killing me. In fact, they seem interested in getting away from me as quickly as possible, at least if the squeaking of their sneaker soles on the polished floor is any indication as they flee.

Then, the New York College fight song (*Hail to thee New York College / Colors gold and white / We will honor you forever / Bite them, Cougars, bite!*—the words to the song not having been changed after New York College lost its Division I standing and mascot) playing dimly in the background, I sink to my knees at the side of the injured man, trying to remember what I'd learned in the emergency first-aid seminar Dr. Jessup had over Winter Break. It was only what information they could cram into an hour, but I do recall that first and foremost, it's important to call for help—a feat I accomplish by whipping out my cell phone and dialing Cooper's cell number, the first one that pops into my head.

It takes him three rings to answer. I guess Lindsay's tribute must be especially moving.

"Somebody's been stabbed by the squash courts," I say into the phone. It's important to stay calm in an emergency. I learned that during my assistant hall director training. "Call for an ambulance and the cops. The guys who did it are wearing basketball masks. Don't let anyone in basketball masks leave. And get a first-aid kit. And get down here!"

"Heather?" Cooper asks. "Heather—what? *Where* are you?"

I repeat everything I've just said. As I do, I look down at the stabbed man, and realize, with sudden horror, that I know him.

It's Manuel, Julio's nephew.

"Hurry!" I shriek into the phone. Then I hang up. Because the blood from Manuel's body is starting to pool around my knees.

Whipping off my sweater, I stuff it into the gaping hole in Manuel's stomach. I don't know what else to do. The emergency first-aid course we took didn't cover multiple stab wounds to the gut.

"You're going to be all right," I tell Manuel. He's looking up at me with half-lidded eyes. The blood around him is gelatinous and almost black as it seeps into my jeans. I stuff my sweater more deeply into the biggest hole I can find, keeping my fingers pressed over it. "Manuel, you're going to be fine. Just hang on, okay? Help will be here in a minute."

"H-Heather," Manuel rasps. Blood bubbles up out of his mouth. I know this is not a good sign.

"You're going to be fine," I say, trying to sound like I believe it. "You hear me, Manuel? You're going to be just fine."

"Heather," Manuel says. His voice is nothing more than a wheeze. "It was me. I gave it to her."

Pressing hard against the wound—blood has soaked through my sweater and is gathering under my fingernails—I say, "Don't talk, Manuel. Help is on its way."

"She asked me for it," Manuel says. He's obviously delirious with blood loss and pain. "She asked me for it, and I gave it to her. I knew I shouldn't've, but she was crying. I couldn't say no. She was . . . she was so . . ."

"Would you shut up, Manuel?" I say, alarmed by the amount of blood coming out from between his lips. "Please? Please don't talk."

"She was crying," Manuel keeps saying, over and over again. *Where is Cooper?* "How could I say no to her when she was crying? I didn't know, though. I didn't know what they were going to do to her."

"Manuel," I say, hoping he can't hear that my voice is shaking. "You have to stop talking. You're losing too much blood. . . ."

"But they knew," he goes on, clearly off in his own world. A world of pain. "They knew where she got it—"

At that moment, Cooper turns the corner, Pete and Tom right behind him. Pete, seeing me, pulls out his security walkie-talkie, and begins squawking into it about how they've found me, and to get a stretcher down to the squash courts ASAP.

Cooper falls to his knees beside me and, miraculously, reveals a first-aid kit he's snagged from somewhere.

"Ambulance is on the way," he says, while Manuel, beneath my blood-soaked fingers, rambles feebly on.

"I gave it to her, don't you see, Heather? It was me. And they knew it was me."

"Who did this to him?" Cooper demands, pulling a huge roll of Ace bandages from the first-aid kit. "Did you get a look at him?

"They all had basketballs on their heads," I say.

"What?"

"They had basketballs on their heads." I grab the roll of bandages from him, pull away my sweater, and ram the roll of bandages into the biggest wound. "Half a basketball, over their faces, with little eye holes cut out—"

"My God." Tom, looking pale, blinks down at us. "Is that . . . is that *Manuel?*"

"Yes," I say, as Cooper leans forward and pulls down one of Manuel's eyelids.

"He's going into shock," Cooper says, pretty calmly, in my opinion. "You know him?"

"He works at Fischer Hall. His name is Manuel." Julio, I know, is going to flip out when he sees this. I pray that he doesn't come looking for his nephew.

"They did this as a warning," Manuel says. "A warning to me not to tell that I gave it to her."

"Gave what to who, Manuel?" Cooper asks him, even as I'm shushing him, telling him to save his breath.

"The key," Manuel says. "I know I shouldn't have, but I gave her my key."

"Who?" Cooper wants to know.

"Cooper," I say. I can't believe this. I can't believe he's interrogating a dying man.

But he ignores me.

"Manuel, who'd you give your key to?"

"Lindsay," Manuel says. Manuel shakes his head. "I gave Lindsay my key. She was crying . . . she said she'd left something in the cafeteria, something she needed to get. At night, after it was closed—"

His eyelids drift shut.

Cooper says, "Damn."

But then the EMTs are there, shoving us both out of the way. And I'm actually relieved, thinking everything is going to be okay.

Which just goes to show how much I know.

Which is nothing.

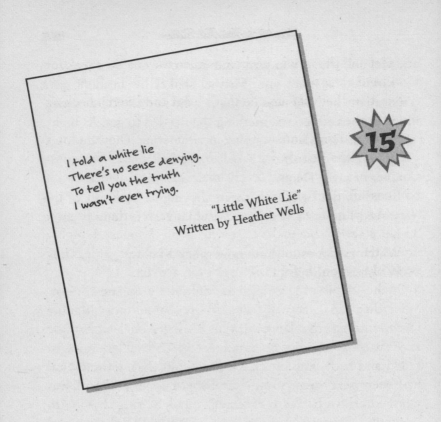

I told a white lie
There's no sense denying.
To tell you the truth
I wasn't even trying.

"Little White Lie"
Written by Heather Wells

15

You know what happens when someone nearly gets murdered during a Division III college basketball game that is being televised live on New York One?

Everyone keeps right on playing.

That's right.

Oh, they posted cops at all the exits, and after the game—which the Pansies lost, twenty-four to forty. They just never came back after the second half. And not even because they heard about what happened to Manuel. Because no one told them. No, basically, the Pansies just suck—the cops made everybody stop on their way out and show them their hands and feet and the insides of their bags, so they could check for blood and weapons.

Not that they *told* anyone that's what they were checking for, of course.

But they didn't find anything incriminating. They couldn't even hold the people with half-basketball masks for questioning, because roughly every male in the audience had a half-basketball mask.

And it was pretty obvious—to me, anyway—that the guys who'd stabbed Manuel were long gone. I mean, I highly doubt they stuck around to watch the rest of the game. They probably got out before the cops even arrived.

So they didn't even witness the Pansies' humiliating defeat.

Neither did I, actually. Because no sooner was Manuel loaded into an ambulance with his heartsick uncle at his side and carted away—the paramedics said he had lost a lot of blood and had some internal injuries, but that nothing vital had been punctured, so he'd probably be okay—than I was whisked off to the Sixth Precinct to look at mug shots with Detective Canavan, even though I EXPLAINED to him I hadn't seen their faces, due to the masks.

"What about their clothes?" he wants to know.

"I told you," I say, for the thirtieth time at least. "They were wearing regular, everyday clothes. Jeans. Flannel shirts. Nothing special."

"And you didn't hear them say anything to the victim?"

It's kind of irritating to me that Detective Canavan keeps referring to Manuel as "the victim" when he knows perfectly well that he has a name, and what that name is.

But maybe, like Sarah's gallows humor, saying "the victim" is a way of distancing himself from the horror of acts of such violence.

I wouldn't mind distancing myself from it, either. Every time I close my eyes, I see the blood. It wasn't red like blood on TV. It was dark brown. The same color the knees of my jeans are now.

"They didn't say anything," I say. "They were just stabbing him."

"What was he doing there?" Detective Canavan wants to know. "By the soda machines?"

"How should I know?" I ask with a shrug. "Maybe he was thirsty. The line at the concession stand was really long."

"What were *you* doing there?"

"I told you. I had to go to the bathroom, and the line at the other ladies' room was too long."

When Detective Canavan arrived at the sports complex—because of course we called him, to tell him what Manuel had said, about giving a key to Lindsay—I had suggested that he stop the game and question every single person present—particularly Coach Andrews, whom I now had reason to believe was more deeply involved than previously thought.

But President Allington—who unfortunately had to be informed of what was going on, given how many cops were lurking in the building—balked, saying that New York One would be on the story in a red-hot minute, and that the college had had enough bad publicity for one week. The last thing the school needed was reporters going around asking questions about a crime that, for all we knew, might in no way be connected to Lindsay—despite what I told everyone Manuel had said.

Then President Allington went on to assure us that, bad publicity aside, New York One would also be within their rights to sue if the game were stopped, claiming they stood to lose a million dollars in advertising if the game didn't continue.

I honestly never suspected those Bowflex commercials brought in so much revenue, but apparently Division III college basketball is considered must-see TV by those folks most likely to be interested in purchasing exercise equipment for the home.

"One thing I want to be sure everyone understands," President Allington also said to Detective Canavan, unfortunately (for him) within my earshot, though he was speaking softly so that no lurking reporters might overhear, "is that New York College is in no way responsible for either the death of that girl or the injuries sustained by Mr. Juarez this evening. And if he did give her a key with which she might have accessed the cafeteria, we are in no way responsible for that, either. Legally, that's still trespassing."

Which caused Detective Canavan to remark, "So what you're saying, Mr. Allington, is that if Lindsay used Manuel's key to gain access to the cafeteria, she damn well deserved to get her head chopped off?"

President Allington looked understandably flustered by this statement, and one of his flunkies stepped in to say, "That is not what the president meant at all. What he meant was, the college cannot be held responsible for the fact that someone in our employ gave his keys to a student who later got herself killed on college property. . . ."

Detective Canavan didn't stick around to hear more. And, to my everlasting relief, he took me away with him.

Or at least it was a relief at first. Because it meant I could put off having to talk to Cooper about my dad for that much longer.

Unfortunately, it meant I had to talk to Detective Canavan instead.

"And that's it? That's all you can remember? Jeans, flannel shirts, basketballs on their heads. What about their shoes? Were they wearing tennis shoes? Loafers?"

"Sneakers," I say, remembering the squeaking on the floor.

"Well." He blinks at me. It's late, and he's probably been at the precinct all day. The number of Styrofoam cups littering the floor by his desk indicates how he's managed to sustain his energy level for so long. "That narrows it down."

"I'm sorry. What do you want me to say? They were—"

"Wearing basketballs on their heads. Yes. You mentioned that."

"Are we done here?" I want to know.

"We're done," Detective Canavan says. "Except for the usual warning."

"Warning?"

"Not to involve yourself in the investigation into Lindsay Combs's murder."

"Right," I say. I can be just as sarcastic as he can. "Because I so stumbled across poor Manuel getting stabbed by her killers on purpose."

"We don't know the attack on Mr. Juarez and Lindsay's murder are connected," Detective Canavan points out. Seeing my raised eyebrows, he adds, "Yet."

"Whatever," I say. "Can I go?"

He nods, and I'm out of there like a shot. I'm tired. All I want to do is go home. And change my pants, which are stiff with Manuel's blood.

I go out into the lobby of the Sixth Precinct, expecting to see Cooper there, sitting in the same seat he always takes when he's waiting for me to come out of one of my many visits with Detective Canavan (today is a new record, twice in less than twelve hours).

But the seat is empty. In fact, the lobby is empty.

That's when I notice it's snowing really hard outside. I mean, *really* hard. I can barely make out the shape of the Range Rover parked in front of the station. But when I go outside and peer through the driver's-side window, I recognize Patty's husband Frank. He starts when I tap on the window, and puts it down.

"Heather!" Patty leans over from the passenger seat. "There you are! Sorry, we didn't see you, we're listening to a book on tape. One about parenting that the new nanny recommended."

"The nanny who terrifies you?" I ask.

"Yes, that's the one. God, you should have seen her face when we told her we were coming here. She nearly . . . Well, never mind. Get in, you must be freezing!"

I hop into the backseat. The interior is warm and smells faintly of Indian food. That's because Frank and Patty had been enjoying some samosas as they waited for me.

"How'd you know where I was?" I ask, as they pass me one, loaded with tamarind sauce. Yum.

"Cooper called," Frank explains. "Said he had to run and could we pick you up. Off on one of his cases, I guess. What's he working on, anyway?"

"How should I know?" I ask, with my mouth full. "Like he's going to tell me."

"Did you really see someone get stabbed?" Patty asks, turning around in her seat. "Weren't you scared? What is that all over your jeans?"

"I didn't have time to be scared," I say, chewing. "And that's blood."

"Oh, God!" Patty turns quickly around to face the windshield again. "Heather!"

"It's okay," I say. "I can just get new ones." Although, with my luck, I'll have gone up a size, thanks to all the holiday cheer in which I imbibed.

Size 14 is still average for an American woman. Still, you don't want to have to buy all new jeans to accommodate your new size. That can be hard on the wallet. What you want to do instead is maybe reduce intake on the bodega fried chicken. Maybe.

Although it depends on how you look in the new jeans.

"It's really coming down hard," Frank observes, as he pulls out of his primo parking space. In ordinary circumstances, that space would be instantly taken by some waiting vehicle. But it's a blizzard, and no one is out on the streets. The flakes are falling thick and fast, already coating the street and sidewalks with an inch of fluffy white stuff. "I can't imagine Cooper's going to be able to do any real detecting in this weather."

Frank is just slightly obsessed with the fact that Cooper is a private detective. Most people fantasize about being rock stars. Well, it turns out rock stars fantasize about being private detectives. Or, in my case, being a nonvanity size 8 and still able to eat anything I want again.

Although I'm not actually a rock star. Anymore.

"Heather, I hope you're being careful this time," Patty frets, from the front seat. "I mean, about this dead girl. You aren't getting involved in the investigation, are you? Not like last time?"

"Oh, heck, no," I say. Patty doesn't need to know about my trip to the Tau Phi House. She has enough to worry about, being a former model and rocker's wife, not to mention the mother of a toddler who, at last reportage, ate an entire H & H everything bagel—almost as big as his own head—in one sitting.

The nanny hadn't been too happy about that one.

"Good," Patty says. "Because they don't pay you enough to get yourself nearly killed, like last time."

When Frank pulls up in front of Cooper's house, I see that a few of the lights are on . . . which surprises me, since it means Cooper must be home.

But before I can get out of the car, Frank says, "Oh, Heather, about the gig at Joe's—"

I freeze with my hand on the door handle. I can't believe— what with all the blood and everything—I'd forgotten about Frank's invitation to jam with him and his band.

"Oh," I say, frantically trying to think up an excuse. "Yeah. About that. Can I get back to you? 'Cause I'm really tired right now, and can't really think straight—"

"Nothing to think about," Frank says cheerfully. "It's just gonna be me and the guys and a hundred and sixty or so of our friends and family. Come on. It'll be fun."

"Frank," Patty says, apparently having caught a glimpse of my face. "Maybe now's not the best time to ask about that."

"Come on, Heather," Frank says, ignoring his wife "You're never gonna get over your stage fright if you don't get back up there. Why not do it among friends?"

Stage fright? Is that my problem? Funny, I thought it was just fear of having people boo and throw things at me. Or, worse . . . snicker, the way Jordan and Cooper's dad did, when I played them my own songs that fateful day in the Cartwright Records offices. . . .

"I'll think about it," I say to Frank. "Thanks for the ride. See ya."

I plunge from the car before either Patty or her husband can say anything, then run to the front door, ducking my head against the onslaught of flakes.

Phew. Talk about narrow escapes.

Inside, Lucy meets me in the foyer, excited to see me, but not in an *I gotta go out right this minute* kind of way. Someone's already let her out.

"Hello?" I call, shedding my coat and scarf.

No one answers. But I smell something unusual. It takes me a minute to place the scent. Then I realize why: it's a candle. Cooper and I are not candle people—Cooper because, well, he's a guy, and me because I've seen them cause so many fires in Fischer Hall that I'm paranoid I, too, will forget and leave one burning unattended.

So why is someone burning a candle in the house?

The smell is coming from upstairs . . . not the living room or kitchen, and not Cooper's office. It's coming from upstairs, where Cooper sleeps.

Then it hits me. Cooper must be home, and entertaining. In his room.

With candles.

Which can only mean one thing: He's got a date.

Of course. That's why he couldn't wait for me down at the precinct, and had to call Frank and Patty! He's got a date.

I pause at the bottom of the stairs, trying to sort out why this realization has made me suddenly so upset. I mean, it's not like Cooper KNOWS about the enormous crush I have on him. Why SHOULDN'T he see other people? Just because he HASN'T seen anyone (that I know of . . . he certainly hasn't brought anybody back to the house) since I moved in doesn't mean he SHOULDN'T or CAN'T. Now that I think of it, we never really did discuss the issue of overnight guests. It's just not something that ever came up.

Until now.

Well, so what? He's having a sleepover. It doesn't have anything to do with me. I'll just creep up to the third floor and go to bed. No reason to stop and knock and ask him how he's doing. Even though I'm dying to see what she looks like. Cooper has a reputation in his family for always dating super-intelligent, incredibly beautiful, even exotic women. Like brain surgeons who are also former models. That kind of thing.

Even if I thought I ever had a chance with Cooper romantically, one look at his many exes would cure me. I mean, what guy would want a washed-up ex-pop star who now works as an assistant residence hall director and wears vanity size 8 jeans (or possibly 10s) when he could have a physicist who was once Miss Delaware?

Yeah. Right. No one. I mean, unless the physicist happens to be really boring. And maybe doesn't like Ella Fitzgerald (I've got all her songs memorized, including the scat). And maybe isn't the warm, funny human being I just happen to believe I am. . . .

Stop. STOP IT.

I'm creeping up the stairs to the second floor as quietly as I can—Lucy panting at my side—when I notice something strange. The door to Cooper's bedroom is open . . . but there's no light on. Whereas the door to the guest room down the hall from Cooper's bedroom is open, *and* there's a light on, *and* the light is flickering. Like a candle flame.

Who on earth would be in our guest room with a candle?

"Hello?" I say again. Because if Cooper's entertaining lady friends in our guest room, well, that's just his tough luck if I come busting in. His room is his inner sanctum—I've never dared venture into it . . . if only because he's so rarely to be found in it. Also because thousand-dollar sheets scare me.

But the guest room?

The door is really only slightly ajar. Still, it's technically open. Which is why I push on it to open it a little farther, and say, "Hello?" for a third time. . . .

. . . then shriek at the sight of my father doing the downward-facing dog.

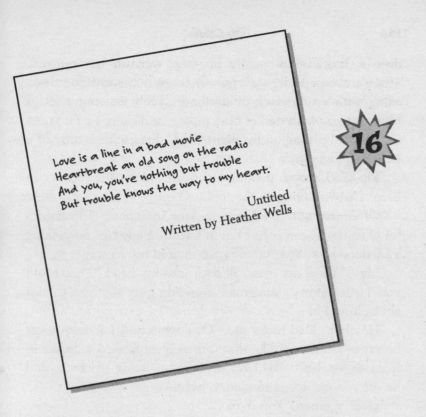

16

Love is a line in a bad movie
Heartbreak an old song on the radio
And you, you're nothing but trouble
But trouble knows the way to my heart.

Untitled

Written by Heather Wells

"I find yoga extremely relaxing," Dad explains. "Back at camp, I did it every morning and every night. It's really rejuvenated me."

I stare at him from across the room. It's strange to hear your father call jail camp. Especially while he's doing yoga.

"Dad," I say. "Could you quit that for a minute and talk to me?"

"Of course, sweetheart," Dad says. And comes back to his feet.

I can't believe this. He's clearly moved in. His suitcase is open—and empty—on the window seat. His shoes sit by the dresser, lined up as neatly as if he were in the military. There's a typewriter—a typewriter!—on the antique desk, along with a tidy stack of stationery. He's wearing a set of blue pajamas with darker blue piping, and there's a fat green tea candle burning on his nightstand, along with a copy of a Lincoln biography.

"My God," I say, shaking my head. "How did you get in here? Did you *break* in?"

"Of course not," Dad says, looking indignant. "I learned a lot of things at camp, but I didn't acquire any tips on picking a Medeco lock. Your young man invited me to stay."

"My—" I feel my eyes roll back into my head. "Dad. I told you. He is not my young man. You didn't say anything to him about how I lo—"

"Heather." Dad looks sad. "Of course not. I would never betray a confidence like that. I merely expressed a dislike in front of Mr. Cartwright for my current living situation, and he offered me accommodation here—"

"Dad!" I groan. "You didn't!"

"Well, the Chelsea Hotel was hardly a suitable place for a man in my position," he says patiently. "I don't know if you're aware of this, Heather, but many people with criminal records have resided in the Chelsea Hotel. Actual murderers. That's not the kind of environment a person who is trying to rehabilitate himself should be in. Besides which, it was quite noisy. All that loud music and honking horns. No, this"—he looks around the pleasant white bedroom happily—"is much more *me*."

"Dad." I can't help it. I can't stand up anymore. I sink down onto the side of the queen-sized bed. "Did Cooper say how long you could stay?"

"In fact," Dad says, reaching out to ruffle Lucy's ears, since she's followed me inside, "he did. He said I could stay as long as it took in order for me to get back on my feet."

"Dad." I want to scream. "Seriously. You can't do that. It's not that I don't want to work on our relationship—yours and mine, I mean. It's just that . . . you can't take advantage of Cooper's generosity this way."

"I'm not," Dad says matter-of-factly. "I'm going to be working for him, in exchange for rent."

I blink. "You're . . . what?"

"He's taking me on as an employee of Cartwright Investigations," Dad says . . . a little proudly, I think. "Just like you, I'm working for him. I'm going to help him tail people. He says I've got just the right looks for it . . . sort of unnoticeable. He says I blend."

I blink some more. "You *blend*?"

"That's right." Dad opens up the drawer to his nightstand and takes out a small wooden flute. "I'm trying to take it as a compliment. The fact that I'm so unnoticeable, I mean. I know your mother often felt that way, but I wasn't aware it was true of the world in general. Oh, well. Listen to this little tune I learned at camp. It's quite restful. And after the night you've had, I'm sure you could use a little relaxation." He proceeds to lift the flute to his lips and begins to play it.

I sit there for a minute more as the notes—plaintive and, as he'd mentioned, oddly restful—wash over me. Then I shake myself and say, "Dad."

He immediately stops playing. "Yes, dear?"

It's the endearments that are killing me. Or possibly making me want to kill HIM.

"I'm going to bed now. We'll talk about this again in the morning."

"Well, all right," he says. "But I don't see what there is to talk about. Cooper is obviously a man of good sense. If he wants to hire me, I don't see why you should object."

I can't see why I should object, either. Except . . . how am I going to get Cooper to realize I'm the woman of his dreams if my DAD's around? How am I ever going to make him that romantic steak dinner for two I'd been planning? There's nothing romantic about steak for *three*.

"I realize I haven't been the best father to you, Heather," Dad goes on. "Neither your mother nor I provided you with very good role models growing up. But I hope the damage isn't so serious that you are incapable of forming loving relationships now. Because it's my sincerest wish that that is what you and I can have with one another. Because everyone needs a family, Heather."

Family? Is that what I need? Is that what's wrong with me? I don't have a family?

"You look tired," Dad says. "Which is understandable, after the day you've had. Here, maybe this will help soothe you." Then he starts playing the flute again.

Okay. *This* I don't need.

I lean down, blow out Dad's green tea candle, and snatch it from the nightstand.

"These are a fire hazard," I snap, in my most assistant residence hall directory voice.

Then I stalk from the room and upstairs to my own apartment.

The snow doesn't stop. When I wake up in the morning, I look out the window and see that it's still coming down—slower now, and less of it. But still in big fluffy flakes.

And when I get out of bed—which isn't easy, considering how snug it is in there, with Lucy sprawled half across me—

and go to the window, I find myself looking out at a winter wonderland.

New York City looks different after a snowfall. Even an inch can make a difference—it covers all the dirt and graffiti, and makes everything look sparkly and new.

And twenty inches—which is what it appears we got overnight—can make the city look like another planet. Everything is quiet . . . no honking horns, no car alarms . . . every sound is muffled, every branch straining under the weight of so much fluffy white stuff, every windowsill coated in it. Gazing out at it, I realize, with a sudden zing to my heartstrings, what's going on:

It's a Snow Day.

I realize it even before I pounce on the phone and call the college's weather hotline. Oh, yes. Classes are canceled for the day. The school is closed. The city, in fact, is shut down. Only necessary emergency personnel should be on the streets. *Yes.*

Except, of course, when you live two blocks away from where you work, you can't exactly plead that you couldn't get in.

But still. You can be late.

I take my time bathing—because why stand up if you don't have to?—and getting dressed. I have to resort to the backup jeans because of the bloodstains on my primary pair, and I am dismayed to find they are slightly snug. Okay, more than slightly. I have to pull my old trick of stuffing wadded-up socks along the waistband of my jeans to stretch them out, while doing deep knee bends. I tell myself it's because they just came out of the dryer. Two weeks ago.

And when I remove the socks before going downstairs, they are a little less tight. At least I can breathe.

It's as I'm breathing that I realize I'm smelling something unfamiliar. At least, unfamiliar in this house.

Bacon. And, if I'm not mistaken, eggs.

I hurry down the stairs—Lucy at my heels—and am horrified when I walk into the kitchen and find Cooper there, reading the paper, while my dad stands at the stove in a pair of brown cords and a woolly sweater. Cooking breakfast.

"This," I say loudly, "has to stop."

Dad turns around and smiles at me. "Good morning, honey. Juice?"

Cooper flicks down one side of the paper. "Why are you up?" he wants to know. "They just said on the news New York College is closed."

I ignore him. But I can't ignore Lucy, who is at the back door, scratching to be let out. I open the door, letting in an arctic blast. Lucy looks disappointed by what she sees out there, but bravely soldiers ahead. I close the door behind her and turn to face my father. Because I've come to a decision. And it has nothing to do with the wooden flute.

"Dad," I say. "You cannot live here. I'm sorry, Cooper. It was nice of you to offer. But it's too weird."

"Relax," Cooper says, from behind his newspaper.

I feel my blood pressure shoot up another ten points. Why does this always happen whenever anyone says the word *relax*?

"Seriously," I say. "I mean, I live here, too. I'm also an employee of Cartwright Investigations. Don't I get a say in this?"

"No," Cooper says, from behind his newspaper.

"Honey," Dad says, turning around and handing me a steaming mug of coffee. "Drink this. You never were a morning person. Just like your mother."

"I am not like Mom," I say. Though I take the coffee. Because it smells delicious. "Okay? I am *nothing* like her. Do you see, Cooper? Do you see what you've done? You've invited this man to live here, and he's already telling me I'm like my mother. And I am nothing like her."

"Then let him stay here," Cooper says, still not looking out from behind his paper, "and find that out for himself."

"Your mother is a lovely person, Heather," Dad says, as he puts two sunny-side-up eggs and some bacon on a plate. "Just not in the mornings. Rather like you. Here." He hands the plate to me. "This is how you used to like them as a little girl. I hope you still do."

I look down at the plate. He has arranged the eggs so that they are like eyes, and the bacon is a smiling mouth, just like he used to do when I was a kid.

Suddenly I am overwhelmed by an urge to cry.

Damn him. How can he *do* this to me?

"They're fine, thanks," I mutter, and sit down at the kitchen table.

"Well," Cooper says, finally lowering the paper, "now that that's settled, Heather, your dad is going to be staying with us for a while, until he figures out what his next move is going to be. Which is good, because I can use the help I have more work than I can handle on my own, and your dad has just the kind of qualities I need in an assistant."

"The ability to *blend*," I say, chomping on a strip of bacon. Which is, by the way, delicious. And I'm not the only one who thinks so. Lucy, whom Dad lets back in after she scratched on the door, is enjoying a strip I snuck her, as well.

"Correct," Cooper says. "An ability which should never be

underestimated when you are in the private investigative field."

The phone rings. Dad says, "I'll get that," and leaves the kitchen to do so.

The second he's gone, Cooper says, in a different tone, "Look, if it's really a problem, I'll get him a room somewhere. I didn't realize things were so . . . unsettled . . . between you two. I thought it might be good for you."

I stare at him. "*Good* for me? How is having my ex-con dad live with me *good* for me?"

"Well, I don't know," Cooper says, looking uncomfortable. "It's just that . . . you don't have anyone."

"As I believe we have discussed before," I say acidly, "neither do you."

"But I don't need anyone," he points out.

"Neither do I," I say.

"Heather," he says, flatly. "You do. No one died, left you their townhouse, and made you independently wealthy. And, no offense, twenty-three thousand dollars a year, in Manhattan, is a joke. You need all the friends and family you can get."

"Including jailbirds?" I demand.

"Look," Cooper says. "Your dad's an extremely intelligent man. I'm sure he's going to land on his feet. And I think you're going to want to be around when that happens, if only to inflict enough guilt on him to get him to throw some money your way. He owes you college tuition, at least."

"I don't need tuition money," I say. "I get to go free because I work there, remember?"

"Yes," Cooper says, with obviously forced patience. "But you wouldn't have to work there if your dad would agree to pay your tuition."

I blink at him. "You mean . . . quit my job?"

"To go to school full-time, if getting a degree is really your goal?" He sips his coffee. "Yes."

It's funny, but though what he's saying makes sense, I can't imagine what it would be like not to work at Fischer Hall. I've only been doing it for a little over half a year, but it feels like I've been doing it all my life. The idea of *not* going there every day seems strange.

Is this how everybody who works in an office feels? Or is it just that I actually *like* my job?

"Well," I say, miserably, staring at my plate. My empty plate. "I guess you're right. I just . . . I feel like I take enough advantage of your hospitality. I don't want my family sponging off you now, too."

"Why don't you let me worry about protecting myself from spongers," Cooper says wryly. "I can take care of myself. And besides, you don't take advantage. My accounts have never been so well organized. The bills actually go out on time for a change, *and* they're all accurate. That's why I can't believe they're making you take remedial math, you do such a great job—"

I gasp at the words *remedial math*, suddenly remembering something. "Oh, no!"

Cooper looks startled. "What?"

"Last night was my first class," I say, dropping my head into my hands. "And I spaced it! My first class . . . my first course for college credit . . . and I missed it!"

"I'm sure your professor will understand, Heather," Cooper says. "Especially if he's been reading the paper lately."

Dad comes back into the kitchen, holding the cordless phone from the front hallway. "It's for you, Heather," he says.

"Your boss, Tom. What a charming young man he is. We had a nice chat about last night's game. Really, for a Division Three team, your boys put on quite a show."

I take the phone from him, rolling my eyes. If I have to hear one more thing about basketball, I'm going to scream.

And what am I going to do about what Kimberly said last night? Was there something going on between Coach Andrews and Lindsay Combs? And if so . . . why would he *kill* her over it?

"I know the school's closed," I say to Tom. "But I'm still coming in." Because, considering my newest housemate, a monsoon couldn't keep me away, let alone a little old nor'easter.

"Of course you are," Tom says. Clearly, the idea that I might do what all the other New Yorkers are doing today— staying in—never even occurred to him. "That's why I'm glad I caught you before you left. Dr. Jessup called—"

I groan. This is not a good sign.

"Yeah," Tom says. "He called from his house in Westchester, or wherever it is he lives. He wants to make sure a representative from Housing shows up at the hospital to visit Manuel today. To show we care. Also to bring flowers, since there are no florist shops open, thanks to the storm. He says if you buy something from the hospital gift shop, I can reimburse you from petty cash. . . ."

"Oh," I say. I'm confused. This is a sort of a high-profile assignment. I mean, Dr. Jessup doesn't usually ask his assistant hall directors to step in as representatives of the department. Not that he doesn't trust us. Just that . . . well, I personally haven't been the most popular person on staff since I dropped the Wasser Hall assistant hall director during that trust game. "Are you sure *I'm* the one he wants to go?"

"Well," Tom says, "he really didn't specify. But he wants someone from the Housing Department to go, to make it look like we care—"

"We *do* care," I remind him.

"Well, of course *we* care," Tom says. "But I think he meant *we* as in the Housing Department, not *we* as in the people who actually know Manuel. I just figured since you and Manuel have a previously existing relationship, and you're the one who, in effect, saved his life, and—"

"And I'm two blocks closer to St. Vincent's than anyone else at Fischer Hall right now," I finish for him. It's all becoming clear now.

"Something like that," Tom says. "So. Will you do it? Swing over there before coming here? You can take a cab there and back—if you can find one—and Dr. Jessup says he'll reimburse you if you bring back the receipt. . . ."

"You know I'm happy to do it," I say. Anytime I get to spend money and charge it to the department is a happy day for me. "How are *you* doing, though?" I ask, trying to sound nonchalant, even though the answer is vitally important to my future happiness. There's no telling what kind of heinous boss I might get assigned if Tom left. Possibly someone like Dr. Kilgore. . . . "Are you still thinking . . . I mean, the other day you mentioned wanting to go back to Texas—"

"I'm just trying to take this one day at a time, Heather," Tom says, with a sigh. "Murder and assault were never covered in any of my student personnel classes, you know."

"Right," I say. "But, you know, in Texas they don't have fun blizzards. At least, not very often."

"That's true," he says. Still, Tom doesn't sound convinced of New York's superiority over Texas. "Anyway, I'll see you in a bit. Stay warm."

"Thanks," I say. And I hang up . . .

. . . to find Cooper looking at me strangely over his coffee.

"Going to St. Vincent's to visit Manuel?" he asks lightly. Too lightly.

"Yes," I say, averting my gaze. I know what he's thinking. And nothing could be further from the truth. Well, maybe not *nothing*. . . . "I doubt I'll find a cab, so I better go bundle up—"

"You're just going to give Manuel get-well wishes," Cooper says, "and then head back to work, right? You wouldn't, say, hang around and try to question him about who attacked him last night and why, would you?"

I laugh heartily at that. "Cooper!" I cry. "God, you're so funny! Of *course* I wouldn't do that. I mean, the poor guy was brutally stabbed. He was in surgery all night. He probably won't even be awake. I'll just sneak in, leave the flowers—and balloons—and go."

"Right," Cooper says. "Because Detective Canavan told you to stay out of the investigation into Lindsay's murder."

"Totally," I say.

Dad, who has been watching our exchange with the same kind of intensity he watched the basketball game the night before, looks confused. "Why would Heather interfere with the investigation into that poor girl's death?"

"Oh," Cooper says, "let's just say that your daughter has a tendency to get a little overinvolved in the lives of her residents. And their deaths."

Dad looks at me gravely. "Now, honey," he says, "you really

ought to leave that sort of thing to the police. You don't want to be getting hurt, now, do you?"

I look from Dad to Cooper and then back again. Suddenly it hits me: I'm outnumbered. There's two of them now, and only one of me.

I let out a frustrated scream and stomp out of the room.

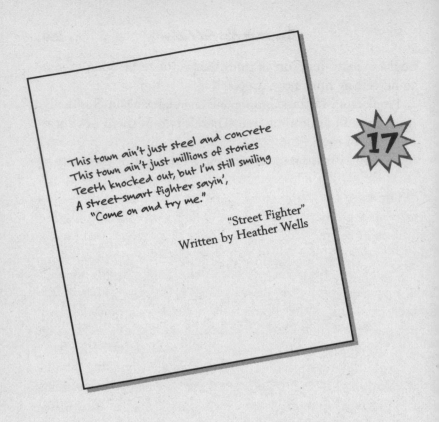

17

This town ain't just steel and concrete
This town ain't just millions of stories
Teeth knocked out, but I'm still smiling
A street-smart fighter sayin',
"Come on and try me."

"Street Fighter"
Written by Heather Wells

The gift shop is open, thank God. The flowers aren't exactly very fresh-looking, though—no delivery that morning, on account of the road conditions, which are so bad I not only couldn't get a cab, but had to walk in pretty much the center of the street in order to avoid drifts up to my knees.

Still, they have balloons of every size and description, and the helium tank is working, so I have fun making an enormous balloon bouquet. Then I have them throw in a GET WELL SOON bear for good measure, after first making sure the GET WELL SOON banner comes off, so Manuel can regift the bear to a girlfriend or niece. You have to think about these things when you're giving stuffed toys to a man.

I make my way up to ICU, which is where Manuel is being held, to find him awake, but groggy, with a lot of tubes coming in and out of him. There are a lot of people in his room, including a woman who appears to be his mother, who is slumped exhaustedly in a chair near Julio, who is also dozing. While I see two cops—one posted at either entrance to the intensive care unit—I don't see Detective Canavan anywhere. He either hasn't made it into the city yet, or was already here and left.

There are two law enforcementy-looking guys leaning against the wall by the door to Manuel's room, both in suits that are damp up to the knees from their walks through the snowdrifts outside. They're holding Styrofoam cups of coffee. One is saying, as I approach, "Canavan get anything out of 'im?"

"Nothing he could make any sense of." The younger man is wearing a tie in a festive tropical print. "Asked him if he knew why he'd been stabbed. All he did was groan."

"Canavan ask him about the key?"

"Yep. Got about the same response. Nothing."

"What about the girl?"

"Nothing."

"Maybe we should get the kid's uncle to ask him," the older one says, nodding at a dozing Julio. "Might be he'll respond better to a face he recognizes."

"The kid's completely out of it," his colleague says with a shrug. "We're not getting shit out of him."

Both men notice me at the same time. I'm kind of hard to miss, with my enormous balloon bouquet. Also, I'm clearly eavesdropping.

"Can we help you, miss?" the younger one asks, sounding bored.

"Oh, hi," I say. "I didn't mean to interrupt. I'm here to see Manuel Juarez? I'm from the Housing Department, over at New York College, where Manuel works. They sent me to see how he's doing."

"You got ID?" the older detective, or whatever he is, asks, in as bored a voice as his colleague has used.

I fumble for my staff ID. I have to have the younger one hold the balloons while I do so.

"Nice bear," he comments dryly.

"Thanks," I say. "I thought so."

They check the ID. Then the older one hands it back and says, "Knock yourself out," while nodding toward Manuel's room.

I take back my balloons and, with some difficulty, maneuver them through the door, then quietly approach Manuel's side. He watches me the whole time, without making a sound. The only noise I can hear, as a matter of fact, is the steady breathing of his uncle and a woman I assume is his mother. And the clicking of all the machines next to his bed, doing whatever they're doing to him.

"Well, hey, there, Manuel," I say with a smile, showing him the balloons. "These are for you, from all of us over at Fischer Hall. We hope you feel better soon. Sorry about the bear, I know it's a bit, you know. But they were out of flowers."

Manuel manages a slight smile. Encouraged, I go on, "You aren't feeling so hot, are you? I'm so sorry those guys did this to you, Manuel. It really stinks."

Manuel opens his mouth to say something, but the only thing that comes out is a grunting noise. I see his gaze go to the brown pitcher on the table by his bed. There are some paper cups next to it.

"You want some water?" I ask. "Did anybody tell you that you weren't supposed to have any? Because sometimes they don't want you to drink, if you're going to have more surgery or something."

Manuel shakes his head. So, after letting the balloons drift to the ceiling so I don't have to hang on to them anymore, I pour some of the water into a paper cup.

"Here you go," I say, and hold the cup out to him.

He's too weak to lift his hands, though—they're weighted down by all the tubes going into them anyway—so I put the cup to his lips. He drinks thirstily.

When he finishes the first cup, he looks pointedly at the pitcher, so, figuring he wants a refill, I pour him another one. He drinks that one, too, only slower. When he's done with that one, I ask if he wants more. Manuel shakes his head, and is finally able to speak.

"I was so thirsty," Manuel said. "I tried to tell those guys—" He nods at the two detectives in the hallway. "But they didn't understand me. I couldn't talk, my throat was so dry. Thank you."

"Oh," I say. "No problem."

"And thank you for what you did last night," Manuel says. He can't seem to speak very loudly—though Manuel, even in the peak of health, was never a loud talker—so it's hard to hear what he's saying. But I lean forward and am able to catch most of it. "Uncle Julio says you saved my life."

I shake my head. "Oh, no," I say. "Really, that was the paramedics. I was just in the right place at the right time, is all."

"Well," Manuel says, managing a smile, "lucky for me, then. But no one will tell me . . . did we win?"

"The basketball game?" I can't help laughing. "No. We got creamed in the second half."

"It was my fault," Manuel says, looking pained.

"It wasn't your fault." I'm still laughing. "The Pansies suck, is all."

"My fault," Manuel says again. His voice cracks.

That's when I stop laughing. Because I realize he's crying. Fat tears are beading up under his eyelids, threatening to come spilling out any minute. He seems to want to lift his hands up to wipe them away, but he can't.

"It's *not* your fault, Manuel," I say. "How can you even think such a thing? The guys on the team didn't even know what happened to you until later. Coach Andrews didn't tell them—"

"No," Manuel says. The tears are sliding out from beneath his eyelids and streaming down his face. "I meant it's my fault about Lindsay. My fault that she died."

Whoa. "Manuel," I say. "It isn't your fault that someone killed Lindsay. It isn't your fault at all."

"I gave her the key," Manuel insists. And he does manage to move one of his hands then. He curls his fingers into a fist and thumps the mattress, pathetically softly.

"That doesn't mean you killed her," I assure him.

"She wouldn't be dead if I hadn't given it to her. I should have said no when she asked. I should have said no. Only . . . she was crying."

"Right," I say. I glance at the two detectives outside the room. They've disappeared. Where did they go? I want to run out after them, tell them to get in here . . . but I don't want Manuel to stop talking. "You said that last night. When did she come to you crying, Manuel? When did she ask you for the key?"

"It was right before I went home," he says. "Monday night. After the cafeteria was closed at seven. I was pulling a double, because Fernando had to go to his grandmother's birthday party. The holiday. You know. And she came up to me, as I was putting on my coat to go home, and said she needed to borrow the key to the cafeteria, because she'd left something in there."

"Did she say what?" I ask, glancing at the door. Where were those guys? "What it was she left, I mean?"

Manuel shakes his head. He's still crying.

"I should have gone with her. I should have gone and opened the door for her and waited until she got whatever it was. But I was supposed to meet someone"—from the way he says the word *someone*, it's clear he means a girlfriend—"and I was running late, and she's . . . well, she was Lindsay."

"Right," I say encouragingly. "We all knew Lindsay. We all trusted her." Though I'm starting to think maybe we shouldn't have.

"Yeah. I know I shouldn't have given it to her," Manuel goes on. "But she was so pretty and nice. Everybody liked her I couldn't imagine she wanted the key for anything bad. She said it was really important—something she had to give back to . . . the people she borrowed it from. Or they'd be angry, she said."

My blood has run cold. That's the only way I can think of to explain why I suddenly feel so chilly. "She didn't say who *they* were?"

Manuel shakes his head.

"And she definitely said *they*, plural, like it was more than one person?"

He nods.

Well, that was weird. Unless Lindsay had said *they* instead of *him* or *her* to hide the sex of whoever it was she was talking about.

"So you gave her the key," I say.

He nods miserably. "She told me she'd give it back. She said she'd meet me by the front desk the next morning at ten o'clock and give the key back. And I waited. I was out there waiting when the police came in. Nobody told me what was going on. They just walked right past me. I was waiting for her, and the whole time, she was inside, dead!"

Manuel breaks off. He's choking a little, he's crying so hard. One of the machines that's hooked up to him by a tube starts beeping. The woman I assume is his mother stirs sleepily.

"If . . ." Manuel says. "If—"

"Manuel, don't talk," I say. To the woman who has just woken up, I say, "Get a nurse." Her eyes widen, and she runs from the room.

"If . . ." Manuel keeps saying.

"Manuel, don't talk," I say. By now Julio is up, as well, murmuring something in Spanish to his nephew.

But Manuel won't calm down.

"If it wasn't my fault," he finally manages to get out, "then why did they try to kill me?"

"Because they think you know who they are," I say. "The people who killed Lindsay think you can identify them. Which means Lindsay must have said something to you to make them think that. Did she, Manuel? Try to remember."

"She said . . . she said something about someone named—"

"Doug?" I cry. "Did she say something about someone named Doug? Or maybe Mark?"

But the beeping is getting louder, and now a doctor and two nurses come rushing in, followed by Manuel's mother . . . and the two detectives.

"No," Manuel says. His voice is getting fainter. "I think it was . . . Steve. She said Steve was going to be so mad. . . ."

Steve? Who's *Steve*?

Manuel's eyelids drift closed. The doctor barks, "Get out of the way," and I jump aside, while she messes around with Manuel's tubes. The beeping, mercifully, goes back to its normal, much quieter rate. The doctor looks relieved. Manuel, it's clear, has drifted off to sleep.

"Everyone out," says one of the nurses, waving us toward the door. "He needs to rest now."

"But I'm his mother," the older woman insists.

"You can stay," the nurse relents. "The rest of you, out."

I feel horrible. I shuffle out, along with the two detectives, while Julio and Mrs. Juarez stay with Manuel.

"What happened to him?" the younger detective asks me, when we hit the hallway.

And so I tell him. I tell him everything Manuel said. Especially the part about Steve.

They look bored.

"We knew all that," the older one says—sort of accusingly, like I'd been wasting their time on purpose.

"No, you didn't," I say, shocked.

"Yeah, we did," the younger one agrees with his partner. "It was all in the report. He said all that stuff last night, about the key."

"Not the stuff about Steve," I say.

"I'm pretty sure there was a Steve in the report," the older detective says.

"Steve," the younger one says. "Or a John, maybe."

"There's no John," I say. "Only a Doug. Or maybe a Mark. Mark was the dead girl's boyfriend. Well, except she was seeing a guy named Doug on the side. And now there's Steve. Only there's no Steve that I know of—"

"We already got all that," the younger detective says again, looking annoyed.

I glare at them. "Where's Detective Canavan?"

"He couldn't get into the city this morning," the older one says. "On account of the road conditions where he lives."

"Well," I say, "are you going to call him and tell him about this Steve guy? Or do I have to do it?"

The younger detective says, "We already told you, miss. We know about—"

"Sure, we'll call him," the older one interrupts.

The younger one looks startled. "But Marty—"

"We'll call him," the older one says again, with a wink at the younger one. The younger one goes, "Oh, yeah. Yeah. We'll call him."

I just stand there and stare at them. It's clear Detective Canavan already told them about me. It's also clear he didn't say anything good.

"You know," I say truculently, "I have his cell number. I could just call him myself."

"Why don't you do that?" Marty, the older detective says. "I'm sure he'd love to hear from you."

The younger one cracks up.

I feel myself blush. Am I really that big a pain in Detective Canavan's ass? I mean, I know I am. But I never thought he went around complaining about me to the rest of the detectives. Am I the joke of the Sixth Precinct?

Probably.

"Fine," I say. "I'll just be going now." And I turn to leave.

"Wait. Ms. Wells?"

I turn back to face them. The younger detective is holding out a pen and a notepad.

"Sorry, Ms. Wells, I almost forgot." He looks totally serious. "Can I have your autograph?"

I narrow my eyes at him. What kind of joke is this?

"Seriously," he says. "I told my kid sister you hang around the station a lot, and she asked me to get your autograph for her, if I could."

He *looks* sincere. I take the pen and notepad, feeling a rush of embarrassment for having been so huffy to him.

"Sure," I say. "What's your sister's name?"

"Oh, she just wants your signature," the detective says. "She says autographs don't sell as well on eBay when they're personalized."

I glare at him. "She wants my autograph just so she can sell it?"

"Well, yeah," the detective says, looking as if he can't believe I'd think anything else. "What else is she going to do with all those old CDs of yours? She says she has a better chance of selling hers if she can throw in an autograph. She says it'll make her stand out from all the millions of other people selling their Heather Wells collection."

I hand the pad and pen back to him. "Goodbye, Detectives," I say, and turn to go.

"Aw, come on," the detective calls after me. "Heather! Don't be that way!"

"Can't we all just get along?" Marty wants to know. He's laughing so hard, he can barely get the words out.

When I get to the elevator, I turn and tell them what I think of them. With my middle finger.

But this just makes them laugh harder.

They're wrong, what they say about a crisis bringing out the best in New Yorkers. It so doesn't.

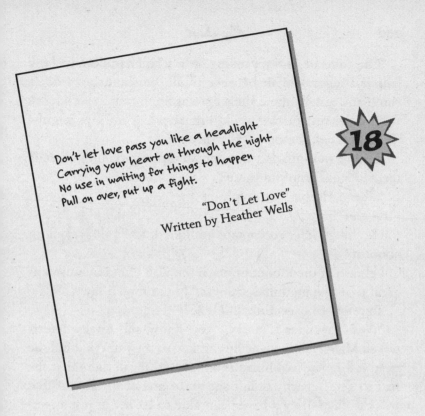

Don't let love pass you like a headlight
Carrying your heart on through the night
No use in waiting for things to happen
Pull on over, put up a fight.

"Don't Let Love"
Written by Heather Wells

I make it back to Fischer Hall in one piece . . . more or less.
I can't find a cab—there just aren't any. The few cars I see on
the road are cop cars. One of them bottoms out on Sixth Avenue, then sits there, its rear wheels spinning, while a bunch
of people come out of the nearby coffee shop and Gap to
help them get unstuck.

Not me, though. I've had my fill of cops for the day.

I'm still grumpy about the autograph thing when I finally
step into my office . . . only to find Tom in my seat, and the
door to his office closed. Behind it, I hear the murmur of Dr.
Kilgore's voice.

"Oh, come *on*," I say, yanking off my knit hat. I can feel my hair floating in the air because of all the static, but I don't care. "You're telling me she's here again?"

"For the rest of the week, I'm afraid," Tom says glumly. "But cheer up. Tomorrow's Friday."

"Still." I pull off my coat and slump into Sarah's chair. "I feel violated. Who's in there?"

"Cheryl Haebig," he says.

"Again?"

He shrugs. "Her roommate got killed. She's all broken up about it."

I glower at the Monet print on the wall. "Lindsay wasn't as great as everyone thinks she was," I hear myself say.

Tom raises his eyebrows. "Hello?"

"Well, she wasn't," I say. "You know she totally sweet-talked Manuel into giving her his key to the caf. What did she need it for? She told him she left something in there that she had to get. But why didn't she go to one of the RAs if that was the case? They'd have been able to let her in just as easily as Manuel, if all she needed to do was grab something. No, she went to him because he was on his way out to a date and she knew he didn't have time to wait for her to get whatever it was, and would just hand over the key if she asked for it. So then she'd have it all night. She was working him. The way she worked all the boys. And the girls, even. I mean, Magda was gaga for her."

"You seem to have a lot of issues with Lindsay," Tom says. "Maybe you need to talk to Dr. Kilgore next."

"Shut up," I advise him.

He grins wickedly. "You got some messages." And hands them to me.

Jordan Cartwright. Jordan Cartwright. Jordan Cartwright. Tad Tocco.

Wait. Who's Tad Tocco?

"I'm getting coffee," Tom says, getting up with his mug. "You want any?

"Yeah," I say, barely paying attention. "Coffee'd be good." Who is Tad Tocco, and why is his name so familiar?

Then, after Tom's left the office, I yell, "Put some hot cocoa in it!"

"Okay," Tom yells back.

Tom's office door is tugged open, and Dr. Kilgore sticks her head out to look at me.

"Could you," she says testily, "keep your voice down, please? I have a very distraught student in here."

"Oh, sure," I say guiltily. "Sorry."

She glares at me and slams the door.

I slump more deeply into my seat. Sarah has left a copy of the school paper on her desk, open to the sports page. There's a photo of Coach Andrews on it, clapping his hands and yelling at a blur on the court in front of him. The caption reads, *Steven Andrews shouts encouragement to his players.*

And my blood goes cold in my veins.

Steven. Steven *Andrews.*

And the next thing I know, I'm on the phone to the Athletic Department.

"Uh, hi," I say, when someone finally answers the phone. "Is Coach Andrews in today?"

Whoever answers sounds cranky . . . possibly because he, like me, was forced to come in to work on a Snow Day.

"Where else would he be?" the cranky person asks. "He's got another game this weekend, you know."

The guy hangs up on me. But I don't care. Because I've found out what I need to know. Coach Andrews is around. Which means I can go over to the Winer Complex and question him about his relationship with Lindsay. . . .

No, wait. I can't do that. I promised. I promised everyone I wouldn't get involved this time. . . .

But I promised Magda I wouldn't let Lindsay's name be dragged through the mud. And if Coach Andrews was sleeping with her, as Kimberly suggested, then that meant Lindsay was being taken advantage of by a person in a position of power. Well, as much power as a basketball coach can have over a cheerleader. At the very least, the relationship was completely inappropriate. . . .

But what could Lindsay possibly have left in the cafeteria that she'd needed to give back to Coach Andrews so desperately?

There's really only one way to find out. Which is why I get up from Sarah's desk and, after stopping by the recycling pile at the bottom of the basement stairwell and snagging a good-sized box, I hurry out into the lobby, winding my scarf back around my neck and nearly colliding with my boss, who is carrying two mugs of coffee out of the cafeteria.

"Where are you going?" Tom wants to know, eyeing the box.

"Lindsay's parents called," I lie. It is seriously scary how easily these things trip off my tongue. It's no wonder I can't seem to find the guts to sing in front of anyone. It's becoming more and more clear my true talent lies in a completely different direction than vocal performance. "They want somebody to clean out her locker over at the Winer Complex."

Tom looks confused. "Wait . . . I thought Cheryl and her friends did that already. When they got the sweater."

"I guess not," I say, shrugging. "I'll be back in a bit. 'Bye!"

Before he can say another word, I throw myself out into the wind and cold, using the box to shield my face from the snow. It's slow going—no one has had a chance to shovel the sidewalks yet, due to the fact that the snow has only slowed down a bit, not stopped. But I have my Timberlands on, so my feet stay dry and relatively warm. And anyway, I like the snow. It covers the empty marijuana baggies and nitrous oxide canisters that litter the sidewalks, and muffles the sounds of sirens and honking car horns. True, car owners won't be able to dig out their vehicles for a week, since the snowplows—their lights blinking orange and white, orange and white, as they go by, reflecting against high drifts piled on either side of the street—will just cover them again.

But it sure is pretty. Especially in Washington Square Park, where snow now completely fills the basin of the fountain, and has capped the statues of George Washington with wigs of winter white. Icicles glisten on the twisted black branches of trees from which, in another age, criminals were hanged. Only squirrels disturb the white expanse of snow beneath those trees, where once paupers' graves, not green benches, rested. The dog run is empty, as are the play areas, swings dangling forlornly back and forth in the wind. The only signs of life come from the chess circle, which is, as always, occupied, by homeless people who eschew the dubious safety of the local homeless shelter, and diehard players who are willing to brave the elements in order to get in a good game.

This is how I like my city: all but empty.

God, I really *am* a jaded New Yorker.

Still, pretty as the town looks, I'm relieved when I pull open the door to the sports complex and am able to stomp the snow off my boots and onto the rubber-backed mats inside. My face slowly defrosts as I pull out my ID and show it to the security guard, who waves me through the hand scanner. The building, as always, smells of sweat and chlorine, from the pool. It's pretty empty—most students don't seem to feel the need to brave the elements in order to get in their daily workout.

Not so with the Pansies basketball team, though. I spot them as I look over the atrium railing, down on the parquet court below, practicing the slam dunks they aren't allowed to try during a game, hanging on the rim, that sort of thing. The court looks bigger with all the bleachers pushed back. As I watch, someone passes Mark—I recognize his flattop— the ball.

"Shepelsky," his teammate says. "Go for a layup."

Mark expertly catches the ball, dribbles, then shoots. I swear there are three feet of air at least between the soles of his sneakers and the court. When he lands, I hear the same squeak of rubber on a smooth, shiny surface that I heard last night, when Manuel's masked assailants fled the scene.

Not that that means anything. I mean, all sneakers sound like that. Besides, Mark and his friends were probably in the locker room while Manuel was being stabbed, getting reamed out by their coach. They couldn't have had anything to do with what happened to him.

Unless.

Unless Coach Andrews was the one who sent them to do it.

I'm letting my imagination run away with me. Best to take myself and my box to Coach Andrews's office and see if there's actually anything to this crazy idea of mine before I start making up scenarios in which Steven Andrews is a Svengali with the ability to convince late-adolescent boys to do his smallest bidding. . . .

Maybe in Division I schools, where the basketball coach is second only to God—even more important than the university president—would someone like Coach Andrews have his own personal assistant to guard his privacy. As it is, there's just a snarky student worker sitting in the outer part of the Athletic Office, reading a battered copy of *The Fountainhead*.

"Hey," I say to him. "Coach Andrews around?"

The kid doesn't even look up from his book, just jerks a thumb in the direction of an open door.

"In there," he says.

I thank him and approach the doorway, through which I see Steven Andrews sitting at a desk covered with what looks like playbooks. He's got his head in his hands, and is staring dejectedly down at a piece of paper with a number of *X*'s and *O*'s on it. He looks, for all the world, like Napoleon planning a battle.

Or maybe me, making room assignments, since I still haven't figured out how to work the Housing Department computer system.

"Um, Coach Andrews?" I say.

He looks up. "Yes?" Then, as I pull my hat off and all of my hair tumbles down in a staticky mess around my face, he seems to recognize me. "Oh, hi. You're . . . Mary?"

"Heather," I say, lowering myself into the chair across from his desk. I don't mind pointing out that the office furniture in the Winer Sports Complex is way nicer than the furniture in my office. No orange vinyl couches here, no sirree. Everything is black leather and chrome.

I'm betting Coach Andrews makes more than twenty-three thousand five hundred a year, too.

Although he doesn't get all the free Dove Bars he can eat. Probably.

"Right," he says. "Sorry. Heather. You work over in Fischer Hall."

"Right," I say. "Where Lindsay lived."

I watch his reaction to the name *Lindsay* carefully.

But there is no reaction. He doesn't flinch or go pale. He just looks questioning. "Uh-huh?"

Man. This is one tough nut to crack.

"Yes," I say. "I was just wondering . . . did anybody clean out her locker?"

Now Coach Andrews looks confused. "Her locker?"

"Right," I say. "Her locker here at the sports complex. I mean, I assume she had one."

"I'm sure she did," Coach Andrews says. "But that's something you'd probably be better off asking the cheerleading coach, Vivian Chambers? She'd be the one who'd be able to tell you which locker was Lindsay's, and what the combination is. She's got an office down the hall. Only I don't think she made it in today. On account of the snow."

"Oh," I say. "The cheerleading coach. Right. Only . . . well, I'm here now. And I've got this box."

"Well." Coach Andrews looks like he really wants to help me. Seriously. I mean, the guy has a big game coming up, and he's actually willing to take the time to help out a fellow New York College employee. One who makes way less money than he does. "I think I could probably get the number and combination from Facilities. Let me give them a call."

"Wow," I say. Is he being so super-helpful because he's actually a nice guy? Or because he feels guilty over what he did to Lindsay? "That is so nice of you. Thanks."

"No problem," Coach Andrews says, as he picks up his

phone and dials. "I mean, as long as the guys made it into work today . . ." Someone on the other end picks up, and Steven Andrews says, "Oh, Jonas, great, you made it in. Look, I got a woman from the Housing Department who needs to clean out Lindsay Combs's locker. I was wondering if you guys had access to the combination. Oh, and also which locker it was, since Viv didn't make it to work this morning. . . . You do? Great? Yeah, that'd be great. Okay, yeah, call me back."

He hangs up and beams at me. "You're in luck," he says. "They're gonna look it up and call back with it."

I'm stunned. Seriously. "That's . . . thanks. That was really nice of you."

"Oh, no problem," Coach Andrews says again. "Anything I can do to help. I mean, what happened to Lindsay was so terrible."

"Wasn't it?" I say. "I mean, especially since Lindsay—well, she was so popular. It's hard to believe she had any enemies."

"I know." Coach Andrews leans back in his chair. "That's the part that gets me. She was, like, universally liked. By everyone."

"Almost everyone," I say, thinking of Kimberly, who honestly doesn't seem to have been all that fond of her.

"Well, right," Coach Andrews says. "I mean, besides whoever it was who did that to her."

Hmmm. He doesn't seem to be aware of the animosity between Kimberly and Lindsay.

"Yeah," I say. "Clearly someone didn't like her. Or was trying to shut her up about something."

Steven Andrews's blue eyes are wide and guileless as they gaze into mine. "About what? I mean, Lindsay was a good kid. That's what's been so hard about all this. For me, I mean. For you guys, I'm sure it's worse. I mean, you and your boss . . . what's his name again? Tom Something?"

I blink. "Snelling. Tom Snelling."

"Yeah," the coach says. "I mean . . . he's new, right?"

"He started last month," I say. Wait. How did we get off the subject of Lindsay, and on to Tom?

"Where'd he come from?" Coach Andrews wants to know.

"Texas A & M," I say. "The thing about Lindsay is—"

"Wow," the coach says. "That must be a big change for him. I mean, going from College Station to the Big Apple. I mean, it's been rough for me, and I just came down from Burlington."

"Yeah," I say. "I imagine that was tough. But Tom's handling it." I don't mention the part about how he wants to quit. "About Lindsay, what I was wondering was—"

"He's not married, is he?" Coach Andrews asks. Casually. Too casually.

I stare at him. "Who? *Tom?*"

"Yeah," he says. Suddenly I notice his cheeks are turning sort of . . . well, pinkish. "I mean, I didn't see a ring."

"Tom's *gay*," I say. I realize he's a Division III college basketball coach and all. But really, how dense can this guy be?

"I *know*," Coach Andrews says. Now his cheeks are red. "I was wondering if he's in a relationship with anyone."

I find myself shaking my head at him, blinking. "N-no. . . ."

"Oh." The coach looks visibly relieved—even happy—to hear this news. "Because I was thinking, you know, it's hard moving to a new city and starting a new job and all. Maybe he'd want to grab a beer sometime, or something. I don't—"

His phone rings. Coach Andrews answers it. "Andrews," he says. "Oh, great. Here, let me grab a pen."

I sit there while Steven Andrews jots down Lindsay's locker number and combination, trying to understand what I think I've just learned. Because unless I'm mistaken, Coach Andrews is *gay*.

And seems to want to date my boss.

"Great, thanks so much," the coach says, and hangs up the phone.

"Here you go," he says, sliding the piece of paper he's written toward me. "Just go on down to the women's locker room, and you'll find it. Number six twenty-five."

I take the paper, fold it, and slip it into my pocket in a sort of daze. "Thanks," I say.

"No problem," Coach Andrews says. "Where were we, again?"

"I . . . I . . ." I feel my shoulders sag. "I don't know."

"Oh, right, Tom," he says. "Tell him to call me sometime. You know. If he ever wants to hang out."

"Hang out," I echo. "With you."

"Yeah." Coach Andrews must see something in my face that alarms him, since he asks, looking suddenly anxious, "Wait, was that totally inappropriate? Maybe I should just call him myself."

"Maybe," I say faintly, "you should."

"Right." The coach nods. "You're right. I should. I just felt like—well, you know. You seem cool, and maybe you'd . . . but never mind."

This was, I decided, either the most elaborate attempt ever to draw suspicion away from a murder suspect, or Coach Steven Andrews was, in fact, gay.

Had Kimberly lied to me? It's starting to look like it. Especially when Steven Andrews leans forward and whispers, "Not to sound like a girl or anything, but . . . I *totally* have all your albums."

I blink at him one last time. Then I say, "Great. I'll just be going now."

" 'Bye," he says happily.

And I take my box and leave. Fast.

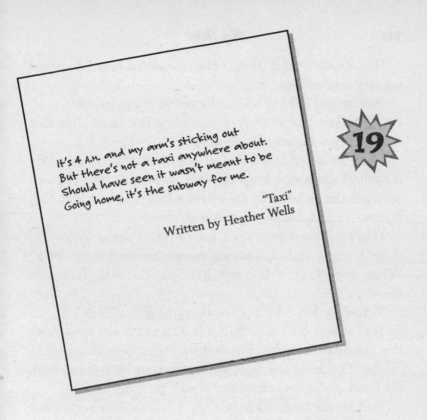

It's 4 A.M. and my arm's sticking out
But there's not a taxi anywhere about.
Should have seen it wasn't meant to be
Going home, it's the subway for me.

"Taxi"

Written by Heather Wells

19

"Call Coach Andrews," I say to Tom, when I get back to the office.

He looks up from his computer—or I should say, *my* computer. "What?"

"Call Steve Andrews," I say, collapsing into Sarah's chair and tossing my box—empty; someone had already cleaned out Lindsay's locker, just like Tom had said—onto the floor. "I think he has a crush on you."

Tom's hazel eyes goggle. "You are fucking shitting me."

"Call him," I say, unwinding my scarf, "and see."

"The coach is *gay*?" Tom looks as stunned as if I'd walked up and slapped him.

"Apparently. Why? Doesn't he set your gaydar off?"

"Every hot guy sets my gaydar off," Tom says. "But that doesn't mean it's actually *accurate*."

"Well, he asked about you," I say. "Either it's all part of a diabolical scheme to keep us from suspecting him in Lindsay's murder, or he really does have a little crush on you. Call him, so we can find out which it is."

Tom's hand is already reaching for the phone before he stops himself and says, giving me a confused look, "Wait. What does *Coach Andrews* have to do with Lindsay's murder?"

"Either nothing," I reply, "or everything. Call him."

Tom shakes his head. "Nuh-uh. I'm not doing something this important in front of an audience. Not even an audience of you. I'm doing this from my apartment." He scoots back his (well, really, my) chair, and stands up. "Right now."

"Just let me know what he says," I call, as Tom hurries out the door and toward the elevator. When he's gone, I sit there and wonder just how far Andrews will be willing to take this thing, in the event he isn't actually gay. Would he put out for Tom? All in an effort to throw off investigators? Could a straight guy even do that? Well, probably, if he's bi. But Coach Andrews didn't seem bi.

Of course, he hadn't seemed gay to me, either, until today. He did an excellent job of hiding it. But then, maybe if you're a gay basketball coach, you *have* to be good at hiding it. I mean, if you want to keep your job.

I'm wondering if President Allington has any idea that his golden boy is a gay boy, just as Gavin McGoren strolls into the office.

"Wassup?" he says, and throws himself onto the couch across from my—I mean, Tom's—desk.

I stare at him.

"How should I know what's up?" I say. "It's a Snow Day. No one has class. Why are you here? Shouldn't you be off in a bar somewhere in SoHo, drinking yourself blind?"

"I would be," Gavin says, "except that boss of yours says I have to see him for"—he digs a much-folded, very grimy disciplinary letter from his back pocket—"follow-up counseling pertaining to an incident involving alcohol."

"Ha," I say happily. "You loser."

"Has anyone ever told you that you don't have a very professional attitude towards your job?" Gavin wants to know.

"Has anyone ever told you that trying to drink twenty-one shots in one night is extremely dangerous, not to mention stupid?"

He gives me a *no-duh* look. "So how come they haven't caught the guy that iced Lindsay?" he asks.

"Because no one knows who did it." And some of us are driving ourselves crazy trying to figure it out.

"Wow," Gavin says. "That makes me feel so safe and secure in my living environment. My mom wants me to move to Wasser Hall, where people don't get their heads chopped off."

I stare at him, genuinely shocked. "You're not going to, are you?"

"I don't know," Gavin says, not making eye contact. "It's closer to the film school."

"Oh, my God." I can't believe this. "You're thinking about it."

"Well, whatevs." Gavin looks uncomfortable. "It's not cool, living in Death Dorm."

"I would imagine it would be very cool," I say. "To a guy who aspires to be the next Quentin Tarantino."

"Eli Roth," he corrects me.

"Whatever," I say. "But by all means, move to Wasser Hall if you're scared. Here." I lean down and pick up the empty box I'd lugged to the Winer Sports Complex and back again. "Start packing."

"I'm not scared," Gavin says, shoving the box away and sticking his chin out. I notice that the straggly growth on it is getting less straggly and more bushy. "I mean . . . aren't you?"

"No, I'm not scared," I say. "I'm angry. I want to know who did that to Lindsay, and why. And I want them caught."

"Well," Gavin says, finally looking me in the eye, "do they have any leads?"

"I don't know," I say. "If they do, they aren't telling me. Let me ask you something. Do you think Coach Andrews is gay?"

"Gay?" Gavin lets out a big horse laugh. "No!"

I shake my head. "Why not?"

"Well, because he's a big jock."

"Historically, there have been a few gay athletes, you know," I say.

Gavin snorts. "Sure. Lady golfers."

"No," I say. "Greg Louganis."

He stares at me blankly. "Who's that?"

"Never mind." I sigh. "He could be gay and just not want everyone to know. Because it might freak out the players."

"Gee, ya think?" Gavin asks me sarcastically.

"But you don't think he's gay," I say.

"How would I know?" Gavin asks. "I never met the guy. I just know he's a basketball coach, and they aren't gay. Most of the time."

"Well, have you ever heard anything about Coach Andrews and Lindsay?"

"What, like, romantically?" Gavin wants to know.

"Yeah."

"No," he says. "And, might I add, gross. He's, like, thirty."

I narrow my eyes at him. "Yeah. That's ancient."

Gavin smirks, and says, "Whatever. Besides, I thought Lindsay was all hot-and-heavy with Mark Shepelsky."

"They've cooled off, apparently," I say. "Lately she's been hooking up with a kid named Doug Winer. Do you know him?"

"Not really." He shrugs. "I know his brother, Steve, better."

And the earth suddenly seemed to tilt on its axis.

"What?" I can't believe what I've just heard.

Gavin, startled by my response, stammers, "St-Steve. Yeah. Steve Winer. What, you didn't know—"

"Steve?" I stare at him. "Doug Winer has a brother named *Steve?* Are you *serious?"*

"Yeah." Gavin looks at me strangely. "He was in one of my film classes last semester. We worked together on a project. It was kind of lame—which makes sense, since Steve's kind of lame. But we hung out some. He's a senior. He lives over at the Tau Phi House."

"He's a Tau Phi, too?" I can't seem to digest any of this.

"Yeah. He's, like, president of the house, or something. Well, he should be, 'cause he's the oldest guy there. The dude's twenty-five, and he's still taking classes like Intro to Social Work and shit. Steve wants to be a big-time breadwinner, like Daddy. But he's too stupid and lazy to think of any way to do it except through dealing. So . . ." Gavin shrugs. "He deals coke and shit to college party kids, while

Dad—and New York College, as far as I can tell—turns a blind eye. I mean, it makes sense the school won't do anything about it, because old man Winer donated the sports complex." He chuckles. "Too bad his own kids are too fucked up most of the time to use it."

"So the Winer boys are big-time dealers?" I ask. Suddenly Coach Andrews isn't interesting me half as much as he was earlier.

"I don't know about big-time," Gavin says, with a shrug. "I mean, they both deal, and all, which is fine. But you aren't supposed to sample your own wares. But back when I had class with him, Steve was using, all the time. And so he was always asleep—crashing, you know—when we were supposed to be working on the project. I had to do the whole thing myself, practically. We got an A, of course. But no thanks to Winer."

"So what's he deal?" I ask.

"You name it, the Winer can get it. Though he's got principles. He only sells to people who are ready to experience the alternative planes of reality that drugs can help them achieve. It's like this thing." Gavin rolls his eyes. "Some principles. You know what that guy's hobby used to be when he was a kid? Burying cats up to their necks in dirt in the backyard, then runnin' over their heads with the lawn mower."

"That," I say, wide-eyed, "is disgusting."

"That's not all. Steve'd tie a brick to their tails and throw 'em in the pool. That guy is a maniac. Plus, he's got this thing about money. See, their old man made a pile of money in construction. And he wants his boys to do the same. You know, find their own entrepreneurial fortunes, and shit? So soon as they graduate from college, they're cut off. That's why Steve's trying to keep the gravy train go as long as he can."

I eye him. "Gavin," I say. "How do you know all this stuff?"

"What stuff?"

"All this stuff about the Winers."

Gavin looks blank. "I dunno. I've partied with them."

"You've *partied* with them?"

"Yeah," Gavin says. "You know. I think Steve's a loser, but the guy's got connections. That is one bridge I'm not burning, even if he did totally fuck up our project. But, you know, when I get my own production company going, I'll need investors. And drug money is better than no money. I don't have to ask where it came from. Plus, some great-looking chicks show up at those Tau Phi parties. There's one tonight. . . ." His voice trails off, and he looks at me warily. "I mean, women. Not chicks. Women."

"There's a party at the Tau Phi House tonight?" I ask.

"Um," Gavin says. "Yes?"

And suddenly I know where I need to be tonight.

"Can you get me in?"

Gavin looks confused. "What?"

"Into the party. To meet Steve Winer."

Gavin's perpetually sleepy brown eyes actually widen. "*You* wanna score some coke? Oh, man! And I always thought you were straight! All those anti-drug ads you did when you were a star—"

"I don't want any *coke*," I say.

" 'Cause coke's no good for you. Reefer's the way to go. I can get you some excellent reefer, mellow you right out. 'Cause you can be a real tight-ass sometimes, you know that, Heather? I always noticed that about you."

"I don't want any reefer," I say, through gritted teeth.

"What I want is to ask Steve Winer a few questions about Lindsay Combs. Because I think Steve might know something about it."

Gavin's eyelids droop back down to their normal width. "Oh. Well, shouldn't the police be doing that?"

"You would think so, wouldn't you?" I give a bitter laugh. "But the police don't really seem to care, as far as I can make out. So. What do you say? Do you think you can score me an introduction?"

"Sure," Gavin says. "I can do that. I mean, if you want me to. I can take you with me tonight to the party."

"Really?" I lean forward on Sarah's desk. "You would really do that?"

"Uh," Gavin says, looking as if he doubts my sanity, "yeah. I mean, it's no big deal."

"Wow." I stare at him. I can't tell if he's trying to get into my good graces to pull some kind of scam, or if he sincerely wants to help. "That'd be . . . great. I've never been to a frat party before. What time will it start? What should I wear?" I try not to think about the FAT CHICKS GO HOME sign. Will it still be there? What if they won't let me in because they think I'm too fat? God, how embarrassing.

I mean, for them.

"You've never been to a frat party before?" Now Gavin looks shocked. "Jesus, even when you were in college?"

I decide to let that one slide. "Slutty, right? I should dress slutty?"

Gavin isn't making eye contact anymore. "Yeah, slutty usually works out good. Things don't usually start going until eleven. Should I pick you up then?"

"Eleven?" I practically scream, then remember Dr. Kilgore,

who, I can tell from the murmuring behind the grate, is meeting with someone in Tom's office, and lower my voice. "Eleven?" By eleven o'clock, I've usually got out my guitar, for a few pre-bedtime rounds of whatever song I'm currently working on. Then it's lights out. "That's so late!"

Now Gavin looks back at me, grinning. "Gonna have to set the alarm, huh, Grandma?"

"No," I say, frowning. Who's he calling Grandma? "I mean, if that's the earliest—"

"It is."

"Well, fine. And no, you can't come pick me up. I'll meet you outside Waverly Hall at eleven."

Gavin smiles. "What's the matter? You afraid of your boyfriend seeing us?"

"I told you," I say. "He's not my—"

"Yeah, yeah, yeah," Gavin says. "He's not your boyfriend. Next thing you're gonna be saying, this isn't a date."

I stare at him. "It isn't. I thought you understood that. It's an exploratory mission, to get to the bottom of Lindsay Combs's murder. It isn't a date at all. Although I really appreciate your—"

"Jesus!" Gavin explodes. "I was just messing with you! Why you gotta be like that?"

I blink at him. "Like what?"

"All professional and shit."

"You said a minute ago I *wasn't* very professional," I point out.

"That's just it," he says. "You run all hot and cold. What's up with that?"

He says all this just before Tom walks in, beaming.

"What's up with what?" Tom wants to know, sliding into

the seat behind my desk. I can tell from his expression that his phone call with Steve Andrews had gone well.

What does this mean? Did I have the wrong Steve, after all?

But why would Kimberly lie to me?

"This thing," Gavin says, waving the disciplinary letter in Tom's face. "Man, look, I know I screwed up. But do we really have to go through all this? I don't need no alcohol education, I already got it in the St. Vinnie's ER, man."

"Well, Gavin," Tom says, leaning back in my chair. "You are a lucky man, then. Because, due to the fact that I currently have no access to my office—and happen to be in an excellent mood—you are off the hook from alcohol counseling this week."

Gavin looks shocked. "Wait . . . I *am*?"

"For *this* week. I *will* reschedule. For now . . . fly," Tom says, waving his hand toward the outer door. "Be free."

"Holy shit," Gavin says happily. Then he turns and points at me. "I'll see you later, sweetcheeks."

And he runs out.

Tom looks at me. "Sweetcheeks?"

"Don't ask," I say. "Really. So, I take it you and Steve—"

"Seven o'clock tonight," Tom says, grinning ear to ear. "Dinner at Po."

"Romantic," I say.

"I hope so," Tom gushes.

So do I . . . for his sake. Because if it turns out I am wrong, and Steven Andrews isn't gay, that means there is actually something to what Kimberly told me in the ladies' room last night.

Until I know for sure, though, I'm concentrating on the

only other lead I have . . . Manuel's mysterious "Steve," which all too coincidentally turns out to be the name of Doug Winer's brother. If he knows something about Lindsay's death, I'll be able to tell . . . at least I hope so.

If I don't get thrown out for being a fat chick, first.

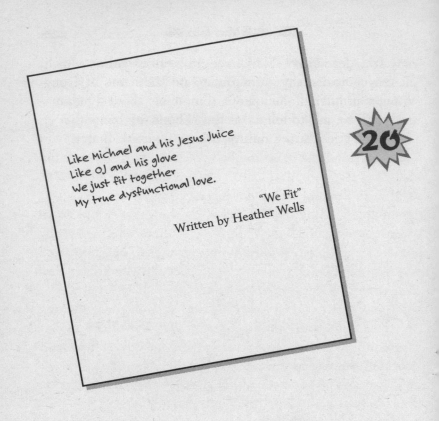

Like Michael and his Jesus Juice
Like OJ and his glove
We just fit together
My true dysfunctional love.

"We Fit"

Written by Heather Wells

20

Never having been to a frat party before, it's sort of hard to figure out what to wear to one. I understand sluttitude is in order. But to what degree? Plus, it's cold outside. So do I really want to venture out in pantyhose and a mini? Is a mini even appropriate on a woman of my age, not to mention one with as many thigh dimples as I seem to have developed recently?

And it's not like I even have anybody I can ask. I can't call Patty, because then she'll remember I never gave Frank an answer about the gig at Joe's, and Magda's no help at all. When I call and ask her if I should wear a mini, she just says, "Of course." And when I ask if I should wear a sweater with it, she explodes, "Sweater? Of course not! Don't you have anything mesh? What about leopard print?"

I settle for a black mini that fits a little snug, but with a diaphanous (though not mesh) top from Betsey Johnson, you can't see the little bulge my belly makes as it hangs over the skirt's waistband in spite of my control-top pantyhose. I throw on a pair of skinny black knee boots (which will be instantly trashed by the salt from the snowplows) and go to work on my hair. I want to look very different from the way I'd looked the last time I'd been at the Tau Phi House, so I opt for an updo, sexily mussed . . . since it will end up that way when I pull off my hat, anyway.

A few spritzes of Beyoncé's latest—hey, I know it's wrong to wear a rival pop star's signature scent, but unlike Tania's (or Britney's), Beyoncé's actually smells good . . . like fruit cocktail, yum—and I'm ready to go.

I just don't anticipate running into Jordan Cartwright on my way out.

Seriously. Why me? I mean, I sneak all the way downstairs—making it safely past the other two men in my life without either of them suspecting a thing, Dad in his room tootling his flute, and Cooper in his room doing whatever it is he does in there after dark, which God only knows what that is, but I think it must involve headphones because I don't see how he could stand doing whatever it is while listening to whatever it is Dad is playing—and out the front door, only to encounter a freakishly bundled-up Sasquatch-like figure trying to figure out how to climb the stoop with cross-country skis on.

"Heather?" Sasquatch squints up at me in the light spilling from the door I've just opened. "Oh, thank God it's you."

Even though his voice is muffled because of all the scarves he's wrapped around his neck and face, I recognize it.

"*Jordan*." I hasten to close and lock the front door behind me, then make my way carefully down the steps—not an easy feat in three-inch spiked heels, given the ice. "What are you doing here? Are those . . . *skis*?"

"You wouldn't return my calls." Jordan lowers the scarves so I can see his mouth, then raises the ski goggles that were hiding his eyes. "I really need to talk to you. And Dad's got the limo, and none of the car services can get over the bridges, and there were no cabs. So I had to ski down Fifth Avenue to get here."

I stare at him. "Jordan," I say, "you could have taken the subway."

His eyes widen in the light streaming down from the street lamp overhead. "The *subway*? This time of night? Heather, there are *muggers*."

I shake my head. It's finally stopped snowing, but it's still bitterly cold. My legs are already frozen, with just a thin layer of nylon to protect them.

"Jordan," I say impatiently, "what do you want?"

"I . . . I'm getting married day after tomorrow," Jordan says.

"Yes," I say. "You are. I hope you didn't come all the way down here to remind me about it and to beg me to come to your wedding. Because I'm still not going."

"No," Jordan says. It's hard to tell in the streetlight, but he looks a little peaked. "Heather. I'm getting *married* day after tomorrow."

"I know," I say. Then, all at once, I realize what he's doing there.

Also that he's drunk.

"Oh, no." I show him the flat of my gloved palm. "No. You

are not doing this to me now. I don't have time for this, Jordan. I have to meet someone."

"Who?" Jordan's eyes look moist. "You do look kinda . . . dressed up. Heather . . . do you have a boyfriend?"

"God!" I can't believe this. Fortunately my voice doesn't carry very far along the street. The two feet of snow blanketing the tops of all the parked cars—not to mention the clouds, hanging so low that they're reflecting the light of the city with a pinkish hue—muffle it. "Jordan, if you changed your mind about marrying her, tell *her*, not me. I don't care what you do. We broke up, remember? *You* broke up with *me*, as a matter of fact. For *her*."

"People make mistakes," Jordan murmurs.

"No, Jordan," I say. "Our breaking up wasn't a mistake. We needed to break up. We were *right* to break up. We don't belong together."

"But I still love you," Jordan insists.

"Of course you do," I say. "The same way I love you. Like a sibling. That's why we *had* to break up, Jordan. Because siblings aren't supposed to—you know. It's gross."

"It wasn't gross that night we did it up there," he says, nodding toward Cooper's front door.

"Oh, right," I say sarcastically. "That's why you ran so fast when we were done. Because it wasn't gross."

"It wasn't," Jordan insists. "Well . . . maybe it was weird. A little."

"Exactly," I say. "Jordan, you only want to be with me because I'm familiar. It's easy. We were together so long . . . we grew up together, practically. But that's not a good reason for two people to stay together. There has to be passion. And we don't have that. Whereas I think you and Tania do."

"Yeah." Jordan looks bitter. "She's chock-full of passion, all right. I can barely keep up."

This is so not what you want to hear about your ex's new girlfriend. Even if you DO think of him as a brother. Mostly.

"Well, ski on back uptown," I say, "and take an aspirin and go to bed. You'll feel better about things in the morning, I promise."

"Where are you going?" Jordan asks mournfully.

"I have to go to a party," I say, opening my purse to make sure I've brought my lipstick and my new can of pepper spray. Check, and check.

"What do you mean, *have* to?" Jordan wants to know, skiing beside me as I carefully pick my way along the sidewalk. "What's it for, work or something?"

"Something like that," I say.

"Oh." Jordan skis with me until we reach the corner, where a traffic light blinks forlornly along a trafficless street. Not even Reggie is out in weather like this. The wind from the park whips around us, making me reconsider this entire venture, and wish I were in my tub with the latest Nora Roberts instead of out on this empty street corner with my ex.

"Well," he says finally. "Okay, then. 'Bye."

" 'Bye, Jordan," I say, relieved that he's finally going away.

As he skis slowly off toward Fifth Avenue, I start across the park, bitterly regretting my decision not to wear jeans. True, I wouldn't look as alluring. But I'd be a heck of a lot warmer.

Getting across the park is murder. I no longer admire the beauty of the new-fallen snow. The paths are plowed, but not well, and new snow has covered them. My boots aren't waterproof, being designed primarily for indoor use, preferably in front of a roaring fire on a bearskin rug. At least, that's what the girl in the catalog was doing in the picture. I knew

I should have ventured over to the gazillion shoe stores on Eighth Street instead of ordering them online. But it's so much safer to order online. There's no Krispy Kreme sign blinking HOT NOW on my computer.

I'm half hoping that when I get to Waverly Hall, Gavin won't be there and I can turn around and go home.

But he's there, all right, shivering in the arctic wind from the park. As I totter toward him in my high heels, he says, "You owe me, woman. I'm freezing my 'nads off."

"Good," I say, when I reach him. "Your 'nads get you into too much trouble, anyway."

I have to place a hand on his shoulder to steady myself as I knock snow from my boots. He looks down at my legs and whistles.

"Jesus, sweetcheeks," he says. "You clean up good."

I drop my hand from his shoulder and smack him on the back of the head with it instead.

"Eyes forward, Gavin," I say. "We're on a mission, here. There'll be no ogling. And don't call me sweetcheeks."

"I wasn't," Gavin insists. "Oggl—ogle—what you said."

"Come on," I say. I know I'm flushing. That's because I'm beginning to have strong reservations about all of this—not just the miniskirt, but enlisting Gavin's aid. Is this really the way a responsible college administrator behaves, meeting students—even ones who are twenty-one—in the dead of night outside of frat parties? Gavin's already shown a marked immaturity when it comes to handling his alcohol consumption. Isn't my agreeing to accompany him to an event like this just reinforcing his poor judgment? Am I an enabler? Oh, God, I *am*!

"Look, Gavin," I say, as we move through the courtyard of the building toward the front door. I can't see the underwear in the shrubbery anymore because it's all covered with snow, but I can hear the pounding music coming from an upper floor, so loud it seems to reverberate inside my chest. "Maybe this isn't the best idea. I don't want to get you into trouble. . . ."

"What are you talking about?" Gavin asks, as he pulls the door open for me—always a gentleman. "How am I going to get in trouble?"

"Well," I say. A blast of warm air from inside the lobby hits us. "With the drinking thing."

Gavin shudders, despite the warmth. "Woman, I am never drinking again. You think I didn't learn my lesson the other night?"

"Come in or close the door," the guard roars from the security desk. So we hurry inside.

"It's just," I whisper, as we stand there stamping our feet under the glare of the security officer, "if Steve and Doug really are behind what happened to Lindsay, they're extremely dangerous individuals. . . ."

"Right," Gavin says. "Which is why you shouldn't drink anything, either, once we get in there, that you didn't open or pour yourself. And don't leave your beer alone, even for a second."

"Really?" I raise my eyebrows. "You really think—"

"I don't think," Gavin says. "I *know*."

"Well, I—"

Behind us, the outer door opens, and Nanook of the North follows us inside.

Except it isn't Nanook. It's Jordan.

"Aha!" he says, flipping up his goggles and pointing at me. "I knew it!"

"Jordan." I can't believe this. "Did you just *follow* me?"

"Yes." Jordan is having some trouble getting his skis inside the door. "And good thing I did. I thought you said you didn't have a boyfriend."

"Close the door!" the crusty old security guard bellows.

Jordan is trying, but his skis keep getting in the way. Annoyed, I go to him to help, giving one of his ski poles a vicious tug. The door finally eases shut behind him.

"Who's *this* guy?" Gavin demands. Then, in a different tone of voice, he says, "Oh, my God. Are you *Jordan Cartwright*?"

Jordan removes the ski goggles. "Yes," he says. His gaze flicks over Gavin, taking in the goatee and Dumpster-wear. "Rob the cradle much, Heather?" he asks me bitterly.

"Gavin's one of my *residents*," I sniff. "Not my boyfriend."

"Hey." Gavin is wearing a tiny smile on his lips. I should have taken this as a sign that I wasn't going to like what he was about to say. "My *mom* really enjoyed your last album, man. So did my grandma. She's a huge fan."

Jordan, most of his scarves halfway unwound, glares at him. "Hey," he says. "Fuck you, kid."

Gavin feigns offense. "Is that any way to talk to the son of one of the only people who bought your last CD, man? Dude, that is cold."

"I'm serious," Jordan says to Gavin. "I just cross-country skied down here from the East Sixties, and I am in no mood for shenanigans."

Gavin looks surprised. Then he grins at me happily. "Jordan Cartwright said *shenanigans*," he says.

"Stop it," I say. "Both of you. Jordan, put your skis back on. We're going to a party, and you're not invited. Gavin, buzz up so we can get someone to sign us in."

Gavin blinks at me. "The frats don't have to sign anyone in."

"Don't be ridiculous," I say to him. "The sign-in policy is

campus-wide. I'd show my ID to get us in, but, you know, I don't want them knowing a housing official is on the way up." I look at my ex, who is still unwinding his various scarves. "Jordan. Seriously. Gavin and I are here on a mission, and you're not invited."

"What kind of mission?" Jordan wants to know.

"One that involves keeping a low profile," I say. "Which we aren't going to be able to do if we waltz in there with Jordan Cartwright."

"I can keep a low profile," Jordan insists.

"The sign-in policy doesn't include the Greek system," Gavin says, in a bored voice.

I glance at the security guard. "Really?"

"Anyone can go up there," the guard says, with a shrug. He looks almost as bored as Gavin. "I just don't know why they'd want to."

"Does this have something to do with that dead girl?" Jordan wants to know. "Heather, does Cooper know about this?"

"No," I say, through gritted teeth. I can't help it, I'm so annoyed. "And if you tell him, I'll . . . I'll tell Tania you cheated on her!"

"She already knows," Jordan says, looking confused. "I tell Tania everything. She said it was okay, so long as I didn't do it again. Listen, why can't I go with you guys? I think I'd make an awesome detective."

"No, you wouldn't," I say. I'm still reeling from the information that his fiancée knows he cheated on her. I wonder if she knows it was with me. If so, it's no wonder she always gives me such dirty looks whenever she sees me.

On the other hand, dirty looks are the only kind Tania ever gives anyone.

"You don't *blend*," I accuse Jordan.

Jordan looks insulted. "I do, too, blend," he insists. He looks down at the skis he's holding, then hastily leans them, and the ski poles, against the wall, along with his goggles. "Can you watch these?" he asks the security guard.

"No," the guard says. He's gone back to whatever it is he's watching on his tiny desk-drawer television.

"See?" Jordan holds his arms out. He's wearing a shearling coat, multiple scarves, jeans, ski boots, a woolly sweater with a snowflake pattern stitched into it, and a balaclava. "I blend."

"Can we go up already?" Gavin wants to know, giving a nervous look out the door. "A whole bunch of people are coming. The max capacity of the elevator is three. I don't want to wait."

Tired of arguing with Jordan, I shrug and point to the elevator. "Let's go," I say.

I'm almost positive Jordan says, "Goodie!" under his breath.

But that's not possible.

Is it?

When night ends
At breaking dawn
You know you've been partying
way too long.

"Party Song"
Written by Heather Wells

21

I've never really liked parties. The music's always turned up too loud, and you can never hear what anyone is saying to you.

Although at a party like the one at the Tau Phi House, that might actually be a good thing. Because no one here looks like much of a scintillating conversationalist, if you know what I mean. Everyone is super-attractive—the girls with stick-straight blow-outs, the guys with product carefully layered through their rumpled locks, to give them the appearance of having bed head, when you so know they just got out of the shower.

And though it might be below freezing outside, you wouldn't know it by the way the girls are dressed—spangly halter tops and low-riders so low they'd make a stripper blush. I don't see a single pair of Uggs. New York College kids are nothing if not up on their Hot or Not lists.

I am dismayed when we come off the rickety elevator to see that the words FAT CHICKS GO HOME are still spray-painted along the hallway, though it looks as if a little progress has been made in removing them. They're not quite as fluorescent as they were last time I was here.

But they're still there.

And I certainly don't see anyone above a size 14 at the party. If I had to guess, I'd say the average size present is a 2.

Although I don't know how these girls find thongs in the children's section, which is undoubtedly where most of them have to shop in order to find anything that fits them.

But not everyone seems to find their incredibly slim waists (how do all their internal organs even *fit* in there? I mean like their liver, and everything? Isn't it all squashed? Don't you need at least a twenty-nine-inch waist in order for everything in there to have enough room to do its job?) freakish. Jordan is soon having a very nice time, since the minute he walks through the door, a size 2 runs up to him and is all, "Ohmigod, aren't you Jordan Cartwright? Weren't you in Easy Street? Ohmigod, I have all your CDs!"

Soon more size 2s are gathered around him, wriggling their narrow, nonchildbearing hips and squealing. One of them offers Jordan a plastic cup of beer from a nearby keg. I hear him say, "Well, you know, after my solo album came out, there was a bit of a backlash from the media, because people aren't comfortable with that which isn't familiar," and I know he's gone, sucked into the Size 2 Zone.

"Leave him," I say to Gavin, who is staring at Jordan in concern—as who wouldn't? Those girls look as if they haven't eaten in days. "It's too late. He's going to have to save himself. Have you seen Doug anywhere?"

Gavin looks around. The loft is so crowded with people—and the lights are turned so low—that I don't see how he could recognize anyone. But he manages to spy Doug Winer in a corner over by the wide windows, making out with some girl. I can't tell if the girl is Dana, his paramour of the other morning. But whoever she is, she is keeping Doug occupied . . . enough so that I don't have to worry about him lifting his head and spotting me for the time being.

"Great," I say. "Now, which one is Steve?"

He looks around again. This time he points in the direction of the billiards table and says, "That's him. Playing pool. The tall one, with the blond hair."

"Okay," I say. I have to shout in order for him to hear me, because the music is pulsing so loud. It's techno pop, which I actually sort of like. To dance to. Sadly, no one is dancing. Maybe it's not cool to dance at college parties? "We're going in. You're going to introduce me, right?"

"Right," Gavin says. "I'll say you're my girlfriend."

I shake my head. "He'll never believe that. I'm too old for you."

"You're not too old for me," Gavin insists.

I'm unbuttoning my coat and pulling off my hat. "You called me Grandma!"

"I was joking," Gavin says, looking sheepish. "You couldn't really be my grandma. I mean, how old are you, anyway? Twenty-five?"

"Um," I say. "Yeah." Give or take four years. "But still. Tell him I'm your sister."

Gavin's goatee quivers indignantly. "We don't look anything alike!"

"Oh, my God." The techno pop is starting to give me a headache. What am I even doing here? I should be home, in bed, like all the other late-twenty-somethings. *Letterman* is on. I'm missing *Letterman*! I fold my coat over my arm. I don't know what else to do with it. There's no coat check, and I don't dare leave it lying around. Who knows who might throw up on it? "Fine. Just say I'm a friend who's looking to alter her state of consciousness."

Gavin nods. "Okay. But don't go off with him alone. If he asks."

I can't help preening. Just a little. I finger the tendrils that have escaped from my updo. "Do you think he will?"

"Steve'll do anything that moves," is Gavin's disconcerting reply. "He's a dog."

I stop preening. "Right," I say, giving my miniskirt a tug to make it a millimeter longer. "Well, let's go."

We make our way through the crowd of writhing bodies to the pool table, where two guys are taking turns shooting, in front of an appreciative audience of size 2s. Where did all these tiny girls come from? Is there some kind of island where they're all kept, and only let out at night? Because I never see them during the daytime.

Then I remember. The island is called Manhattan, and the reason I never see them in the daytime is because they're all busy at their internships at Condé Nast.

Gavin waits politely for a tall guy to put the six ball in the corner pocket—much to the appreciative sighing of the size 2s—before going, "Steve-O."

The tall guy looks up, and I recognize Doug Winer's pale blue eyes—but that's it. Steve Winer is as lanky as his little brother is stocky, a basketball player's body to Doug's wrestling frame. Wearing a black cashmere sweater with the sleeves pushed up to reveal a set of very nicely tendoned forearms, and jeans so frayed they could only be designer, Steve sports the same carefully mussed hairdo as all the other guys at his party—with the exception of Gavin, whose hair is mussed because he really didn't comb it after he got up.

"McGoren," Steve says, a smile spreading across his goodlooking face. "Long time no see, man."

Gavin saunters forward to shake the hand Steve's stretched out across the table. Which is when I notice that Steve's jeans are hanging low enough on his hips to reveal a few inches of his washboard stomach.

It's the sight of the stomach that does it—plus the fact that there are a few tawny tufts of hair sticking up from under his waistband, as well. I feel as if someone just kicked me in the gut. Steve Winer may be a student and potential murderer, and therefore off-limits.

But he's got a wicked bod.

"Hey, dude," Gavin says, in his habitually sleepy drawl. "How's it goin'?"

"Good to see you, man," Steve says, as the two of them clasp right hands. "How's school? You still a film major?"

"Aw, hells yeah," Gavin says. "Made it through Advanced Experimental last semester."

"No shit?" Steve doesn't seem surprised. "Well, if anyone could make it, it'd be you. You ever see that Mitch guy who was in our group in Tech Theory?"

"Not so much," Gavin says. "Got busted for meth."

"Shit." Steve shakes his head. "That fuckin' sucks."

"Yeah, well, they sent 'im to minimum security federal, not state."

"Well, that's lucky, anyway."

"Yeah. They let 'im take two pieces of sporting equipment, so he packed his hacky-sack and a Frisbee. He's already got a killer Frisbee team started. First one in the prison system."

"Mitch was always an overachiever," Steve observes. His gaze strays toward me. I try to adopt the same vacuous expression I see on the faces of the size 2s around me. It's not hard. I just imagine I haven't eaten in twenty-four hours, like them.

"Who's your friend?" Steve wants to know.

"Oh, this is Heather," Gavin says. "She's in my Narrative Workshop."

I panic slightly at this piece of improvisation by Gavin—I know nothing about film workshops. But I lean forward—making sure my boobs, in their black frilly demicup bra, plainly visible beneath the diaphanous shirt, strain against the material as hard as possible—and say, "Nice to meet you, Steve. I think we have a mutual friend."

Steve's gaze is hooked on my boobs. Oh, yeah. Take that, you size 2s.

"Really?" he says. "Who would that be?"

"Oh, this girl Lindsay . . . Lindsay Combs, I think her name is."

Beside me, Gavin starts choking, even though he hasn't had anything to drink. I guess he doesn't appreciate my improv any more than I'd appreciated his.

"Don't think I know anyone by that name," Steve says, tearing his gaze from my chest and looking me straight in the eye. So much for what those body language experts in *Us Weekly* are always saying, about how liars never make direct eye contact while they're telling a fib.

"Really?" I'm pretending like I don't notice how all the size

2s around us are elbowing one another and whispering. *They* know who Lindsay Combs is, all right. "God, that's so weird. She was telling me all about you just last week. . . . Oh, wait. Maybe she said *Doug* Winer."

"Yeah," Steve says. Is it my imagination, or has he relaxed a little? "Yeah, that's my brother. She must have meant him."

"Oh," I say. And giggle as brainlessly as possible. "Sorry! My bad. Wrong Winer."

"Wait." One of the size 2s, who appears to be slightly drunker—or whatever—than the others, hiccups at me. "You heard what happened to her, right? To Lindsay?"

I try to look as wide-eyed and expressionless as she does. "No. What?"

"Ohmigod," the girl says. "She got, like, totally murdered."

"Totally!" agrees the size 2's friend, who looks as if she might be pushing a size 4. "They found her head in a pot on the stove in Death Dorm!"

To which all the size 2s and 4s around the pool table respond by going, "Ewwww!"

I gasp and pretend to be shocked. "Oh, my God!" I cry. "No wonder she hasn't been in Audio Craft lately."

Gavin, beside me, has gone pale as the white ball. "Lindsay was an accounting major," he murmurs, close to my ear.

Damn! I forgot!

But it's okay, because the music is pounding loud enough, I don't think anyone heard me but him. Steve Winer, for his part, has reached for his martini glass—seriously, the guy is drinking martinis at a frat party—while his opponent lines up a shot that requires those of us around the pool table to back up a little.

I feel that I've lost the momentum to the conversation, so

when we all gather back around the table to watch Steve take his next shot after his opponent misses, I say, "Oh, my God, why would somebody do that? Kill Lindsay, I mean? She was so nice."

I see several of the size 2s exchange nervous glances. One of them actually leaves the table, muttering something about having to pee.

"I mean," I say. "I did hear something about her and the basketball coach. . . ." I figure I'll just throw this out there and see what happens.

What happens is pretty predictable. The size 2s look confused.

"Lindsay and Coach *Andrews*?" A brunette shakes her head. "I never heard anything about *that*. All I heard was that you didn't leave your stash lying around in plain sight when Lindsay was around—"

The brunette breaks off as her friend elbows her and, with a nervous glance at Steve, says, "Shhhh."

But it's too late. Steve's shot has gone crazily wild. And he's not happy about it, either. He looks at Gavin and says, "Your friend sure does talk a lot."

"Well," Gavin says, seeming abashed, "she's a screenwriting major."

Steve's pale blue gaze fastens on mine. I don't think it's my imagination that, good-looking as he is, there's something genuinely creepy about him—hot abs aside.

"Oh, yeah?" he says. "Anybody ever tell you that you look a lot like what'sername? That pop star who sang in all the malls?"

"Heather Wells!" The size 4 isn't as drunk—or whatever—as anyone else (undoubtedly due to having slightly more body fat, in order to absorb the alcohol), and so is pretty swift on the uptake. "Ohmigod, she DOES look like Heather Wells! And . . . didn't you say her name was Heather?" she asks Gavin.

"Heh," I say weakly. "Yeah. I get that a lot. Since my name is Heather. And I look like Heather Wells."

"That is so *random*." One of the size 2s, markedly unsteady on her feet, has to cling to the side of the pool table to stay upright. "Because you are not going to believe who's here. Jordan Cartwright. From Easy Street. Not just a look-alike with the same name. The *real* one."

There are excited squeals of disbelief from the other girls. A second later, they're all asking their friend where she'd seen Jordan. The girl points, and the majority of the spectators of Steve Winer's game of eight ball, have tottered off to get Jordan's autograph . . . on their breasts.

"God," I say to the guys when the girls have all gone. "You'd never guess Jordan Cartwright was that popular by the sales of his last album."

"That guy's a queer," Steve's opponent assures us. He's taken control of the table since Steve missed his last shot, and is picking off Steve's balls one by one. Steve, down at the far end of the felt, doesn't look too happy about it. "I heard this whole wedding thing with Tania Trace is to cover up the fact that he and Ricky Martin are butt buddies."

"Wow," I say, excited that there's a rumor like this going around, even though I know it's not true. "Really?"

"Oh, yeah," Steve's opponent says. "And that hair of his? Transplants. Guy's going bald as this cue ball."

"Wow," I say again. "And they do such a good job of covering it up whenever he's on *Total Request Live*."

"Well," Gavin says, taking my arm for some reason, "sorry to interrupt your game. We'll just be going now."

"Don't go," Steve says. He's been leaning on his pool cue, staring at me, for the past two minutes. "I like your friend here. Heather, you said your name was? Heather what?"

"Snelling," I say, without skipping a beat. Why my boss's last name should come so trippingly to my lips, I have no idea. But there it is. Suddenly my name's Heather Snelling. "It's Polish."

"Really. Sounds British, or something."

"Well," I say, "it's not. What's Winer?"

"German," Steve says. "So you met Lindsay in one of your screenwriting classes?"

"Audio Craft," I correct him. At least I can keep my lies straight. "So what was that girl talking about, back there? About Lindsay only being nice so long as you don't leave your stash lying around in plain sight?"

"You sure are interested in Lindsay," Steve says. By this time, his opponent has finally failed to sink a shot and is waiting impatiently for Steve to take his turn, saying, "Steve. Your turn," every few seconds.

But Steve is ignoring him. The same way I'm ignoring Gavin, who continues to tug on my arm and say, "Come on, Heather I see some other people I know. I want to introduce you," which is a total bald-faced lie anyway.

"Well," I say, looking Steve dead in the eye, "she was a special girl."

"Oh, she was special, all right," Steve agrees tonelessly.

"I thought you didn't know her," I point out.

"Okay," Steve says, dropping his pool cue and moving swiftly toward me—and Gavin, whose grip has tightened convulsively on my arm. "Who the fuck *is* this bitch, McGoren?"

"Jesus Christ!" The voice, coming from behind us, is, unfortunately, familiar. When I turn my head, I see Doug Winer, one arm around the shoulders of a very scantily garbed non-vanity size 8 (it's nice to see the Winer boys aren't sizeist). Doug's pointing at me, his face very red. "That's the chick who was with the guy who tried to break my hand yesterday!"

All the amiability has vanished from Steve's face. "Soooo," he says, not without some satisfaction. "Friend from class, huh?" This is directed at Gavin. And not in a friendly way.

I instantly regret the whole thing. Not the fact that I'm not home on my bed, strumming my guitar, with Lucy curled at my side. But the fact that I've gotten Gavin involved. Granted, he volunteered. But I should never have taken him up on his offer. I know that the minute I see the glint in Steve's eyes. It's as cold and hard as the frozen metal statues of George Washington in the park below us.

I don't know if this is the guy who killed Lindsay. But I do know we're in trouble. Big trouble.

Gavin doesn't appear to be as convinced as I am that we're in for it. At least if the calm way he's going, "What're you talkin' about, man?" is any indication. "Heather's my friend, man. She was just hoping to score some blow."

Wait. *What? I was what?*

"Bullshit," scoffs Doug. "She was with that guy who came to my room and asked me all those questions about Lindsay. She's a fuckin' cop."

Since Gavin genuinely has no idea what Doug is talking about, his indignation is quite believable. "Hey, man," he says, turning to glare at the smaller Winer. "You been samplin' a little too much of your own wares? Crack is whack, ya know."

Steve Winer folds his arms across his chest. In contrast to

his black sweater, his forearms look darkly tanned. Steve has obviously been in a warm climate recently. "I don't deal crack, nimrod."

"It's an *expression*," Gavin says with a sneer. I watch him in admiration. He may be in film school because he wants to direct, but as an actor, he's not half bad. "Listen, if you're gonna go ape-shit on me, I'm outta here."

Steve's upper lip curls. "You know what you are, McGoren?"

Gavin doesn't look the least bit concerned. "No. What am I, man?"

"A narc." As Steve speaks, two bodies disengage themselves from a couple of black leather couches, where, previously unnoticed by me, they'd apparently been sitting for some time, staring at a basketball game on the wide-screen TV. The girls who'd run off to get Jordan's autograph are trickling back, but have stopped giggling, and now stand gaping at the drama unfolding before them, as if it were an episode of *Real World*, or something.

"We don't like narcs," one of the Tau Phis says. A little younger than Steve, this one has considerably large biceps.

"Yeah," says his twin. Well, bicep-size-wise.

I glance from one to the other. They aren't related, probably, and yet they look exactly alike, same cashmere-sweater-and-jeans combo Steve favors. And same blue eyes without a hint of warmth—or intelligence—in them.

"Jesus, Steve-O," Gavin says, scornfully enough to sound like he really does resent the implication. He jerks a thumb in my direction. He hasn't let go of my arm. "She's just a friend of mine, lookin' to score. But if you're gonna act like assholes about it, forget it. We're outta here. C'mon, Heather."

But Gavin's attempt at a retreat is cut short by Doug Winer himself, who steps directly into our path.

"Nobody threatens a Winer and gets away with it," Doug says to me. "Whoever you are . . . you're gonna be sorry."

"Yeah?" I don't know what comes over me. Gavin is trying to drag me away, but I just plant my high heels on the parquet and refuse to budge. To make matters worse, I actually hear myself ask, "The way somebody made Lindsay sorry?"

Something happens to Doug then. His face goes as red as the lights on the aerial towers I can see blinking in the dark windows behind him.

"Fuck you," he yells.

I probably shouldn't have been too surprised when, a second later, Doug Winer's head met my midriff. After all, I *had* been asking for it. Well, kind of.

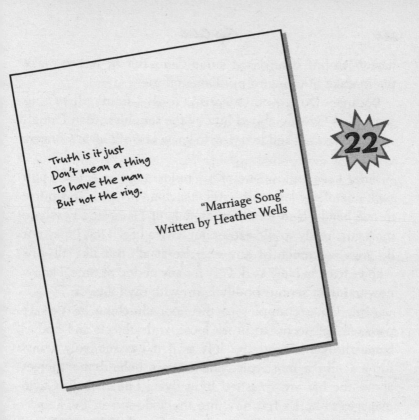

Truth is it just
Don't mean a thing
To have the man
But not the ring.

"Marriage Song"
Written by Heather Wells

22

Having two hundred pounds of frat boy hit you in the gut is a special feeling, one that's hard to describe. To tell you the truth, it's actually a good thing I'm as big a girl as I am. I might not actually have survived if I'd been a size 2.

But since (truth be known) Doug doesn't actually outweigh me by all that much—plus, I saw him coming, and so had time to reflexively clench—I just lie on the floor with the breath knocked out of me. I haven't sustained any internal injury. That I can detect, anyway.

Gavin, on the other hand, doesn't do as well. Oh, he'd

have been fine if he'd just stood there. But he has to make the mistake of trying to pry Doug off me.

Because Doug—no surprise, really—fights dirty. No sooner has Gavin grabbed him by the shoulders than Doug's whipped around and is trying to gnaw one of Gavin's fingers off.

Since I can't allow one of my residents to be eaten, I pull back one of my legs and—still clenching my coat and purse in one hand—land a heel in an area of Doug's body where most guys really would rather not have a heel. Hey, I may not do yoga—or much of any exercise at all. But like all girls who've lived in New York City for any period of time, I know how to inflict serious bodily harm with my footwear.

After Doug crumples to the floor clutching his private parts, all hell seems to break loose, with objects and bodies being thrown around the loft as if it has suddenly transformed into a mosh pit. The mirrors behind the shelves above the bar are smashed by a flying billiard ball. Gavin manages to hurl a frat boy into the wide-screen TV, knocking it over with a crash and a burst of sparks. The size 2s are squealing and fleeing out into the hallway past the FAT CHICKS GO HOME sign, just as one of the pinball machines collapses under Jordan's weight (I don't ask what he was doing on top of it . . . or why his pants are halfway around his ankles).

Fortunately there's so much chaos that I'm able to grab Gavin and shriek, "Let's go!" Then the two of us each throw one of Jordan's arms around our neck (he is in no condition to walk on his own) and drag him from the loft and down the hall . . .

. . . just as the sprinkler system goes off due to the fire started by the knocked-over television.

As the size 2s in the hallway shriek because their blow-outs are starting to curl, we duck through an exit marked STAIRS, and don't stop running—and dragging a semiconscious ex–boy band member—until we burst out onto the street.

"Holy crap," Gavin yells, as the cold air sucks at our lungs. "Did you see that? Did you *see* that?"

"Yeah," I say, staggering a bit in the snow. Jordan isn't exactly dead weight, but he's not light, either. "That was not cool."

"Not cool? Not cool?" Gavin is shaking his head happily as we slip and slide along Washington Square North, trying to make our way west. "I wish I'd had my video camera! None of those girls was wearing a bra. When the water hit them—"

"Gavin," I say, cutting him off quickly, "look for a cab. We need to get Jordan back to the Upper East Side, where he lives."

"There are no cabs," Gavin says scornfully. "There's no one even out on the street. Except for us."

He's right. The park is a dead zone. The streets around it have barely been plowed at all. There isn't a car to be seen, except way over on Eighth Street. None of the cabdrivers there can see us, however, no matter how frantically I wave.

I'm flummoxed. I don't know what to do with Jordan. I believe his claim that none of the car services are able to make it over the bridges. And no way am I calling his dad— the man who told me nobody wants to listen to my "angry-rocker-chick shit"—to see if he can swing by in the family limo.

Jordan himself is happy as a clam, stumbling along between us, but he's definitely the worse for wear. I can't just leave him on someone's doorstep—tempting as the idea seems. He'll freeze to death. And it's blocks—*long* blocks, not short ones—to the subway, and in the opposite direction— we'd have to go past Waverly Hall to get to Astor Place.

And I'm not risking running into any angry frat boys. Especially since I can hear sirens in the distance. The fire department must be automatically notified when the sprinkler system goes off.

Between us, Jordan raises his head and cries happily, having heard the sirens as well, "Oh, hey! Here come the cops!"

"I can't believe you were ever engaged to this guy," Gavin says in disgust—revealing, albeit accidentally, that he's been Googling me. "He's such a tool."

"He wasn't always like this," I assure Gavin. Although the truth is, I think Jordan probably *was* always like this. I just never noticed, because I was so young and stupid. And besotted with him. "Besides, he's getting married the day after tomorrow. He's a little nervous."

"Not day after tomorrow," Gavin says. "Tomorrow. It's past midnight. It's officially Friday."

"Crap," I say. The Cartwrights have to be wondering what happened to their youngest son. Tania's probably frantic. If she's even noticed he's gone, that is. I can't send him back to her like this—with his pants half open and lipstick marks all over his face. God, why can't he be just a *little* more like his brother?

Oh, God. His brother. Cooper is going to *kill* me when he finds out where I've been. And I'm going to have to tell him. I can't drag Jordan home like this and not explain.

And I *have* to take Jordan home. It's the only place I can bring him. I don't think I can carry him much farther. Plus, I'm freezing to death. Pantyhose are definitely not suitable legwear the night after a blizzard in Manhattan in January. I don't know how those girls in the low-riders could stand it. Weren't their belly buttons cold?

"Okay," I say to Gavin, as we reach the corner of Washington Square Park North and West. "Here's the deal. We're taking him to my house."

"Are you serious? I get to see where you live?" Gavin's grin, in the pink glow of the street lamps, alarms me. *"Sweet!"*

"No, it's not sweet, Gavin," I snap. "It's the *opposite* of sweet. Jordan's brother is my landlord, and he's going to be upset—*very* upset—if he hears us come in and sees Jordan like this. So we've got to be quiet. Super-quiet."

"I can do that," Gavin says gallantly.

"Because it's not just Cooper I don't want to wake up," I tell him. "My, um, dad is staying there, too."

"I get to meet your *dad?* The one who was in *jail?*" Oh, yes. Gavin's definitely been Googling me.

"No, you don't get to meet him," I say. "Because hopefully he, like Cooper, will be asleep. And we're not waking him up. Right?"

"Right," Gavin says, with a sigh.

"Heather." Jordan is dragging his feet a bit more.

"Shut up, Jordan," I say. "We're almost there."

"Heather," Jordan says again.

"Jordan," I say. "I swear to God, if you throw up on me, I will kill you."

"Heather," Jordan says for a third time. "I think someone slipped something into my drink."

I look at him in some alarm. "You mean this isn't how you always are after a party?"

"Of course not," Jordan slurs. "I only had one beer."

"Yeah," I say. "But how many glasses of wine did you have before you got downtown?"

"Only ten," Jordan says innocently. "Hey. Speaking of which. Where are my skis?"

"Oh, I'm sure they're fine, Jordan," I say. "You can pick them up in the morning. Why would someone put something in your drink?"

"To take advantage of me, of course," Jordan says. "Everyone wants a piece of me. Everyone wants a piece of Jordan Cartwright pie."

Gavin, who gets a faceful of Jordan's beery breath as he says this, wrinkles his nose. "Not me," he says.

We've reached Cooper's house. I stop to dig my keys from my purse, and give a mini-lecture as I do so.

"Now, when we get inside," I say to Gavin, "we're just going to dump Jordan on the couch in the living room. Then I'm taking you back to Fischer Hall."

"I don't need no escort," Gavin says scornfully, his street slang coming back now that there are no Tau Phis in sight and he's feeling cocky again.

"Those frat boys are angry," I say. "And they know where you live—"

"Aw, hell, woman," Gavin says. "Steve-O don't know shit about me except my name. I was never cool enough for him 'cause I don't like putting chemicals in my body."

"Except twenty-one shots."

"I mean except for alcohol," Gavin amends.

"Fine," I say. "We'll argue about it later. First we'll put Jordan down on the couch. Then we'll worry about getting you home."

"It's two blocks away," Gavin says.

"Heather."

"Not now, Jordan," I say. "Gavin, I just don't want you—"

"Heather," Jordan says again.

"*What*, Jordan?"

"Cooper's looking at us."

I look up.

And sure enough, there's Cooper's face in the window by the door. A second later, we hear the locks being thrown back.

"Okay," I say to Gavin, my heart beginning to pound. "Change of plans. On the count of three, we ditch Jordan, then run like hell. One. Two."

"Don't even think about it," Cooper says, as he comes out onto the stoop. He's wearing cords and a wool sweater. He looks warm and calm and sensible. I long to throw myself at him, bury my head against his hard chest, breathe his Cooper-y scent, and tell him what a terrible evening I've had.

Instead, I say, "I can explain."

"I'm sure you can," Cooper says. "Well, come on. Get him inside."

We drag Jordan inside, with effort—especially since Lucy appears and begins jumping excitedly all over us. Well, me, actually. Fortunately, my thighs are so frozen I can't feel her nails as they rake my nylon stockings.

It's as Lucy leaps up in an effort to lick Jordan's hand that he suddenly becomes very vivacious, saying, as we haul him past Cooper, into the foyer, "Hi ya, bro! What's happenin'?"

"Your fiancée called," Cooper says, as he closes the door behind us and begins working all the locks. "That's what's happening. Did you just take off without telling anyone where you were going?"

"Pretty much," Jordan says, as we let him go and he flops back against his grandfather's somewhat dilapidated pink couch, where Lucy begins licking him in earnest. "Ow. Nice doggie. Make the room stop spinning, please."

"How did he even get down here?" Cooper wants to know. "There aren't any cabs. And no way Jordan took the subway."

"He skied," I explain lamely. It's mercifully warm in the house. I can feel my thighs twitching as they defrost.

"He skied?" Cooper raises both eyebrows. "Where are his skis?"

"He lost them," Gavin says.

Cooper seems to notice Gavin for the first time. "Oh," he says. "You again, eh?"

"You shouldn't be mad at Heather," Gavin begins. "It was all that guy's fault. See, she was trying to sober him up with a brisk walk around the park, but he wouldn't go for it. Fortunately I was passing by and was able to help get him here, or who knows what would have happened. Guy could have frozen. Or worse. I hear there's a doctor who jumps on any drunks he finds in the park and harvests their kidneys to donate to wealthy Bolivians on dialysis. You wake up in the morning all achy and you don't know why—and boom. Turns out someone stole your kidney."

Wow. Gavin really is the king of the improv. He lies with such ease, and so convincingly, I can't help wondering how many of the stories he's fed me over the months I've known him were fabrications like the one he just came up with.

Cooper, however, doesn't look impressed.

"Right," he says. "Well, thank you for your aid. I think we can handle it from here, though. So goodbye."

"I'll walk you back," I start to say to Gavin, but a voice from the hallway interrupts me.

"There she is!" My dad comes in, dressed in pajamas and a robe. It's clear from the way a tuft of what's left of his hair is sticking up in the back that he'd been asleep, but Tania's call had wakened him as well as Cooper. "Heather, we were so worried. When that Tania person phoned, and then we couldn't find you—don't you ever do that again, young lady! If you're going to go out, you had better darn well tell one of us where you're going."

I blink, looking from my father to Cooper and back again. "Are you serious?" I ask incredulously.

"*I'll* walk Gavin back," Cooper says, making it evident that he's anticipated my next move—avoidance. "Heather, get some blankets for Jordan. Alan, call Tania back and tell her Jordan's crashing here for the night."

Dad nods. "I'll say he was at an impromptu bachelor party," he tells us. "And came here to sleep so as not to disturb her."

I just stare—mostly because I've forgotten my dad has a first name, and that Cooper had just used it. But also at the preposterousness of what Dad's just said.

"Jordan doesn't have any friends," I say. "Who's going to throw him a bachelor party? And he'd never be that considerate, not to disturb her."

"I do so have friends," Jordan insists from the couch, where Lucy has progressed to licking his face. "You two are my friends. Or six. Or however many you are."

"I don't need anyone to walk me back," Gavin declares, as Cooper reaches for his coat.

"Maybe not," Cooper says grimly. "But I need some fresh air. Come on."

The two of them go out, leaving me alone with Jordan and my father—two men who both abandoned me when I needed them most, and then both came crawling back when I didn't need—or want—them at all.

"You owe me," I say to Jordan, after I've stalked back into the living room with a blanket—and a salad bowl to throw up in—for him. Even though I'm fairly positive he won't re-member any of this in the morning, I add, "And I'm still not coming to your wedding." To my dad, I say, "Don't tell Tania I was with him when you call her."

"I may have been in prison for the past two decades, Heather," Dad says, with wounded dignity. "But I still have some idea how these things work."

"Well, good for you," I say. Then, calling for Lucy, I hurry up the stairs to my own apartment, hoping if I lock the door and get in bed fast enough, I'll miss Cooper's return. I know Sarah would accuse me of practicing avoidance techniques.

But hey, when it comes to Cooper sometimes avoidance is the only way to go.

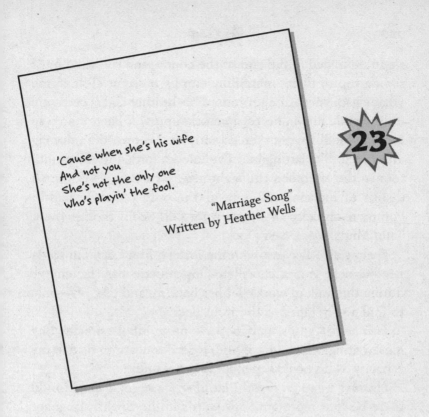

'Cause when she's his wife
And not you
She's not the only one
Who's playin' the fool.

"Marriage Song"
Written by Heather Wells

23

I sneak away the next morning to avoid Cooper. I do this by rising at the ungodly hour of eight, and manage to get bathed and dressed and out the door by eight-thirty. This is so unlike my usual schedule—of not appearing downstairs before eight fifty-five—that I avoid everyone in the house, including my dad, who is still tootling his Indian flute "tribute to the morning" song when I creep by his room, Timberlands in hand so as not to cause the floorboards to creak.

There's no sign of Cooper—a peek through his partly open bedroom door reveals a neatly made bed—or, more ominously, Jordan. The blankets beneath which Jordan had slept are folded at the end of the couch, and the salad bowl sits on top of them, mercifully empty. It seems clear to me what's happened: Cooper roused his brother and is currently transporting him in his own vehicle uptown. There's no way Jordan would have woken so early on his own the morning after a tear like last night's. I've known Jordan to sleep until four in the afternoon the night after a carouse. Our mutual dislike of morning was one of the only traits we had in common—besides an affection for Girl Scout cookies (him: Thin Mints. Me: Do-Si-Does).

Feeling as if I've just won the lottery, I let Lucy out to do her business, grab a chocolate-chip protein bar (for energy during the walk to work), let her back in, and take off—only to find a note taped to the front door.

Heather, it reads, in Cooper's neat, infinitesimally tiny handwriting, which I have been forced to learn to read in my capacity as his bookkeeper, *we've got to talk*.

Heather, we've got to talk? Heather, we've got to talk? Could there be four more ominous words in the English language than *we've got to talk?* I mean, seriously, who wants to see a note that says THAT taped to their front door?

No one, that's who.

Which is why I pull it off and crumple it into my pocket on my way out the door.

What could Cooper want to talk to me about? The fact that I dragged his brother home last night, dead drunk, to sleep it off on his couch, when Cooper's made it more than clear he wants nothing to do with his immediate family? The fact that I snuck out to investigate Lindsay Combs's murder, without telling any-one where I was going and after I'd sworn that this time I would leave the detecting up to the professionals? Or possibly the fact that I endangered the life of one of my residents while doing so?

Or maybe it didn't even have anything to do with what happened last night. Maybe Cooper's decided he's sick of putting up with the Wellses and all of their quirks—Dad's Indian flute and my tendency to drag home drunk pop stars and twenty-one-year-old baggy-panted wannabe gangstas. Maybe he's going to toss us all out on our ears. Some of us would certainly deserve that kind of treatment.

And I'm not talking about Lucy or my dad.

My walk to work is reflective and sad. Even the protein bar tastes a lot more like cardboard and a lot less like a Kit Kat bar than usual. I don't want to get kicked out of Cooper's house. It's the only home I've ever known, really, not counting the apartment Jordan and I lived in together, now forever tainted by the memory of seeing him with Tania Trace's lips locked around his—

"Heather!" Reggie, back on his usual corner, seems surprised to see me out and about so early. *I'm* surprised to see him back at work. Though the snow has stopped and the plows have made some headway, the streets are still mere narrow strips between vast mountains of piled-up snow.

"Morning, Reggie," I say, coming out from behind a six foot drift covering some unfortunate person's car. "That was some storm, huh?"

"I wasn't too happy about it," Reggie says. He's bundled up against the cold in a gold Tommy Hilfiger parka. A paper cup of coffee steams in his gloved hands. "Sometimes I think it might be better to return to the islands."

"But what would you do there?" I ask, genuinely interested.

"My parents have a banana plantation," Reggie says. "I could help manage it. They have wanted me to come home to do so for a long time. But I make more money here."

I can't help but mentally contrast the Winer boys and their family situation with Reggie's. Doug and Steve Winer's dad wants them to make their own fortunes, and so the boys have turned to selling drugs. Reggie's parents want him to take over the family business, but he makes more money selling drugs. The whole thing is just . . . stupid.

"I think you'd be better off on the banana farm, Reggie," I say. "For what it's worth. It'd be a lot less dangerous."

Reggie seems to consider this. "Except during hurricane season," he finally concedes. "But if I were back there, I would miss seeing your happy face every morning, Heather."

"I could come visit," I say. "I've never been to a banana farm."

"You wouldn't like it," Reggie says, with a grin that shows all his gold teeth. "We get up very early there, before light. Because of the roosters."

"God," I say, horrified. "That sounds awful. No wonder you prefer it in New York."

"Plus, if you can make it here, you can make it anywhere," Reggie says, with a shrug.

"Totally," I say. "Hey, did you hear anything about that Doug Winer guy I asked you about?"

Reggie's smile fades. "I did not," he says. "Although I did hear there was a bit of a ruckus in one of the fraternities last night."

I raise my eyebrows. "Really? Wow. What kind of ruckus?"

"One that apparently involved your ex, Jordan Cartwright," Reggie says. "But that must be just a rumor, because what would the famous Jordan Cartwright be doing at a fraternity party two nights before his wedding?"

"You're right," I say. "That must be just a rumor. Well, I better go. Don't want to be late!"

"No," Reggie agrees gravely. "Not you."

"See you later! Stay warm!" I wave cheerfully, then duck around the corner onto Washington Square West. Phew! That was close. I can't believe word about what happened last night has already reached the drug dealers. I wonder if it will make Page Six. Thank God the Greeks don't have a sign-in policy. I'd be in so much trouble at work if it got out I'd been there. . . .

When I walk through the front door of Fischer Hall at twenty of nine, Pete, who is at the security desk, nearly chokes on his bagel.

"What happened?" he asks, with mock worry. "Is it the end of times?"

"Very funny," I say to him. "I've been here on time before, you know."

"Yeah," Pete says. "But never *early*."

"Maybe I'm turning over a new leaf," I say.

"And maybe I'll get a raise this year," Pete says. Then laughs heartily at his own joke.

I make a face at him, check in with the student front desk worker to collect the briefing forms from the night before, and head to my office. I see, to my relief, that the outer door is closed and locked. Yes! I'm the first one in! Won't Tom be surprised when he sees me!

I strip off my coat and hat, then head to the caf for coffee and a bagel. Magda, I'm happy to see, is back at her regular post. She looks better than she has all week. Her eye shadow is fluorescent pink, her hair standing its normal six inches off her forehead, and her eyeliner is unsmudged and black as coal. She smiles at me when I come in.

"There she is," she cries. "My little pop star. Did you miss your Magda?"

"Yes, I did," I say. "Have a good day off?"

"I did," Magda says, growing sober. "I needed it. You know what I mean? It was nice not to think about this place—and what happened here—for a change." She heaves a shudder, then, as two students come up behind me, cries, in a completely different voice, "Oh, look. Here come two of my movie stars. Good morning, little movie stars!"

The students eye her uneasily as she runs their meal cards—which double as their IDs—through her scanner. When she's handed them back and the kids are gone, Magda says, in her normal voice, "I heard you went to visit Manuel. How is he?"

"Um, when I was there yesterday, not so good," I say. "But when I left last night, I heard he'd been moved out of the ICU and was being listed as stable."

"Good," Magda says. "And the police still haven't caught the people who did it to him?"

"No," I say. I'm tempted to tell Magda *I* have a pretty good idea who they were. But I need to see how Tom's date went first. "But I'm sure they're working on it."

Magda scowls. "They aren't working to find who killed little Lindsay," she says. "Three days it's been, and no arrest. It's because she's a girl," she adds, glumly resting her chin in her hands. "If it were a man's head they found in there, they'd have someone under arrest already. The police don't care what happens to girls. Especially girls like Lindsay."

"Magda, that's not true," I assure her. "They're working as hard as they can. I'm sure they'll be making an arrest soon. I mean, they got snowed in yesterday, just like you did."

But Magda just looks skeptical. I realize it's futile to try to change her mind when she's so convinced she's right. So I get my bagel—with cream cheese and bacon, of course—and cocoa-coffee and return to my desk.

I'm sitting there wondering who Tad Tocco is and why he wants me to call him—he has a New York College office extension—when Tom stumbles sleepily into the office, looking surprised to see me.

"Whoa," he says. "Is this an illusion?"

"No," I say. "It's really me. I'm here on time."

"You're here *early*." Tom shakes his head. "Will miracles never cease?"

"So." I'm watching him carefully. "How'd it go? With Coach Andrews, I mean."

He's pulling out his keys to unlock his office door, but I see the swift, secret smile before he can hide it.

"Fine," he says tonelessly.

"Oh, right," I say. "Come on. Spill."

"I don't want to jinx it," Tom says. "Seriously, Heather, I have a tendency to rush into things. And I'm not doing that this time. I'm just not."

"So . . ." I study him. "If you're going to take things slow with him, that means things must have gone pretty well."

"They went great," Tom says. He can't hide his smile anymore. "Steve's just . . . well, he's amazing. But like I said, we're taking things slow."

We. He'd already started saying *wo*.

I'm happy for him, of course. But a little bummed out for myself. Not because I'd like to be part of a *we* someday—though I would, naturally.

But because now I have to wonder just why Kimberly so obviously lied to me . . . I mean, unless Steven Andrews is as good an actor as Heath Ledger, which I sort of doubt.

Still, I can't help but feel happy for Tom.

"So if you're taking things slow," I say, "that means you must be planning on sticking around for a while after all, right?"

He shrugs, blushing. "We'll see," he says. And goes into his office.

Which reminds me of something else. "So where's Dr. Death? She coming in today?"

"No, thank God," Tom says. "Counseling Services has decided that if any more students need to work with grief counselors, they can go across the park."

"Let me guess," I say. "Cheryl Haebig stopped by to see Dr. Kilgore a few too many times."

"I think Cheryl nearly drove Dr. Kilgore to distraction," Tom says happily. "My office is mine again. All mine! I'm going to the caf to get a tray—a *tray*—and have breakfast *at my desk*."

"Enjoy," I say happily, thinking how nice it is to have a boss who thinks eating breakfast at his desk is totally appropriate in the workplace. I have really scored in the boss department with Tom. I'm glad he's not going anywhere. At least, for now.

I am going over the briefing forms when Gavin appears, looking strangely uncomfortable.

"Um, hi, Heather," he says, standing stiffly in front of my desk. "Is Tom around? I'm supposed to reschedule my alcohol counseling appointment."

"Yeah, he's here," I say. "He just went into the caf to grab something to eat. Have a seat. He should be right back."

Gavin sits down on the couch next to my desk. But instead of sinking into it, his legs splayed apart obscenely, as he's tended to do in the past, Gavin sits very straight in his seat, keeping his gaze straight ahead. He doesn't mess around with the paper clips or McDonald's *Toy Story 2* action figures on my desk, the way he usually does, either.

I stare at him. "Gavin? Are you okay?"

"What?" He blinks at the Monet print on the wall, resolutely not looking at me. "Me? Sure, I'm fine. Why?"

"I don't know," I say. "You just seem sort of . . . distant."

"I'm not being distant," Gavin says. "I'm just giving you space."

It's my turn to blink. "You're what?"

Finally, he looks at me.

"You know," he says. "I'm giving you space. Your friend Cooper told me last night that you really need your space. So I'm trying to give it to you."

Something cold passes over me. I think it's foreboding.

"Wait," I say. "Cooper told you I need space?"

"Yeah," Gavin says with a nod. "Last night. When he was walking me back here. Which I didn't need, by the way. I mean, I'm twenty-one years old. I don't need anyone to escort me back to my dorm."

"Residence hall," I say. "And what else did Cooper tell you about me?"

"Well, you know." Gavin shrugs uncomfortably and turns back to the Monet on the opposite wall. "That you were really, really hurt when his brother Jordan cheated on you, and that you were confused, and you're still getting over the loss, and aren't ready for any new romantic relationships—"

"*WHAT?*" I've risen to my feet. "He said *what?*"

"Well," Gavin says, turning his head to look at me quizzically, "you know. I mean, on account of how you're still in love with him—"

My heart seems to explode inside my chest. "*In love with WHO?*"

"Well, Jordan Cartwright, of course." Gavin looks taken aback. "Oh, shit," he adds, when he sees my expression. "I forgot. Cooper said not to tell you what he said—you won't tell him I told, will you? That guy kinda scares me. . . ."

Gavin's voice trails off as he stares at me in alarm. I can't imagine why. Maybe it's because of the way I'm hanging over my desk with my mouth wide open and my eyes spinning around in their sockets.

"Well, I mean, isn't that why you don't want to go to Jordan's wedding tomorrow?" Gavin is starting to babble. "Because you're still so in love with him, you can't stand to see him marry someone else? Because that's what your friend Cooper thinks, anyway. He thinks that's why you haven't been able to move on to someone else, because you're still mourning Jordan's loss, and that it will be a while before you get over it—"

The scream starts at the bottom of my feet and rises steadily, like steam from a kettle. I'm about to tilt my head back to let it out when Tom comes staggering into the office, his face white as the snow outside. He's not carrying a tray with breakfast on it.

"They just found the rest of her," he says, right before he collapses onto the couch beside Gavin.

The scream disappears.

"The rest of who?" Gavin wants to know.

"Lindsay," Tom says.

They say that only time will tell
Until then, I'm in a living hell
What can I do, what can I say
I can't BELIEVE how much I weigh.

"Scale"

Written by Heather Wells

Magda is at her cash register, weeping.

"Magda," I say, for what has to be the fifth time, "just tell me. Tell me what happened."

Magda shakes her head. Against all laws of physics and hairspray, her hair has collapsed. It droops sadly to one side of her face.

"Magda. Tell me what they found. Tom won't talk about it. Gerald won't let anybody into the kitchen. The cops are on their way. Just *tell* me."

Magda can't speak. She is constricted with grief. Pete doesn't have to argue with any of the residents he is busy herding from the cafeteria—they're leaving of their own volition, with many nervous glances in Magda's direction.

Considering the fact that she's practically keening, I don't blame them.

"Magda," I say. "You're hysterical. You've got to calm down."

But Magda can't. Which is why, after heaving a sigh, I haul off and slap her.

And why she, in turn, slaps me back.

"Ow!" I cry, outraged and clutching my cheek. "What did you do *that* for?"

"You hit me first!" Magda declares angrily, clutching her own cheek.

"Yeah, but you were hysterical!" Magda has some arm on her. I'm seeing stars. "I was just trying to get you to snap out of it. You didn't have to hit me back."

"You aren't supposed to slap hysterical people," Magda snaps back. "Didn't they teach you anything in all those fancy first-aid courses they made you take?"

"Magda." My eyes finally stop swimming in tears. "Tell me what they found."

"I'll show you," Magda says, and holds out the hand she hadn't used to smack me in the face. There, in her palm, is nestled a strange-looking object. Made of gold, it resembles an earring, only much larger, and curved. There's a diamond on one end of it. The gold is pretty banged up, like it's been chewed on.

"What is that?" I ask, gazing down at it.

"WHERE DID YOU GET THAT?"

Both Magda and I are startled by the reaction of Cheryl Haebig as she and her boyfriend Jeff pass us on the way out of the cafeteria. Cheryl's eyes are wide, her gaze glued to the object in Magda's hand. Pete, who is trying to herd everyone out of the place, looks frustrated.

"Cher," Jeff says, tugging on his girlfriend's arm, "come on. They want us to leave."

"No," Cheryl says, shaking her head, her gaze still fixed on what Magda is holding. "Where you did get that? Tell me."

"Do you recognize it, Cheryl?" I ask her—though it's obvious from her reaction that she does. Also that I probably don't want to know why. "What is it?"

"It's Lindsay's navel ring," Cheryl says. Her face has gone as white as the blouse she's wearing. "Oh, God. Where'd you get it?"

Magda presses her lips together. And closes her fingers. "Oh, no," she says, in the singsong voice she only uses when students are around. "Never mind. You go to class now, or you'll be late—"

But Cheryl takes a step forward and says, her eyes going hard as the marble floor beneath us, *"Tell me."*

Magda swallows, glances at me, then says, in her normal voice, "It was stuck at the bottom of the garbage disposal. The one that hasn't been working right all week. The building engineer finally got around to taking a look at it. And he found this."

She flips it over. On the other side of the gold, the word LINDSAY is engraved—hard to make out, after all the mashing. But still there.

Cheryl gasps, then seems to find it difficult to stand. Pete and Jeff help her to a nearby chair.

"Tell her to put her head between her knees," I tell Jeff. He nods, looking panicky, and makes his girlfriend lean forward until her long, honey-colored hair is sweeping the floor.

I turn back to Magda and stare down at the ring. "They put the rest of her down the disposal?" I whisper.

Magda shakes her head. "They tried. But bones won't grind up."

"Wait, so . . . *they're still down there?*"

Magda nods. We're whispering so Cheryl won't overhear. "The sink was stopped up. No one thought to wonder why— it's always stopped up. We just used the other one."

"And the police didn't look in there, either?"

Magda wrinkles her nose. "No. The water was all . . . well, you know how it can get back there. Plus they served chili Monday night. . . ."

I feel a little bit of vomit rise into my throat.

"Oh, my God," I say.

"I know." Magda looks down at the belly button ring. "Who could do such a thing to such a nice, pretty girl? Who, Heather? *Who?*"

"I'm going to find out," I say, turning away from her and striding blindly—because my eyes are filled with tears— toward Cheryl, still sitting with her head between her knees. I squat down beside her so that I can ask her, "Cheryl. Were Lindsay and Coach Andrews sleeping together?"

"WHAT?" It's Jeff who looks astonished. "Coach A and Lind—NO WAY."

Cheryl raises her head. It's very red from all the blood that's rushed into it while she was hanging upside down. There are tear tracks down her cheeks, and unshed tears still glisten on her long eyelashes.

"Coach Andrews?" she echoes, with a sniff. "N-no. No, of course not."

"Are you *sure*?" I ask her.

Cheryl nods. "Yeah," she says. "I mean, Coach A, he . . ." She looks up at Jeff. "Um."

"What?" Jeff looks frightened. "Coach A *what*, Cher?"

Cheryl sighs and looks back at me. "Well, none of us are sure," she says. "But we always just assumed Coach A is gay."

"*WHAT?*" Now Jeff looks as if *he's* the one who's about to cry. "Coach Andrews? No way. *NO WAY.*"

Cheryl blinks up at me tearfully. "You can see why we kept that suspicion to ourselves," Cheryl says.

"I can," I say. I give Cheryl a pat on the wrist. "Thank you."

And then I'm gone, brushing past Pete to head out of the caf and toward the elevator.

"Heather?" Magda trots after me in her stilettos. "Where are you going?"

I jab at the UP button, and the elevator door slides open.

"Heather." Pete follows me out into the lobby, gazing after me in concern. "What's going on?"

I ignore them both. I get in the elevator and stab the button for the twelfth floor. As the doors close, I see Magda tottering toward me, trying to stop me from going alone.

But it's just as well she doesn't come with me. She isn't going to like what I'm about to do. *I* don't like what I'm about to do.

But someone has to do it.

When the doors open on the twelfth floor, I get off the elevator and stalk toward Room 1218. The hallway—which the RA has decorated in a Tigger the Tiger motif, being a Pooh fan . . . only an ironic Tigger, since she's given him dreadlocks—is silent. It's just past nine in the morning, and the kids who aren't in class are asleep.

But one of them I fully intend to wake up.

"Director's Office," I yell, thumping on the door once with my fist. We are not allowed to enter any room unannounced.

But that doesn't mean we have to wait for the resident to answer the door. And I don't. I insert my master key into the lock and turn the knob.

Kimberly, as I hoped, is curled up in her bed. Her roommate's matching twin—they've even got the same bedspreads, in New York College gold and white—is empty. Kimberly is sitting up, looking groggy.

"Wh-what's going on?" she asks sleepily. "Omigod. What are *you* doing in here?"

"Get out of bed," I say to her.

"What? Why?" Even when just waking from a dead sleep, Kimberly Watkins looks pretty. Her face—unlike my own, when I'm just waking up—isn't smeared with various anti-zit-and-wrinkle creams, and her hair, instead of standing comically on end, falls into perfectly straight planes along either side of her face.

"Is there a fire?" Kimberly wants to know.

"There's no fire," I say. "Come on."

Kimberly has clambered from her bed and is standing there in an oversized New York College T-shirt and a pair of boxers. On her feet are a pair of baggy gray socks.

"Wait," she says, tucking a lock of hair behind one ear. "Where are we going? I have to get dressed. I have to brush my—"

But I've already got her by the arm and am dragging her out the door. She tries to resist, but let's face it: I'm a lot bigger than she is. Plus, I'm fully awake, and she isn't.

"W-where are you taking me?" Kim stammers, as she trots to keep up with me as I haul her toward the elevator. Her alternative is to let me drag her, which she apparently realizes I am totally willing to do.

"I've got something to show you," I tell her in reply.

Kimberly blinks nervously. "I—I don't want to see it."

For a minute, I consider throwing her up against the nearest wall as if she were a handball. Instead, I say, "Well, you're going to see it. You're going to see it, and then you and I are going to have a talk. Understand?"

The elevator cab is still waiting at the twelfth floor. I pull her into the car and jab the button for the lobby.

"You're crazy," Kimberly says, in a shaky voice, as we glide down. She's starting to wake up now. "Do you know that? You're going to get fired for this."

"Oh, yeah?" I laugh. That's the best one I've heard all day.

"I mean it. You can't treat me like this. President Allington's gonna be mad at you when he finds out."

"President Allington," I say, as we reach the lobby and the elevator doors open, "can kiss my ass."

I drag her past the door to my office, and down the hall toward the front desk, where the student worker actually looks up from the copy of *Cosmo* she's snagged from somebody's mailbox to stare at me in shock. Pete, who is waving firemen into the building—why, no matter what we call 911 for, from a resident freaking out on meth to human bones in a garbage disposal, does the New York City Fire Department always manage to show up first?—pauses in his coordination efforts to stare at me.

"I hope you know what you're doing," he says, as I drag Kimberly past him.

"Don't just stand there," Kimberly shouts at him. "Stop her! Don't you see what she's doing? She's holding me against my will! *She's hurting my arm!*"

Pete's walkie-talkie crackles. He lifts it to his lips and says, "No, it's all clear here in the lobby."

"Stupid rent-a-cop!" Kimberly sneers at him, as I thrust her through the cafeteria doors.

Magda, who is standing at the entrance next to her boss, Gerald, and several firemen, looks startled. Her hand is open to show the firemen her discovery. Cheryl, I see, is still sitting nearby, a very white-faced—but solemn—Jeff Turner at her side. I grab Kimberly by the back of her neck and shove her face toward Magda's open palm.

"See that?" I demand. "Do you know what that is?"

Kimberly is squirming to escape my grasp. "No," she says sullenly. "What are you talking about? You better let me go."

"Show her," I say to Magda, and Magda very nicely holds the belly button ring right up to Kimberly's face.

"Recognize it?" I ask her.

Kimberly's eyes are as wide as quarters. Her gaze is riveted on the object Magda is holding.

"Yeah," she says faintly. "I recognize it."

"What is it?" I ask, letting go of her neck. I don't need to hold on to her anymore to make her look. The truth is, she can't look away.

"It's a navel ring."

"Whose navel ring is it?"

"Lindsay's."

"That's right," I say. "It's Lindsay's. Do you know where we found it?"

"No." Kimberly is starting to sound congested. I wonder if she's starting to cry or merely coming down with something.

"In the garbage disposal," I say. "They tried to grind your friend's body up, Kimberly. *Like she was garbage*."

"No," Kimberly says. Her voice is growing even fainter. Which is unusual, for a cheerleader.

"And you know what the person who killed Lindsay did to

Manuel Juarez at the game the other night," I say. "Just because they were afraid Lindsay might have said something to him about them. What do you think about that, huh, Kimberly?"

Kimberly, her voice still faint, her face now swollen with tears, mumbles, "I don't see what that has to do with me."

"Don't mess with me, Kimberly," I say. "First you tried to tell me Lindsay's roommate might have killed her out of jealousy. Then you tried to make me think Coach Andrews and Lindsay were romantically involved, when you know perfectly well Coach Andrews is same-sex oriented—"

I hear, from behind me, a little gasp. I know it's come from Cheryl Haebig.

"Face it, Kimberly," I say, not turning around. "You know who killed Lindsay."

Kimberly is shaking her head, hard enough that her hair has fallen into her eyes. "No, I—"

"Do you want to see it, Kimberly?" I demand. "The disposal they tried to stick Lindsay down? It's all clogged up. With her blood and bones. But I'll show it to you, if you want."

Kimberly lets out a little moan. The firemen are staring down at me like I'm some kind of sick freak. I guess they're right. I *am* a sick freak. I don't feel bad at all about what I'm doing to Kimberly. Not even a tiny bit.

"You want to know what they did to Lindsay, Kim? Do you want to know?" She shakes her head some more, but I go on anyway. "First, someone strangled her—so hard and for so long, the capillaries around her eyes burst. She was probably gasping for air, but whoever had hold of her didn't care, and didn't let go. So she died. But that wasn't enough. Because then they chopped her up. Chopped her up and put the different parts of her body down the disposal. . . ."

"No." Kimberly is sobbing now. "No, that isn't true!"

"It is so true. You know it's true. And you know what else, Kimberly? You're next. They're coming after you next."

The tear-filled eyes widen. "No! You're just saying that to scare me!"

"First Lindsay. Then Manuel. Then you."

"No!" Kimberly jerks away from me—but unfortunately ends up in front of Cheryl Haebig, who has risen to her feet and is standing there, eyes blazing, glaring at Kimberly.

Only Kimberly doesn't seem to notice the glare. She cries, "Oh, thank God," when she sees Cheryl. "Cheryl, tell her— tell this bitch I don't know anything."

But Cheryl just shakes her head.

"You told her Lindsay and Coach A were involved?" she snaps. "Why would you do that? Why? You know it wasn't true."

Kimberly, seeing she's not going to get any support from Cheryl, backs away from her, still shaking her head. "You . . . you don't understand," she hiccups.

"Oh, I understand, all right," Cheryl says. For every step she takes forward, Kimberly takes another step back, until Kimberly's back is up against Magda's desk, where she freezes, looking fearfully up into Cheryl's face. "I understand you were always jealous of Lindsay. I understand you always wanted to be as well liked and popular as Lindsay. But it was never going to happen. Because you're such a fucking—"

Only Cheryl doesn't get to finish. Because Kimberly has collapsed against the cashier's desk, sliding slowly down it until she's on the floor, a puddle in New York College white and gold.

"No," she sobs. "No, I didn't do it. I didn't do anything. I didn't kill her!"

"But you know who did," I step forward to say. "Don't you, Kimberly?"

She's shaking her head. "I don't! I swear I don't! I just—I know what Lindsay did."

Cheryl and I exchange puzzled glances.

"What did Lindsay do, Kimberly?" I ask.

Kimberly, her knees curled up to her chest, murmurs softly, "She stole his stash."

"She *what*?"

"She stole his stash! God, what are you, dense?" Kimberly glares up at us through her tears. "She stole his entire stash, about a gram of coke. She was mad at him, 'cause he was so stingy with it. Like, she'd blow him and he'd just give her a line or two. Plus he was seeing other girls, too, on the side. It was pissing her off."

Cheryl takes what seems like an involuntary step backward when she hears this. "You're lying," she says to Kimberly.

"Wait," I say, confused. "Whose stash? Doug Winer's? Are you talking about Doug Winer?"

"Yes." Kimberly nods miserably. "She didn't think he'd miss it. Or if he did, he'd think one of his frat brothers took it. Oh, don't look at me like that, Cheryl!" Kimberly is glaring at her fellow squad member. "Lindsay wasn't a fucking saint, you know. No matter what you and the other girls want to think. God, I don't know why you guys could never see her for what she was . . . a coke whore. Who got what she fucking deserved!"

Kimberly's sobbing has risen to hyperventilation level. She's clutching her arms to her stomach as if she were suffering from appendicitis, her knees to her chest, her forehead to her knees.

But while Cheryl has backed off, looking horrified, I'm still not about to let Kimberly off the hook.

"But Doug did miss the coke," I say. "He missed it, and he came looking for it, didn't he?"

Kimberly nods again.

"That was why Lindsay needed to get into the caf. To give him his coke back. Because she hid it in here, didn't she? Because she didn't think it would be safe to leave in her room, where Ann might find it." Nod. "So she got the key from Manuel, let herself in here, smuggled Doug into the building somehow, and . . . Then what? If she gave it back . . . why'd he kill her?"

"How should I know?" Kimberly lifts her head slowly, as if it were very heavy. "All I know is that Lindsay ended up getting what she deserved after all."

"You . . ." Cheryl is glaring down at the other girl, her chest rising and falling rapidly with emotion, her eyes bright with unshed tears. "You . . . you . . . *bitch!*"

Which is when Cheryl draws her arm back to slap Kimberly, who cowers—

But Cheryl's hand is seized before she can bring it down across Kimberly's face.

"That," Detective Canavan, who has come up behind us, says calmly, "is enough of that, *ladies.*"

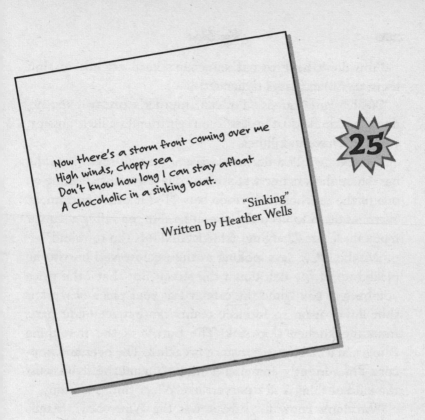

Now there's a storm front coming over me
High winds, choppy sea
Don't know how long I can stay afloat
A chocoholic in a sinking boat.

"Sinking"
Written by Heather Wells

"So there you go," I say to Pete, as we sit at the sticky table in the back of the Stoned Crow after work. "There's your motive, plain as day."

A glance at the security guard's face reveals that he's at least as confused as Magda. "*What?*" they both say at the same time.

"That's why he killed her," I explain patiently. "Lindsay was going around, shooting her mouth off to her friends about his drug dealing. He had to silence her, or risk getting caught eventually."

"You don't have to cut someone's head off just to shut them up," Magda says indignantly.

"Yeah," Pete agrees. "I mean, murder's pretty extreme, don't you think? Just because your girlfriend's a little gossipy, you don't have to kill her."

"Maybe he killed her as a warning," Sarah says, from the bar where she's sitting watching a college basketball game on one of the overhead television sets. "To his other customers. Warning them to keep their mouths shut, or suffer a similar fate. Oh, Jesus! Charging! CHARGING! Is the ref blind?"

"Maybe," Pete says, poking at the microwaved burrito he picked up in the deli down the street. But that's the price you have to pay when the cafeteria at your place of work is shut down again so forensic teams can extract body parts from the kitchen slop sink. The burrito is the first thing Pete's had a chance to eat since breakfast. The beer and popcorn I'm currently enjoying is mine. "Or maybe it was just the kind of thing a sick pervert like Winer thinks is funny."

"We don't know for sure it was the Winer boy," Magda points out.

Both Pete and I stare at her.

"Well," she says, "you don't. Just because that girl said he was the one Lindsay was supposed to meet doesn't mean he was the one who *did* meet her. You heard what the detective said."

"He said we should mind our own business," I remind her. "He didn't say anything about whether or not he thought Doug—or his brother—did it." Even though I'd taken him aside and, after telling him what I'd observed at last night's frat party, had added, "It's obvious that Doug—and Steve, remember what Manuel said, that Steve was the name Lindsay mentioned—killed her for shooting off her mouth about their drug dealing, then left her head as a warning for the rest of their clients. You have to arrest them. You HAVE to!"

Detective Canavan, however, hadn't appreciated being told that he "had" to do anything. He'd just frowned down at me and said, "I should have known that was you at that party last night. Can't you go *anywhere* without causing bedlam?"

At which I took umbrage. Because I've been lots of places where fights didn't break out. Lots of them. Look at me here at the bar across from Fischer Hall.

And okay, it's only, like, four minutes after five, so hardly anyone else has gotten off work yet and the place is pretty much empty except for us.

But no bedlam has broken out. Yet.

"So when are they going to do it?" Magda wants to know. "Arrest those boys?"

"*If* they're going to arrest them," Pete corrects her.

"But they have to," Magda says, blinking rapidly over her alcoholic beverage of choice—a White Russian. Pete and I can't even look at it without gagging a little. "I mean, they took that Kimberly away with them to interview her after she said all those things in front of us . . . even if she lied to them later, they heard what she told us in the cafeteria."

"But is that evidence?" Pete asks. "Isn't that—what do they call it on *Law and Order*? Hearsay?"

"Are you telling me they didn't get one fingerprint from that kitchen?" Magda demands. "Not one stray hair they can get DNA from, to find out who did it?"

"Who knows what they found?" I say, mournfully shoving a handful of stale barroom popcorn in my mouth. Why is stale barroom popcorn so delicious, anyway? Especially with a cold beer. "We'll probably be the last to find out."

"At least Manuel's going to be all right," Pete says. "Julio says he's getting better every day. Although they still have policemen posted outside his hospital room."

"What's he going to do when they discharge him?" Magda wants to know. "They aren't going to post a policeman by his house, are they?"

"They'll *have* to have arrested Doug by then," Sarah says, from the bar. "I mean, Doug has to be the one who strangled her. The only question is, did he do it accidentally? Like did he asphyxiate her during sexual play, then panic? From what you told me, he doesn't seem like the type who has much control over his temper—"

"Yeah. Did I mention he totally head-butted me in the gut?" I ask.

"But putting her limbs down a disposal to get rid of the evidence?" Sarah shakes her head. "Doug doesn't have the brains for something like that—even if it did turn out not to work thanks to the disposal breaking. Oh, my God, foul! FOUL!"

I look up from the empty popcorn basket and notice that Pete and Magda aren't the only ones staring at Sarah in disbelief. The bartender, Belinda, a punk rock waif with a shaved head and overalls, is blinking at her with astonishment as well.

Sarah notices, looks around, and says defensively, "Excuse me, a person can have multiple interests, you know. I mean, I can be interested in psychology and sports, too. It's called being well-rounded, people."

"More popcorn?" Belinda asks her, looking pretty scared for someone with so many nose rings.

"Uh, no," Sarah says. "That stuff is stale."

"Um," I say, "I'll take some. Thanks."

"On that note," Pete says, rising from his chair, "I have to get home before my kids tear the place apart. Magda, you want a ride to the subway?"

"Oh, yes," Magda says, getting up as well.

"Wait," I protest. "I just got more popcorn!"

"Sorry, honey," Magda says, struggling into her faux-rabbit fur coat. "But it's about twelve degrees out there. I'm not walking to the subway. See you on Monday."

"See you guys," I say mournfully, watching them leave. I'd leave, too, but I still have half a beer left. You can't just leave a beer like that. It's un-American.

Except a minute later I'm regretting not having made my escape when I had the chance, since the door opens, and who should walk in but . . .

Jordan.

"Oh, there you are," he says, spotting me at once. Which isn't hard, since I'm the only one in the bar, with the exception of Sarah and a couple of Math Department types, who are playing pool. Jordan slides into the chair Pete just vacated, and explains, as he peels off his jacket, "Cooper told me you sometimes come here after work."

I glare at him over my beer. I don't know why. I guess it's just that he mentioned Cooper's name. Cooper's not high on my list of favorite people right now.

Actually, neither is his brother.

"Nice place," Jordan says, looking around. It's clear he's being sarcastic. Jordan's idea of a nice place is the bar at the Four Seasons. Which isn't exactly in my price range. Anymore.

"Well, you know me," I say, more lightly than I feel. "Only the best."

"Yeah." Jordan stops looking around and looks at me instead. This is somehow worse. I know I'm not exactly ravishing at the moment. Last night's wild ride didn't do much for the bags under my eyes, and I didn't actually wash my hair this morning. Instead, I washed it the night before, to get the smell of Tau Phi House cigarette smoke out of it. Sleeping on my hair while wet has a way of making it look . . . well, sort of matted the next day. Add that to the fact that I'm wearing my second-best pair of jeans—I still haven't managed to replace the ones with the blood-stained knees—which aren't exactly loose, to the point where I have to constantly worry about camel toe, and you have the picture.

But Jordan's no prize today, either. He's got dark circles where I've got bags, and his case of hat head is even worse than mine. His blond hair is sticking up in tufts all over his head.

"You want a beer?" I ask him, since Belinda is looking over at us questioningly.

"Oh, God, no," Jordan says, and shudders. "I'm never drinking again after last night. I seriously think someone slipped something in my drink. I only had that one—"

"You told me you had ten glasses of wine before you even got downtown," I remind him.

"Yeah," Jordan says, with a *So what?* look on his face. "That's what I have most nights. I've never been as blotto as I was last night."

"Why would someone roofie you?" I ask. "It's not exactly like you're unwilling to have sex with strangers."

He glares at me. "Hey, now," he says. "That's not fair. And I don't know why someone would do it. Maybe it was, like, an ugly girl, or someone I wouldn't ordinarily go with."

"I didn't see any ugly girls at that party." Then I brighten. "Maybe it was one of the guys! Frats are known hotbeds of latent homosexuality."

Jordan makes a face. "Please, Heather . . . let's just drop it, okay? Suffice it to say, I'm never drinking again."

"Well, that will make the champagne toasts tomorrow a bit of a letdown," I say.

Jordan fingers the initials someone has carved into the tabletop, not meeting my gaze. "Look, Heather," he says. "About last night—"

"I don't know where your skis went, Jordan," I say. "I called Waverly Hall and the guard said no one left any skis there, so obviously someone stole them. I'm really sorry, but you know—"

He flinches. I think it's because I've spoken so loudly.

"I don't care about the stupid skis," he says. "I'm talking about us."

I blink at him. Then I remember that Cooper must have driven him home this morning.

Oh, no.

"Jordan," I say quickly. "I am *not* still in love with you. I don't care what Cooper told you, okay? I mean, sure, I used to be in love with you. But that was a long time ago. I've moved on—"

He blinks at me. "Cooper? What are you talking about?"

"Didn't he give you a ride home this morning?"

"Yeah. But we didn't talk about you. We talked about Mom and Dad. It was nice. I haven't talked to Cooper—just one-on-one—like that in a long time. I think we worked out some things. Our differences, I mean. We both agreed that we're nothing alike—but that that's all right. Whatever his relationship with Mom and Dad . . . well, it's no reason he and I can't get along."

I stare at him. I can't quite believe what I'm hearing.

Cooper can't stand Jordan. I mean, to the point of refusing to take his calls or open the door when he comes over.

"Wow," I say. "That's . . . that's . . . well, progress. Good for you."

"Yeah," Jordan says. He continues to finger the graffiti. "I think I talked him into coming to the wedding tomorrow. I mean, he didn't agree to be my best man, like I asked, but he said he'd come."

I'm genuinely shocked. Cooper can't stand his family, and now he's planning on attending a big blowout wedding at St. Patrick's Cathedral, with a reception at the Plaza, in their company? Those are so not his type of events. . . .

"Well," I say. Because I really don't know what else to say. "That's . . . that's amazing, Jordan. Really. I'm so happy for you."

"It really means a lot to me," Jordan says. "The only thing better would have been if . . . well, if you would have agreed to come tomorrow, Heather."

I clutch my beer. "Oh, Jordan," I say. "That's so sweet. But—"

"That's why it's so hard for me to say what I'm about to say," Jordan goes on, as if I hadn't spoken. "And that's this. Heather." He reaches across the table to grip the hand that isn't curled around my pint glass, then looks earnestly into my eyes. "It really hurts me to say this, but . . . I can't let you come to my wedding tomorrow."

I blink at him. "Jordan," I say. "I—"

"Please let me finish," Jordan says, squeezing my hand. "It isn't that I don't want you there, Heather. More than anyone in the world, I want you there. You're the person I've been closest to for the longest in my life. If there's anyone I want to be by my side for the most important event of my life, it's you."

"Um, Jordan," I say. "I'm flattered. I really am. But shouldn't the person you most want at your side for this be—"

"It's Tania," Jordan interrupts.

"Right," I say. "That's what I mean. Shouldn't Tania be the person you most want at your side? Considering she's the one you're—"

"No, I mean Tania is the one who doesn't want you there," Jordan says. "Not after last night. See, she wasn't too happy when she found out I spent the night with you—"

"Oh, my God, Jordan!" I burst out, yanking my hand away from him, and glancing quickly toward Sarah and Belinda to make sure they haven't overheard. "You didn't spend the night with me! You spent it on your brother's living room couch!"

"I know that," Jordan says, having the dignity to flush. "But Tania doesn't believe it. See, Tania thinks you're still in love with me, and—"

"Oh, my God!" I cry again. "What is it with everybody thinking I'm still in love with you? I'm so not! I fell out of love with you way before I ever walked in and saw Tania with your—"

"Hey, now," Jordan says, ducking his head as the two math geeks look over at us interestedly. "No need for that kind of language."

"Seriously, though, Jordan," I say. "I fell out of love with you that time we were touring in Japan, remember, and you kept going to visit all those temples. Only they weren't really temples, were they?"

Jordan's flush deepens. "No. I didn't know you knew. You never said anything."

I shrug. "What was there to say? Besides, I thought maybe you'd work it out of your system. But you didn't."

"I just never knew any woman could do that with a ping-pong ball," Jordan says, in a dreamy voice.

"Yes," I say briskly. "Well, fortunately for you, Tania is a girl of many talents."

His fiancée's name snaps him out of his reverie, as I'd known it would.

"So you're really all right with it?" he asks me, with a worried expression. "Not coming to the wedding?"

"Jordan, I never had any intention of coming your wedding tomorrow. Remember? I *told* you that. Like five times."

He reaches out to grasp my hand again. "Heather," he says, gazing into my bloodshot eyes with his own. "I can't tell you what this means to me. It proves that, no matter what you say, you do care about me . . . at least a little. And I hope you'll believe me when I say I'm sorry things turned out this way. But it's time for me to start my new life, with my new partner. If it's any comfort to you at all, I hope that someday you, too, will find someone to share your life with. . . ."

"Jordan," I say, leaning forward to pat his hand. "I *have* found that someone. Her name is Lucy."

Jordan makes a face and lets go of my hand. "I mean a man, Heather, not a dog. Why do you always have to make a joke out of everything?"

"I don't know," I say, with a sigh. "That's just the kind of girl I am, I guess. You're lucky you escaped when you did."

Jordan looks at me sadly, shaking his head. "You'll never go back to the way you used to be when we first met, will you? You were so sweet back then. Never cynical."

"That's because back then my boyfriend didn't feel like he was missing out on the fact that I never did vaginal tricks with a ping-pong ball," I tell him.

"That's it," Jordan says, putting his jacket back on and standing up. "I'm leaving. I'll see you . . . well. Later."

"After you get back from the honeymoon," I say. "Where are you going, anyway?"

Jordan can't seem to make eye contact. "Japan. Tania's touring."

"Well," I say. "*Ja mata.*"

Scowling, Jordan storms from the bar. Only when he's gone does Sarah turn her attention from the game (there's a commercial), and says "Jesus Christ. What did you say to him, anyway?"

I shrug. "Goodbye."

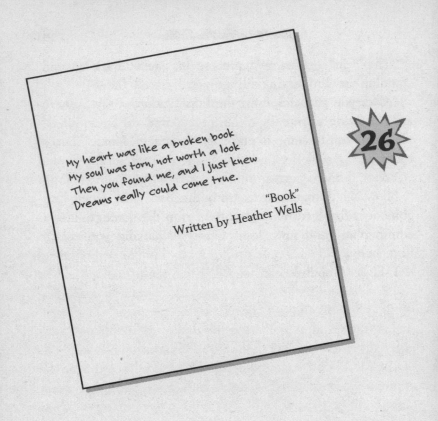

My heart was like a broken book
My soul was torn, not worth a look
Then you found me, and I just knew
Dreams really could come true.

"Book"

Written by Heather Wells

26

After the day I've had, I'm looking forward to an evening alone. I plan on taking out the old guitar and giving it a thorough workout, then lighting a fire and curling up on the couch to watch all the TV shows I've DVR'd through the week. I think there's some leftover Indian takeout in the fridge. I'm going to chow down on samosas and nan and *America's Next Top Model* reruns. Could there be a better plan for a Friday night? Especially a Friday night coming after a week of dealing with bodyless corpses and frat boys.

Except that when I walk through the front door of

Cooper's place, I realize there's something I forgot to factor into my plan.

And that's that I now live with my father.

The smell hits me the minute I step into the foyer. It's unmistakable. Someone is cooking the steaks I snuck out of work to buy at Jefferson Market. The steaks I got for me and Cooper, but never got around to cooking for him, on account of . . . well, everything that was going on.

Wrenching off my coat, I stalk into the kitchen. Dad is there in an apron in front of the stove, cooking my steaks in a cast-iron pan with the mushrooms and onions I also picked up. He's set the kitchen table for two, with napkins and lit candles and everything. Lucy, curled in one of her many dog beds (Cooper's the one who keeps buying them, not me. He thinks they're cute), raises her head when I come in and wags her tail, but that's all. She's obviously already been out.

"Well," I say. I have to speak loudly to be heard over the Bollywood music Dad's playing on Cooper's stereo system. "Expecting company?"

Dad jumps and turns around. He's drinking one of my Diet Cokes. Some of it slops out of the can because he turns so abruptly.

"Heather!" he cries. "There you are! I didn't hear you come in."

I'm glaring at the steaks. I can't help it. Those were in *my* fridge in my apartment upstairs. Which it's true I never lock, but that doesn't mean I welcome strange men prowling around up there, poking through my stuff.

Because Dad *is* a strange man. To me. I mean, relatively speaking.

"I hope you don't mind," Dad says, apparently noticing the direction of my gaze. "I figured somebody better fry these up,

or they were going to spoil. I was in your apartment, looking
for your mother's number."

"In the *refrigerator*?" I ask.

"I was just wondering what you eat," he says affably. "I feel
like I barely know you. I'm sorry, were you keeping these
steaks for some special occasion? Because if so, you really
ought to have stuck them in the freezer. They'll last longer
that way."

The smell of sizzling meat and onions is delicious, it's
making me a little dizzy.

"I was kind of saving them . . . but it doesn't matter," I say,
a little mournfully. It doesn't matter because, at least according to Gavin, Cooper thinks I'm still head over heels for his
brother, anyway. Making him dinner isn't going to change
that. I'm probably going to have to resort to shooting ping-
pong balls from my ying yang onstage before anyone ever believes I'm over Jordan. Including Jordan.

"Well, that's good," Dad says. "Because they're almost
done. You like your steak a little rare, right?"

I raise my eyebrows, genuinely surprised. "Wait . . . you
cooked them for *me*?"

"Who else?" Dad looks a little surprised.

"Well." I chew my lower lip. "A lady friend, maybe?"

"Heather, I've only been out of prison a week," Dad says.
"That's hardly enough time to make a lady friend."

"Well, then, Cooper," I say.

"Cooper is busy with his latest case," Dad says. "So I'm
afraid it's just you and me. I wasn't sure when you'd be
home, of course, but I took a chance. Have a seat. There's a
bottle of wine there. I hope you don't mind drinking alone.
I'm sticking with soda these days."

Shocked, I pull out a chair and sink down into it, as much

because I'm not sure I can stand up anymore as because he asked me to.

"Dad," I say, looking at the carefully set table, "you don't have to cook dinner for me. Or breakfast, either, for that matter."

"It's the least I can do," Dad says. He takes the steaks out of the pan and sets them on two plates, along with the mushrooms and onions. "I'll just let these sit a minute," he explains. "They're better that way. Juicier. So." He pulls out the chair across from mine and sits down in it. "How was your day?"

I stare at him for a minute. I'm tempted actually to tell him, *Well, Dad, not so good, actually. We found out what they did with the rest of Lindsay Combs, and it wasn't pretty. Then I manhandled a student and when the higher-ups find out about it, I'll probably be fired.*

But instead I say, "It was fine, I guess. How was your day?" Because I really don't want to get into it.

"Fine, fine," Dad says. "Cooper had me follow a man from his office to his lunch appointment, then back to his office."

My eyebrows go up. Way up. I can't believe I'm finally learning something about what Cooper does all day.

"Really? Who hired him to follow the guy? What's the guy supposed to have done?"

"Oh, I can't tell you any of that," Dad says pleasantly. "Here." Dad pours me a glass of red wine and hands it to me.

"But I work for the company," I say. "Client-detective privilege should extend to me."

"Oh, I don't think so," Dad says, shaking his head. "Cooper was quite explicit about me not telling you anything."

"But that's not fair!" I cry.

"He said you'd say that. I'm sorry, honey. But he seems really to prefer that you don't know. I think it's due to your tendency to get yourself involved in situations you really ought to stay out of. Like this murder at your dorm. I think the steaks are ready now."

Dad pops up to get them. I sip my wine, scowling into the candle flames.

"Residence hall," I say, as he plops a plate filled with perfectly cooked steak down in front of me.

"I beg your pardon?"

"It's a residence hall," I say. "Not a dorm. Saying *dorm* does not foster a warm sense of community, which is what we're aiming for. Well, aside from all the senseless killing." I cut off a piece of meat and chew. Heaven. Marinated to perfection.

"I see," Dad says. "That's very like how we called Eglin a camp and not what it was—prison."

"Right," I say, taking a sip of wine. "Made you forget about the shivs, and concentrate on all the lavalieres."

"Oh, no one had a shiv," Dad says, with a chuckle. "How do you like your steak?"

"It's great," I say, swallowing another bite. "Okay, so as long as we're exchanging pleasantries about our places of work— or incarceration—what's the deal? Why are you here, Dad? It's not really because you have nowhere else to go, because I know you've got plenty of rich friends you could be shacking up with instead of me. And this getting-to-know-your-daughter-better thing—sorry, I'm not buying it. So level with me. What's the scam? And please keep in mind that I'm pretty sure I outweigh you."

Dad puts down his fork and lets out a sigh. Then he takes a sip of Diet Coke and says, "You're so like your mother, it's uncanny."

I feel the usual bubble of animosity that pops up every time he says this. But this time, I tamp it down.

"Yeah, I think we've established that you believe that," I say. "So let's move on. Why were you looking for Mom's number in my apartment today?"

"Because," Dad says, "for some years now, I've been working a sort of . . . program. It has certain steps that its practitioners must follow if, by the end, they hope to achieve spiritual enlightenment. And one of the steps is that they must make amends with those they have harmed. That is why I wanted to phone your mother. To try to make amends."

"Dad," I say. "Mom *left* you. Don't you think *she*'s the one who needs to be making amends? With both of us?"

Dad shakes his head. "I promised your mother when I married her that I would love and support her. That didn't just mean emotionally. I promised to support her financially, as well, especially while she stayed home and raised you. When I went to prison, I was forced to renege on my part of that bargain. It's my fault, really, that your mother had to take you out on the road in order to support you both."

"Right," I say sarcastically. "She couldn't just get a job as a receptionist in a doctor's office somewhere. She had to parade her freakishly musical kid around in front of the masses at various malls."

Dad makes a *tsk-tsking* sound.

"Now, Heather," he says. "Don't try to rewrite history. You loved performing. We couldn't keep you *off* the stage. Believe me, I tried. Your mother only did what she felt she had to . . . and you certainly never complained."

I lay down my fork. "Dad. I was eleven. Do you really think that was the kind of decision that should have been left to me?"

Dad looks down at his food. "Well, that's an issue you're

going to have to work out with your mother. I'm afraid by that time, I was no longer in a position to be actively involved in your parenting."

"True," I say. And fat chance of me ever having an opportunity to "work out" my issues with Mom. That's something that's a little hard to do over the phone. Though Dad seemed perfectly willing to try. "So. Did you find the number?"

"Yes," Dad says. "It was in your address book. Some of the addresses in there are quite old, you know. You should think about getting a new book. If you want, I could do that for you tomorrow."

I ignore this offer.

"Did you call her?"

"I did," Dad says.

"And did you make amends?"

"I tried to," Dad says. "But your mother can, as you know, be very difficult. She refused to admit that I had hurt her in any way. In fact, she reminded me—as you did, just now—that it was she who left *me*, and that if anyone should be making amends, it's her. But that she doesn't care to, because, according to her, I deserve everything I got."

I nod. "Yeah, that sounds like Mom, all right. It really sucks when you say I'm like her, by the way. If you tried to make amends with me, I'd be much more receptive."

"Well," Dad says. "That's good, because you're next on my list."

I shrug. "Amends accepted."

"I haven't even made them yet."

"Yeah, you have," I say. "This dinner is enough. It's totally delicious."

"This dinner is hardly enough," Dad says. "You were basically deprived of a father figure during your formative teen years. That's the kind of hurt that can't be cured with a single steak dinner."

"Well," I say, "now that you're living here, maybe you can cure it with multiple steak dinners. Like every Friday night, or something. Although you might want to vary the menu a little. I like pork chops, too. Oh, and fried chicken."

"Heather," Dad says, sounding sad. "Food can't serve as a balm for all the harm I've caused you. I understand that, of all the people I hurt when I broke the law, you are the one who suffered the most. Leaving you alone with your mother, who then put you on that mall tour. Even if you did enjoy it, that's no way for anyone to spend her childhood, living in a trailer and traveling from mall to mall, being exploited by the one person who should have been looking out for your best interests."

"It *was* more fun than going to school," I point out. "And, like you said—it was hard to get me off the stage back then."

"But you were deprived of the normal joys of childhood. And I can't help but feel that that deprivation is partially responsible for the way you are today."

I stare at him. "What's wrong with the way I am today?" I ask.

"Well, for one thing, you're nearly thirty and you don't have a husband or children. You don't seem to realize that family is the most important thing in the world—not that guitar I hear you plinking late into the night, and not your job. *Family*, Heather. Take it from someone whose lost his—family is what matters."

I lay my fork down again and say gently, "There are lots of different types of families nowadays, Dad. They don't all consist of a husband and wife and kids. Some of them consist of a girl, her dog, a PI, her dad, her best friend, and the various people she works with. Not to mention the drug dealer down the street. My feeling about it is, if you care about someone, doesn't that person automatically become your family?"

"But don't you worry," Dad says, after he spends a moment digesting this information, "that if you don't have children, there'll be no one to care for you in your old age?"

"No," I say. "Because I could have children, and they could turn out to hate me. The way I see it, I have friends who care about me now, so I'll probably have friends who'll care about me when I'm old, too. We'll take care of each other. And in the meantime, I'm putting the max into my 401(K), and setting aside as much as I can into a SEP IRA as well."

Dad gazes at me over his steak. I'm disturbed to note that there are tears in his eyes.

"That's very profound, Heather," he says. "Especially since I sense that, in many ways, these so-called family members of yours have been kinder to you than your actual blood relations."

"Well," I admit, "at least none of them has stolen all my money and fled the country. Yet."

Dad raises his Diet Coke can. "I'll drink to that," he says. I clink his can with my wine glass. "So you really don't mind," he says, when we're done clinking, "if I stick around and try to make amends—even though you say I don't have to?"

"I don't care," I say. "Just so long as you aren't expecting me to take care of you in your old age. Because I've only been contributing to my 401(K) for a couple of months. I don't have enough money in it to support myself, let alone an aged parent."

"I'll tell you what," Dad says. "Why don't we agree to support each other emotionally only?"

"Sounds good to me," I say, spearing the last of my steak.

"Looks like you're ready for salad," Dad says, getting up and going to the fridge, from which he takes the salad bowl into which Jordan did not, thankfully, barf. In it is what appear to be various types of lettuce, some cherry tomatoes, and—much to my delight—croutons.

"I'll toss," Dad says, proceeding to do so. "I hope you like blue cheese dressing." Without waiting for an answer (because, really, why would he need one? Who doesn't like blue cheese dressing?), he goes on, "Now. About you and Cooper."

I nearly choke on the sip of wine I've taken.

"This is just my opinion," Dad says, "and I've been out of the dating scene for a long time, I'll admit. But if you really want things to progress to a romantic level with him, I'd suggest not spending quite so much time with his younger brother. I realize you and Jordan were together for a terribly long time, and that it's hard to let go. But I sense a certain amount of friction from Cooper concerning his family, and if I were you, I'd limit my interactions with them. Especially Jordan."

I stab at some of the lettuce he's spooned onto my plate.

"Gee, Dad," I say, "thanks for the tip." Because what else can I say? I'm not going to get into my love life—or lack thereof—with my *dad*.

But he apparently doesn't realize this, since he goes on.

"I think that once Jordan is married, and Cooper realizes you're finally over him, you'll have a much better chance with him." Dad sits back down and starts on his own salad. "Though it wouldn't hurt if you'd make a little more effort to be pleasant in the mornings."

I eat more salad. "Good to know," I say. "I'll take it under advisement."

"Although you did seem to make quite a positive impression last night," Dad comments.

I stop chewing. "Last night? You mean when Cooper caught me hauling his dead-drunk brother in the door?"

"No," Dad says amiably. "I meant the fact that you were wearing a skirt. You should do that more often. Young men appreciate a girl in a skirt. I saw Cooper staring."

I don't bother telling my dad that the reason Cooper was staring wasn't because I was in a skirt and he appreciated it, but because I was in *such a short skirt* that I looked like a hooker. Probably Cooper was trying not to laugh.

Still, these aren't the kinds of things you can say to your father.

"I never even asked you," Dad says, a little while later, over dessert (Dove Bars, of course). "Did you have plans for tonight? Am I keeping you from something?"

"Just *America's Next Top Model*," I say.

"What's that?" Dad asks innocently.

"Oh, Dad," I say. And show him. I mean, if he really wants to make amends, watching *ANTM* with me is an excellent way to start.

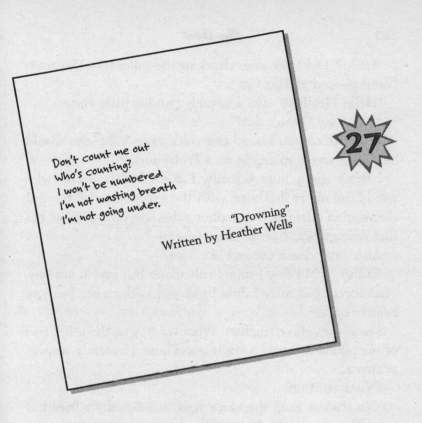

Don't count me out
Who's counting?
I won't be numbered
I'm not wasting breath
I'm not going under.

"Drowning"
Written by Heather Wells

27

Dad is asleep after our fourth episode of *ANTM* in a row. I guess I can't really blame him. While women find watching pretty girls play complicated mind games with one another endlessly fascinating—like today in the caf, with Cheryl and Kimberly—your average heterosexual man can only take so many hours of it before he—like Dad, and Patty's husband, Frank—passes out from sheer boredom.

He's sleeping hard enough that when the phone rings, it doesn't even wake him. There might be something to this yoga stuff after all, if it makes you sleep so hard even a ringing phone can't wake you.

"Hello?" I whisper, after checking the caller ID—*Unknown Number*—and picking up.

"Hello, Heather?" asks a vaguely familiar male voice.

"Yes," I say. "Who's this?"

"Oh, I think you know," the voice says. "Who else would be calling you at midnight on a Friday night?"

I think about this. Actually, I don't know anyone who would call me at this hour, with the exception of Patty. But she wouldn't dare pick up a phone this late, now that she has that disapproving live-in nanny.

Also, Patty doesn't sound like a guy.

"Is this . . ." I know I sound ridiculous, but I say it anyway. "Tad Tocco? I'm sorry I didn't call you back earlier, but I've been busy."

I hear convulsive laughter. Whoever it is on the other end of the phone is having a really good time. I instantly suspect students.

Drunk students.

"No, it's not Tad," the voice says. "It's actually a friend of yours from last night. Don't tell me you don't remember."

And suddenly the memory of those ice-blue eyes on mine comes flooding back.

And all the blood seems to leave my extremities. I'm sitting there, frozen to the spot, holding the phone with my dad asleep on one side of me, and Lucy asleep on the other.

"Hello, Steve," I manage to say, through lips that have gone cold. "How did you get my number?"

"How'd I figure out your last name and look it up, you mean?" Steve asks, with a laugh. "A little bird told me. Do you want to speak to him? He's right here."

The next thing I know, a voice that is unmistakably Gavin McGoren's is swearing—steadily, and with much imagination—

into the phone. I'd recognize those "motherfuckin's" any-where. They are the same ones Gavin regularly uttered back when I used to catch him elevator-surfing.

Then I hear a smacking sound—like skin on skin—and a second later, Steve is saying, "Tell her, goddamn you. Tell her what we told you to say."

"FUCK . . . YOU," is Gavin's response. This is followed by a scuffling sound, and more smacking. When I hear Steve's voice again, it's out of breath.

"Well, I think you get the idea, anyway," he says. "We're having another party. And this time, you're actually invited. And to make sure you show, we have your friend Gavin here. Unless you do exactly what I tell you, he's going to suffer some bodily injury. And you wouldn't want that, now, would you?"

I'm so horrified I can barely breathe. I say, "No."

"I didn't think so. So here's the dealio. You come here. Alone. If you call the cops, he will get hurt. If you don't show, he—"

"HEATHER, DON'T—" I hear Gavin start to bellow, but his voice is quickly smothered.

"—could get very, very hurt," Steve finishes. "Got it?"

"I got it," I say. "I'll be there. But where's here? The Tau Phi House?"

"Please," Steve says, sounding bored. "We're *here*, Heather. I think you know where."

"Fischer Hall," I say, my gaze going toward my living room windows, which look out at the back of the twenty-story building that is my place of work. It's still early, by New York College residence hall standards, which means that most of the lights in the windows are blazing as the building's occu-pants prepare to go out, apparently completely unaware that down on the first floor, in the closed and locked cafeteria, something unspeakable is about to take place.

Which is when I stop feeling cold, and start feeling angry. How dare they? Seriously. How dare they think they can get away with this *again*? Do they really believe I'm going to sit idly back and *let* them turn Fischer Hall into Death Dorm?

And okay, maybe it already *is* Death Dorm. But I'm not going to let it stay that way.

"Heather?" Steve's voice is warm in my ear. It's amazing how charming psychopathic killers can be, when they put their minds to it. "Are you still there?"

"Oh, I'm here," I tell him. "And I'll be right over."

"Good," Steve says, sounding pleased. "We'll be looking forward to seeing you. Alone, like I said."

"Don't worry," I assure him. "I'll be alone." Like I need any help kicking his skinny ass. Steve Winer is making an extremely bad decision, challenging me to a confrontation on my own turf. He might have been able to off a girl as tiny as Lindsay without getting caught, but if he thinks a girl like me is going to go down without a fight—a fight loud enough to bring the entire building banging on the cafeteria doors—he's got another think coming.

But then again, he, like his brother, doesn't strike me as the sharpest knife in the drawer.

"Good," Steve says. "And remember. No cops. Or your boyfriend's a dead man."

I hear a thump, and then a scream. The scream comes from Gavin.

And I know that, stupid though he might be, Steve Winer isn't someone to underestimate.

I slam down the receiver and spin around to see my dad sitting up, blinking groggily.

"Heather?" he says. "What's the matter?"

"Something's going down at the dorm," I say, grabbing a piece of paper and writing a number on it. "I mean, residence hall. Something bad. I need you to call this person and tell him he needs to get over there as fast as possible. Tell him I'll meet him in the caf. Tell him to bring backup."

Dad squints down at the number. "Where are you going?"

"I'm going to Fischer Hall," I say, grabbing my coat. "I'll be back as soon as I can."

Dad looks confused. "I don't like this, Heather," he says. "They don't pay you enough for you to be hurrying over there in the dead of night like this."

"Tell me about it," I say, and I'm out the door.

The walk to Fischer Hall has never seemed so long. Even though I'm half running, it seems to take forever to get there. Partly because of the slick sidewalks I have to navigate, but also, I'm convinced, because of how hard my heart is hammering inside my chest. If they did anything to hurt Gavin . . . if they so much as bruised him—

I'm so intent on getting where I'm going that I don't even see Reggie until I crash into him.

"Whoa, little lady," he cries, as we collide. "Where would you be off to in such a hurry so late at night?"

"Geez, Reggie," I say, struggling to catch my breath. "Don't you ever go home?"

"Fridays are my best nights," Reggie says. "Heather, what's the matter? You're white as—well, a white girl."

"It's those guys," I pant. "The ones I told you about. They have one of my residents. In the caf. They're going to hurt him if I don't get there, fast—"

"Whoa, whoa, whoa." Reggie has hold of both my arms

and doesn't seem eager to let go. "Are you serious? Heather, don't you think you should call the police?"

"I did!" I have to windmill both my arms before I manage to break free of his grip. "My dad's calling them. But someone has to get in there in the meantime—"

"Why does that someone have to be you?" Reggie wants to know.

But it's too late. I'm already off and running again, my Timberlands pounding on the newly shoveled sidewalk, my heart pounding in my throat.

When I throw open the door to Fischer Hall, the mystery of how Doug and his fellow frat brothers—not to mention his real brother—got into the building to kill Lindsay without actually being signed in is cleared up the minute I walk through the door and see the security guard.

"You!" I cry. It's the crusty old guard from the security desk in Waverly Hall.

"ID," he says. *He doesn't even recognize me*.

"You were at Waverly Hall last night," I pant, pointing at him accusingly.

"Yeah," Crusty Old Guard says, with a shrug. "That's my regular spot. I fill in other places when there's an opening. Like here, tonight. I need to see your ID before I can let you in."

I'm flipping open my wallet to show him my staff identification. "I'm the assistant director of this building," I say to him. "I know you let a bunch of Tau Phis in here tonight without making them sign in. Just like you did Monday night, when they killed someone."

Crusty Old Guard—his name tag says Curtiss—grunts. "I don't know what you're talking about," he says grumpily.

"Yeah," I say. "Well, you'll find out in a minute, believe me.

In the meantime, I want you to phone up to the building director and tell him to head to the caf. And when the cops show up, send them there, too."

"Cops?" Crusty Curtiss looks startled. "What—"

But I'm already running past him.

I don't head for the main doors to the caf, though. I'm not about to go walking blindly into their trap—lame as it might be. Instead, I dash down the hall, past my office, then the student government's office—closed and locked, as always—and finally past the dining manager's office, to the back entrance to the kitchen. The door, as I'd known it would be, is locked.

But I have my master key. I slip it from my pocket and—cradling a can of pepper spray in my free hand—unlock the door as quietly as I can and let myself into the kitchen.

It's dark. As I'd expected, they're in the dining hall itself. They don't have anyone stationed in the kitchen. They haven't even bothered turning the lights on in here. Amateurs.

I creep along the galley, straining my ears. I can hear the murmur of male voices out in the dining area. There's a light on there, as well . . . but not the lights in the chandeliers. They haven't turned on the overheads. Instead, they've got some kind of flickering lamp on . . . flashlights?

Or flames?

If they're burning candles in there, they are in so much trouble. Burning candles isn't allowed in any of the residence halls.

I'm not really sure what my plan is. I figure I'll creep as close as I can behind the service counters, then peer out over them to see what the boys are up to. Then I'll creep back and report what I've seen to Detective Canavan when he arrives with backup. That way they'll have a good idea how many people they're dealing with.

I crawl along behind the steam tables, thinking that I'm really going to have to have words with Gerald, because it is just disgusting back there. Seriously, the knees of my jeans are getting filthy, and my hand lands on something squishy that I sincerely hope is a furry Tater Tot.

Except that Tater Tots don't make squeaking noises and jump away.

It's all I can do to restrain a scream.

Good thing I go to the trouble, though. Because when I peek up over the top of the steam tables, I see something that both horrifies and stuns me.

And that's a dozen figures in deeply hooded robes—like monks wear—only blood red, standing around one of the dining tables, which has been dragged from its normal place and put in a position of prominence in the center of the room, and covered with a blood-red cloth. On top of it are various items I'm too far away to identify. One of them, though, has to be a candelabra or something. The flickering light I'm seeing really is candlelight.

I'm not too far away to identify the figure that's sitting off to one side, his wrists tied to the arms of one of the dining chairs. It's Gavin. With duct tape over his mouth.

That is totally going to hurt when I pull it off. I mean, when it catches on his goatee.

Of course, I know right away what I'm looking at. I subscribe to all the premium cable channels, after all. It's some kind of fraternity initiation ritual, like in that movie *The Skulls*.

And I want no part of it. Gavin appears to be all right—at least, he doesn't seem to be in any imminent danger. I decide the best thing to do might be to retreat and wait for reinforcements.

Which is why I'm crawling back toward the kitchen when my coat pocket catches on a steel mixing bowl stashed way too low on a shelf. It falls to the (grimy) floor with a clatter, and the next thing I know, there are a pair of Adidas in front of me, peeping out from the hem of a red robe.

"Look what we have here," a deep male voice says. And a second later, hard hands slip beneath my armpits and pull me to my feet.

Not that I go quietly, of course. I lift my hand to direct a stream of pepper spray inside the hood, only to have the canister knocked from my hand. I am, however, wearing Timberlands, the footwear of choice for the intrepid Manhattan assistant dorm director. I level one of my steel-encased toes at the shins of my captor, causing him to swear colorfully.

Sadly, however, he doesn't release me, and the only result is that another robed guy comes up and grabs me, too. Plus a lot more mixing bowls fall down, making a horrendous racket.

But a racket is what I *want* to make now. I want everyone in the building to come running. Which is why I start screaming my head off as I'm dragged over to the ceremonial table the Tau Phis have set up.

At least until Steve Winer—or a guy I assume is him; he's the tallest and has fancy gold trim around the cowl of his robe, as befitting the president of a frat house—walks over to where Gavin is sitting and smacks him, hard, across the face with some kind of scepter he's holding.

I stop screaming. Gavin's head has snapped back at the blow. For a minute it stays that way. Then, slowly, he turns his neck, and I see the gash that's opened up on his cheek . . . and the fury blazing in his eyes.

Along with the tears.

"No more screaming," Steve says, pointing at me.

"She kicked me, too," says Adidas, beside me.

"No more kicking," Steve adds. "You kick and scream, the kid gets whacked again. Understand?"

I say, in what I consider a relatively calm voice, "The cops are going to be here any minute. I know you said not to call them, but . . . too late."

Steve pushes back his hood so he can see me better. The only light source—it really is a candelabra, sitting on the middle of the altar he's created—isn't exactly bright, but I can see his expression well enough. He doesn't, however, look alarmed.

And this alarms *me*.

Especially when, a second later, the double doors to the caf are thrown open, and Crusty Curtiss comes shuffling in, looking annoyed. He's got a half-eaten sandwich in his hand. It appears to be a Blimpie Best.

Which just happens to be one of my favorites, especially with sweet and hot pickles.

"Can't you keep her quiet?" he asks Steve, in an irritated voice. "People are wondering what the hell is going on in here."

I stare at him in horror. Seeing my expression, Steve chuckles.

"Oh, yes," he says. "There are loyal Tau Phis all over the world, Heather. Even working as security guards at major urban colleges."

"Some cops showed up," Curtiss says to me, taking another bite from his sandwich and speaking with his mouth full. "I told 'em I didn't know what they was talkin' about, that I'd been here all night and hadn't see you. So they left. They looked kinda pissed off. I don't think they'll be back."

I glare at him. "You," I say, "are so fired."

Curtiss laughs at that. He seems to genuinely be enjoying himself.

"Fired," he says, chuckling. "Right."

He turns around and shuffles back the way he'd come.

I look at Steve. "Okay," I say. "Let's get this over with. But let Gavin go. Your problem's with me, not him."

"We don't have a *problem*," Steve explains politely, "with either of you."

"Well." I look around the room at the assorted Tau Phis, wondering which one is Doug. "What am I doing here, then?"

"Oh, did I not explain over the phone?" Steve wants to know. "I guess I forgot." He steps forward and lifts a long, ornamental knife from the altar he's made. Ornamental in that the handle is gold and covered with semiprecious stones.

The blade, however, looks plenty real. And sharp.

"Pledges," Steve says, "it's time."

And from out of the shadows step another half dozen robed figures, who'd apparently been lurking in the back, over by Magda's register.

"Time for what?" I ask curiously.

"Initiation," Steve informs me.

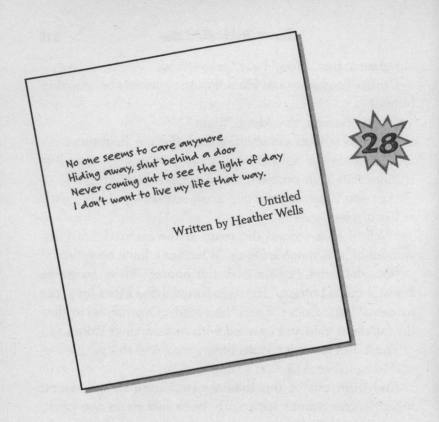

No one seems to care anymore
Hiding away, shut behind a door
Never coming out to see the light of day
I don't want to live my life that way.

Untitled

Written by Heather Wells

"Oh, you have got to be kidding me with this" I say disgustedly.

"Pledges," Steve says, ignoring me, "now is the time when you will be given the opportunity to prove your dedication to the house of Tau Phi Epsilon."

"Seriously," I say. "This is freaking stupid."

Steve finally looks over at me. "If you don't shut up," he says, "we'll off your boyfriend first, then you."

I blink at him. I want to be quiet. I really do. But . . .

"Gavin's not my boyfriend," I say. "And seriously. Don't you think there's been enough killing?"

"Um." One of the pledges throws back his hood. I'm astonished to see Jeff Turner, Cheryl Haebig's boyfriend, standing there. "Excuse me. What's she doing here?"

"Shut up!" Steve whirls around to glare at Jeff. "No one gave you permission to speak!"

"But, dude," Jeff says. "She's the assistant director of the building. She's gonna tell—"

"She isn't going to tell," Steve interrupts. "Because she's going to be dead."

This news appears to come as a shock to more than just Jeff. A few of the other pledges stir uneasily.

"Dude," Jeff says, "is this some kind of joke?"

"SILENCE, PLEDGES!" Steve thunders. "If you want to be a Tau Phi, you must be prepared to make sacrifices for the cause!"

"Oh, right," I say quickly, while I still have the pledges—or Jeff, at least—on my side. "Is that what Lindsay Combs was, Steve? A sacrifice? Is that why you killed her?"

More nervous movement from the pledges. Steve turns his head to glare at me.

"That bitch betrayed a member of our order," he snaps. "She had to be punished!"

"Right," I say. "By chopping off her head and grinding her body up in a garbage disposal?"

Jeff throws a shocked look in Steve's direction. "Dude. That was *you*?"

"Oh, it was Steve, all right," I say. "Just because Lindsay stole—"

"Something that didn't rightfully belong to her," Steve barks. "Something she wouldn't give back—"

"She tried," I insist. "She let your brother in here—"

"And it was gone!" Steve shouts over me. "She claims someone must have stolen it. Like we were supposed to believe that! She was a liar as well as a thief. She deserved to be put to death for her betrayal!"

"Dude." There's hurt as well as disbelief in Jeff's face. "Lindsay was my girlfriend's *best friend*."

"Then you ought to be thanking me," Steve says imperiously. "For if your girlfriend had continued to consort with the likes of that woman, she'd have eventually learned her ways and betrayed you, too, the way she betrayed one of our brothers."

It seems to take a minute for this to sink in for Jeff. But when it finally does, he doesn't hesitate a second longer.

"That's it." Jeff Turner shakes his head. "I'm out. I only joined this stupid frat 'cause my dad was in it. I did not sign on to go around killing people. You want to hit my butt with a paddle? Fine. You want to force me to chug a twenty-four-pack? No problem. But kill chicks? No way. You guys are fucking nuts—"

As he's saying this, he's reached down to pull off his robe. Steve, watching, shakes his head sadly. Then he nods at two of the robed figures in the circle around his altar, and they cross the room to deliver several blows to Jeff's midriff— while he's still floundering around in his robe, no less—until he finally falls to the ground, where they begin kicking him, heedless of his screams of pain. The other pledges, seeing this brutal treatment of one of their peers, stand frozen in place, watching.

They're not the only ones who feel frozen. I cannot believe what I am seeing. Where are the cops? They couldn't really have believed that idiot Curtiss, could they?

Knowing there's only one person who's going to be able to put a stop to this—or die trying, anyway—I say loudly to the other pledges, who are just standing there watching their friend get the snot kicked out of him, "Just so you guys know, the thing Lindsay stole? It was Doug Winer's stash of coke."

It's impossible to tell what the boys' reaction to this information is, since their faces are still hidden beneath their hoods. But I see them stir even more uneasily.

"Don't listen to her," Steve instructs them. "She's lying. It's what all of them do—try to demonize the order by spreading malicious lies about us."

"Um, we don't have to demonize you guys," I say. "You do a good enough job of that on your own. Or are you saying your brother Doug didn't strangle his girlfriend to death because she stole his nose candy?"

One of the people kicking Jeff Turner stops, and a second later Doug Winer is striding toward me, his hood down.

"You take that back!" he cries, eyes blazing. "I didn't! I didn't kill her!"

Steve reaches out to grab his little brother's arm. "Doug—"

"I didn't!" Doug cries. "You have no proof!" To Steve he says, "She has no proof!"

"Oh, we have plenty of proof," I say. I'm stalling for time. Steve has to know that. But he seems to have forgotten about Gavin and using him as a means to keep me silent. And that's all I want. "We found her body today, you know. What was left of it, anyway."

The look Steve throws me is one of total incredulity. "What the fuck are you talking about?"

"The body. Lindsay's body. See, the thing you didn't take into account was the fact that disposals don't grind up bones . . . or navel rings. We found Lindsay's this morning."

Doug makes the kind of noise girls sometimes make when I tell them they can't have a single next year. It's a sound between a sigh and a protest, and comes out like, "Nuh-uh!"

Steve's grip on the knife tightens. The blade flashes in the candlelight. "She's bluffing. And even if she's not . . . so what? There couldn't have been anything to lead them to us. Not after the way we cleaned up."

"Yeah." I'm sweating now, I'm so hot in my winter coat. Or maybe it isn't heat. Maybe it's nerves. My stomach is in knots. I probably shouldn't have had that second Dove Bar. Jeff is lying totally still now. I don't know if it's because he's unconscious, or just pretending to be so the kicking will stop. "You guys may be good at partying and putting on fancy initiation rites, but at cleaning, you really suck. They totally found hairs."

Doug throws a startled look at his brother. "Steve!"

"Shut up, Doug," Steve snaps. "She's bluffing."

"She's not!" Doug has gone white as a ghost in his robe. "She knew! She knew about the stash!"

"Leaving the head was your first mistake," I go on conversationally. "You might have gotten away with it, if you hadn't left the head on the stove like that. They'd have noticed the bones and belly button ring and all, but chances are they wouldn't have known what they were. It would have been like Lindsay had just disappeared. No one would have known you guys had been there, so no one would have wondered about how you got in. That was your second mistake, trying to off Manuel. He wouldn't have told anybody about the key if you hadn't scared him like that. And if he had, what difference would it have made? He's just a janitor. Nobody listens to the janitor." I shake my head. "But no. You had to get cocky."

"Steve," Doug whines. "You said no one would know it was us. You said no one would know! If Dad finds out what we did—"

"Shut up," Steve yells. I jump a little at the volume of his tone. So do the guys who still have hold of my arms. "For once in your life, shut the fuck up, you little shit!"

But Doug's not about to do as his brother says. "Christ, Stevie!" he cries, his voice breaking. "You told me Dad'd never know. You told me you'd take care of it!"

"I *did* take care of it, you little shit," Steve snaps. "Just like I take care of all your stupid fuckups."

"Don't worry about it, you said. Leave everything to me, you said." Doug's practically crying. "You son of a bitch! You didn't take care of *shit*! Now Lindsay's dead, we're gonna get busted—and I *still* don't know what happened to my stash."

Apparently oblivious to the fact that his sibling has just incriminated them all, Steve shouts, "Yeah, well, who's the asshole who fucking killed the bitch in the first place? Did I tell you to kill her? Did I tell you to fucking kill her? No, I did not!"

"It wasn't my fault she died!" Suddenly Doug is stumbling forward and, to my abject horror, clamps both his hands on the front of my coat. A second later, he's sobbing into my face. "I didn't mean to kill her, lady. Honest I didn't. She just made me so goddamned mad, stealing my coke like that. And then she wouldn't give it back! That whole thing, telling me someone musta stole it out of here—it was such bullshit. If she'd just given it back when I asked . . . but no. I thought Lindsay was different, you know. I thought Lindsay really liked me, not like those other girls, who only hang out with me because of my last name. I didn't mean to choke her so hard—"

"Shut up, Doug." Steve's voice is hard again. "I mean it. Shut the fuck up."

Doug lets go of me and spins around to appeal to his older

brother, tears streaming down his face. "You told me you'd take care of it, Steve! You told me not to worry. Why'd you hafta do that with her head, huh? I told you not to—"

"Shut up!" Steve, I can tell from the way his hands are shaking, is losing it. The knife he's holding points one minute at me, and the next at Doug. A detached part of my brain wonders if Steve Winer would really stab his own brother.

The same part kind of hopes he will.

"What did you expect me to do, huh, you little shit?" Steve is so mad, his voice is now no louder than a hiss. "You call me in the middle of the fucking night, crying like a baby, and say you killed your fucking girlfriend. I have to get up, come all the way over here, and clean it up for you. And you have the nerve to criticize *me*? You have the goddamned *audacity* to question *my* methods?"

Doug gestures helplessly at me. "Jesus Christ, Steve! This fucking DORM MANAGER figured it out. How long do you think it's gonna be before the police catch on?"

Steve blinks at me, then licks his lips nervously, his tongue darting out like a snake's. "I know. That's why we have to get rid of her."

Which is when one of the red-robed figures beside me stirs and says, "Uh, dude. You said we were just gonna scare 'em, like we did the janitor guy—"

"Scare him? He nearly bled to death!" I cry.

"If you say one more word," Steve says, pointing the knife blade at me, "I'll kill you now, where you stand, instead of letting you out the easy way." The tip of the knife travels away from me, and ends up pointing at the glass on the altar. It appears to be filled with water. "Drink that," Steve commands.

I look at the glass. I have no idea what's in it. But I can guess, judging by what happened to Jordan the other night.

Rohypnol, otherwise known as roofies, a popular sedative on the college circuit. One dose, already dissolved in water, ought to make me much more malleable, when it comes time for cutting.

It's right about then that I decide I've had about enough. I'm hot, my stomach hurts, and I'm pretty worried about Gavin and Jeff. I wish I had let Cooper kill Doug Winer when he'd had the chance. I wish I myself had taken one of Doug's pillows and stuffed it over his head and held on until the kid stopped struggling.

No. That's too kind. I wish I had wrapped my own hands around that thick neck and squeezed, squeezed the life out of him the way Doug had squeezed the life out of Lindsay. . . .

"Come on, Heather," Steve says, beckoning impatiently with the knife. "We don't have all night."

"Uh, Steve," the other guy next to me says. "Seriously, man. This is getting weird."

"Shut up," Steve says to his fellow Tau Phi. He grabs the glass, brings it over to me, and shoves it under my nose. "DRINK IT."

I turn my face away. "No."

Steve Winer gapes at me. "*What?*"

"No," I say. I can feel that I have the support of the room. The Tau Phis are starting to realize their leader has lost it. They won't let him hurt me. I'm pretty sure. "I am not going to drink it."

"What do you mean, you aren't going to drink it?" The shadow of a smile returns to Steve's face. "Are you blind? I'm holding a knife to your throat."

"So?" I shrug. "What's the difference to me? I'm gonna get killed anyway."

This is not what Steve wants to hear. The smile fades from his lips, and there isn't a hint of humor in his face when he hands the glass to the guy on my right, turns around, walks over to Gavin, grabs him by the hair, yanks his head back, and raises the knife toward his exposed throat—

"Steve, man, don't!" one of my guards yells, just as I say, "Whoa, I'll drink it, I'll drink it," grab the glass, and down its contents.

"That's it," the guy who'd been holding the glass says. "I'm out of here. Jeff's right, you guys are fucking crazy."

And he begins striding from the cafeteria—along with several other Tau Phis—including all the pledges but Jeff Turner, who is still lying on the floor, still as death.

"Don't let them go," Steve barks at the Tau Phis who'd kicked Jeff into unconsciousness. But even they hesitate.

"Did you hear me?" Steve lets go of Gavin's hair and stands there, staring confusedly as his frat brothers begin to leave him, one by one. "You guys. You can't do this. You took a pledge. A pledge of total loyalty. Where are you . . . you can't—"

Doug is starting to look scared. "Jesus, Steve," he says. "Let 'em go. Just—"

Doug breaks off midsentence, though. That's because Steve has dropped the knife, and, from somewhere deep inside his robe, he's managed to bring out a small handgun, which he is now holding level with his brother's chest.

"Douglas," Steve says. "I am getting fed up with you and your whining."

"Jesus, Steve!" Doug cries again. But this time the fear and tears in his voice cause his fellow Tau Phis to turn around to look.

Which is when I do what I know I have to. After all, no

one's paying the least bit of attention to me. Everyone's gaze is on Steve, whose back is to me.

Which is why, as soon as I see his index finger tighten on the trigger, I dive, my arms spread wide, at the floor. Because I know something about the floor of the caf of Fischer Hall that Steve Winer will never know: it is squeaky clean. Julio may not be in charge of the floors behind the steam tables, but he's in charge of the cafeteria floor, and he's waxed it until it's slick as ice. Which means I slide across it like an Olympic skater doing a belly flop, until I've collided with the elder Winer's legs, which I then throw my arms around, pulling him down.

Then I reach up, seize Steve's wrist, and sink my teeth into it, forcing him to drop the gun. Also to scream and writhe in pain and terror.

Doug seems to get over his astonishment at what I've just done first—perhaps because he's the only one who didn't have the sense to duck when Steve was waving that gun around, and so is the only person in the room still standing. He stumbles forward until his hand closes over the butt of the gun his brother has dropped. His fingers trembling, he raises the pistol and aims it—

Well, at me.

"No," cries Steve hoarsely. "Don't shoot, you little fuck! You might hit me!"

"I *want* to hit you!" Doug screams. Really. He screams it. Tears are streaming down his face. "I am so sick of you always telling me what a fuckup I am! And okay, I may be a fuckup . . . but at least I'm not a freak! Yeah, I killed Lindsay— but I didn't mean to. You're the sick fuck who thought it would be a good idea to leave her head on the stove. Who even fucking does shit like that, Steve? *Who*? And then you made us stab that poor janitor . . . and now you want us to kill this lady here . . . and why? To make yourself look like a badass in front of your frat buddies. Because *Dad* was a badass when *he* was a Tau Phi."

The mouth of the gun Doug is pointing at us keeps straying from me to Steve in a very unnerving manner. Steve, beneath me, is beginning to sweat. Copiously.

"Doug," he says. "Dougie. Please. Give me the—"

"But Dad didn't kill people, Steve!" Doug goes on, as if he hadn't heard. "He didn't cut people up! He was a badass without doing shit like that! Why can't you see that? Why can't you see that no matter what you do, *you're never going to be like Dad*?"

"Fine," Steve says. "I'm never going to be like Dad. Now put the gun down—"

"No!" Doug screams. "Because I know what's going to happen! You're going to turn this all around and blame it on me somehow. Like you always do! Like you've always done! And I'm not putting up with it anymore! Not this time!"

Which is when he points the gun in the dead center of Steve's forehead.

And also when a calm, slightly familiar voice says from the cafeteria's doorway, "Drop it, son."

Doug looks up, his expression one of mingled astonishment and indignation. I turn my head as well, and am quite confused to see Reggie—yes, drug dealer Reggie—leveling a very large and shiny Glock 9mm at Doug Winer's chest.

"Drop the weapon," Reggie says. Strangely, his Jamaican accent is completely gone. "I don't want to have to hurt you, but if I have to, I will. I think we both know that."

Steve, still pinned beneath my body, cries, "Oh, Officer,

thank God you're here! This guy went berserk and was trying to kill me!"

"Uh-huh," Reggie says tonelessly. "Give me the gun, son."

Doug glances down at his brother, who nods encouragingly beneath me. "Go on, Dougie. Give the gun to the nice policeman."

By this time, Doug is crying too hard to shoot anyway. "You're such a fuck, Steve," he says, as he hands the gun to Reggie, who passes it to Detective Canavan, who is looming in the doorway behind him, his gun drawn as well.

"You may not know it, Officer, but you just saved all our lives," blathers Steve Winer. "My brother was trying to kill me. . . ."

"Right," Reggie says, reaching to his belt for his handcuffs. "Heather, please get off Mr. Winer."

Obligingly, I roll off Steve Winer. As I do, I notice that the room kind of spins around. But in a pleasant manner.

"Reggie!" I cry, from where I'm splayed on the floor. "You're an undercover cop? Why didn't you *tell* me?"

"Because he's a Fed." Detective Canavan is standing over me, directing about twenty uniformed officers to handcuff everyone in a red robe. "With your usual aplomb, Wells, you managed to stumble into the middle of a sting operation the DEA's been working on for months. Congratulations on that, by the way."

"Detective!" I cry happily, staring up at Detective Canavan. "What took you so long?"

"We had a little trouble getting in," he explains. "The security guard was being . . . resistant. And no one could find a key." He rolls his eyes. "Typical of this place, by the way. Why are your pupils so big?"

"'Cause I'm so happy to see you!" I cry, sitting up to fling my arms around his neck as he leans down to help me to my feet. "I just love you so much!"

"Uh," Detective Canavan says, as I cling to him—because the room is spinning around quite a bit by now. "Wells? Are you on something?"

"They made her drink something." This comes from Gavin, who has been untied by the maid/undercover DEA agent, and whose facial gash is being examined by a pair of EMTs who've come in, apparently from nowhere. As I'd expected, the duct tape has left an angry red mark across his mouth, and taken away some of his soft, wispy mustache, making it even wispier-looking.

"Gavin!" I cry, letting go of Detective Canavan and throwing my arms instead around him—much to the annoyance of the paramedics trying to clean him up. "I love you, too! But only as a friend."

Gavin doesn't look as happy to hear this as I think he should be. "I think it's roofies," he says, attempting to extricate himself from my embrace. Which I find rude, to say the least.

"Okay," Detective Canavan says, taking me by the arm. "Come on."

"Where are we going?" I want to know.

"Oh," Detective Canavan says, "I think the hospital will be a good place to start. Get some fluids into you."

"But I'm not a bit thirsty," I assure him. "I could use some ice cream, though. Hey, want a Dove Bar? They're right in the freezer over there. Hey, everyone should have a Dove Bar. Hey, everybody," I turn to yell. "Have a Dove Bar! On me!"

"Come on, Wells," Detective Canavan says, keeping a firm grip on my arm. "That's enough."

And then, as he's leading me out of the cafeteria and into

the lobby, I see a sight that makes me forget all about the Dove Bars. And it's not Crusty Curtiss in handcuffs—although that's very pleasant to see. And it's not half the residents standing there, trying to see what's going on, and Tom and the RAs, along with Sarah, trying to talk them into going about their Friday night business.

No. It's my father.

"Dad!" I cry, breaking free from Detective Canavan's grasp and throwing myself into my waiting father's arms.

"Heather!" he says, seeming very surprised by my greeting, but not unhappy about it. "Thank God you're all right!"

"I love you *so much*," I tell him.

"She loves everyone quite a bit at the moment," I hear Detective Canavan explain. "She's on Rohypnol."

"That's not why I love you," I assure my father, worried his feelings will be hurt otherwise. "And it's not just because you called the cops and kept me from getting decapitated, either."

"Well," Dad says, with a chuckle, "that's good to know. Her mouth is bloody. Why is her mouth bloody?"

And that's when I notice Dad's not standing there alone. Cooper is by his side! He's reaching for one of his ubiquitous handkerchiefs. Handkerchiefs are apparently a very important tool in the private investigations field.

"Oh," Detective Canavan says. "She bit a guy. That's all."

"Cooper!" I cry, throwing my arms around his neck next, as Cooper reaches to dab Steve Winer's blood from my mouth. "I'm so glad to see you!"

"I can tell," Cooper says. He's laughing, for some reason. "Hold still, you've got some—"

"I love you *so much*," I tell him. "Even though you told Gavin I'm still in love with your brother. Why did you do that, Cooper? I'm not in love with Jordan anymore. I'm *not*."

"Okay," Cooper says. "We'll take your word for it. Here, hold still."

"I'm not, though," I assure him. "I don't love Jordan. I love *you*. I really, really do."

Then Reggie steps into my line of vision one more time, just as Cooper is finishing washing me up, and I shout, "Reggie! I love you! I love you so much! I want to come visit you on your banana plantation!"

"I don't actually have a banana plantation, Heather," Reggie says. He's laughing, too. Why is everyone laughing? Seriously, maybe I should give up the songwriting thing and go into stand-up comedy, since I'm apparently so hilarious. "I'm from Iowa."

"That's okay," I say, as some EMTs gently pry my arms from around Cooper's neck. "I still love you anyway. I love *all* of you! You, Tom—and Sarah—and even Dr. Kilgore. Where *is* Dr. Kilgore, anyway?"

And then the room starts spinning fast—I mean, *really* fast—and my sleepiness becomes too much to resist anymore.

And I don't remember anything more after that.

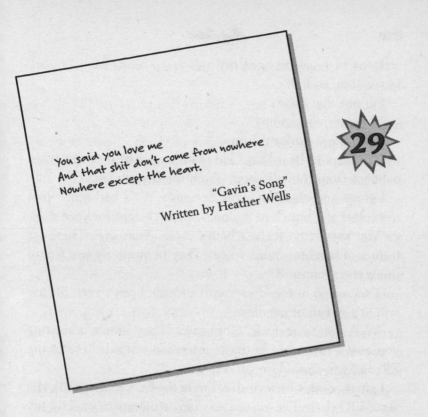

You said you love me
And that shit don't come from nowhere
Nowhere except the heart.

"Gavin's Song"
Written by Heather Wells

My head is POUNDING.

Seriously.

It isn't funny.

I can't believe people do this drug recreationally. If this is how Jordan felt yesterday—was it only yesterday?—at the Stoned Crow, well, it's no wonder he turned down a beer. I never want to drink again. Anything. Not even water. Not even—

"Heather."

I open one eye. I can't believe who I see standing there beside my gurney. My boss. Of all the people in the world to wake up to, I have to open my eyes to my boss's face? I mean, I love Tom, and all.

But not *that* much.

"How are you feeling?"

"Like crap," I inform him.

"I'm sorry to hear that." He holds up a fistful of GET WELL balloons from the gift shop. "From the department."

I groan and close my eyes. Seriously, it's a bad sign when the colors of a bunch of balloons are too bright for your eyes.

"You should be feeling better soon," Tom says. There's a tremor of laughter in his voice. "They're pumping you full of fluids and vitamin B."

"I wanna go home," I say, with a moan. I can't even lift my arm, it's so full of needles.

"Well, you're in luck," Tom says. "They aren't admitting you. Just a few more hours of intravenous fluids here in the ER, and you should be good to go."

I groan. I can't believe this. I'm in the St. Vincent's ER, the same ER where I've visited so many students in exactly my current condition.

But I never realized they felt this crappy.

"Listen," Tom says, in a voice that's got no laughter left in it. "I wanted you to be the first to know."

I open one eye. "You really are quitting?" I ask.

"Not at all," Tom says, with a chuckle. "I'm getting promoted. To area coordinator."

I open my other eye. "*WHAT?*"

"Stan was so impressed by how I handled the whole Lindsay situation," Tom explains excitedly, "that he promoted me. I'll still be in Housing, but now I'll be assigned to Waverly Hall. The frats, Heather. Stan says he realizes now that the building needs an on-site adult presence . . . it's a ten-

thousand-dollar-a-year raise. Of course, I'll have to be working with pills like the Tau Phis . . . but they shouldn't be so
hard to handle, now that Steve and Doug are under arrest.
And Steven—Coach Andrews—says he'll be happy to
help. . . ."

I close my eyes. I can't believe this. I finally get a boss I
like, and they take him away.

And excuse me, but Tom didn't handle the Lindsay situation. *I* did. I'm the one who nearly got killed getting her
killers to fess up. Where's *my* promotion?

In a way, I kind of wish they *had* killed me. At least my
head wouldn't hurt so much.

"Wow," I say. "That's great, Tom."

"Don't worry," Tom says. I feel him pat my hand. "I'll make
sure we get you a really kick-ass new boss. Okay?"

"Yeah," I say. "Okay."

I must have fallen back asleep, because when I open my eyes
again, Tom is gone. In his place are Magda, Sarah, and Pete.

"Go away," I say to them.

"Oh, thank God," Magda says, looking relieved. "She's all
right."

"I'm serious," I say. "My head is killing me."

"That's the benzodiazepine wearing off," Sarah says chip-
perly. "It's a central nervous system depressant. You're going
to feel like crap for a while."

I glare at her. "Thanks."

"We just wanted to see how you were doing," Pete says.
"And to tell you not to worry."

"Yes," Magda says, grabbing the side of my gurney and
bouncing excitedly. "They found the cocaine!"

"Right," Pete says. "They found the cocaine. Doug Winer's
stash. The one Lindsay stole."

This makes me open my eyes more fully. "Really? Where was it?"

"Where do you think?" Sarah asks. "In Kimberly Watkins's room."

"But . . ." I know I'm out of it. But I can't believe I'm *that* out of it. "Kimberly and Lindsay were in on it together?"

Sarah shakes her head. "No. Lindsay taped the bag under her favorite cafeteria table—which is why it wasn't there when she went looking for it, to give it back to Doug when he figured out she was the one who had it. Because someone else had already found it. Someone who regularly shares that table with Lindsay. Or used to, anyway."

I stare at her. "*Kimberly Watkins*? Kimberly had Doug's coke the whole time?" When Sarah nods, I ask, "How did you find out?"

"Cheryl," Magda explains. "She was so angry—over what Kimberly said about Lindsay and Coach Andrews, and then, later, over what happened to her poor Jeff—who is going to be all right, just a few broken ribs—that she went to confront Kimberly, and . . . well . . . let's just say they didn't act like a couple of movie stars."

"Well, unless you mean Paris Hilton and Nicole Richie," Sarah says.

"Cheryl beat the crap out of Kimberly," Pete says. "And Kimberly confessed. She was going to start her own little drug-dealing operation, it seems. She saw Lindsay hide the coke, and stole it next chance she got. Only after what happened to Lindsay, she was too scared to do anything. She was terrified the Winer boys would find out she was the one who had the stuff, and do to her what they did to Lindsay."

"That's why she kept trying to throw me off their scent," I murmur.

"Exactly," Sarah says. "Anyway, Cheryl went straight to the cops with what she found out, and now Kimberly's under arrest, as well. I guess the DEA'd been working for months to bust what they considered the biggest student drug ring on campus. Only, until Lindsay's murder, they really didn't have any idea where the kids were getting the stuff. That's why they had Reggie working undercover in the park. They were hoping he'd pick up some clues . . . which he finally did, when you asked him about the Winer boys. But even then, they still didn't have proof. . . ."

Sarah shrugs. "Now, in addition to possession and dealing, the Winer boys have murder and attempted murder charges against them . . . along with a couple of the other guys from their frat. Daddy Winer has already hired the top criminal lawyer in town. But I don't see how they're gonna beat the rap with you around to testify. Oh, and Kimberly, who's turned state witness in exchange for them dropping the possession charges against her. . . ."

"So Kimberly's kicked out of school?" I murmur.

"Uh," Magda says, "yeah. They all are. Even the Winers."

"Good," I say faintly, as my eyelids drift closed again. "That's more spaces for me to make room changes into next week, when the housing freeze lifts."

Everything goes mercifully black for a while—that must be my central nervous system depressing again. When I open my eyes again, I find myself looking up at Detective Canavan and Reggie.

"You," I say to Reggie. "You lied to me."

He smiles. I am heart-struck to note the gold teeth are gone.

"Sorry," he says. "It was in the line of duty."

"Brian's a special agent with the Drug Enforcement

Agency, Heather," Detective Canavan explains. "He's been working undercover for nearly a year in the park, trying to figure out where the influx of party drugs on campus was coming from. Thanks to your tip about the Winers, Brian was able to direct his people to send in a fellow agent disguised as a maid"—the maid I'd seen in the hallway at the Tau Phi House scrubbing the FAT CHICKS GO HOME sign—"and get all the evidence they needed to bust the Winers not just for drug trafficking, but eventually for murder and assault as well."

I look at Reggie. "Brian?"

He shrugs. "Reggie sounds more street, you know?"

"Have you ever even been to Jamaica?" I ask him.

"Oh, God, no," he says. "I get any vacation time, I head straight for the mountains. I'm a skier."

I look back at Detective Canavan. "Do I get a medal or something?"

"Um," Detective Canavan says. "No. But I got you this." He holds up a dark chocolate Dove candy bar. "The ice-cream kind would have melted," he explains.

I lift my hand—the one with all the IVs in it—and snatch the candy bar away from him.

"This city," I say, "is getting pretty cheap with the rewards for valor."

They go away, and I eat my candy bar. It's delicious. So delicious that I fall back asleep. When I wake up again, Gavin McGoren is leering down at me.

"Well, well, well," he says, with a grin. "Isn't this a fine turn of events? For once *you're* the one on the gurney, instead of me. I have to say, I like it a lot better like this."

"Who let you in here?" I want to know.

Gavin shrugs. "I'm a fellow patient, not a visitor," he says.

He turns to show me his cheek where Steve hit him. "Seven stitches. What do you think? That'll leave a pretty sweet scar, huh?"

I close my eyes. "Your mother is going to *kill* me."

"What are you talkin' about, woman?" Gavin scoffs. "You saved my life."

"I caused you to be kidnapped and beaten," I say, opening my eyes again. "Gavin, I—I can't tell you how sorry I am. Really. I never should have involved you in any of this."

The red marks are gone from around Gavin's mouth. So is the goatee. He apparently took the time to shave before coming in to see me. Which I should have taken as a sign of what was about to come, but my faculties are still slightly befuddled from the drug.

"There's a way you can make it up to me, if you want," he says.

"Yeah? How?" I genuinely think he's going to ask for a single with a view of the park.

Instead, he asks me out.

"You know," he says. "Just sometime. We could kick it together. Play pool or something. When you're feeling better. It doesn't have to be a date," he adds hastily. "I know you're still all in love with Jordan Cartwright, and shit. But, you know. Just to try it out. Just to see."

"Gavin." I'm not positive, but I'm fairly sure I'm the first assistant director of a New York College residence hall to be asked out while lying on a gurney in the St. Vincent's ER recovering from being roofied. "I can't date you. You're a resident. I'm not allowed to date residents."

Gavin considers this. Then he shrugs. "I'll get an apartment."

I open my eyes wider. "Gavin. Do you have any idea how much rents are in Manhattan? Besides, you're still a student.

New York College administrators are forbidden from dating students."

Gavin thinks about this for a minute. Then he says evenly, "Okay, well, then, after I graduate. Next year. Will you go out with me then?"

I'm too tired to resist. "Yes, Gavin," I say, closing my eyes again. "Next year, after you graduate, I will go out with you."

Gavin looks pleased. "Cool. You said you loved me, you know."

My eyes fly open. "Gavin, I was under the influence."

"I know," he says, still looking pleased. "But that shit don't come from nowhere. Nowhere except the heart."

When I open my eyes next, I see Patty and Frank.

"Hi," I croak.

"You could have just told me you aren't ready to play in front of anyone yet," Frank says, "instead of going to all this trouble to get out of doing the gig."

"Frank!" Patty sounds exasperated. "Don't listen to him, Heather. We just heard. How are you doing?"

"Oh," I say. My voice still sounds awful. "Great."

"Seriously," Frank says. "We'll be playing the pub all week. So if you aren't feeling up to it tonight, there's tomorrow night. And the night after that, too."

"Frank," Patty says, looking annoyed. "Leave her alone. Can't you see that singing is the last thing she's got on her mind?"

"No," I surprise myself by saying.

Frank and Patty both look at me strangely. "No, what, honey?" Patty asks.

"No, I want to," I say. It is only as the words are coming out of my mouth that I realize I mean it. "I want to play with you guys. Just one song, though."

Patty shakes her head. "Oh, Heather. You're still on drugs."

"No, she's not," Frank says, grinning. "She means it. You mean it, Heather, don't you?"

I nod. "Not tonight, though, okay? Because I've got a headache."

Frank grins some more. "Totally fine," he says. "So whatcha gonna sing? Something you wrote? Something new?"

"No," I say. "Something Ella."

Frank's grin fades. "You're right," he murmurs to Patty. "She *is* still on drugs."

"She means Ella Fitzgerald," Patty hisses at him. "Just smile and nod."

Frank smiles and nods. "Okay, Heather. Night-night, Heather."

I close my eyes, and they go away. When I wake up, later, my dad is peering down at me.

"Honey?" He looks worried. "It's me, Dad."

"I know." Every word is like a stab wound to my head. I close my eyes again. "How are you, Dad?"

"I'm good," Dad says. "I'm so glad you're all right. I called your mother, to let her know."

This causes me to open one eye. "Dad. Why would you do that? She didn't even know I was—whatever."

"I think she has a right to know," Dad says. "She's still your mother. She loves you, you know. In her own way."

"Oh," I say. "Right. I guess. Well. Thanks for getting hold of Detective Canavan."

"Well, that's what family's for, honey," he says. "Listen, I was just talking to the doctor. They're going to let you go home soon."

"Are they going to give me anything for this headache first?" I ask. "I can barely see, my head's pounding so hard."

"Let me see if I can go find the doctor," Dad says. "Heather . . . what you did. I'm really proud of you, honey."

"Thanks, Dad," I say. And the tears in my eyes aren't just from the pain in my temples. "Dad. Where's Cooper?"

"Cooper?"

"Yeah. I mean, everybody else has been by to see me, except Cooper. Where is he?" He hates me. I know it. I said something to him—I can't remember what it was. But I know I did. And he hates me for it.

"Well, he's at Jordan's wedding, honey. Remember? It's Saturday. He was here for a long time while you were sleeping, though. But finally he had to leave. He promised his brother, you know."

"Oh," I say. The disappointment I feel is ridiculous. And crushing. "Sure."

"Oh, here comes your doctor," Dad says. "Let's see what he has to say."

They let me go that evening. Over twelve hours of intravenous fluids, and, while I don't feel a hundred percent by any means, at least my headache is gone and the room has stopped spinning around. A look in the ladies' room mirror tells me more than I want to know about what Rohypnol does to a girl's complexion—my face is chalky white, my lips chapped, and the circles under my eyes look like bruises.

But, hey. I'm alive.

That's more than poor Lindsay Combs can say.

I sign my discharge papers and head out, a sample packet of Tylenol my only souvenir—Tylenol, that was the best they could do—expecting to see my dad waiting for me in the lobby.

But instead of Dad, I find Cooper.

In a tux.

I almost turn around and check myself back in, considering the way my heart turns over in my chest at the sight of him. Surely that isn't normal. Surely that's a sign that my central nervous system needs more fluids, or something.

He stands up when he sees me, and smiles.

Oh, now, see. Smiles like that should be against the law. Considering what they do to a girl. Well, a girl like me.

"Surprise," he says. "I let your dad go home. He'd been here all night, you know."

"I heard you were, too," I say. I can't make eye contact, both on account of the way my heart is hammering and because I'm so embarrassed. What had I said to him earlier? I'm pretty sure I'd told him I loved him.

But Dad said I'd been saying that to everyone—including the twin planters outside Fischer Hall.

Still, surely Cooper had to know it had only been the drugs.

Even though of course in his case, it hadn't.

"Yeah," Cooper says. "Well, you do have a tendency to keep me on my toes."

"I'm sorry," I say. "You must be missing the reception."

"I said I'd go to the wedding," Cooper says. "I didn't say anything about the reception. I'm not the hugest salmon fan. And I do not do the chicken dance."

"Oh," I say. I can't really picture him doing the chicken dance, either. "Well, thank you."

"You're welcome," Cooper says.

And we head out into the cold, to where he's parked his car along Twelfth Street. Once inside, he starts the engine and lets the heater run. It's dark out—even though it's barely five o'clock—and the streetlights are on. They cast a pinkish glow over the drifts piled up alongside the street. The snow, so beautiful when it first fell, is fast turning ugly, as soot and dirt stain it gray.

"Cooper," I hear myself saying, as he finally puts the car in gear. "Why did you tell Gavin I'm still in love with your brother?"

I can't believe I've said it. I have no idea where the question came from. Maybe there's some residual Rohypnol in my central nervous system. Maybe I need to check back into the hospital to get the rest of it out.

"That again?" Cooper asks, looking amused.

The amusement sends a spurt of irritation through me.

"Yes, *that* again," I say.

"Well, what did you want me to tell him?" Cooper asks. "That he has a chance with you? Because I hate to be the one to break it to you, Heather, but that guy has a major crush on you. And the more you ask him to take you to frat parties and the like, the more you're just reinforcing it. I had to tell him something to try to nip his little infatuation in the bud. I thought you'd be grateful."

I am careful not to make eye contact with him. "So you don't believe that. About me and your brother, I mean."

Cooper is quiet for a minute. Then he says, "You tell me. I mean, it's kind of hard to believe there's nothing there when every time I turn around, you two are together."

"That's him," I say adamantly. "Not me. I do not have feelings for your brother. End of story."

"All right," Cooper says, in the soothing tone in which one might speak to the mentally disturbed. "I'm glad we got that straightened out."

"We haven't," I hear myself say. What am I doing? WHAT AM I DOING?

Cooper, who'd been about to pull out of the parking space, puts his foot on the brake. "We haven't what?"

"Got it straightened out," I say. I cannot believe the words that are coming out of my mouth. But they just keep coming. There's nothing I can do to stop them. This has to be the Rohypnol. It *has* to be. "How come you've never asked me out? Is it because you're not interested in me that way, or what?"

Cooper sounds amused when he replies, "You're my brother's ex-fiancée."

"Right," I say, beating a fist on the dashboard. "*Ex. Ex*-fiancée. Jordan's married now. To someone else. You were there, you saw it for yourself. So what's the deal? I know I'm not really your type . . ." Oh, God. This is going from bad to worse. Still, I can't go back. "But I think we get along. You know. For the most part."

"Heather." Now there's a hint of impatience creeping into Cooper's voice. "You've just come out of a really bad long-term relationship—"

"A *year* ago."

"—started a new job—"

"Almost a year ago."

"—reconnected with a father you barely know—"

"Things with Dad are cool. We had a nice talk last night."

"—are struggling to figure out who you are, and what you're going to do with your life," Cooper concludes. "I'm pretty sure the last thing you need right now is a boyfriend. In particular, your ex-fiancé's brother. With whom you live. I think your life is complicated enough."

I finally turn in my seat to look at him. "Don't you think I should be the judge of that?" I ask him.

This time, he's the one who looks away.

"Okay," he says. "*My* life is too complicated. Heather—I

don't want to be your rebound guy. That's just . . . that's not who I am. I don't chicken dance. And I don't want to be the rebound guy."

I'm flabbergasted. "Rebound guy? Rebound guy? Cooper, Jordan and I broke up a year ago—"

"And who have you dated since?" Cooper demands.

"Well, I . . . I . . ." I swallow. "No one."

"There you go," Cooper says. "You're ripe for a rebound guy. And it's not going to be me."

I stare at him. *Why?* I want to ask him. *Why don't you want to be my rebound guy? Because you don't actually want me?*

Or because you want something more from me than that?

Looking at him, I realize I'll probably never know.

At least . . . not yet.

I also realize I probably don't want to know. Because if it's the latter, I'll find out, one of these days.

And if it's the former. . . .

Well, then, I'll just want to die.

"You know what," I say, averting my gaze, "you're right. It's okay."

"Really?" Cooper asks.

I look back at him. And I smile.

It takes every last little bit of strength I've got left. But I do it.

"Really," I say. "Let's go home."

"Okay," he says.

And smiles back.

And it's enough.

For now.

**Tad Tocco
Assistant Professor
Office Hours
2–3 P.M. weekdays**

That's what the sign on the door says.

Which is why I don't understand what, when I open the door, a Greek god is doing there, sitting in front of me.

Seriously. The guy sitting at the computer behind the desk has long, golden hair—like as long as mine; a healthy, ruddy glow of good health about him; a placard on his desk that says KILLER FRISBEE 4-EVER; and the sleeves of his button-down shirt pushed back to reveal a set of forearms so muscular and gorgeous that I think I must have walked into some snowboard shop, or something.

"Hi," the guy behind the desk says, with a smile. A smile that reveals a set of white, even teeth. But not so even that they're, like, perfect. Just even enough for me to be able to guess that he'd probably fought with his family over not wanting to get braces.

And that he'd won.

"Wait, don't tell me," he says. "Heather Wells, right?"

He's my age. Maybe a little older than me. Thirty, thirty-one. He has to be, even though he's wearing reading glasses . . . adorable gold-rimmed ones, though. Still, there's a *Scooby Doo* lunch box on a shelf above his head. Not a new one, either. An original *Scooby Doo* lunch box, the ones kids had when I was in the first grade.

"Um," I say. "Yeah. How did you . . ." My voice trails off. Right. I forget, sometimes, that my face was once plastered all over the bedroom walls of teenage girls—and some of their brothers.

"Actually, I saw you perform the other night with Frank Robillard and his band," the guy says cheerfully. "Over at Joe's Pub?"

My stomach lurches. "Oh. You saw that?"

"Jazz isn't really my thing," the guy says. "But I liked that song you did."

"It was an Ella Fitzgerald cover," I say. I really want to throw up now. Rodgers and Hart's "I Wish I Were in Love Again" happens to be one of Cooper's favorite songs. Which isn't necessarily why I chose to sing it, but . . . well, it might have been one of the reasons.

Thank God he'd been called away at the last minute by some kind of PI emergency. I don't think, in the end, that I could have gotten up there if I'd known he was in the audience.

"Frank and I—" I stammer. "W-we were just fooling around."

Well, *Frank* had been fooling around. I'd been deadly serious . . . at least until no one booed us. Then I began to relax and have a little fun with it. Afterward, people clapped . . . but of course they were applauding for Frank (even though Patty assures me they were also clapping for me. But only for having the guts to get up there, I'm sure. I'd been rusty . . . and I hadn't missed the fact that my dad, in the audience, had been clapping the hardest of anyone. I guess it's nice to know, whatever else happens, I've got one parent watching my back).

"Well, it sounded great to me," Mr. Gorgeous says. "So, you finally got my messages?"

I blink at him. "Um, I guess so. I got a message from someone named Tad Tocco—"

"That's me," Tad says. The smile gets even bigger. So does he, as he stands up and holds out his right hand. He's taller than me. And possibly even outweighs me. He's a big, muscular guy. "Your remedial math professor." His hand swallows mine. "I was going to introduce myself after the show the other night, but you seemed to disappear right after your song."

I say something. I have no idea what. His hand is callused. From playing so much killer Frisbee, no doubt.

"Anyway, I have to say," he says, letting go of my hand, finally, and sinking back into his chair, just as my knees give out and I sort of fall back into the one on the other side of his desk, "you have a way better excuse for blowing off my class than most of my students. I mean, I've never had anyone miss the first week of school because they were busy catching a murderer."

My jaw drops. "You're my . . . you're my . . ." I've forgotten how to formulate words.

"I'm your remedial math professor," Tad says cheerfully. "I

wanted to get in touch with you about scheduling some makeup sessions. You know, for the classes you've missed? I don't want you falling behind. So I figured we could meet. At your convenience, of course. How's after work? There's a bar near that place you work—Fischer Hall? The Stoned Crow. A bunch of us plays darts down there, so it would be convenient for me if we could meet there, seeing as how we're both over twenty-one." Then he winks at me. *He winks at me.* "I find algebra goes down a lot easier with popcorn and beer. That okay with you?"

I can only stare at him. He's just so . . . hot.

Way hotter than Barista Boy.

Suddenly I think I'm going to like college.

A lot.

"That sounds *great* to me," I say.

Visit **www.panmacmillan.com** to read more about all our books and to buy them. You will also find features, author interviews and news of any author events, and you can sign up for e-newsletters so that you're always first to hear about our new releases.

www.panmacmillan.com

GIFT SELECTOR
YOUR ACCOUNT
WISH LIST
WAITING LIST

| HOME | ABOUT US | IMPRINTS | TRADE/MEDIA | CONTACT US | ADVANCED SEARCH | SEARCH | GO |

BOOK CATEGORIES | WHAT'S NEW | AUTHORS/ILLUSTRATORS | BESTSELLERS | READING GROUPS

Coming Soon...

Reading Groups

Competitions
Feeling Lucky?

Extracts
Sneak Previews

Interviews

Events
Meet Our Stars

Reviews
What The Critics Say

News & Awards

Editor's Choice
What We're Reading

ACCESSIBILITY   HELP   TERMS & CONDITIONS   PRIVACY POLICY   SEND PAGE TO A FRIEND